A Superfluous Woman

by

Emma Frances Brooke

edited with an introduction and notes
by Barbara Tilley

Victorian Secrets 2015

Published by

Victorian Secrets Limited
32 Hanover Terrace
Brighton BN2 9SN

www.victoriansecrets.co.uk

A Superfluous Woman by Emma Frances Brooke
First published in 1894
This Victorian Secrets edition 2015

Introduction and notes © 2015 by Barbara Tilley
This edition © 2015 by Victorian Secrets
Composition and design by Catherine Pope

The cover image is *Portrait of a Lady* by William Merritt Chase (1890).

A catalogue record for this book is available from the British Library.

ISBN 978-1-906469-56-6

CONTENTS

INTRODUCTION

Emma Frances Brooke was a prolific writer and a political activist; she was an educated woman whose career spanned thirty-one years, during which time she also played a pivotal role in organizing and running the Fabian Society, a powerful socialist group that is still in existence today. In 1894, when her most famous novel, *A Superfluous Woman,* was published she had been a self-supporting author for over twelve years, yet she did not have a large public audience for her work. During the 1880s she had already published five novels, an epic poem in blank verse, and several political articles, which focused on the rights of women and her early socialist theories. But it was *A Superfluous Woman* that, simply put, made her famous. This novel quickly became enormously popular, so much so that from January to June of 1894 the novel went quickly into five printings; four of those in three-volume editions, a rare occurrence at a time when publishers were phasing out the three-decker novel due to the expense of printing and the demise of the circulating libraries.[1] Initially published anonymously, literary critics clamored to learn the identity of the author, but she remained unknown to the general public until after the publication of her overtly socialist novel, *Transition,* in 1895. The revelation that Brooke was the author of *A Superfluous Woman* significantly changed her literary career; biographical entries about her from this time forward mentioned only those ten novels published after this seminal work.[2] The important influence of this one novel on Brooke's writing career is even seen in her obituary, which describes it as "her first book".[3] Upon her death on November 28, 1926, the novel went out of print and has not been available until now in this new critical edition.

Brooke was born on December 22, 1844 and was brought up in the town

---

1   For a history of the circulating library system in England see Guinevere L. Griest. *Mudie's Circulating Library and the Victorian Novel.* Bloomington: Indiana University Press, 1970.

2   Brooke wrote ten novels after *A Superfluous Woman*: *Transition* (1895), *Life the Accuser* (1896), *The Confession of Stephen Whapshare* (1898), *The Engrafted Rose* (1899), *The Poet's Child* (1903), *The Twins of Skirlaugh Hall, A Mystery* (1903), *Susan Wooed and Susan Won* (1905), *Sir Elyot of the Woods* (1907), *The Story of Hauksgarth Farm* (1909) and her final novel, *The House of Robershaye* (1912).

3   "Miss Emma Brooke Obituary." *Manchester Guardian Weekly,* 2 December 1926: 4.

of Bollington, near Macclesfield, Cheshire in the north of England. She came from two well-established local families who were a part of the cotton mill industry. Little is known about her childhood, but an 1895 essay about her in *The Sketch*, written by the literary critic Arthur Waugh, offers some insight into her early years.[4] Her father Joseph Brooke was a wealthy cotton spinner and is described by Waugh as "a landlord and capitalist" (19). According to an entry in *Who's Who* from 1903, her mother was "descended from [an] old yeoman family" in Cheshire (167).[5] Waugh describes Brooke's childhood as "very religious, with a leaning towards the ascetic and austere" (19). Evidently she lived a rather "gloomy and repressed" life in her "out-of-the-way village", but it was an upbringing that allowed her to see "the rougher side to human nature" (19). These early influences are evident in her fiction; she drew on her experience and knowledge of the cotton mill industry to create thought-provoking narratives, which focused on class disparities and the inequalities that workers and women faced in their daily lives.

In 1872 her father died and she inherited enough money to pursue her education formally. That same year, she joined a pioneering group of eight women at Newnham College, Cambridge to study literature, psychology, political economics and logic.[6] She stayed at Newnham until 1874 and then returned to Bollington where, according to Waugh, she "passed some excessively troubled years" (19). A biographical entry about Brooke in *The Labour Annual* of 1895 states that during this time at home she lost "by a sudden blow almost her entire fortune" (163).[7] The reason for this event is not given, but when she moved to London in 1879 she became a self-supporting author, writing anonymously or under a pseudonym, E. Fairfax Byrrne.[8] She remained financially independent all her life, choosing never to marry or to have children.

In 1881 her first major work was published, a lengthy poem in blank verse called *Millicent*. She then turned to writing prose and spent the early

---

4 Arthur Waugh. "The Book and Its Story." *The Sketch: A Weekly Review for Literature and the Arts* Vol. X, May 1 (1895): 19-20.

5 *Who's Who: An Annual Biographical Dictionary.* "Brooke, Emma Frances." Vol. 55 (1903): 167.

6 Newnham College was established as a women's college in 1871. Women began to take degrees in 1879.

7 *The Labour Annual: A Year Book of Industrial Progress and Social Welfare.* Brighton: The Harvester Press Limited, 1971.

8 It is not clear how she came to choose this name, except that Byrrne may be a play on the Scottish word "burn," which means brook (85). And, of course, E. Fairfax Byrrne retains her initials, E. F. B. Adrian Room. *Dictionary of Pseudonyms: 13,000 Assumed Names and their Origins.* 5th ed. Jefferson: McFarland, 2010.

part of her career establishing herself as a novelist. Writing anonymously for the Religious Tract Society, she explored religious and romantic themes in *God's Gift to Two; or Margaret Redfern's Discipline* (1883) and *Reaping the Whirlwind, A Story of Three Lives* (1885). Brooke's familiarity with the north of England, specifically the Cheshire countryside and the mill towns she grew up in and around, found their way into several of her early novels in either the plot or descriptions of place. For example, in *God's Gift to Two*, the heroine, Margaret Redfern, is a working-class girl whose job is in the cotton mills of Cheshire. Brooke's interests in class dynamics, the economic welfare of the worker, women's rights, a woman's rejection of motherhood, and religious freedoms all surfaced in varying degrees in her early work. Novels with more overt political and socialist viewpoints were written under her pseudonym during this time: *A Fair Country Maid* (1883), *Entangled* (1885), and *The Heir Without a Heritage* (1887). In *A Fair Country Maid*, one of the male characters is a radical socialist who is alienated in his own community because of his political ideals. *The Heir Without a Heritage* focuses attention on Brooke's growing interest in exploring religion, specifically the rigid doctrines of Evangelicalism.

Brooke lived in the north London neighborhood of Hampstead from 1879 onward and there found several organizations, which spoke to her developing interests in class disparities, women and worker's rights, and socialist politics. By 1882 she was already involved in campaigning for the Female Middle Class Emigration Society (FMCES) of which she was one of two Honorary Secretaries. In a letter to the editor in the *Southland Times*, a New Zealand newspaper, Brooke explained that the society helped "educated, middle-class women" find employment in the colonies (4).[9] She held her secretary position until 1884, at which time she turned her attention to other projects. In this same year Charlotte Wilson, a fellow Newnham College student, invited her to read Karl Marx's *Das Kapital* with likeminded middle-class intellectuals who were interested in examining the topics of economics, capitalism and labor politics in Britain. Initially called the Karl Marx Club, but soon renamed the Hampstead Historic Club, this group lasted for four years (1884–1888), during which time Brooke acted as secretary. Waugh writes that to "study social questions, and especially the theories of Socialism" were the main goals of this group of writers, intellectuals and revolutionaries (20). Brooke described the Hampstead Historic Club as a "little band of comrades who worked so long and so harmoniously together" (20). These early

---

9   Emma Brooke and Jane E. Lewin. "Female Middle Class Immigration Society." *The Southland Times*, 20 January 1883: 4.

"comrades," who included the Irish playwright George Bernard Shaw, and the socialists Sidney and Beatrice Webb, Graham Wallas, and Sydney Olivier, would remain her lifelong friends.

The Fabian Society formed in January 1884 and drew many of its members from the Hampstead Historic Club. As Waugh points out "the Hampstead Historic Club gradually melted into the Fabians . . . For the conspicuous members of the smaller club became the giants of the Fabian Society" (20). The Fabian Society consisted of middle-class men and women whose initial mission, according to Edward Pease's *The History of the Fabian Society*, was to explore through discussions and giving papers "how to reconstruct society" (23).[10] This idealist and somewhat utopian agenda transitioned into more realistic and pragmatic work as the society began to coalesce into an active and self-supporting political group. In the 1880s and 1890s, the society focused much of its attention on writing about the rights of laborers, restructuring the economics of wealth among the classes, and working to move away from privatizing businesses and capitalist interests. The early members ranged in age and occupation, but most were university educated and male.

Brooke became a member of the Fabian Society on October 2, 1885;[11] in this group she developed her interests in and promotion of the rights of workers, women and children. She was one of the few women who helped to organize and run the Fabian Society and it was she who in 1889 "hawked ... to the doors of two or three publishers" the famous *Fabian Essays* before the society had to self-publish the work and sell it by subscription to its members (Waugh 20). Furthermore, her interest in socialist politics extended into her own neighborhood of Hampstead where she held the influential position of Secretary to the Hampstead Fabian Group for eight years (1885–1893). Brooke was also elected to the Executive Committee of the Fabian Society from 1893–1896, during which time she published her famous novel, *A Superfluous Woman*.[12] At the time of her election she was one of only two women on the Executive Committee.[13]

---

10 Edward R Pease. *The History of the Fabian Society.* Teddington: The Echo Library, 2006.

11 Lecture and Business Meeting Minute Book. Fabian Society Collection: London School of Economics and Political Sciences. 24 October 1883–6 July 1888. Vol. C36.

12 In *Chamber's Biographical Dictionary* of 1898, Brooke is described as "a prominent member of the Fabian Society" (136). David Patrick. Ed. *Chambers's Biographical Dictionary: The Great of All Times and Nations.* London: J. B. Lippincott Company, 1898.

13 Executive Committee Minute Book. Fabian Society Collection: London School of Economics and Political Sciences. 3 March 1893–January 1895, Vol. C5.

Her involvement with the Fabian Society was all encompassing and influenced both the subject matter in her fiction and her political essays. In 1888, she published "Women and Their Sphere" in Annie Besant's socialist journal *Our Corner*.[14] A critically important work for Brooke, this article lays out her perspective on women according to their roles and economic positions in society, particularly in relation to motherhood. She believed that motherhood served as a means to subjugate women's sexuality and their economic strength in society as independent wage earners. Brooke argues that society does not recognize a woman as an individual with free will, but as a "woman who is performing the function of motherhood" (69). She goes on to explain, "Even in the present day, though sentimentally motherhood is endowed with dignity, it has certainly not been recognised in its important bearing as a responsible piece of social work" (70). Her arguments in this article show how she merges her feminist and socialist views about women with her interest in economics and labor politics.[15]

In 1908, the Fabian Women's Group formed and Brooke was one of its founding members. The overall mission of this group was to recognize class differences between women, to find ways to expand upon women's economic power through education and jobs, and to work with the larger suffrage movement to support women's rights. Brooke immediately took a leadership role in the group and was made Chair of the Studies Sub-Committee. She was at heart a student of economics and so it seems appropriate that she headed up this group, whose task it was to examine a woman's position in society and how she could develop and retain her economic independence. Brooke contributed to several important papers during her time in the Fabian Women's Group, one of which is particularly interesting as it revisits her arguments about economic power for women, but especially for mothers. On June 25, 1909, along with five other women in the Fabian Women's Group, Brooke presented "A Summary of Six Papers and Discussions Upon the Disabilities of Women as Workers" to other Fabian members.[16] Brooke

---

14 E. Fairfax Byrrne. "Women and Their Sphere." *Our Corner*. January Vol. IX (1888): 5–13 and February Vol. IX (1888): 64–73. See Appendix C.

15 In keeping with her interests in women and the economy, she studied at the London School of Economics (LSE) in the late 1890s and there wrote, *A Tabulation of the Factory Laws of European Countries in so far as they relate to the Hours of Labour, and to Special Legislation for Women, Young Persons, and Children*, a small volume published in 1898 in London by Grant Richards. This work explores the way women and children were treated as economic entities in other countries.

16 "Disabilities" in this instance refers to economic disadvantages, not physical or mental problems.

read the first paper in the series, declaring that although women had made great strides in their own education, there was still one area of "women's emancipation" that remained, "the stigma attached to sex" (108).[17] She argues that a woman can only be seen as equal to a man if her "potentiality for motherhood" is recognized as an economic contribution that has merit and worth to society (108). The acknowledgement of motherhood as more than an ideal and as actual social work was, for Brooke, a very important cause and one that she worked tirelessly to promote. She believed that since all women were potential mothers, this "was in itself a cogent reason why the claim of women to full social recognition, economic and political, should be acknowledged" (154–155). These provocative ideas about women were explored in great detail in *A Superfluous Woman* and in her later fiction, particularly *Transition* (1895) and *Life the Accuser* (1896).

A Superfluous Woman was published at a point in history when writers were exploring the "woman question" through political plots and ideas in literature. A sub-genre emerged in the 1880s and 1890s called New Woman fiction, out of which began to develop an idea of womanhood understood as "new" and applied to women as a descriptor, so that the character in fiction became known as a "New Woman." This genre began to appear in the early 1880s; Olive Schreiner's *The Story of an African Farm* (1883) is commonly considered by contemporary literary critics to be the first New Woman novel. Authors explored images of women who embraced a desire to be educated, to pursue employment, to explore artistic and sexual freedoms, and to choose whether to marry or to have children outside of marriage. Because the nature of these desires required a measure of economic freedom, the New Woman tended to be represented in fiction as middle and upper class. New Woman authors also readily critiqued marriage and motherhood by exploring the effect of the sexually degenerate male, often a husband, on the physical health of the female body, typically that of a wife who then becomes a mother.

As Michelle Elizabeth Tusan explains in her article "Inventing the New Woman: Print Culture and Identity Politics During the Fin-de-Siecle,"[18] the term "New Woman" came into being, as a full-fledged named identity and as a capitalized title on August 17, 1893 in the feminist newspaper, *The Woman's Herald*. In a short entry called "The Social Standing of the "New Woman"" the author, a Mr. Ham, declares "Without warning woman suddenly appears on the scene of man's activities, as a sort of new creation, and demands a share

17 *Women's Fabian Tracts*. Ed. Sally Alexander. Routledge: London, 1988.
18 Michelle Elizabeth Tusan. "Inventing the New Woman: Print Culture and Identity Politics during the Fin-de-Siecle." *Victorian Periodicals Review*. Vol. 31, No. 2 (Summer 1998): 168 – 182.

in the struggles, the responsibilities, and the honours of the world" (410).[19] This image of the New Woman was adopted by feminist presses for the express purpose of shouldering the responsibility and the future of civilized society for women. Tusan argues that the New Woman was represented in the pages of the women's presses "as a reasonable and thoughtful woman who had only the best interests of the British state at heart" (170). This image of womanhood was a "symbol of new female political identity" that was embraced by women writers exploring feminist issues of the day (168).

In March of 1894, Sarah Grand, the feminist and popular novelist published her article, "The New Aspect of the Woman Question" in *The North American Review*. In this article she explores the reasons why man, or "the Bawling Brotherhood," has embraced the "cow-woman and the scum-woman" but not the "new woman" (Patterson 30).[20] Grand argues that it is the new woman who "has solved the problem and proclaimed for herself what was wrong with Home-is-the-Women's Sphere, and prescribed the remedy" (30). For Grand the "remedy" and the "solution for the Woman Question" is a woman who is "stronger and wiser" than her male counterpart (30-34). She and other New Woman authors used fiction to drive the larger political discussion about women's rights and their roles in British society. They created an image of woman in literature, the New Woman, who was morally and physically healthy, educated and self-directed. This was quite a different image than the one written about and appropriated by the mainstream presses and anti-feminist writers.

In May of 1894, two months after Grand's article was published, a new voice was heard in the discussions about the "new woman". This perspective was from an anti-feminist, sensation fiction novelist named Ouida in an essay, simply entitled: "The New Woman". Responding vehemently to Grand's article, she declared that there are "two unmitigated bores" being discussed by writers, the "Workingman and the Woman, the New Woman" (Patterson 35). Ouida's point of view about how British women have failed to live up to society's standards of femininity is most fiercely leveled at the New Woman who she sees as having "vanity . . . undigested knowledge . . . [and an] overweaning estimate of her own value" (Patterson 39).[21] Her response to Grand encapsulates much of what became fodder for political parody and critique of

19 "The Social Standing of the New Woman." *The Woman's Herald*. 17 August 1893, 410.
20 Grand, Sarah. "The New Aspect of the Woman Question." in *The American New Woman Revisited: A Reader, 1894 – 1930*. Martha H. Patterson, Ed. New Brunswick: Rutgers University Press, 2008, 30 – 34.
21 Ouida. "The New Woman" in Patterson, 35 – 42.

the New Woman by the popular presses in the 1890s.

Brooke entered into the controversy and political discussions about the New Woman at the height of the phenomenon with the publication of *A Superfluous Woman*. When her novel was introduced to readers in January 1894 they were already familiar with Schreiner's earlier novel, along with such works as Mona Caird's *The Wing of Azrael* (1889), George Egerton's *Keynotes* (1893), Sarah Grand's *The Heavenly Twins* (1893), and George Gissing's *The Odd Women* (1893). Interestingly, Brooke's initial anonymity caused a stir for literary critics who associated the prose and the plot with both Olive Schreiner and Sarah Grand. For example, a critic writing in *The Athenaeum* on February 3, 1894 (one month after the publication of *A Superfluous Woman*), states that the heroine of Brooke's novel "faintly recalls Miss Schreiner's immortal Lyndall, at times, but she has neither the strength nor the poetry of that extravagant little spirit" (144).[22] In W. T. Stead's *The Review of Reviews* (1894), a critic observes the common themes that connect Brooke's novel with other writers, specifically the heroine's marriage to a degenerate aristocrat, which "recalls the 'speckled toad' episode in the 'Heavenly Twins' by Sarah Grand" (192).[23] Critics clearly associated the subject matter in Brooke's novel with other more established and well-known New Woman authors of the time. These associations spurred on the popularity of *A Superfluous Woman* and it became one of the most well read New Woman novels of the early 1890s.

A Superfluous Woman is a complex novel, which reflects Brooke's interests in socialist ideologies and the "woman question". Although she employed many of the standard tropes used by other so-called New Woman authors, her novel begins not with the New Woman, but with a commentary and critique of social classes through the introduction of the character, Dr. Cornerstone. He acts as Brooke's voice through which we hear her Socialist theories and agenda, which focus mainly on a woman's right to individual choice, free will, and intellectual development. It is through Dr. Cornerstone that we learn about the concept of "mind-energy as the one thing to be trusted in, cherished, and cultivated above all other qualities, and in all persons, without distinction of sex" (35). Without the stimulation of the mind women will not thrive in society, nor ever hope to be independent individuals. Dr. Cornerstone argues for the education of the aristocratic woman, "the idle

---

22 Olive Schreiner's feminist heroine in *The Story of an African Farm* (1883) is Lyndall. She is a philosophical character who envisions a world in which a woman does not have to define herself as a sexual being in order to be in a relationship with a man. Yet she takes a lover, gets pregnant, loses the child in labor and slips away into death. See Appendix A for the *Athenaeum* review.

23 See Appendix B for *The Review of Reviews* review.

lady–"the superfluous female" to exercise her "mind-energy" (38). Later, he expounds, in conversations with his intellectual friend, Carteret, and his wife, Mrs. Cornerstone, on his (Brooke's) socialist viewpoint about women's rights, their need to be intellectually stimulated in order to be productive members of society, and the political and economic differences between the sexes.

Dr. Cornerstone acts as the medium for change that takes place in Jessamine Halliday, the heroine of the narrative. At the beginning of the novel, she is wasting away and dying from self-induced ennui. Dr. Cornerstone is summoned when other, more traditional doctors have failed to help her; he administers the "pill, which they call Reality" by sharing a story of the plight of a working-class mother who can barely support her ill children on the wages she makes in a leather factory (32). Jessamine is revived by the awareness of extreme suffering and class disparities, so that she is filled with a desire to change herself and her purpose in life. As Dr. Cornerstone becomes her "Mentor," he introduces her to feminist, political, and socialist readings that affect the way she looks at herself and her position in society as a woman (42). The readings influence her and Jessamine shows her "force of mind" by becoming a "new" woman. She leaves behind her old identity in London as a "pretty piece of sexuality" to live a life of "good and useful thing[s]" through work in the Scottish Highlands (32, 48-49). "*To do good*" is Jessamine's ultimate goal and one that Brooke equates with the socialist ideas of an individual's ability to work with and for others in a community (Brooke's emphasis 48).

In Brooke's socialist view, the only way for a woman to live a productive, free, and healthy life is through education, physical labor and a rejection of rigid societal conventions; Jessamine must abandon her decadent upper-class lifestyle and embrace a more physically and emotionally edifying existence. As an aristocratic woman, Jessamine's sole purpose in life has been to get married. But with the introduction of Dr. Cornerstone and his socialist leanings, she begins to understand that in order for change to occur she must "step into the real … [and] … try vigorous work" (47). Brooke also ties Jessamine's emotional change in herself to a literal change in the environment. She flees London and goes to a farming community in the Scottish Highlands, where she meets Colin MacGillvray, a peasant farmer with whom she falls in love. In the Highlands, unlike London, she learns what it means to work alongside and to be on equal footing with a man. Colin plays an important role in Jessamine's change and development from a "*recherché* morsel" in a London drawing room to a woman who works with "vigorous application" (73, 56). Moreover, the environment of the Highlands offers a place where

Jessamine believes a sexual relationship with Colin and the birth of a child might occur outside of marriage.

Her greatest desire in her newfound love for Colin is to break from the culture of conventionality and embrace her own sexual freedom. She envisions a new future for herself when she might return to London to declare, "This is the child of the man I love … I could not marry him … but, yes, I loved him so that I united myself to him with trembling joy. And this is my baby" (132). This utopian vision, however, does not come to pass because Colin cannot see Jessamine as anything but "'My wife—*my wife!*'" (171). Jessamine has "abandoned herself and all her preconceived ideas" about marriage during her time in the Scottish Highlands; however, when confronted with Colin's possessive declaration, their vast division of class, and the knowledge of the inevitable "bargain", she finds her "passion flying from her" heart (171, 169). She rejects his offer of devotional love because it is tied to "The contract—the contract!" and returns to London where she instead marries the physically diseased and morally degenerate Lord Heriot to whom she had been promised by her Aunt Arabella before leaving that life behind her (169). Brooke uses the story of Jessamine's marriage to Lord Heriot to make a political argument about the imperative need for choice and free will for all women.

A popular subject explored in New Woman novels was the effect of the diseased male body and a man's morally degenerate behavior on a woman who becomes his wife and eventually has children in an unhealthy marriage. The final part of *A Superfluous Woman* is similar in subject matter to other New Woman plots of the time, especially Sarah Grand's *The Heavenly Twins* (1893).[24] In Grand's novel a discussion about the dangers of motherhood unfolds in the story of Edith and her marriage to a syphilitic man, Sir Mosely Menteith. Edith gives birth first to a son who seems to be "healthy when he was born" but "rapidly degenerate[s]" (277). She is pregnant with her second child when she returns home and gives birth to a "speckled toad" (301). Edith goes mad after giving birth and dies a painful death. She is characterized as a victim of society's desire that she remain ignorant of her husband's sexual and immoral behavior before their marriage.

Brooke also explores marriage to a physically and morally unhealthy husband but instead she gives Jessamine more insight and control over her life choices. Unlike Edith, Jessamine is not ignorant of her husband's degenerate family history or of his past debauched sexual behavior. She declares to Dr. Cornerstone that she "married him of my own free will. My eyes were wide

---

24 Grand, Sarah. *The Heavenly Twins*. Ann Arbor: University of Michigan Press, 1993.

open—wider than you think—than you dream" (199). She chose to marry Lord Heriot because although she "was conscious of degradation, yet [she] had not the force to resist" (197). She cannot fight against society's rigid expectations and conventions placed on aristocratic women to marry for status and economic profit. Moreover, Lord Heriot has "the Church and the clergy behind [him], and the support of society" (118). Like Grand's portrayal of Edith, Brooke is clearly equating Jessamine's unfortunate marriage with her victimization by society of which Lord Heriot is a part. Yet, Brooke is also interested in exploring what it means for Jessamine to change her fate as a woman and as a mother through the power of free will and personal choice.

In the third volume of *A Superfluous Woman,* the narrative moves forward by ten years. Jessamine is pregnant for the third time and explains to Dr. Cornerstone "from dreaming over [motherhood] as a half hope, I have come to think of it with concentrated horror" (199). She already has a daughter and a son, "aged respectively ... eight and six years" (200). The "idiot" daughter has a "drooping head" and is described by her mother as "malicious"; the son is a "poor malformed thing—a child who lived in pain" (200). Jessamine feels a strong sense of duty to her children who are alive, but only loathing for the growing child inside of her. She asks Dr. Cornerstone to "Give me the means of dying, so that my baby does not see the light of day . . . I am bound with chains. Give me the death which is my only release" (201). When Dr. Cornerstone refuses to help her die, Jessamine asks whether he believes in free will. Effectively, she believes she has a right to a self-induced abortion; she declares, "I will cancel it—from *within.* I will repudiate it—reject it—from *within* ... I myself will annul it ...Who has a right to his will, if not I? ... There is nothing ... stronger than a mother" (202). Motherhood was to be, for Jessamine, the salvation in her marriage to Lord Heriot, but instead children brought with them "an irresistible, irrevocable claim" upon her that she could not escape, except through their deaths and her own (211).

In this narrative, Brooke's socialist views about women and their children challenge British society's sentimentality surrounding motherhood at the time. She believed that motherhood, but especially pregnancy, led to the enslavement of women and the loss of their personal and economic independence. She wrote in 1888 that "a woman who is performing the function of motherhood is hopelessly handicapped; her force, whether she will or not, is going forth in an object apart from her own personal ends" ("Women and Their Sphere" 69). Jessamine's children are symbolic of her complete subjection to her husband. She thinks of the child inside of her as a "shadow—small, still, insignificant, but containing within itself monstrous possibilities" (210). Yet, through the use of the very "mind energy" that Dr. Cornerstone has declared is important for all women, Jessamine makes the choice to rid herself of her child; her "first quiet sense of achievement" is felt when her third child dies, as she willed it (218). And then she chooses death too.

However, Brooke lingers over Jessamine's self-analysis and self-awareness of her life before death. Effectively, Jessamine enters into a dream state in which she describes her discovery that she is pregnant again with an unhealthy child, her labor and birth of that child, its death, and her initial survival. When Jessamine comes out of this dream state under the care of Dr. Cornerstone "she realised what a frenzy of willing she had thrown into her desire that the baby should not live; fixing her thought on it … and filling day and night and space and time with the relentless demand for the extinction of that life" (218). She also remembers that in a sudden moment of violence, she has lost both of her other children at the hands of one another. Jessamine's "idiot" daughter kills her crippled brother and then in the frenzy dies herself. There is no sentimentality surrounding the deaths of her children nor is there any pain of loss; death is characterized for all involved as a means of release from suffering. Jessamine, herself, chooses death because "the needs of the body were over … she had dropped Life—dropped it like a heavy stone … There was no reason why she should go on living" (217). Death is positioned as a choice of the individual will, rather than a punishment for bearing unhealthy children and living in a loveless marriage.

Interestingly, Brooke does not end the novel with Jessamine's death, but interrupts her story to spend the penultimate chapter exploring issues concerning the nature of equality for men and women and the reasons for women to be educated, independent thinkers in society. This political discussion occurs away from London in the "most beautiful of all places, a fir-wood" while Dr. Cornerstone is on summer holiday with his wife, Mrs. Cornerstone, and their friend, Carteret (223). Dr. Cornerstone is relating the story of Jessamine, "the superfluous woman" as he refers to her, when he declares that it is time to "talk now as on an equality" (224). Mrs. Cornerstone asks the two men if their discussion will be as "though we were three men … or as though we were three women?" (223-224). This provocative question sets the tone for a frank examination among the three characters about the political and economic disparities between the sexes. Mrs. Cornerstone does not wait for an answer from them, but declares that she "will consent to listen. And in the end I shall perhaps decide whether to keep my own standpoint, or to condescend to yours" (224). In their conversation, she is positioned as a thinking woman on equal footing with both her husband and Carteret. She has barely entered into the narrative so far, but in this chapter Brooke uses her to show the strength, personal independence and intellectual rigor of the emancipated middle-class woman.

Mrs. Cornerstone's role in this chapter, besides being the voice of reason and moderation in their discussions about gender equality, is to argue that the description of "the superfluous woman" as applied to Jessamine is a misnomer. She anchors their conversation about women's equality by supporting Jessamine: "I, if I had known her, would have told her she was no more superfluous than the beautiful flower she was called by. I would have shown her how to believe it" (223). She clearly has faith in the solidarity of women and like Jessamine, has a mind of her own; she believes that every woman has the right to choose her own intellectual path in life, but "all women shall not have the same" educational options (227). She, Dr. Cornerstone and Carteret agree that choice is paramount to women's emancipation and that without it "women … are socially condemned to a too exclusive development of one side of the nature" (224). Presumably, as Brooke has argued throughout the narrative, the "one side of the nature" is the reproductive side that contributes to a woman being seen as "merely a function" in society and nothing more (225).

Illustrating the integrity and strength of women, Mrs. Cornerstone shows that she identities with Jessamine as a wife and a mother when she declares, "If I had known her, I would not have let her be beaten. I would have taught her that no man had a right to call her "superfluous"" (227). Hers is the voice to remind her husband and Carteret that all women are not "superfluous" but instead are "reasonable and adults" (228). Brooke seems to suggest that if one woman is unable to speak for and defend herself, there are other women who will come forward to speak for her. This is emphasized in Mrs. Cornerstone's final declaration about the way she perceives Jessamine: "I am going where I can think about her and not theorize. Perhaps—who knows?—I may discover that she is not so very distant from me, after all. If so, I shall have the opportunity I wish for of telling her that she is not superfluous" (229). Her desire to speak to Jessamine suggests an inherent link between the two, even beyond the grave, that has to do with the political unity of women across classes. This socialist viewpoint foreshadows Brooke's later work in The Fabian Women's Group, an organization which focused much of its attention on equalizing "class differences among women" in order to change their economic positions in society (Alexander 6).

Brooke had a clear socialist agenda in *A Superfluous Woman,* but she also explored issues concerning the "woman question." She did not see these subjects as separate from one another but integral to an understanding of a woman's economic and social position in British culture. Writing in the early twentieth century, Brooke declared, "there need be no question to the Socialist woman whether Socialism or the women's movement comes first. The women's problem cannot be truly solved without Socialism, while the success of Socialism itself lies as a germ in the heart of that problem" (Alexander 109). Throughout her career she argued that women were defined more often by their sexual roles in society and, therefore, inherently by their reproductive role. However, even if women became mothers, whether they embraced this responsibility or not, Brooke believed they could still achieve economic success through education, and in fact, they had a fundamental right to these advantages in society. The plot of *A Superfluous Woman* reflects Brooke's political viewpoints and offers much more than just a simple love story or a tale of a degenerate lord and his unsuspecting wife. Instead, she infuses the narrative with discussions that focus on the inequalities between men and women, the needs of women to be educated, to have personal independence, and to make informed choices in life. Indeed, it is the integration of her socialist and feminist views in her writing that make Brooke such a provocative author to examine in the twenty-first century.

BARBARA TILLEY
October 18, 2014

WORKS BY EMMA FRANCES BROOKE

Brooke, Emma. *A Superfluous Woman*. 3 vols. London: Heinemann, 1894.

__. *A Superfluous Woman*. New York: Cassell Publishing Company, 1894.

__. *Life the Accuser*. London: Heinemann, 1897.

__. *Sir Elyot of the Woods*. London: Heinemann, 1907.

__. *Susan Wooed and Susan Won*. London: Heinemann, 1905.

__. *The Confession of Stephen Whapshare*. London: Hutchinson & Co., 1898.

__. *The Engrafted Rose*. London: Hutchinson & Co., 1899.

__. *The House of Robershaye*. London: Smith, Elder & Co., 1912.

__. *The Poet's Child*. London: Methuen, 1903.

__. *The Story of Hauksgarth Farm, A Novel*. London: Smith, Elder & Co., 1909.

__. *The Twins of Skirlaugh Hall, A Mystery*. London: Hurst and Blackett, 1903.

__. *Transition*. London: Heinemann, 1895.

Byrrne, E. Fairfax. *A Fair Country Maid*. London: Richard Bentley and Sons, 1883.

__. *Entangled*. London: Hurst and Blackett, 1885.

__. *God's Gifts to Two Or Margaret Redfern's Discipline*. London: Religious Tract Society, 1883.

___. *Millicent, A Poem*. London: C. Kegan Paul & Co., 1881.

___. *The Heir Without a Heritage, A Novel*. London: Richard Bentley and Sons, 1887.

___. *Reaping the Whirlwind: A Story of Three Lives*. London: Religious Tract Society, 1904.

A NOTE ON THE TEXT

Published first in the classic, but fading three-decker volume form in January 1894, Brooke's novel quickly went into five printings ending with a one-volume edition in which she made many drastic changes to shorten the story. This final edition was published in June 1894 and includes a *Preface* that does not exist in any of the other editions, but is included here in the Appendix. Cassell Publishing Company of New York also published the American edition of *A Superfluous Woman* in 1894. The American edition follows the three-decker English printings in terms of the plot, but unfortunately changes significant words, phrases, and punctuation throughout the novel's narrative; moreover, the English spelling has been Americanized.

This Victorian Secrets edition follows the first edition of the novel, which was published on January 10, 1894 by William Heinemann and is to be found in the British Library.

ACKNOWLEDGEMENTS

In the very long process that it is has taken to bring this project to fruition, there are many people to thank and for whom I am grateful. First, I must say thank you to Catherine Pope for being willing to bring this wonderful work back into light once again. To Jay Jenkins at Valancourt Books, I must also say thank you because without him there would be no project at all and he connected me to Catherine in the kindest of ways. Key friends and family members lent their support as well: my best friend Margaret and my sister, Terry, read the introduction at pivotal points and gave much needed help and advice. And to my mother, Susan, I am grateful for her feedback in helping me to choose the most perfect cover for this edition. A special note of thanks goes to Ann Heilmann who has been a real mentor and guiding force in helping me to strengthen my argument in this introduction. Lastly, I must acknowledge the one person with whom I once lived and whom I loved for so long; she encouraged and supported me during the days, weeks, months, and years of research and writing about Emma Brooke: to Rita this book is dedicated.

ABOUT THE EDITOR

Barbara Tilley is a Visiting Assistant Professor at DePaul University in Chicago. She is in the Writing, Rhetoric and Discourse department where she teaches a range of first year writing courses. Her literary background is in the long nineteenth century and she has published short pieces on John Keats and the Lake School poets. She is currently working on a critical biography of Emma Brooke, which focuses on Brooke's socialist politics as they relate to her interests in and promotion of women and worker's rights during her lifetime. Tilley is examining Brooke's central and active leadership within the Fabian Society and the Fabian Women's Group between 1885 and 1918. Included in the book will be an exploration of Brooke's most important relationships with those writers and intellectuals whom she befriended in the early years of the Fabian Society, including George Bernard Shaw, Sidney and Beatrice Webb, and Edward Pease.

A Superfluous Woman

PART I

CHAPTER I

'DYING? H'm!' said the Doctor.

He was a short square man with great shoulders; and he stood with his hands thrust into the pockets of his coat, and with his legs a little apart; he had forgotten to turn down his trousers before coming into the room, so that a pair of large strong boots, much splashed with mud, planted themselves only too visibly upon the carpet. He was not a West-End[1] doctor, and had made his way to this West-End mansion by short stages in omnibuses and by short stages on foot. His practice lay amongst the sores which devour the flesh of Lazarus.[2] Most of his hours were spent in those hospitals where the maimed worker seeks a little respite from misery before he passes from the cruelty of the world, and much of his leisure in gratuitous labour amongst the fetid dens of the poor. He seemed in his own eyes to be as a gatherer who binds together perpetually fallen sheaves of blighted corn, and his constant fight with death had brought a grim look into his face.

But not into his eyes. These were large, brown, soft and penetrating, and had the look of one who brings a message, or who entreats a favour. They called this man Dr. Cornerstone.

'Dying, Doctor!' repeated the lady with whom he was in converse, wiping from her eye the moisture of sentiment, while her mind with really strong feeling repudiated his boots.

'Madam,' said Dr. Cornerstone, 'perhaps I can see my patient?'

---

1   The West-End of London was considered the more upper-class and wealthy part of the city. This would be the "area of London lying west of Charing Cross and including the fashionable shopping district around Oxford Street and Regent Street as well as Mayfair and the Parks". A. D. Mills, *Oxford Dictionary of London Place Names.* Oxford: Oxford University Press, 2004, 245.

2   The story of Lazarus is from the New Testament and the Gospel of Luke (16:19-31). He is the beggar who was given nothing as he stood outside the gates of the rich man. When both men die, it is Lazarus who goes to heaven; the rich man suffers from everlasting thirst and is tormented by heat and fire. In Brooke's context Lazarus represents the London poor to whom Dr. Cornerstone ministers. *The Bible, Authorized King James Version with Apocrypha.* Robert Carroll and Stephen Pricket, Eds. Oxford: Oxford University Press, 1997.

Upon which the lady brought her pocket-handkerchief from her face, and rose, and led the way from the room.

The house through which the Doctor followed her was full of pleasant airs and pleasant scents; through the open windows of the staircase he caught glimpses of trees in blossom (for it was May), and the sound of the city came to the ear only as a pleasing hum. For the mansion was in one of the best parts of London, and round about blew the breezes of the open park, so that in a moment, as by enchantment, he who entered here was set apart from the noise and the disgrace of the streets.

They paused at the door of a chamber. Here the lady turned round once more, and once more wiped the tear of sentiment from her eye.

'Dying, Doctor!' said she. 'The most beautiful woman in England, and one of the richest! The world was at her feet. Indeed, there is no doubt that, had not this illness intervened, Lord Heriot——'

'Madam, shall we proceed?' said the Doctor with a singular look.

And the lady opened the door.

He found himself in a large chamber so disposed for luxury that the senses of one who breakfasted, dined and supped on misery might well stagger for the moment. A wide and beautiful window showed trees full of blossom; opposite the window, but at some distance back in the room, was a comfortable couch upon which the patient lay, covered with a pearl-coloured silk eiderdown. By the side of the couch was a table with flowers and fruit; a nurse appropriately dressed in the exquisite garb of her profession stood near, holding a cup of fragrant soup. Another nurse flitted in the background of the room, where the Doctor rather surmised than saw a bed, and the elegant litter of a luxurious toilet. The prettinesses of the chamber alone, gathered there merely to please the eye of the occupant, must, the Doctor reflected, have diverted labour sufficient to have produced the clothes and food for a whole street of starving people for a year's time.

He advanced towards the couch and planted himself somewhat sturdily before it, his hands again in his coat-pockets, and his muddy boots a little apart, and he looked down at the face and figure which the pearl-silk eiderdown partially concealed.

The lady who had accompanied him stood meanwhile a little behind, with her hands folded together and her head inclined, and wearing an expression of anxiety which was conventional rather than deep.

Contrasts are apt to be trying, and, by the side of the sturdy Doctor, anything tutored and compressed in deference to fashion fell away from the lines of humanity into caricature. And one half of this lady's personality had been purchased, it is to be feared, in shops; Worth, the hairdresser, perfumer and dentist were responsible for her more striking features, while, though God may have been the shaper of her bones in the first instance, they had suffered from the corset-maker's processes. As to her mind, if the exterior were any index to it, this, with the smile and tear, was probably Society's own product.

Such was the woman within whose hands had lain the shaping of the earlier years of the girl who reposed beneath the eiderdown upon the couch; she it was who had been the ruling spirit, the educator and influence.

It was in the Doctor's mind that it had been so, as he stood gazing at the unsolved enigma of his patient; and the thought threw him upon a reverie so deep that he forgot either to move or speak; and presently the lady unclasped her hands and drew up her head, the attitude of appropriate sorrow being prolonged further than endurance could bear. At the same moment a nurse set a cup of broth down on a table. The chink of the china roused the Doctor; he raised his head and looked round.

'Remove these women,' said he.

The lady signalled with her hand, and the attendants disappeared, closing the door behind them with the caution of long practise. When they had gone, she found herself confronted by an open-eyed and steady look. This unaccustomed steadfastness and truth in the eye confounded her like an accusation; her nerves shrank and her spirits took a panic, and all the artifice slipped off her face, as the colour will wash from the cheek of a doll.

'I must request you also to leave me alone with my patient,' said the Doctor, in a cool clear whisper.

Whereupon the woman's scared senses fled straight away to the book of etiquette; it was her rock of ages, and she clung there with tenacity.

'Impossible, Doctor! Impossible! I could not do such a thing! It is not customary!' she returned in emphatic sibilants.

A ray of sardonic humour gleamed in the man's eye, and alarmed her once more with the sense of the unusual.

'Madam,' said he, 'you tell me that three physicians have tried their hands on this case and failed. You tell me that, hearing my name by chance, you proposed to call me in to assist. And your physicians consented to permit this last resource. But they informed you that my methods were unusual and unorthodox, and that it was impossible for them to meet me professionally, or to take the responsibility of applying them. In other words, in spite of my doctor's degree, I am a quack. You have, madam, sufficiently outraged custom by calling me in at all, and a trifle more or less will do no harm. Custom, you will understand, does not apply to quacks.'[3]

He began to walk at her as he spoke, with his head raised, and with his eyes steady. And she went before him as though a wind had blown, carrying a shaft of fear to her heart. When she had gone, he turned the key in the door.

The patient had not so much as lifted an eyelid.

Dr. Cornerstone went first to a table where the prescriptions and medicine-bottles stood, and where pens and ink were placed in readiness for himself. He read the prescriptions in a leisurely manner, and then took up the notes of the nurses. The prescriptions he swept aside; upon the notes he made a few concise comments. And then once more he came to the side of the couch and gazed at the patient. Then he drew a chair near and sat down, and stretched out his hand and took hers into it.

She lay there as beautiful and as still as a marble statue. Her dark hair fell upon the pillow and over the edge towards the carpet; her dark lashes rested on her cheek; her features were small, and there was a dimple near her mouth, and a dent in her chin; her eyebrows were wide and beautiful as a bird's wing. She was called Jessamine Halliday. One wasted hand lay outside on the quilt, and held a sprig of the white jessamine blossom loosely. Only by the scarcely visible motion of the lace about her throat and breast could one have told that she lived. The Doctor kept her hand in his silently for a few minutes. And he looked towards the garden, where the wind came and went softly amongst the May blossoms, and where the bees already hummed.

Then, in a low voice, he spoke:

'The Reaper goes,' said he, 'over the Great City. His wings are Famine and Overwork, but his eyes are merciful. He stands now upon the threshold of a room; none who are in the room see him or think of him; he is their deliverer, the only one they have, or can have, but their whole life is spent in keeping him at bay. They think only how they shall manage to live—to exist. They think of that, though there is nothing in life which they can hope for to make it pleasant and worth living. They ask for nothing but to work hard—hard— and to gather a few pence at the end. The fear that the hard work will fail them is the haunting fear of their lives. The room is a low attic, with a slanting roof and a small window. The window is open, but just outside is a wall with other small windows; the one opposite has a broken pane stuffed with rags. There is a stifling smell in the room, for it is filled with people at work. Under the window are two men cutting pieces of fur into shape on a wooden

---

3   As a "quack," Dr. Cornerstone's methods set him apart from his peers and enable him to treat patients of all classes; he clearly does not embrace the hierarchical structure of class that exists in English culture and society. His view of class reflects Brooke's own Socialist views, as we shall see throughout the novel.

table; across the fireplace is a board on trestles, and here a lad nails the fur and stretches it. In another corner is an old wooden bedstead, worm-eaten, moth-destroyed, and revolting; here a sick woman sits, and her shaking fingers hold some strips of the fur. She never raises her head; she sews and sews, and looks at the work; when she coughs badly she has to wait for a minute, but her trembling fingers set to the work again feverishly. At the other end of the room are two other women sewing as she does. They are all three elderly, and all three are leaden-eyed and pale and exhausted. They are working now as they have worked all their lives; the sick woman on the bed has two children to keep. Her husband died five months ago; but for two years before his death he was ill, and could not work. She kept him, too. She is thinking now of the two little ones locked in the garret in the opposite court, and waiting for her to come back to feed them. All her life she has worked as she works now, but she has never made for herself or for them one wholesome set of clothes, nor cooked one satisfying meal. And now there are sores upon her face, her hair has been cut away in patches, her eyes are half blind, and her cheeks are sunken, so that the bones threaten to pierce them, and her skin burns with fever. Once she looks up, and in her eyes is a horrible fear; something frightens her. The women at the other end of the room have been talking loudly and complainingly, and the man at the table is answering them angrily. "You can do it or not, as you like," he says in a rough voice; "is it my fault, I asks? What does the governor say to me? He says I may take the furs at two and six a dozen less, or I may leave them alone. He says he knows a chap that will do them lower than that. 'It's nothing to me,' he says, 'who does them, or who doesn't. I'm not going to waste my time talking,' he says. And if he knocks off my pay, where am I? Is it my fault that I take a penny here or a penny there off yours? How am I to live, I want to know? There are plenty of women waiting to take your places, and you know that as well as I do." He swears as he talks, and the women are silent after a time. She on the bed has never spoken. Her eyes sink back to her work, and her cheek has gone deadly pale. She lays her hand on her breast for a moment. The baby at home is but six months old, and how is it to be fed?

'Night comes. At last the lights are put out in the work-room, and the woman can go home. She creeps upstairs to the garret in the opposite court, full of sick fear and misery. She is always frightened when she leaves them so long alone. To-night, when she opens the door, she finds the eldest child wailing on the floor, and the baby lying in the cradle, white and weak, with scarcely a breath passing between its lips. And the fear comes into the mother's face again, and she feels at her breast, and cries to one who has come up the stairs behind her: "Doctor! doctor! for the Lord's love give me a drink of broth! For the child's sake, doctor!"

'But the Reaper, unseen and merciful, followed her from the work-room; he stands now beside her in the garret, and his eyes are merciful and tender; he lays his hand upon mother and child. He does it now—for this is no dream—he steps nearer. He gathers these two, and lays them to rest in his bosom.'

The Doctor's voice ceased. And when it had stopped, the wind was heard whispering through the trees. And he still held one of the white hands of Jessamine in his own; the other hand had let fall the blossom.

'The Reaper goes over the Great City,' spoke the Doctor once more; 'and his wings are Idleness and Riches, but his eyes are flames of wrath. And he stands upon the threshold of the room, and he cries: "How long, O Lord, how long?"[4] And a Voice goes out like the whispering of wind in the blossoms of the trees. And the Voice says: "Lay not Thine hand to the root, but give time for repentance, and bid the sick arise, and work, and suffer!"'[5]

The Doctor stopped and turned from the window, and the girl's eyes were wide open and were fixed upon his; and then he lifted her with his arm, and while she lay back against his shoulder he fed her slowly in small sips with the strong and fragrant soup.

'Is the woman dead?' whispered the patient.

'Yes,' said the Doctor.

---

4   The Reaper's quotation is from Psalm 13 in a modified form: "How long wilt thou forget me, O Lord? for ever? How long wilt thou hide thy face from me? How long shall I take counsel in my soul, having sorrow in my heart daily? how long shall mine enemy be exalted over me?" (Psalm 13:1-2). The sentiment here in Psalm 13 relates to the story just told by Dr. Cornerstone of the suffering mother and her children.

5   The quote spoken by the "Voice" is less clear. This seems to be a mix of biblical references, only one of which I could definitely find and even that, it seems, has been interpreted differently by Brooke. This is the last part of the quote: "and bid the sick arise, and work, and suffer." This is most likely from St. Mark: "Whether is it easier to say to the sick of the palsy, Thy sins be forgiven thee; or to say, Arise, and take up thy bed, and walk?" (Mark 2:9).

CHAPTER II

JUST one year and one month passed, and upon a mild June evening Dr. Cornerstone sat talking with a friend in his study. The windows were thrown open and the blinds were not drawn. When for a time the square was silent and no one passed up it with the shriek or the whoop by which born Londoners try to assure themselves of mirth at the heart, a rustle of trees was heard; and from the window (for the room was on the first-story) were to be seen interlaced branches and leaves with the gaslight of the square very prettily shining upon them. In the daytime the trees looked black and dry, and exhausted the spirit rather than refreshed it; but at night they put on something of their pristine character.

Besides the trees, high between the chimneys of the great hospital opposite, one saw a star or two.

Around the square, which was in comparison a well of silence, the roar of the city went like some evil and despairing beast.

Dr. Cornerstone sat on an armchair with his feet stretched out. Business was not quite as brisk with him as usual; in June the people were neither choked with poisonous heat nor nipped to the heart with cold; in June Dr. Cornerstone had a less grim look than ordinary. He appeared quite sweet-tempered now as he enjoyed this unusual leisure with a friend by his side.

From upstairs sometimes—at those moments when no beat of human feet passed up the square—one heard the measured creak of a rocking-chair, and the sound of a sweet voice singing an old song:

> 'Go from the window, love, go,
>   Go from the window, my dear;
> The wind and the rain will not drive you back again;
>   You may not be lodgèd here.'[1]

That was Dr. Cornerstone's wife rocking her baby.

Opposite to the Doctor, on another easy-chair, sat an old friend named Carteret. He was a small man, and he did not stretch himself out, but

---

1   This is a single verse from a longer folk ballad, "Go From My Window," with an extensive oral history. However, it was made popular in Francis Beaumont's 1679 play, *The Knight of the Burning Pestle*.

crumpled his body up and hugged it with his crossed arms; and he thrust forward his thin, eager face, and fixed his eyes steadily on one spot in the carpet, as though a hand wrote something there for him to read.

'And so she did not die, after all?' Carteret was saying.

'Die? Oh dear me no! Certainly not.'

'Have you a name for her illness?'

'I call it a splenetic seizure brought on by ennui and excessive high-breeding.'[2]

'No disease?'

'None. A mere phantasy, a pose. Her imagination had been touched by the picturesque interest of mortal decay upon æsthetic furniture.'

'Faugh! What medicine can purge such sickliness?'

'One only. I administered the pill which they call Reality—in silver wrapping, it may be.'

Carteret grimaced at the carpet.

'A few visits unfolded her nature to me—if, indeed, it be nature. I never saw a creature so fatally feminine. She was just a pretty piece of sexuality. She never thought of herself save as a dainty bit of flesh which some great man would buy.'

'Hum! A professional——'

'*Beauty*,' interposed Cornerstone; 'and with a high price for which she would stand out. Poor wretch! She—they are what society makes them.'

'And they take to it kindly!'

'Some do. As to her, I do not know that. Something tormented her. She had tried every conceivable contortion by which to kill time. She was clever; I never met with a more able nor a more restless little mind. One year she had been artistic, another learned, a third aesthetic, a fourth political, and so on. She was fond of horses, it appears, but not with constancy. She told me that in the autumn she would sometimes shoot and fish like a man. But, in spite of all, the days gaped at her blank and empty.'

'Mortally sick of herself and her amusements, in short.'

---

2 A "splenetic seizure" is applicable to emotions and does not necessarily affect the body in the strictest sense. In the nineteenth century, the spleen was still thought of as "the seat of certain emotions". In this context "splenetic" would be understood as melancholy emotions, rather than the more modern definition of "bad-tempered, [or] irritable" (1374 – 75). *Webster's New World Dictionary of the American Language.* 2nd College ed. Cleveland: William Collins, 1976. Also, in this context ennui is a physical state of listlessness and weariness, though the modern French definition is "boredom" (193). *Larousse French Dictionary.* Boston: Houghton Mifflin Company, 2006.

'And so her final resource was death. I never saw so highly self-conscious a creature, nor one so intuitively aware how the graces of a life-long demeanour may be rounded off at last by a poetic exit from the stage. I fancy the purveyors to fashionable drawing-rooms must have entreated her presence from motives similar to those which prompt them to seek out exotics for the decoration of the table. Her own personality appears to have been her single sustained and successful study. But she had a will! And had she not puzzled the doctors! When I found her she was certainly in danger—floating gracefully down the stream of life to the dark river at the end.'

'And you plucked at her skirts with a rough hand, and saved her?'

'I did so.'

'And when you had set her up on her legs again—if one may surmise legs in so superlative a creature—how did it work?'

'My pill, you mean?'

'Yes; your pill—Reality.'

'"Like madness in the brain."[3] She got well and plunged into new fevers of restlessness. To infuse reality with sober effect one needs a prepared system. She got a sufficient hold of my notions to run new crazes with them. She read Thoreau and Browning's "Waring," and caricatured the ideas in her self-conscious mode.[4] By August she was dressed in unbleached calico and prints at twopence a yard; in the early winter she was running over the East-End[5] with a train of lovers; at the turn of the year I heard of her lecturing on a public platform, the audience chiefly composed of men.'

Carteret shrugged up his shoulders and stretched one lean hand out towards the spot in the carpet, with a derisive grimace.

---

3 Samuel Taylor Coleridge (1772-1834) was a Romantic poet; this line is from the second part of his poem "Christabel" (1798): " . . . And to be wroth with one we love / Doth work like madness in the brain . . ." (412-413). *Norton Anthology of English Literature*. Ed. M. H. Abrams. New York: W. W. Norton & Co., 2000.

4 Henry David Thoreau (1817-1862) was an American transcendentalist writer who is most famous for *Walden, or, Life in the Woods* (1854), which is about his personal experiences living alone in the woods. Among other discussions in *Walden*, he was very interested in the natural world around him. Robert Browning (1812-1889) was a nineteenth-century English poet. He published "Waring," a poem about his very close friend, Alfred Domett (1811-1887) in 1842. The poem concerns Browning's clear admiration and love for Domett as a friend and an artist; Domett was a poet himself. Jessamine is presumably reading both Thoreau and Browning's "Waring" in order to outline for herself the sort of "prepared system" of learning that Dr. Cornerstone refers to earlier in his discussion of her.

5 "The East-End" is a late nineteenth-century term "to describe the heartland of London (the area lying *east* of the city)" (Mills 71-72).

'If,' said he, 'I were a doctor—and it is perhaps a providential dispensation that I am not—I should, Cornerstone, use some discrimination in my art of healing.'

'I agree with you theoretically.'

'I might, for instance,' continued Carteret, 'have thought it scarcely worth while to bring this pretty humbug back to life.'

'But,' said the Doctor, 'a pound or two of healthy human flesh is more valuable in the eyes of our profession than gold of Ophir, and as rare.'[6]

'And she—this artificial minx—is sound?'

'To the core, Carteret. Besides'—the Doctor paused and sighed—'she is a woman.'

'And therefore destined to be "a breeder of sinners."'[7]

Dr. Cornerstone stretched himself out further, folded his hands, leaned his head on the back of his chair, and contemplated the movements of a moth about the ceiling.

'Being a woman,' said he, 'I both pitied and had hopes of her.'

'You were always an optimist.'

'An optimist? No. Try a day's doctoring among the people, and ask yourself if such a thing be possible. But a man whose bitter repast is mitigated by a seasoning of hope—yes.'

'And how did you manage to fish up that bright-coloured thing from the rag-bag of this life?'

'One day I sat thinking, and I got an idea. Carteret, did you ever get an idea?'

'I? Never.'

The Doctor smiled at the moth. Carteret looked up at him with expectation. He was a man whose pleasures lay almost exclusively on the mental side, and his face was worn with the partly conscious martyrdom of deprivation. In thought, in conversation, he was the peer of his fellows, but not elsewhere. An insistence upon the wholeness of human nature, the identity of body and soul, an exhortation from the pagan school to partake of life's feast freely, genially, and without fear, must be irony to some men, and but bitter advice to innumerable women.

6   Ophir is a land of wealth and riches referred to in several places in the Bible. In The First Book of the Kings (9:28) it reads, "And they came to Ophir, and fetched from thence gold, four hundred and twenty talents, and brought it to king Solomon" (*The Bible* 423).

7   This is from *Hamlet,* in which Hamlet says to Ophelia: "Get thee to a nunn'ry, why wouldst thou be a breeder of sinners?" (Act III. Scene I.). *The Riverside Shakespeare.* Boston: Houghton Mifflin Company, 1974.

'The truth is,' said the Doctor, 'we look at things with a too limited eye, and are constitutionally invalided. We are not robust enough to bear to accept the processes of Nature, and we distrust some of our own best faculties.'

'By the last you mean, I presume, that offence against priesthood, mind-energy—that which bids us to dare, do, will, and think. And, one may add, to pull down the house about our ears by way of letting in the skies.'

'Surely energy manifests itself in reserve, self-control, masterly silence and patience, as well as in the more obvious activity? But you are right—it was this mind-energy I alluded to. And I note that the quality is not so much found alarming in a man's own mind as in that of his neighbour—the other man.'

'Or the other woman?'

'Of her chief and foremost,' cried the Doctor, 'whom we are so slow to recognise as our neighbour. Well, the idea that came to me was simply a sudden flashing appreciation of mind-energy as the one thing to be trusted in, cherished, and cultivated above all other qualities, and in all persons, without distinction of sex. It was an inspiration of faith in what we have within ourselves of the best. It was a revolt against invalidish prudence, and an invitation towards robust daring anywhere and everywhere. Even so far as to say that we ought not so much to name mistaken results disaster, as the common practise of servile imitation and faint-hearted acquiescence.'

'The cost being not counted too great, so that genuinely new ideas are opened out to a failing world?'

'Precisely.'

'Well, all I can say is that to a dead certainty the mere suggestion of such a thing will set all our hens, male and female, cackling.'

'Yet I found this sudden premonition of trustworthiness in mind-energy extraordinarily refreshing. It was as though I had lifted up windows in the soul and seen new horizons.'

'It is all very well,' said Carteret; 'but plenty of people will tell you that you can't trust a child with fire nor Phæton with the chariot of the sun.'[8]

---

8 Phæton was the son of Apollo and the nymph Clymene. Phæton questions his parentage, desiring to know whether he really is the son of a god. Clymene directs him to Apollo, who tells Phæton that to prove to him that Phæton is his son, Apollo will grant him any wish that he desires. Phæton wants to drive his father's chariot to the sun, but Apollo cannot allow this wish to be granted because he says that no one can control the chariot except himself. However, Phæton insists, and Apollo gives in to his demand. Phæton cannot control the chariot, and chaos is created in the heavens and upon earth, until Jupiter sends a bolt of lightning and hits the chariot, sending Phæton to his death "like a shooting star" into the river below (40-46). Edmund

'Oh, undoubtedly there might be some ferment and a little danger at first. But the education would be gradual. And in my opinion fewer houses would be burned down, and there would be fewer unpleasant accidents with the fiery elements, if people were guided by explanations, instead of being handed mechanical rules.'

'Possibly,' said Carteret.

'Moreover, life has an odd habit of calling unwilling Phætons to drive ghostly chariots along perilous ways, without any preparation. I propose simply an assiduous cultivation of the mind, so that a man's spirit may be prepared to rise to sudden emergencies. A man's'—here the Doctor paused and sighed—'and also a woman's.'

'Ah! now we return to our Jessamine!'

Carteret settled himself in his chair like a child expecting a story. While the Doctor collected his thoughts, a belated organ-grinder at the end of the square turned on his instrument, played a few bars spasmodically, and left off with the dominant seventh unresolved.

'Yes, here we return to her,' said he at last. 'Life does not exempt these untrained travellers from the usual problems. "Your right decision or your life!" cries that constant and remorseless old highwayman to every soul, male or female alike, and he will take no excuses, nor admit palliations. Yet the education of our Jessamines is into the suppression and rarely into the exercise of mind-energy; it is a prolonged process of curtailment and stunting of the faculties on which right choice and firm vitalizing decisions depend. This leaves the nature pliant to the cultivation of certain characteristics, which, being exaggerated, leave them particularly open to sudden dilemmas.'

'The unfortunate creature! She has never been taught even to shoot at a mark or to do anything with a trigger save scream at it.'

'Just so.'

'It is our infernal selfishness—women crammed inside the coach out of the way of the view, while man bosses it on the box-seat and breathes the air.'

'It is precisely this contact with the fresh air, this command of the wide view, which I claim for all, but demand particularly for women as a necessary condition of their wholesome development. You perceive, Carteret, what a flat catalogue of conventional virtues we impose upon women, assuming them to be the characteristics of the whole sex? Now, I am by no means certain that the catalogue does not include some very deplorable elements, which result in unmitigated harm both racially and socially. At any rate, in varied individualities there must be difference all through, yet one type of

Fuller, Ed. *Bulfinch's Mythology.* New York: Dell Publishing, 1959.

character is handed to all, with the advice "Please *copy*." But no virtue is effective that is not living and spontaneous. And how can a set of fictitious rules give these women any guidance in self-management?'

'You see,' said Carteret, 'it was a man who bore the sins of the world.[9] The woman has the far more onerous office of going into the wilderness as a scapegoat, bearing its virtues.'

'Just so,' said Cornerstone.

'I have always held,' continued Carteret dryly, 'that our great national improvidence lies in the two departments of our refuse and our women. The distinctions of sex where they are arbitrary are in themselves a waste. Why squander individuality in rules? The manner of a woman's thoughts, deeds, and words is prescribed, as you say, beforehand by society; her very love must be according to platitudes and the code. It must be a beautiful fidelity, affection, sentiment, but not a passion like a man's. But supposing a woman fall into something indecorously natural?'

'Well, then comes the rub, for which their education has not prepared them. All coercion and restriction, from outside instead of from within, is merely painful without fruitful result. When I first saw Jessamine, I was considering this very point. I went one day to the Park at the fashionable hour to watch the faces.'[10]

'Hum!'

'After ten minutes I knew I had got fast amongst a circle of the damned. I saw that the place was a wheel round which, in slow immortal weariness, souls damned for idleness were being drawn.'

> *"L'ennui fruit de la morne incuriosité,*
> *Prend les proportions de l'immortalité,"*[11]

murmured Carteret.

---

9   This is a reference to Jesus Christ. In John we read, "The next day John seeth Jesus coming unto him, and saith, Behold the Lamb of God, which taketh away the sin of the world!" (1:29). Carteret's comment underscores the dilemma about a woman's place in the world and society that the two men are discussing.

10 "The Park, at the fashionable hour" refers to Rotten Row in Hyde Park, Westminster. It was common for upper-class men and women to ride in carriages and on horseback to be seen by others at a particular hour of the day.

11   Charles Baudelaire (1821-1867) was a French poet. This is from his poem "Spleen II" (1857). Translation: "When boredom, slow fruit of total apathy, / Takes on the dimensions of immortality" (17-18). *Poison and Vision: Poems and Prose of Baudelaire, Mallarmé and Rimbaud*. Ed. David Paul. New York:Vintage Books, 1974.

'It was a bad sort of sight. I found only the very young girls at all tolerable. Youth in itself is a triumph and a hope. But even there the indefinable tracing of pain and coercion had begun; not one, even of the girls, carried her fetters unconsciously. The iron entered into their souls. I fancied they leaned back in their carriages with closed lips in despair!'

'Lord, how you exaggerate!' exclaimed Carteret.

'I think not,' replied the Doctor; 'not when you make allowances for exceptions. I've nothing to say, for instance, of the *emancipated* woman of the well-to-do middle-class, beyond a friendly grip of the hand such as one bestows on an equal. Neither have I to do just now with the multitude of women-toilers of the masses. And I will leave out of the question also the recognised prostitute. I am occupied simply with the unemancipated daughter of the aristocracy, the plutocracy, and the upper and lower middle classes.'

'With the idle lady—"the superfluous female," in short?'

'Just so. No; I do not exaggerate. I assure you, Carteret, that in all the hours I stood there watching, I never saw one man and woman speak to each other with the free and independent dignity of equals conscious of obligations to the world they lived in. It was all sexuality on the one side, with its correlative sensuality on the other. Whereupon a furious and blinding rage fell upon me; I stood as a stone in my place, wishing that I had the whip of small cords with which the Lord drove the swine down the hill into destruction.'[12]

'Your theology, Cornerstone, is somewhat mixed, but is always efficient.'

'And while I stood thus stupefied, an open victoria drew up by the rails close beside me. I think the Princess was passing. There were two women in the carriage—one quite elderly, the other a girl in her teens. The heart of the old one had perished; she did not suffer, because mortification had set in; but, then, she was no longer human. The other was, as I say, young; I thought at first she did not suffer either. She leaned back and did not lift her eyes. Her face was soft and quiet and beautiful——'

---

12 Dr. Cornerstone has confused his theology here. The first part of the quote, "the whip of small cords," is from St. John: "And when he [Jesus] had made a scourge of small cords, he drove them [the Jew merchants] all out of the temple, and the sheep, and the oxen; and poured out the changers' money, and overthrew the tables" (John 2:15). The second part of the quote—"the Lord drove the swine down the hill into destruction"—is from St. Mark: "Now there was there nigh unto the mountains a great herd of swine feeding. And all the devils besought him, saying, Send us into the swine, that we may enter into them. And forthwith Jesus gave them leave. And the unclean spirits went out, and entered into the swine: and the herd ran violently down a steep place into the sea, (they were about two thousand;) and were choked in the sea" (Mark 5:11-13).

'Ah, Miss Halliday!'

'That was the first time I saw her. Carteret, there are faces which issue from Nature's hand as from a dream. It is as though she sat musing upon an idea as an artist might do, picking up a trait here and a feature there, until it is made perfect, and then she sends it out into a thankless world. What shall we do with our beautiful women? It was a little face—not one of those big, bouncing, full-blown roses; but soft and rare, small and exquisite. And then she had an air which turned the whole place into a picture. Her name is Jessamine, and Jessamine describes her; and she held a spray of the flower in her hand. They say she always has leaf or blossom by her. Well, as I gazed, I became suddenly aware that I impeded the desire of some other person to get near her, and a voice spoke over my shoulder. Ugh! that voice! A thread of vice ran through it like the twang of a broken wire—a thin trickle of disease dropped out with every syllable——'

'But what did the fellow say?'

'Oh, ah! Nothing! nothing! "How do you do, Miss Halliday? So fortunate to catch a glimpse of you! You enjoyed last night? So glad. Going to-night to Lady S——'s? So glad! Shall I be there? Can you ask? Reserve me a waltz. No, no! a *waltz.*"'

The Doctor rose up from his seat and took two or three turns along the room; then he paused opposite Carteret's chair.

'I say the face had an ineffable quality,' he said. 'A violet before now has plucked at my heart. In flowers there are "thoughts too deep for tears."[13] A beautiful face with that indescribable something in it—that poetic suggestion—will stir my soul as a passage of music might; it will lift up my thought for a week. But before my mind had pictured the Paradise about this modern Eve, I saw already the snake lurking in the grass—fatal, horrible.'

The Doctor reseated himself.

'I turned away; but as I turned I heard someone answering for the young girl. The voice said, "*Dear* Lord Heriot, we receive a few *favoured* friends at five this evening for tea. Come round and settle about the dance with dearest Jessamine." I turned again—why, I cannot say. Lord Heriot was occupied with that old Jezebel; the girl had moved her pretty head, and was looking at me. It was the strangest moment. I don't think she saw me really, but she let me read in her face like a book. There was complacent vanity there in large

---

13 This is a modified quote from William Wordsworth's poem "Ode: Intimations of Immortality from Recollections of Early Childhood" (1807). The last four lines of stanza eleven read: "Thanks to the human heart by which we live, / Thanks to its tenderness, its joys, and fears, / To me the meanest flower that blows can give / Thoughts that do often lie too deep for tears" (*The Norton Anthology* 200-204).

measure (they say Heriot is the greatest catch in Europe, so heavily does our beautiful civilization handicap the strong against the weak and diseased), but struggling through this miasmic cloud I saw a look in her eyes. These cried to me plainer than words: "Rescue me! Rescue me!"'

Dr. Cornerstone paused. A thin noise of rain fell amongst the trees in the square, and the step of a man in haste went by.

'When they called me to her bedside I was not astonished,' said the Doctor presently in a low voice; 'it could not surprise me that she had chosen to die.'

'Ah!'

'Her eyes—it was three years or so after the scene in the Park that they called me in—kept always that look. They are astonishingly deep and sombre. They cast a mystery over the face. I have had the conviction sometimes when she turned them towards me, with their inscrutable pathos, that it is humanity itself which cries to one through eyes like that—the sufferings of generations having been concentrated into one pair of orbs; they look at you with the pent-up grief of a race.'

'Or is it prevision of her own?'

Dr. Cornerstone made no reply. He rose once more from his chair, and began once more to perambulate slowly up and down the chamber.

Meanwhile Carteret got his hand into his coat-pocket, and began to fumble in it with a slow, hesitating air. At length he drew out a copy of an evening paper.

'Have you heard the news?' said he.

'What news? Is there anything new under the sun?'

'This paragraph, for instance?'

'What about?'

'It is headed—— It appears to be about Miss Halliday.'

The Doctor stopped in his walk, and his brow contracted uneasily.

'Ah! She has married Lord Heriot!'

'No,' returned Carteret; 'no, not that. The paragraph is headed, "Mysterious Disappearance of Miss Jessamine Halliday."'

CHAPTER III

THE morning after the Doctor's talk with Carteret, a servant entered his consulting-room and handed him a letter. It had no post-mark, and had been pushed into the letter-box by some person unknown. Nor was anyone aware at what hour, for the deliverer had neither rung nor knocked. The Doctor took it without curiosity, supposing it to be one of the constantly received demands for help in illness or poverty.

But a certain prosperous air about the envelope, a suggestion of luxury in the thick creamy paper, above all, the firm characteristic handwriting so expressive of culture, caught his attention. He opened the letter at once, and found it to be one of several sheets in an unknown hand; then he glanced at the signature and read to his infinite surprise the name—'*Jessamine Halliday.*' After which Dr. Cornerstone sat down and immediately perused the contents. They were as follows:

'DEAR DR. CORNERSTONE,

'Before you receive this letter, you will have heard the news. And the news is that I have disappeared. As a rule, when one reads of "mysterious disappearances" in the papers, it really means that the people *appear* for the first time. They come to the surface labelled "Disappeared," and then you hear of their existence. One was not aware of it before, and one certainly would not have missed them.

'But everybody has heard of "Jessamine Halliday," and if, like Helen of Troy, she take it into her head to disappear, it will be a true sensation.[1] One owes it to Society to create an excitement sometimes. All the Society papers will have a leading article, and people will rush to buy; the photographers will make a fortune out of my picture, and all the men at all the clubs will say, "By Jove!"[2] Even royalty will deign to raise a perturbed eyebrow.

---

1 Helen of Troy was considered "the fairest of her sex" and had been promised to Paris by the goddess Venus even though Helen was already married to Menelaus. Paris, with the help of Venus, "persuaded [Helen] to elope with him, and carried her to Troy, whence arose the famous Trojan war" (Fuller 168-169).

2 "and all the men at all the clubs": Jessamine is referring to gentleman's clubs, which were extremely popular in the nineteenth-century. They were places for upper-class men to meet, socialize, drink, eat, smoke, gamble, and read newspapers and journals of the day.

'But not a creature of them all will know where I am, and not a creature of them all will really care twopence.

'But you, Dr. Cornerstone, savage Mentor, you are not "in Society," and perhaps you will care the least little bit in the world; somehow or another I have not the heart to drop quite out of sight without nodding "adieu," and whispering in your ear that "all is well."

'Besides, in some sense, you are at the bottom of this freak of mine, and ought to share a little of the responsibility. Did you not take a great deal on your shoulders when you called me back to life? The world might have been saved much mischief, and I some hurt, if you had let me slide away. Sometimes—do other people feel it?—when I am most gay and triumphant, and most admired and most charming (and, dear Doctor, am I not a charmer?), something stretches out towards me from an immeasurable distance; it comes swift and straight from a far, far place where it waits for me, and it touches me on the heart and on the brow, so that I grow still and afraid. It seems to me as though a future unknown friend or foe steps up to this little soul Jessamine (who is not in the least like Helen of Troy—scratch that out, dear Doctor!) to make a terrible claim upon her.

'What am I—what are we, Doctor—we little women, I mean? You have answered so many questions, but never that. The ancients said we had no souls; and perhaps they were right. The moderns say we care for nothing but an armchair, and a good fire, and a cup of tea, and a novel, and to have some man slaving for us; or else they gird at us for our tiresome desire to be "emancipated," which some call immodest. I think there must be truth in all this, because the moderns have got all the light. People tell us so many things with such an air, and they write them down in print, so that it is no wonder we come to believe them, and to act upon them—if we don't happen to have any extra force of mind, that is.

'And then people who rise to poetry say we would sell our best friend for a diamond, and they give historic instances, which seem to prove everything (though sometimes afterwards I have remembered historic instances of quite the contrary).

'I wonder, Doctor, if I would do so—I love diamonds!

'In those horrid moments, when the Unknown Foe [I think *it* must be a foe] startles me, I feel as though I were a falling star, my heart runs down so quickly—something meant to be set on high in a fixed and constant path, but falling—falling—just anywhere; and I am so frightened that I would (if I could) catch hold of any big virtue to save myself.

'But you said I had no virtues, only inherited tendencies, though you gave me hopes of making up a few if I would exercise tremendous effort.

'I think I have done very well in a year; everybody says I am quite a genius, and in full possession of all the light of the age. And all I did has been reported in the Society papers. "Miss Jessamine Halliday has consented to take a stall at the bazaar for the distressed costermongers."[3] "Miss Halliday insists upon the duty of plain attire, and does not fall into the common error of supposing that luxurious expenditure is good for trade." That was *you*, Doctor, and I went up in everybody's estimation like a rocket. They said it was such a stroke of genius to see that, instead of putting the money into our own fancy dresses we might put it into the fund for the costermongers. You see, Doctor, that people will listen to your "grim" phrases from *my* mouth. How they did stare when I stood on a platform and lectured them on general topics! I looked my best, they say. And how everybody did applaud!

'Dear Doctor, I have one virtue: I like *you*—you who were so savage to me, and who spoke such terrible words! I like your little finger better than the whole heap of trumpery souls that form my range of acquaintances. And I hate the world—yes, I do, Doctor, *I hate it!* I hate it most when the Unknown Foe comes and touches me. I cry then—real tears out of my heart, if I have such a thing. Lord Heriot and Messrs. So-and-So and So say I have not.

'Aunt Arabella does not know one bit how, where, or why I have disappeared. I owe it her to spite her mightily. All my long, long life (I am twenty-one) I can remember nothing but Aunt Arabella's care, and Aunt Arabella's teaching, and Aunt Arabella's *"dearest Jessamine,"* and Aunt Arabella's deportment; so that you will understand I owe her SOMETHING.

'I will tell you just the truth, though it is all quite inexplicable, and it is this:

'I was as near as possible engaged to Lord Heriot. Aunt Arabella said it was more than nearly—that, in real fact, I was engaged to him, and that, after behaving as I had behaved, no honourable girl could draw back. When she says this, she says what is not true. Like Cæsar, "I come, I see, I conquer."[4] But there is not a living soul dares to accuse me of so much as lifting an eyelid to attract any man. Ah, how full of scorn my soul is sometimes! When I enter a drawing-room and see a strange gentleman there, I know that in five minutes he will be beseeching the hostess for an introduction to the dark lady with the jessamine in her hair. Dear Doctor, it is not my fault. I think of them as

---

3   Costermongers: street vendors who sell fresh produce, usually fruits and vegetables.

4   Julius Caesar (100 b.c.-44 b.c.) was a famous Roman leader. Jessamine has modified Caesar's famous line, "veni, vidi, vici; I came, I saw, I conquered" to suit her analysis of her own life and experiences.

if they were whipped curs, and Heriot I loathe.

'Dear Doctor, I did not forget your lessons. I tried to lead a new life of simplicity and usefulness—indeed I did.

'Perhaps I did not quite know the way. Perhaps I shall have more time to think when I have got this business of being married over, and it is off my mind once and for always. Aunt Arabella did so hate you! When I got better she would not let me ask you to the house as a friend; she said it was not proper, and that you wore such strange boots. (Will you give me one to keep in a glass case in my bedroom to help me to be good—the boot that has walked so many miles that the wearer may do so much kindness?)

'When I got better, I heard that a new beauty had arrived in London, and that she was trying to catch Heriot. He is the biggest catch in Europe, you know, Doctor. (I tell you because you are not "in Society," and so perhaps have not heard); and only a real beauty so much as dares to try for him. But I never tried at all, and yet there he was at my feet! Still, I own I felt curious to see the new beauty who was angling for Heriot. And I created a tremendous sensation by going to the Duchess of S——'s ball in a dress made of unbleached calico, and no jewels at all. I did it because of *you,* Doctor. And you never saw such a work of art as that dress was, nor how exquisitely the dull cream colour suited me. They say I never looked so lovely. Well, I saw the new beauty there. She was a large blonde thing in pink and diamonds. And I never lifted even the tail of my eye to Heriot—I *loathe him.* But he followed me all the evening like a dog, and when I talked to any other person he would have my bouquet of jessamine to hold. As for the large blonde thing, I was quite sorry to see how she changed her colour.

'How sick of myself I was when I got home! Aunt Arabella said I had behaved so beautifully—that my conduct was so perfectly ladylike! And there came a feeling into my heart when she was speaking to me that I would rush out into the street in my wonderful calico dress, and dance, and scream, and shout as I had been told the bad girls at the East-End do. Only, of course, I did not. I kissed Aunt Arabella on the cheek, and went upstairs, with my maid behind.

'Dear Doctor, I have so tried to be and to do as you said. But perhaps—very likely—I did not quite know the way. I gave all the money saved from dress (there was not so much) to the Charity Organization. You said the "Charity Organization," did you not? And I read Mill, and Thoreau, and I learnt such quantities of Browning![5] One day I brought a crossing-sweeper

---

5   John Stuart Mill (1806-1873) was an English writer and social activist. Jessamine probably would have read Mill's early feminist work, *The Subjection of Women* (1869),

into the house to be warmed and fed (it was in the Society papers next week); but Aunt Arabella said I must not on any account do such a thing again; he made such a mess, and people talked so, and a small crowd collected, and it upset the footmen. I brought him in at the front-door, and made him stand his broom in the hall; I chose a wet, muddy day on purpose, because of course it is more horrid to be a crossing-sweeper on such a day than any. And you said that "one man was as good as another"; but James and Thomas did not seem to think so, and Aunt Arabella says they gave notice.

'Well, as I said, I LOATHE HERIOT; but he took a great interest in my work, and helped me (dear Doctor, I do so hope you think it really *was* *work?);* and this matter of my marriage is so tiresome until it is settled; and Aunt Arabella said I should be able to do so much more good, and to be so much more useful, if I were Lady Heriot. And, of course, he is the biggest catch in Europe. I only wish there were a bigger! And, then, the large blonde thing was still trying—and she ought to know her place (an American!). And, as I have said, the important thing is marriage, and one must get it over one time or another. And so things went on and on, until one evening, a fortnight ago, when, for once (Aunt Arabella must have arranged it), we were at home, and alone, and Lord Heriot came in to call.

'He brought a present for me. I love jewels. This was really the most splendid jewel I had ever seen. It was a bracelet; and it was in the shape of a snake coiled several times round. The eyes were two enormous diamonds, and the neck and upper part glittered with alternate diamonds and sapphires, and the tail ended in a wonderful sapphire. I never saw such stones and such taste! Lord Heriot unfastened the case, and laid it on the table. He said it was a trifling offering to the most beautiful woman in England, and I stood looking down at it; for though I have plenty of jewels, I always want some more. And just then James came in with candles.

'Of course, nobody ever notices a footman, but somehow on that occasion I happened to do so. He brought the candelabra to the table where the case lay; and I saw him glance at the jewel, and I saw a little significant smile come into his eyes, quite a different look from the servant-look, and it made me furious. But I do not know why. I think if James had not come in, and worn that little smile in his eyes, I might be "married and done for" at this moment.

---

in which he argues that women should be on equal footing with men, including the right to vote and to be educated. He believed in intellectual equality; this argument fits in well with Brooke's own beliefs that women should and must be intellectually stimulated (Dr. Cornerstone's emphasis on "mind energy") in order to live productive lives in society.

'After setting the candelabra on the table, James went round the room drawing the curtains in quite the ordinary way, and Lord Heriot went on talking in a low voice. I do not know what he said, for I was wondering what James meant by his odious smile, and making up my mind that I would tell Aunt Arabella to give him notice next morning. Aunt Arabella—she is always present when Lord Heriot calls, to see that I do not forget my manners; and by my "manners" I mean the woman's way of being soft and sweet and smiling when she is really eaten up with fury and hate—the *slave's* way sometimes, I think, Doctor. But, then, I think such out-of-the-way things, and all the men tell me they are *my* slaves. But Aunt Arabella! She sat in a remote corner, quite oblivious of us, and she was sewing the eternal altar-cloth which makes everyone think her so pious, and Lord Heriot talked.

'But I heard and knew nothing. I was thinking—thinking why James had that odd smile in his eye. And while I thought I became aware that I was holding out my arm unconsciously, and that upon the wrist Lord Heriot was clasping the jewel.

'It was then that the strange mood came upon me in a moment: I felt my Unknown Foe pressing me on the heart and on the brow, and the jewel looked like a fetter on my wrist that was going to chain me up for ever; and just at that moment Lord Heriot's hand gently touched my bare arm.

'And when he touched my arm, I felt as though the snake were a live one, and that it was cold, and slimy, and horrible. I shook my arm free from the jewel in a moment, and it fell clattering upon the table. And I looked at Lord Heriot—I know I did it, because Aunt Arabella sprang up from her seat, dropped the altar-cloth on the floor, and said something—I looked at him as though *he* were a snake. And I heard my own voice saying quite coldly and quietly:

'"Thank you, Lord Heriot; I will not have your jewel. I do not like snakes."

'And then I walked out of the room, but not before I saw him turn pale with fury. And when I got to my bedroom I felt sorry, because the jewel was so pretty, and because I knew he would take it straight to the blonde person. And I began to walk up and down in the twilight.

'It would be all very well if I could have the bracelet without the giver; but a girl can't accept handsome presents like that without being engaged. And it would be all very well if I could be Lord Heriot's widow; but there is such a dark place between. And oh, dear Doctor! I loathe that dark place so—the seeing him day after day, and never any more being able to escape until death comes. I wonder why marriage is so hateful to me! It is not to all girls; for a few—one or two—have told me they were glad. The others were indifferent, or miserable, or frightened, or pious and resigned. I think very few would be married if it were not for the flattery and triumph and the fuss of the wedding-day, and if there were anything else to do. Men play upon our vanity, and that, of course, is prodigious.

'I think sometimes that no girl would be married at all if there were anything else possible. But of course there is not.

'And all these thoughts have only come to me since that fatal bracelet evening. I said many such things to myself then as I walked up and down the room.

'But by-and-by the fury went out of my mind, and the twilight gathered about me, and I began to feel so strange. I began to remember some of the things you had said; only this time, though they were yours, they seemed to be coming back to me through my own heart. You told me to work, and to live simply. I thought I really had been trying; but to-night—to-night—as I walked about in the dusk, it seemed as though it had been all by rote.

'I felt like a shadow—a shadow in a vain world. I am so sick of shadows. And then the Unknown Foe came to me, and I felt my heart swelling and my brow throbbing, and the tears rushed out of my eyes. I stretched my hands about in the darkness feeling for something that I could not find. My heart beat so. I had a feeling of great trouble in my mind. It was no use praying. If you had prayed at Aunt Arabella's knee as a little child, and by her side in church all through your young life, you would never want to pray, nor dream of doing it when trouble comes.

'But after a time I sat down in the big arm-chair in the corner; it began to grow dark, and a moonbeam suddenly came and laid a long thin streak of light upon the carpet and up my dress. And while I sat with my hands tight clasped on my knee, my Great Idea came into my mind. It was like an inspiration; and I remembered you had told me to seize hold of an inspiration, if ever I got one, and to trust to it. A voice out of my own heart said to me:

'"The world is vain: go out of it. You feel like a shadow: step into the real. You are sick of shams: try vigorous work."

'It seemed so simple when it was said, and yet the being able to say it was like the clapping of thunder after a long, still, sultry day. And I thought I would, Doctor. I thought I would leave Aunt Arabella and all my finery, and that I would go out alone into the work-a-day world and see what it is like. I have no idea what it is like, but I mean to see. The having the inspiration to do it was the difficult thing. The moment it got into my brain I made out a whole scheme quickly. The scheme I will not impart even to you, dear Doctor, but only the inspiration. I am telling you so that you may know a cruel fate has not befallen me, but that I am where I have chosen to be.

'As I sat in my arm-chair and made my plans, I began to laugh, and I clapped my hands softly in the darkness. It seemed so charming, so *new*—the best thing I had ever devised, and the most startling. All the Society papers will talk; Heriot will rave; and my Aunt Arabella will——

'Dear Doctor, it was just there that a cruel little thought came and tripped up my joy as it went dancing along the future path I had sketched for it. Supposing—I asked myself—supposing you can never, *never,* NEVER get rid of your Aunt Arabella? Supposing that when you were a little, little child, with heart as soft as the softest clay, and limbs like unkneaded dough, and a mind like an unwritten page, your Aunt Arabella wrote all over it, and gave a twist to your heart and a turn to your limbs that you can never, *never,* NEVER get rid of? Supposing that—hate and hate her as you may—your Aunt Arabella has become part of you, a part which you can never throw off until all your body falls into decay? Perhaps not then—perhaps when your soul flies away even, it will carry your Aunt Arabella with it.

'I thought of this until my heart went cold like a stone from terror. I seemed to be like a creature coming to life for the first moment to find itself, without choice of its own, in a terrible labyrinth without chance of escape. And there I sat down and wept. And my Unknown Foe sat down and wept with me.

'So many thoughts, dear Doctor, had never come into my mind before. It seems to me that when you have opened the way to one inspiration, you cannot close the door before a host of unwished and uninvited followers have entered. But what I thought only made me more determined. I would go away—lose myself—hide. And I wished there had been a Pool of Siloam somewhere, into which I could have stepped down and got rid of the Aunt Arabella in me, and washed myself clean of her, and come out upon the other side just "Jessamine" and no more.[6] How strange that here, on my first venture into an independent life, I should find myself so mixed and fictitious a creature that I knew not how to calculate upon myself!

'But one thing, Doctor, I am certain of. I am going to do a good and useful thing; and perhaps the world will know of it afterwards, and I shall be a leader, and a pioneer; and others will follow me. Dear Doctor, I am going out like the apostles and the teachers of old, *to do good.* Believe it of your little

---

6 The Gospel of John tells the story of the blind man and the Pool of Siloam: "Therefore said they unto him, How were thine eyes opened. He answered and said, A man that is called Jesus made clay, and anointed mine eyes, and said unto me, Go to the pool of Siloam, and wash: and I went and washed, and I received sight" (John 9:10-11).

patient.

'But, oh! promise—*promise* me one thing. Don't tell Aunt Arabella even this one word! She doesn't care in her heart of hearts what happens to me. She has nothing but an ambition for me, by means of which she herself would step up higher. Don't let her come and ferret me out.

'Your grateful and reformed

'JESSAMINE HALLIDAY.'

Dr. Cornerstone finished the letter, folded it up, and placed it in his pocket. And then he sighed.

'Tell Aunt Arabella!' said he. 'I think I would bite my own tongue out first, Jessamine! But oh! my fairest among fair women, that dip into the Pool of Siloam is, as you surmise, no easy business.'

CHAPTER IV

A PEASANT farmer, in a remote district of the Highlands, stood at the door of his cottage conversing with his wife. The man's name was John McKenzie, and the little tract of land which he tilled was named *Drynock*.

The cottage was a roomy place, designed and built by amateur hands, with some assistance from the mason and carpenter. The architecture was primitive and odd; but the whole result was comfort, space, and decency. The owner, a strapping fellow of thirty-five years, with a dark beard and fine gray eyes, leaned against the side of a porch which was creeper-covered with the hardy convolvulus.

The season was unusually hot and dry, and on this glorious July afternoon the sun poured down such mighty rays as are not often felt in the Highlands. The farmers looked thirstily day by day for rain, lamenting the moisture necessary to their light and sandy soil, but accommodating their minds, with the patience of their race, to the perversity of a climate which rarely blesses the efforts of human toil with liberal assistance.

The country was bleak, poor, and yet beautiful, having much natural splendour, though little luxuriance for human needs. A broad valley spread between the hill-ranges; here and there lay a silvery loch; the universal heather ground was broken by the green gold of ripening corn, the verdure of sparse pastures, or bluish drills of turnips and potatoes; every level and brae that would give some return to culture carried its crop; woods of birch (low, gray, and bushy) covered the knolls of unredeemed land, or the glorious growth of heather spread undisturbed; while isolated groups of pine shot sombrely upwards, strengthening the air with their fine aroma. Fir-woods covered the lower hills, where, according to the farmer's opinion, sheep should have been grazing; and the higher hills, with their solemn unapproachable sides, reflected the mute language of the sky in the perpetual change of light and shadow.

On this still July afternoon nothing stirred in the air save here and there the white wing of a loch gull, no sound met the ear save the light domestic noises from inside the cottage, and now and then the shout of a peasant child herding cows at a distance.

'I must be off to fetch the kyes[1] home,' said John McKenzie to some

---

1 John McKenzie means cows. *Concise Scots Dictionary.* Mairi Robinson, Ed. Ed-

person invisible within the cottage.

'Ay,' responded a voice, 'there you stand like a crow in a corn-field, just always ready to be away.'

It was a soft voice, with a musical fall and rise and drawl in it, a measured temperance of long habit conveying sharp words harmlessly, and it belonged to John McKenzie's wife Annie.

'Where will the bonnie wee lassie be?' inquired John, lowering his voice, and peering round curiously.

'She is just drinking her tea in her room.'

'She will soon be through with that,' returned John; 'it is no a very great occupation.'

'Oh yes; she will soon be through.'

'And an awful uncommon hour for tea-drinking Annie.'

'Indeed, we will no be finding fault with new-fangled notions that have their uses. It will just be giving me time to look round and to find myself again.'

'Five o'clock is no a very decorous hour for tea,' insisted McKenzie. 'But she's bonnie,' added he softly.

'And you will have been saying that a good few times, John McKenzie!'

'Annie!'

'A-weel!'

'I was just in a terrification when I was seeing her first. I call her awful bonnie! It fetches a body's breath to see a lassie like that stepping out of a train her lane,[2] and coming up and just saying, "Are you John McKenzie?"'

'Indeed, and it will be making a woman start to see her step into the kitchen like a wraith, and to hear her saying, "Shall I wash up for you, Mrs. McKenzie?"'

'It will be an awful strange dispensation for us, Annie.'

'A-weel. We must be taking the Lord's will as it falls upon us. And she pays well.'

'Oh yes; it's a good in-put. She pays well, though she's but a lassie, and a bonnie one.'

'So bonnie that she casts a shadow.'

'Ay. She makes the wee bit housie look ill-sorted. And such a sight of bonniness going her lane makes a body think.'

'I'm thinking we may just as well think good as ill thoughts.'

'I'm not saying to the contrary. You will be kind to her, Annie?'

---

inburgh: Edinburgh University Press, 2005, 114.

2   Her lane: "without a mate or companion, on one's own, solitary" (*CSD* 356).

'Indeed, I hope so. I shall do my best, whatever.'

'And best brings best along after it.'

'At times, John McKenzie,' replied Annie with deliberation; 'that has a fine-sounding flourish, but I'm not very sure it will fit the uncertainties of this world. It will be an ill thing to be sorry for our wrong-doing, but it is a worse to be sorry for our good.'

John scratched his head.

'I'm not very sure if that will be sound doctrine, Annie. But when she is through with tea, what then?'

'Indeed, she will ever be wearying till I find her a new occupation. I must give her the graip,[3] John McKenzie, and bid her lift a potato for to-morrow's dinner.

'It makes a body giddy to have to bid a rare bonnie leddy lift potatoes. How will she answer, Annie?'

'Just, "Thank you, Mrs. McKenzie." Her voice is soft like honey, and she is aye teachable and gentle. Whiles I turn over in my mind if it's waking or dreaming. But I had[4] on to my pigs and pans and look no further. Biding's better nor spiering,[5] and there's just no time for wonder.'

'A-weel. It is an awful strange dispensation. Has Colin been?'

'Indeed, you would be hearing if he had.'

'Then Colin has not seen her yet?'

'I will not be saying whether he has met her in the road.'

'I made some mention of the matter to Colin.'

'A man's tongue is ever ready with clash.'[6]

'Nay, woman! This is a dispensation that wants a wee bit explanation. It makes a body feel mixtie-maxtie[7] to come upon her sudden-like amidst the pots and pans.'

'And what will Colin be saying?'

'Oh, he will just be saying that there is no inquiring into the new-fangled ways of an ill place like London.'

'Colin thinks himself no sheep-shank.'[8]

'Oh, he will ever be a very discreet douce man.'[9]

---

3   Graip: "an iron-pronged fork used in farming and gardening" (*CSD* 243).

4   Had or haud means "hold" (*CSD* 271).

5   Spiering: "questioning, inquiry; prying interrogation or investigation" (*CSD* 652).

6   Clash: "a tale, story" (*CSD* 99).

7   Mixtie-maxtie: "jumbled, in a state of confusion" (*CSD* 420).

8   Sheep-shank: "a person of some importance" (*CSD* 608).

9   Douce: "sedate, sober, respectable" (*CSD* 157).

'I'm not saying to the contrairy. Whist! John; she will be coming downstairs now. I can hear the jingle of the cups. It is a sore dispensation having a London lassie in and out amongst the kitchen work; but I will not be saying that it is worse than a man standing havering on the doorstep.'

So saying, Mrs. McKenzie, who had been throwing the soft modulations of her voice from some place invisible, appeared on the threshold. She had a matronly figure, soft red hair falling upon each side of her forehead, steady gray eyes with a smile in them, and a beautifully arched head. The effect of her glance upon her husband's face was as the quiet and unnoticeable stirring of conscience within him; the two things had been for so long a period simultaneous that John McKenzie ceased to discriminate between them; he thought it an original stirring of compunction which now reminded him of his cows, and caused him to walk off suddenly with a strong swinging gait.

Mrs. McKenzie turned back into the cottage to welcome with the same general smile of kindliness the entrance of another person.

An inner door which had been closed before was now open, and upon the threshold stood a slim girl, clothed in a gray linsey dress[10] and holding a tray. She had the cautious look of one unaccustomed to the office. Her two small hands grasped the sides firmly, and her eyes were bent in anxious solicitude upon the crockery, while a slight tension in the grace of her figure marked a conscious difficulty of poise. From the ruffled shadowy hair gathered above the arch of the head, to the small foot planted on the ground with elastic firmness, she was a perfect model of a very rare type of beauty. And when she raised her dark lashes and fixed her eyes with a whimsical look of fright in them upon Mrs. McKenzie, she had a marvellous charm.

Some faces distort the expression of beautiful feeling, others fling trifling and even ignoble emotions into a momentary exquisiteness of setting. Some souls beat out their deep and tragic personality in an inherited mould of stupidity; others carry their trivial experiences through a medium of ancestral nobility.

Mrs. McKenzie relieved the girl of her tray, and set it upon the table.

'Shall I wash up the things?' asked the new-comer in musical, well-bred English.

'Oh yes. If you will not be minding it, you can wash up.'

'And when that is done?'

'When that is done,' returned Mrs. McKenzie with a great patience, 'you will be taking the graip——'

'But what is the graip?'

---

10 "A coarse cloth made of linen and wool or cotton and wool" (*Webster's* 823).

Mrs. McKenzie produced an agricultural instrument in the shape of a short iron fork.

'A graip will just be this fork.'

'Oh, thank you.'

'And you will be going down to the potato drill———'[11]

'The drill?'

'In the garden———'

'I think I know, thank you.'

'And you will be lifting a few potatoes for dinner to-morrow.'

'Shall I have to dig deep?' asked the girl with a pretty animation.

'Not deep at all. You will just be gently loosening the roots, and then you will be shaking the plant out of the soil, and you will be finding the potatoes.'

'Thank you. And shall I peel them afterwards?'

'Folks,' returned Mrs. McKenzie with the faintest sign of exasperation, 'will be resting from their labour at eventide.'

'I am not tired.'

'Potato-peeling is hurting to the skin. It will be very hashing[12] to your wee bit hands.'

'I do not mind,' returned the girl with intense earnestness; 'I wish to work. I wish to help you.'

'Oh yes,' returned Mrs. McKenzie with a sigh.

The conversation was broken by the patter of two bare-footed children into the kitchen. It was one of Mrs. McKenzie's secret grievances that, since 'the bonnie leddy's' advent, she had been unable to keep her own little Maysie and Maysie's five or six companions from pattering over the carefully cleaned floors in order to get a fair look at the show.

---

11 Drill: "a furrow in which seeds are planted; a row of planted seeds (*Webster's* 427).

12 Hashing: "fatigue, overwork" (*CSD* 270).

CHAPTER V

WHEN Miss Jessamine Halliday made up her mind to the project of disappearance, which she disclosed in her letter to Dr. Cornerstone, she recalled this patch of country in the Highlands. She had passed through it once when on a journey of pleasure; it was a large district, unattractive to the ordinary tourist as a place of continued residence; the few cottages sprinkled here and there amongst farm-lands were inhabited solely by peasants, and had little or no accommodation for lovers of luxury. This isolation made it precisely the refuge she required. She recollected the cottage of the McKenzies, having stopped to purchase a glass of milk there; and John McKenzie had consented by letter to rent her a couple of rooms in his house, and had also understood that the arrangement included instruction in the household work and a share in the life of the family. He drove to the station—many miles distant—expecting to meet and carry home with him a big lassie, with substantial wrists and a bustling air of management; nor was he without some shrewd apprehension of a bargain advantageous to himself. The contrast between his conception and the amazing actuality threw him into a condition of ecstatic amusement and perplexity, of which he had been unable to rid himself during the drive home, or, indeed, for days afterwards.

Upon Jessamine's part was unmitigated satisfaction. When she got into the trap by McKenzie's side, her modest trunk pushed in behind, she looked round upon the broad stretch of country with a sense of beatitude. After London, with its heat of life, its inconsequent fret and flurry, after Aunt Arabella, the width and grandeur were as the space is to an escaped bird, and the peace and calmness dropped like cold dews on her heart. And then, after this draught of spiritual refreshment, she sat up in the dogcart to glance at the face of the driver.

From class to class, faces are as nothing—mere masks, beyond which nothing can be seen because nothing is surmised. The roving eye, softly aflame with hope and entreaty, seeks out the lineaments of desire, but drops dead and dull beyond the barriers of rank. Here the divine spark fails, the tinder takes it not. Or if any avail to cast it unquenched beyond the pale, that is a sin which society may not condone.

Jessamine, however, had some occasion to study the face of her future host. She found it an intelligent exponent of indispensable human traits;

shrewd, cautious, gentle thoughts had left tracks upon it, while from the eyes a spirit of human kindliness looked leniently upon the world. Besides these general characteristics, an irrepressible smile lurked upon the man's lips, broadening them out and curling them up did any occasion betray the secret humour which tickled his spirit. The reason for his unaccountable mirth was no part of Jessamine's care; she let it alone, and for the rest sank back in her seat satisfied.

It was a part of Jessamine's character to enter into a matter with zest, until the point was reached when she relinquished the whim in favour of the next. The morning after her arrival she proved her mettle by setting to work at once, and kept steadily at it for the next week or so. Mrs. McKenzie found that slimness of figure and fineness of face are not incompatible with persistence in labour, and by degrees she began to accustom herself to the soft, radiant presence amongst her pots and pans and to lose something of her exasperation, though still inwardly bewildered by a sense of unreality invading her prosaic labours, as though a dream should inexplicably involve itself amid high noontide hours.

Meanwhile, the two or three weeks of vigorous application told upon Jessamine's appearance: labour, early rising, and exercise, brought a pink flush into her cheeks and inspired her aspect, while little fierce lines of effort began to pluck up the melancholic Burne-Jones droop of lips and chin.[1] Moving about McKenzie's house or barns or fields, she was—either from the disparity of her surroundings or for a much more subtle and human reason—lovelier and more attractive than in her life before. A look was in her face like to the ripening of fruit when the sun is up.

A whole month passed away, and one evening she sat in her room repairing a rent in her working dress. She had brought no other gowns than these rough linseys, whose simple make suited so admirably not only the labour she had undertaken, but the grace of the wearer. After sewing industriously for some time, she took her scissors and snipped the thread off with a little composed air of self-satisfaction, let the dress fall upon her lap, and looked up idly to the window.

Supposing anyone undertook to distentangle the bare prosaic content of thought from the various and beautiful emotions in which it is transfigured,

---

1 Edward Burne-Jones (1833-1898) was an English painter associated with the late Pre-Raphaelite period. His paintings were in rich, strong colors and his women subjects, especially, were extraordinarily beautiful, but sometimes described as melancholy. Burne-Jones saw his women subjects as ideals of beauty. However, Brooke clearly sees his work in a somewhat negative light if Jessamine is becoming less like these images of women as she works in the Scottish countryside.

the result might be startling to the sensibility. Jessamine's thinking, for all her intense and exalted air, may be briefly summed up as follows:

'I am leading a useful and simple life; I have forsaken the refinement and luxury necessary to a person of my culture to come amongst these poor cottagers, and to give them the benefit of my help and superior influence. Dr. Cornerstone will be pleased with me, and will be more interested in me than ever. I am really endeavouring to be good—and, of course, remarkable at the same time. And as I am a most beautiful and clever woman, my example will be the more striking; people will follow it, and my position in society will be elevated. Meanwhile, it is delightful to spite Aunt Arabella and to torture Lord Heriot, whom I hate, but intend eventually to marry.'

The girl had no idea that these were her thoughts; she felt and looked something so different; indeed, she experienced a warm, subdued glow as she recalled Dr. Cornerstone's profound and austere instructions, and she mistook the reflected fires of his strong spirit for a flame within her own.

After her meditation, she rose and went out to watch the milking of the cows in the barn. When that was over, she came outside to refresh herself and breathe the air.

It was a silent evening; the converse of the fowls, dreamily disputing between the pauses of her thoughts, was the only sound. The sun, though the hour was late, hung softly brilliant in the sky; the tints and shadows were tremulously deep and vivid; a visionary beauty, like some diaphanous covering, enwrapped the hills and woods and valley, and the enchantment dropped even upon the human heart. Jessamine forgot to think, and her mind lay passive to feeling. Her face was turned to the hills; the light mused in her eyes and folded itself like a veil about her head.

And in such a moment as this fell the master-event of her life.

The opening of the wicket-gate into the enclosure had not disturbed her, nor a tread which followed; she supposed McKenzie to be still at his work; but the gradual apprehension of suspended sound at length attracted her attention, and then, looking round, she saw, a few paces from her, a man whom she had not before encountered. He was standing as though arrested, looking upon her with a gaze of unembarrassed concentration, yet so impersonal as to miss effrontery. His dress was that of a peasant farmer. In person he possessed a full share of the strength and height of his race: he had great shoulders and limber straight limbs; moreover, his face was of a fine quality, firm in feature, with steady eyes of a yellowish brown, and throwing out an impression of independence, pride, and unconquerable gentleness. Jessamine, startled into attention, inadvertently permitted her glance to be locked by his, whereupon he merely altered his gaze so far as to throw into it an added steadiness; his expression remained the while placid and unconscious, and his head took a slight inclination from its normal uprightness, so as to suggest his bearing when in church or when in presence of anything curious and uncommon.

Jessamine, who was profoundly sensitive to the impression she produced, perceived, as clearly as though she read it from a printed page, that he who was thus gazing upon her recognised in her no part of his own humanity, but found her a picture, an art-product, an object which it was well for him to have seen, and no more. Indeed, so mirror-like and accurate an impression of herself was reflected back from his eyes and face, that it became a moment of self-revelation.

It touched her mind as with a pin's point, and the finest ripple of feeling passed over her features. The man, remarking it, lifted his cap and removed his eyes; but this was so evidently the exercise of will in casting off an entertaining triviality, that it became a worse misdemeanour than the first. Translated into her own phrase, the voiceless verdict floated thus to the ear of her mind:

'An art-product, a curiosity, very pleasing and unique, which I am glad to have beheld, but it is no affair of mine, and I cannot waste my time upon it.'

As this clear conviction entertained her, the man advanced towards her and passed by; his steps brushed close through the grass, and his shadow fell upon her as he went, and she caught an odour—not of cigars and high living, but as of temperance and a 'fruitful field.'[2]

---

2 There are many references to "a fruitful field" in the King James Bible. Clearly, here, Brooke is emphasizing Colin's difference from what Jessamine has experienced in her previous life in London with men.

CHAPTER VI

JESSAMINE paring apples with Mrs. McKenzie in the kitchen was as pretty as an Academy[1] picture, and about as real. A peat-fire burnt on the hearth, with the kettle swinging over it; on one side the chimney sat Mrs. McKenzie, a bowl of apples grasped in her sturdy knees and an empty one by her side, paring away with prosaic despatch and a murderous sound of steel. Jessamine sat opposite on a wooden bench against the open window; a trellis creeper pinked out the window-frame with a pretty embroidery and cast a chequer of light and shade over her head. She had an earthenware bowl deftly balanced on her knee, and a long riband of peel uncurled itself from her fingers slowly and daintily, for Jessamine worked in some fear of the knife and with care for the finish of the matter. The door as well as the window was thrown open to let in a broad and cheerful beam, and from outside the noises of fowl-life— the hectoring and disputing, the boasting and wise counsel of matrons, the swagger of cocks—assailed the ear with a continual reminder that there are other worlds than ours.

'Mrs. McKenzie,' said Jessamine, breaking the silence, 'who was that man who called last night on your husband?'

The question had been goading the tip of her tongue all the morning.

'That will be Colin Macgillvray you are meaning. Him and John are great friends. Macgillvray Dalfaber,' added Mrs. McKenzie, to be explicit.

'Mr. Colin Macgillvray of Dalfaber,' repeated Jessamine; 'and where is Dalfaber?'

'It will be west to here. Across the fields, on the other side the road.'

'The house lying far off by the loch?'

'That will be it. It lies on the hill above the loch, high on the moor.'

'Ah, I think I know! So near as that? Some barns and a thatched cottage and some oat-fields.'

'That will be Dalfaber, lassie. It will be lying about half a mile distant—a thatched cottage: Macgillvrays have but a poor bit housie.'

'I suppose—is he a farmer?'

'Oh yes, he is a farmer!'

'Does he work for himself ?'

1 The reference here is to the Royal Academy of Art, founded in 1768 by King George III. This is a privately funded institution that still exists today.

'Oh yes; he will be doing all the work on the farm! It will be his father's farm—old Mr. Rorie Macgillvray. He is a very old man.'

Jessamine was silent again; Mrs. McKenzie dropped three apples into the bowl to her one.

'Mr. Colin Macgillvray is married, of course?' said she presently.

'Oh no! Colin is not married; oh no! Indeed, and he is not married! He will be just living with his father and mother.'

'You like this Mr. Macgillvray? He is a respectable man?'

'Oh yes; we like Colin Macgillvray very well! He is just a douce quiet man. His mind's just in his worruk. He doesn't think of much else. There's nothing in him than his worruk. That will be Colin. Oh yes! The farmers about keep themselves very respectable.'

With which Mrs. McKenzie, who saw Macgillvray with the familiar eye of one who looks upon a thing so commonly as to sweep the surface merely and to miss the essence, dropped the last apple in the dish and seemed to reach the end of the subject. Not so Jessamine; for to meet the person who acquaints one with one's self is the great beginning of a very long matter.

Some days passed, and she did not again encounter Macgillvray nor come in his way; but the mind, which runs up and down the earth seeking while the feet halt, went on its quest. There are things so incomplete in themselves that one is tortured until they are rounded by a finish. From the fields, the highway, and the moors, loomed every day a possibility which ended in disappointment; her eyes searched the distance as she walked, and many a passing peasant was startled by her expectant glance into lifting his cap reverently to this presence of high quality and beauty. From no eyes, however, did she catch the critical shaft of Macgillvray's, and this—caustic and cold— still rankled in her heart. It is of the nature of such wounds that the enemy who gives them proves the only physician; it is also in the nature of things that, while many come, the one stays away, and that frequent hands proffer trashy friendship, while the single hand whose smart has made it valuable refrains.

Jessamine walked often somewhere in the direction of Dalfaber; but on one occasion—it was Sunday afternoon—she took that course more frankly. So far, she had hovered on the outskirts of the farm, in the woods or on the moor that flanked it, not venturing beyond the enclosure. A shy dread of repulse kept cancelling her wish for an encounter; she felt the effect of an eye which can succeed better than the law and the police in keeping off intruders and making the owner proprietor of house and land. This Sunday afternoon, however, while man and beast reposed, and the very air sank in vitality under the Sabbath dulness, an urgency of the heart got the better of more retreating instincts. She stepped through the enclosure, and then, like a soul lost beyond the borders of orthodoxy, began to wander about Macgillvray's fields, and beside his rows of barley and oats, and over his pastures, until at last she neared the cottage itself.

The cottage was a roomy and primitive-looking building, a chimney at either side, tolerable windows and a wide door. There was no pretense at adornment nor the faintest hint of a garden; nevertheless the place, with its dark heather thatch, its grave loneliness awatch upon an environment of tumultuously-tumbled hills, had a sombre charm, as though reminiscent of a hundred years of human life braved out within its walls in the bleak solitude.

Jessamine approached; the door was certainly ajar, but a closed, silent, Sabbatarian air, a dulness as though the life within had been nipped, affected her dismally, and the expectation escaping from her heart, left it flat enough to be composed. She took some steps forward, meaning to pass the cottage and go home. At this point, however, a dog, with disconcerting suddenness, rushed from the door and sprang barking upon her. Jessamine, the more startled that she had just been lulled into security, gave a cry, and increased the beast's excitement by running a pace or two towards the cottage. Her sharp and timorous call brought out the master *pêle-mêle*,[2] and before she had time to recall her dignity she found herself shrinking, as is the manner of women in fear, close behind Mr. Colin Macgillvray. At his appearance the dog changed his note to one of excellent temper, and, having done the mischief, now sniffed round the pair inquisitively with a friendly wagging of the tail.

'Had oof with you! Go back!' cried Mr. Macgillvray, smiting in the air with his arm.

Whereupon the collie walked away, glancing back round the corner of his shoulder as he went, as who would say, 'My feelings suffer from this rebuff.'

'The dog would not have hurt you,' said Macgillvray, now turning to Jessamine and looking leniently into her wide-open, startled eyes; 'it's just his way of showing joy.'

'Oh!' returned Jessamine, 'I thought he seemed very angry; I was just a little frightened.'

'Oh, na, na! The dog was not angry. It will just be his play. But you will come in now and rest you awhile?'

Macgillvray's eyes were still lenient while, with a very noble and gracious air, he pushed the door open wider and signed to Jessamine to enter. She

---

2   In a chaotic manner.

walked forward, her heart still beating, partly with physical fear, partly in amaze at finding herself precipitated into the centre of an event which she had intended to approach with a prepared mind.

There were two rooms only on the first-floor of the cottage, but these were divided by a space from whence the staircase mounted to the story above; beneath the staircase was a small cellar. One of the two rooms was the kitchen; the other, to which Colin ushered Miss Halliday, possessed an alcove with a bed in it, and was a combination of bed and sitting room. Colin placed a chair for his guest and took one himself.

'And this is your room?' said Jessamine.

'Oh yes!' answered Colin; 'it will be mine.'

As usual, Miss Halliday's mere presence grouped her surroundings into a picture. She sat in a high-backed chair, her head thrown back, her dark hair rumpled, and a lovely lassitude in limbs and posture. Colin, seated opposite with the ease of a man at home, one arm flung carelessly over the back of his chair, contemplated her steadily. A touch of remorseful sympathy, because of the quick rise and fall of her breast, softened his lips, and when Jessamine's glance, after wandering round the room, paused—large, wistful, shy—upon his, he immediately spoke.

'I'm just most sorry, indeed,' said he; 'my dog has really frightened you.'

'Well, yes,' returned Jessamine, 'he looked very wild and savage, as though he meant to hurt me.'

'Na, na! He will never be doing any harm to anyone. He is just always for rushing, but it means nothing.'

'He is a good watch-dog, at any rate.'

'Oh yes! he's a good watch-dog; but he's most fond of strangers,' said Colin, still anxious for the removal of inhospitable impressions.

'Perhaps I had no right to be where I was?' ventured Jessamine, anxious to bring the conversation to less general topics.

'Indeed!' cried Macgillvray, starting forward with a courteous inclination of the head; 'we are most pleased to see you. We will be most glad if you will be coming just when you like to rest you here, or to sit and walk on the bit of land.'

'Thank you,' returned Jessamine.

And her thanks were accompanied by a grave, luminous glance for which many a high-born gentleman in London would cheerfully have paid a price. Macgillvray inclined his head slightly to one side to facilitate his quite impersonal observation of one pleasing trait the more in a pleasing picture.

Meanwhile, here as everywhere, the poverty of human resource cast itself upon chatter as a refuge. It is only the beasts (and possibly the Chinese) who are sufficiently self-poised to sit opposite each other in Homeric silence,[3] contenting themselves with the occasional embrace of a stolidly friendly eye. In this cottage room, the conversation struggled on through the inequalities of class-habit and class-ideas, like a lop-sided car, Jessamine's alert tongue leaping from topic to topic to find that upon which the peasant's would run easily, while Colin declined to become discursive upon any. It was the lights and touches in his face and manner which revealed his nature, as the sun falling upon a rock will discover its secret beauty. He stood out from the triviality of the conversation with all his qualities large, deep, massive. Miss Halliday's facility in remark began to strike him as—for him, at least—a god-less witchcraft, though possibly an angelic trait in the world of quality; and as he made courteous shift to reply, he was troubled with a haunting recollection of the fourth commandment, which bids men 'remember the Sabbath day to keep it holy.' At length Jessamine, seizing upon the statement in pure nervous hurry to whip up the moment out of this laggard incapacity, assured him of her admiration of the country and her appreciation of the beauty of the hills. Whereupon Colin turned his head and let his eyes rest upon the range of mountains seen through the windows, wearing in his expression a deep sufficiency of familiar content, which seemed to remove him from her presence.

'Oh yes,' said he in his curious sweet voice; 'oh yes, it's a bonnie country. The hills look butifully in an evening; all this summer they really have been looking butifully.'

That was his utmost expansiveness; and his eyes, in their aloofness from her, and their restful familiarity elsewhere, seemed to set her aside; she rose to go, pained and baffled. For a moment she stood hesitating in the whitewashed cottage-room, beautiful and brilliant as some strayed rainbow cloud, while he looked down upon her. But nothing altered in his balance and gravity, and she turned away, an emptiness in her face like the withdrawing of sun from a prism ray. Colin accompanied her to the door and stood upon the threshold; she bade him adieu, and lifted once more a wistful and propitiating eye; but Colin, his glance comprehensively including the hills over her shoulder as well as herself, gravely saluted the high quality which had deigned to visit him, by placing his hand to his forehead and murmuring thanks for her condescension. He kept meanwhile an air of courteous dismissal, and his brow so proud and uncontaminated an independence that it left Jessamine

_____

3 Homer (1200 BC–800 BC) is a Greek poet who is usually credited with writing the epic poems the *Iliad* and the *Odyssey.*

the person abashed.

She did not go home, but sought a lonely spot and sat down on the heather near a group of fir-trees. Some demon chuckled derisively in those regions which conscience makes horrible. It is a discomforting thing to graciously forsake your rank, your high heels, and your paint-pot, in order to follow humanity at the plough, and then to find that humanity at the plough keeps these articles ready to hand back to you with rigid courtesy—putting the china shepherdess back in its right place on the shelf—before proceeding unruffled with its own weighty affairs.

CHAPTER VII

THE morning after her interview with Macgillvray, Jessamine waked restless and dissatisfied. Her pretty scheme, running so merrily along the ways of self-content, had met with something in the nature of an upset. Had Miss Halliday been living in London, or anywhere within call of a fashionable friend who might come in to make the morning hours vapid with talk, her temper might have discharged some sparks; but Mrs. McKenzie's atmosphere and the necessities of the day excluded the privileges of spleen.[1] As well be spiteful in the front of a milch cow as in the eye of Mrs. McKenzie. She lived aloof, irradiating kindliness and vigour, understanding nothing of the ins and outs of sensitiveness and fine feelings, but effacing these distempers by a be-atific wholesomeness. So that Jessamine, who appeared with sombre eyes and brow, and an air of inscrutable melancholy, found herself compelled into an ordinary mood, and was finally driven by the sheer force of circumstance to help in the hay-field.

A day or two after, rather to her astonishment, she found herself on Macgillvray's land, stepping round, as it were, to make inquiries as to the progress of his hay. As she came near him in the hay-field, he looked up, de-sisted from his labour, lifted his straw hat courteously, then, setting the scythe to the ground, took a wide sweep of the steel through the hay, and carried himself by the strong leisurely movement a yard or two from her. Jessamine shrank back hastily. An unconquerable something kept turning its uncouth back upon her.

That evening she somewhat flagged in the ardour of her application. She relieved Mrs. McKenzie from her impetuous energy by going out for a walk. Upon coming back, she heard unusual sounds issuing from the open door of the kitchen. It was her custom to enter by the porch, though her apartments might be reached by another door. The Doctor's counsel had run thus:

'Return to simplicity of life and do serviceable work.'

And Jessamine very carefully practised the maxim by an observance as minute as that of a Pharisee of old.[2] She therefore repudiated the entrance set

---

1   Spleen in this context is "spite [or] bad temper" (*Webster's* 1374). Mrs. McKenzie has a calming effect on Jessamine's unsettled emotions about Colin.
2   In the New Testament the Pharisee was considered to be one who followed rules carefully.

apart for herself, and took by choice the ordinary way. Her step was light—indeed, curiosity prompted caution; the kitchen was filled for the moment by the weird sound which, in the Highlands, is strangely called singing, and she reached the threshold unheard, and stood there unseen to look upon the scene within.

Mr. and Mrs. McKenzie sat side by side; Mrs. McKenzie was knitting, but she glanced now and then at a book which her husband held: both were singing. Little Maysie, their only child, stood between her father's knees listening; her round grave eyes were, however, fixed in awe and admiration upon a fourth figure who sat opposite. Of this visitor Jessamine could see no more than one broad shoulder and a portion of a sturdy neck and head, for he was seated with his back to the window, a little withdrawn behind the door; but in him she at once recognised Colin Macgillvray. There was one other figure which she could see entirely. This was a small boy, one of Maysie's numerous companions; he stood with his small elbows folded upon Colin's knee, and was gazing up into the man's face with a curiously fearless content.

Jessamine beheld this picture undisturbed for the briefest moment; then Maysie spoilt it by catching sight of her and pointing. The change was instantaneous. The song broke off, and both men dropped their books; McKenzie favoured her with the smile of indulgent humour which was his usual greeting, Mrs. McKenzie exhibited faint signs of momentary perplexity, and Colin, rising from his seat with his air of defiant respectfulness, made the peasant's salute by touching his forehead with his hand without inclining his perverse head one inch from its uprightness.

Jessamine's eyes encountered this indifferent, unbending look; and it seemed to her that a tear ran scalding down her heart. She repaid McKenzie's smile by a faint fleeting dimple, and hurried through the kitchen with averted face, closing the inner door behind her. Here she paused, anxious to know if the singing would recommence; it would have been interesting to learn if Colin's voice were rich and deep to suit the colour and quality of his eyes. But no! not a sound. The silence of embarrassment enfolded the kitchen, and before she reached the top of the stairs, Colin's step crunched the gravel outside and retreated from the house.

Then Jessamine entered her sitting-room, threw off her hat, and sat down by the unpropitiating square table, with her elbows on it and her chin in her hands.

'It is almost,' said she to herself, 'as though I had died and been born again—ugly.'

She gazed at the table with blank eyes.

Who cares for pretty Jessamine?' said she dismally.

She listened again; the hushed song made a painful silence in the cottage, and the wind which murmured round did not fill it. Jessamine got up and wandered up and down the very small space of the chamber.

'Oh dear!' said she; 'how *real* they are, and how impossible to get inside it! How they keep me off, and how they reject me! Oh dear! I don't want elegant trifles any more; I want some good, substantial *bread.'*

To one so accustomed to court and welcome wherever she moved, whose lightest word and act had been received with plaudits, the experience was a bewildering one. Colin Macgillvray was the chief offender. She began to wonder whether he really appreciated her beauty; she was quite sure he did not approve of it—of *her.* That last thought set her mind running into all sorts of regions hitherto unexplored. It was a much more severe discipline than Dr. Cornerstone's stern instructions. After all, *that* was a sort of court—for was not Dr. Cornerstone taken up with her? Now, Colin ignored her.

Three days afterwards the hay was gathered in; 'all except,' they said, 'a small field of Macgillvray's.'

And Jessamine, when the shadows lay long upon the ground, and the scents of pine and heather were warm in the air, went down to watch the final carrying. She seated herself upon a bank under a rowan-tree whose berries showed red amongst the leaves, and watched the moving to and fro of the figures at work in the field. Only Colin was there and a boy and a woman; and only a few haycocks remained to be gathered and taken to the cart. Jessamine watched and waited until Colin came and thrust his fork into the haycock near her side. He freed one hand, as he did so, and lifted his cap with his unaltered air of courteous indifference.

'May I help?' murmured Jessamine timidly.

'Thank you, you are most kind; but we are all but finished now.'

The boy led the cart up as he spoke, and he turned with the load of hay suspended upon the fork to pitch it in; but somehow a portion fell to the ground, and Jessamine, rising with a sudden impulse, stooped over it, and gathered it up in her arms. Macgillvray tranquilly deposited his share in the cart, and then, tossing aside his fork, turned to relieve her.

'Thank you,' said he once more as his brown hands freed her from her burden; 'you are most kind.'

But Jessamine lifted her eyes with wistful entreaty in them—the entreaty, not of a vain girl to be sexually flattered, but of one human being to another for a recognition of service; and she fancied that for a second Macgillvray's eye held her at a less distant range than before. It was only for the briefest instant;

before the ripple of pleasure had time to rise in her heart he was standing by his cart again, his back towards her, and was turning his horse's head away from the field. The hay was all lifted, and Jessamine was left alone in the sunny place with thoughts that dimly yearned after austerity and goodness.

After this, during the next three weeks, her encounters with Colin became frequent. With the hay season a habit had been formed of wandering about Dalfaber. When she met the owner, she would pause with a pretty deference, the colour in her cheek and the wistful light in her eye, and ask some question about farming; as these inquiries were at least to the point, he would find leisure to stop and to reply to them carefully. Sometimes a momentary relaxation of his unbending manner recalled the faint beat of pleasure in the hayfield, but oftener beneath his courtesy lurked sturdy defiance. Her acquaintance with the McKenzies had taken a simple cordiality of condition from the first, but her acquaintance with Macgillvray was as a long journey upon an undiscovered winding road that has to be conquered by inches, and where, each corner rounded, the same figure walks before, the back towards one and the face averted.

CHAPTER VIII

ONE afternoon Jessamine had been tempted to take a longer walk than usual, and found herself some miles away from home, over-tired, and dragging exhaustedly along the highway alone. Moreover, the sky threatened storm. While in this evil case she heard behind the sound of wheels, and, turning round, saw Macgillvray approaching in an open trap. As he came up he lifted his hat, and Jessamine signed to him to stop.

'Are you going back home, Mr. Macgillvray?' asked she.

'Oh yes; I am going to Dalfaber.'

'I am very tired. Would you be so kind as to let me drive with you?'

'Indeed, Miss Halliday, and I will be most pleased whatever,' responded Colin with his most courteous air.

Jessamine got into the vehicle by his side. It was a very common dog-cart, ill-hung, and of preposterous height, and the horse that pulled it was an imperfectly broken-in farm beast that started and shied on every small occasion. Nevertheless, she nestled down by the driver with a sense of well-being, thrusting her hands under the rough rug which he folded carefully over her because the air was chill.

It was the first time she had had an opportunity of really long-continued converse with Macgillvray; in all these weeks it seemed to her that she had but nibbled at the outside crust of intercourse; and now, while the horse jogged on at a lurching trot, she feared that he was disposed for silence.

'There is storm in the sky,' she ventured at last.

'Ay,' answered Colin; 'friend or foe?'

And as he spoke he leaned forward, the reins hanging loosely in his hands, and looked skywards. The horse instantly dropped into a walk. Jessamine seized the opportunity of Macgillvray's altered attitude to observe more deliberately the firm line of his profile, the composed folding of his lips, the steady uplift of his eyelid, and the clear depth of his eye.

This was not an intellectual face, but it was a strong one, with the unconquerable quality of mass. His proximity brought with it impressions of warmth, wholesomeness, and power, and his elusive silence piqued curiosity at once by a denial and a promise. After so much clever or vapid chatter, how this reticence spoke to her inmost mind!

'Friend or foe?' repeated Jessamine inquiringly.

'A body gets thinking whiles,' said Colin, still staring upwards.

'Yes,' returned Jessamine.

He glanced down at her, and pointed to the sky with his whip.

'We hoe and dig and drive the plough,' said he, 'but yon is the Great Tiller. Morning by morning we go out to search his face, and then we must be waiting on his smile or frown.'

'Yes.'

'It will be a strange thing to work so hard and be so helpless. Whiles a man's heart feels sore in his body when he stands by the corn-fields to see the grain beaten with the smiting of the showers until the yellow heads lie low on the bit land. And then, come eventide, the clouds open and the sunshine flies and sets the hills laughing under it; and though the grain lies beaten, the sunshine wins.'

'Wins?'

'Ay; wins the soreness from the heart.'

'Is that because it is beautiful?'

'Oh yes, because it is butiful. The smile runs over the heart and makes a body think.'

'Does it?'

'Oh yes; it will be like a book with thoughts in it.'

'But you get tired of always working and always waiting.'

Colin looked over towards his horse's ears with a smile.

'Ay, a body gets tired; but the sky will not be always against us. And when the weather's grand it works for ten.'

'Still, you are obliged to be constantly doing the same thing from year's end to year's end.'

'Oh yes, just so,' returned Colin quietly.

'And do you not wish for something different?'

An odd momentary light shot into Colin's face from some inward source.

'Whiles—a body dreams,' said he.

'And then you want to get away, to do something different,' said Jessamine, leaping to probable conclusions.

'No; it suffices,' answered the man.

'What suffices?' asked Jessamine, discontentedly closing up her idea.

'The dreaming is enough,' repeated Macgillvray. 'It will be a wonder where the thoughts will be coming from that enter a man's head, and how—such strangers to one another and so uncalled-for as they will be—they will just end always in the same thing.'

'And how do they end?'

'In a thankfulness that a man's way is appointed. And in finding that, after all, it looks butifully.'

'Oh,' said Jessamine. 'Well, yes, perhaps, after all, that is the best; perhaps it is beautiful.'

'Oh yes,' returned Colin with delight, 'it will be butiful. The shining that comes into a body's mind from within is a guide, and makes the limits of his path plain. And yet——'

'Yet what?'

The slow rare smile hovered again about his lips. He flicked several flies off his horse as he stared reflectively at it before answering.

'If we bide a wee,[1] who knows?' said he, as though to himself.

He spoke so inwardly that the words were as the shutting of a lid over some secret treasure of the spirit. Jessamine was left on the outside of the closed casket. She wanted to undo the lock and to see that which he would not display, and rash desire precipitated her into indiscretion.

'Do you ever talk like this to your friend Mr. McKenzie?' asked she.

'No,' returned Colin shortly, a light alarm whipping the dreams out of his face.

He flicked his horse sharply over the ears as he answered, and tightened the reins, and the beast resumed its trot.

Jessamine bit her lip in regretful vexation. All her life 'the beautiful Miss Halliday' had blotted out the landscape for her, and it had been so sweet and new a thing to be *forgotten* while this man revealed one corner of the undiscovered treasures of his mind.

After this they drove on for some distance until they encountered a flock of sheep which were being driven along the road to new pastures; they were going in an opposite direction, and had travelled for many miles and many days; the shepherds looked tired and exasperated, and the dogs were wearying of the distinction of their office. Colin, careful of adding to labour because he knew the meaning of labour, drew up against the side of the road; it took several minutes for the flock to pass, and then he drove on again for about a quarter of a mile. The railroad—a single country line—at this point ran parallel to and close upon the road. Colin suddenly brought his horse again to a standstill, and rose up from his seat.

'What is it?' asked Jessamine.

'That will be a sheep from the flock we have just met,' returned Macgillvray,

---

1 This phrase has a range of meanings, typically referring to time. Here it means to remain in a state of emotional reflection or contemplation for a short time (*CSD* 41, 779).

pointing along the line with his whip. 'The poor silly beastie has strayed away, and is running on the railroad.'

'Oh dear!' said Jessamine, standing up too, to look in her turn.

'And there should be a train coming soon,' added Colin, taking out his watch.

'Oh dear me!' cried Jessamine, 'it will be killed! Can't we save it?'

'We will be trying to, whatever,' answered Colin, jumping from the dogcart.

When on the road he hesitated for a second, and glanced up at Jessamine. The glance was doubtful, but the air with which he turned away was unmistakably disparaging.

'I can hold the reins,' said she, mistaking his idea.

'Oh yes,' replied the man; 'but the horse will stand well enough.'

Then he climbed the embankment and ran on until he over-took the sheep. The only result was that the animal slipped past him and raced along the path of peril in the opposite direction. This happened more than once, and at last he stood still, looking vexed and baffled.

Jessamine meanwhile had felt the spur of that single disparaging glance.

'Mr. Macgillvray,' she called from the dogcart, 'cannot I help you?'

Macgillvray, from his place on the embankment, once more surveyed the slim and cultivated grace of her figure as she stood up in the trap; his estimate set her obviously at nought, and he said nothing. But she jumped out of the dogcart, climbed the embankment, and stood by his side; for his look smarted in her heart.

'I might stand here,' said she, making the proposition timidly, 'while you try and drive it back once more.'

'That will do it,' returned Macgillvray cheerily. 'It is most kind of you. It is bound to jump down if there will be one of us on either side. You will be standing here, and will be waving your arms and shouting if it comes your way.'

Having made this proposition, and without waiting for a reply, he ran off again, leaving her with his command upon her conscience. She was considerably startled at the situation, but, nevertheless, stood where he had directed, her arms open and ready to wave (like any automaton scarecrow), and her lips parted ready to shout. Colin had got some two hundred yards distant, and the game began. The sheep proved sillier than is even usual; it ran up and down between them, but clung to the line. At last it made a determined rush towards Jessamine, and she, being inwardly frightened (for, though small, it had horns), instead of dashing at it with such outcry as she could make, shrank back out of the way, drawing her skirts together, and letting it get past to the line beyond. A shout from Macgillvray carried a note of derision; sooner than tolerate it, she recalled her courage, tore after the sheep at her utmost speed, got in front of it again, and drove it back towards him with desperate bravery. It began to be really exciting.

It was the first time Jessamine had tasted real comradeship with a man. Comradeship is impossible where sex is predominant, and in the refined world which she had forsaken sex stands opposite to sex, the stronger with the stirrings of an exhausted sensuality, the weaker comporting itself as a *recherché* morsel which knows its price.[2] But here all was changed. This stalwart peasant saw her only as a serviceable human being; he shouted orders in a peremptory tone as he ran hither and thither, and she made every effort to obey them, sending back shrill retorts when necessary, her voice forsaking in the exigency of the moment that sweet lowness which is an excellent thing in drawing-rooms.

All this rush and scramble was a matter of a few minutes. Suddenly an electric something flashed into Jessamine's face and changed it. In her look and movements great effort had hitherto been discernible, but now a vivid uncontrollable spontaneity animated her. Her quick eye had seen the expected train approaching behind Macgillvray, and at the same moment she saw that, occupied with running and shouting, he heard nothing. He was about fifty yards distant from her, and at the instant of her discovery, abandoning without a shadow of hesitation both the sheep and herself, she dashed forwards at him along the line, her arms wildly outstretched, and a shriek of warning upon her lips. It was a swift, unpremeditated, and scarcely conscious action. She came back to a more normal state to find herself being snatched by Macgillvray from the embankment, the sheep tumbling down headlong beside them, while the train flew past with horrid din.

'Why, what ails the lass?' cried Macgillvray.

His rude grasp was still upon her; her slight figure yielded, and her cheek and hair rested against the rough texture of his coat. When he saw her eyes close and a quiver distort her lips, he forgot the distinction of rank which hitherto he had been so careful to record in the least shade of his bearing, and thought only how tones of the voice and the homely pressure of firm muscle may reassure human terror. The sheep meanwhile began to tear up the road in the right direction, and the train disappeared.

'Why, what will be ailing her?' he repeated with emotion. 'She will be looking as frightened as the poor beastie itself. It will be too much running

---

2 *Recherché:* sought after and cherished for its rare qualities (*Larousse* 439).

for her, after all. Oh, I am most sorry! I am most sorry!'

'Oh, no! no! no!' cried Jessamine, opening her eyes and giving a great sigh. 'I thought you didn't see the train! Oh, I thought you didn't see it! I thought—— Oh, I don't know what I thought!'

And then the 'scales,' as it were, fell from her eyes. She knew that there was no scare, neither had there been danger or alarm. Suddenly she realised that her terror had been the creation of inexperience, and that Macgillvray, treating her as one would treat a foolish terrified child, was holding her in a close embrace. She snatched herself from his arms, the side which he had so rudely pressed blushing unseen with angry shame, and stood defiantly apart, fury flecking her cheeks and dropping a veil upon her eyes.

Macgillvray, when she withdrew from him, let his arms fall, and stood contemplating her with an aspect of quiet wonder. Upon this at last a pucker of amusement stole. It began to dawn upon him that this slight whiff of humanity had supposed his own large and vigorous person to be in danger, and had flung herself forward to save him. It tickled all his heart and filled his whole nature with ecstatic laughter; yet so gentle and tender an expression crossed the mighty amusement of his smile, that it went far to win him forgiveness.

'Oh no,' he said; 'oh no. *I'm* all right'—his voice disparaged himself—'*I'm* all right, whatever.'

Then he turned to his horse, and vaguely touched the harness about its nose. After which he took the reins suddenly into his hand.

'We will be going home now,' said he gravely. 'The sheep is safe, and it is all well over.'

Jessamine, still furious and still shivering, found no method by which to assert her outraged dignity. The mere sense of mass in the nature of this man compelled her; she felt rather than saw the tranquil expectation of his eye, and her resources ran down to nothing. With a completely subdued air she got in by his side, and they drove off in silence.

CHAPTER IX

THE thing discriminated from all else is the point of danger. Ever since the coming of Miss Jessamine Halliday amongst them, Macgillvray had felt her difference from anything he had seen before with the intensity of a dumbly artistic nature; he was profoundly aware of her beauty, he knew it to the slightest expressive turn of her head, and the wilful manner of the smallest of the tresses about her brow. It was only the balance of his mind which kept his feet firmly gripped upon his own standpoint; the rock, however much the light plays tricks with it, is still a rock, and though a mute poetry clung about him, and though gentleness and sweetness grew, lichen-like, upon him, the sturdier qualities which had disturbed Miss Halliday's conclusions were the essential matter. So that, just as he turned a face of unbroken patience to the buffets of the climate under which he toiled, he could confront this Will-o'-the-wisp loveliness, whose sombre eyes carried their own warning, by the inward power which he possessed of reticence over his own thought. Our practised virtues marshal themselves when the tug of trial comes.

Here, dull though it might be, was his road, and nowhere else, such a man and no other was he, and not an inch would he budge from his estimate of himself and his surroundings, but would keep his everyday relation to dry facts undisturbed, damming up the surging element of the imagination with the superb pride of common-sense.

It was on the evening after the incident on the railroad that this attitude was for the first time disturbed. That night he sat in his cottage with his head in his hands. He could not control the spark that seemed to run from his throat to his heart and burn there every time he remembered the manner in which she had risked herself in absurd fears for him: he could not rid himself of a phantom pressure against his side, of an enfolded something within his arms, of every slight shade of the moment's sensation which, unnoticed at the time (for his grasp of her had been rude and unconsidered), now returned and settled upon him as birds come home at eventide to roost. Outside, the hills, which from childhood had reached him the help of their tranquillity, lay in the eternal sameness of their profound and beautiful peace; he scarcely dared lift his glance towards them, so conscious was he that his own eyes were changed.

At last he rose, and went out to stand on the threshold of his home; he pressed his hand upon his brow and eyes, and then his glance travelled slowly and deliberately over the stony, meagre land upon which for a century his fathers before him, and he himself at last, had toiled in stubborn patience, and from which annually they had taken Nature's niggard reward. He surveyed his six poor fields—the barley and the oats, the turnip and potato drills, the scant rough pasture—long and steadily. The herd-boy drove his cows to the shed and the calves gambolled beside them; the lad shouted as he went to the fowls which had got into the oat-field; some doves wheeled from the roof of his barn; the smoke poured down from the ill-built chimney over the side of the house; near at hand was a stack of peat, and there a heap of manure; two horses cropped heather in the hollows; and, close by, his old peasant father, in greasy clothes and with smoke-stained face, crept slowly about, prodding at the earth with the staff in his hand, as though unable to wean himself from a habit of patient interrogation of its stony surface. All these things Colin looked at with a consciously deliberate gaze, teaching himself once more what manner of man he was. And then he remembered with infinite relief that the next day was the Sabbath.

When the sun crept next morning into Jessamine's bedroom and laid a beam like a sword across her breast, she opened her eyes sufficiently to pass into a waking dream, but not enough to gather about her those feints and evasions under which she had been taught to drive Nature into cover. She lay, her eyes shining between her lashes, conscious only of warmth and well-being, and for the moment as bare to feeling as any pagan girl. The feeling was like a dream, and the dream was a memory. At first her mind recalled Macgillvray's words, and played round them, bestowing fanciful meanings; then his rude forceful pressure returned again upon her slender figure with an alluring yet terrifying sweetness; from the chaotic web of light and shade in the room his face rekindled in its kind solicitude; and lower than the obvious blowing of the wind outside was the tender emotion of his voice in her ear.

The next moment the sun, escaping more completely from the clouds, smote her upon the face with another ray which actually wakened her; she started up in bed, and, setting her feet upon the floor, stood with her dark hair tumbling in dishevelled waves to her knees, an angry spark in her eye and a frown upon her brow.

She could hardly have distinguished whether it was against Macgillvray or herself that her wrath was pointed.

It was Sunday, and Sunday with the McKenzies was a scene of dulness.

Jessamine's sitting-room was an uncompromising chamber, a prim square place, in which a Puritan under the Stuarts might have sat nursing his rage against the world and human nature.[1] It had for sole adornment upon the walls a map, not of the country, but of the Calvinistic scheme, drawn out in diagrams for the assistance of the believing few and the terror of the lax many: at the left-hand corner of the map, in a melancholy ellipse, the damned went forth to flames and worms; at the right-hand corner, in a no less sorrowful shape, the elect marched out to thrones and psalms.[2] Beneath this stern relic Jessamine sat, recalling all the defences of society against spontaneity, and pinching the heart out of her timid bit of nature.

The fascination of the life between Drynock and Dalfaber had lain in the element of resistance which met her upon every side. Had she been flattered and easily accepted, it is probable she would have sickened of her experiment before this, and have returned repentant to the bosom of Aunt Arabella. But no second-rate lady had ever struggled more ardently to get into a first-rate aristocratic drawing-room than had Jessamine to penetrate into this inner life of the sturdy Highland peasant; and hitherto she had failed. Failure meant pique, and pique gave zest to higher motives. It was not so much, she felt, the individuals that repulsed her as their common reality of life. This reality in them appeared to reject her as inevitably as a healthy tissue will reject a morbid growth.

But had the taste of it which she had just procured agreed with her? What was the price of becoming as real as these wholesome Highlanders, and bundling the host of fictions and fastidiousnesses in which she had been bred out of doors?

Ah, that price! The fascination of this genuine simplicity and naturalness

---

1   The Stuarts were the House of Stuarts, the monarchs who ruled Scotland from 1371 and then England and Ireland from 1603, with the accession of James I (James VI of Scotland). The House of Stuart's rule ended in 1707 with the Act of Union that formed Great Britain. According to Moira Hook and Arthur MacGregor in *England Under the Stuarts*, "[t]he reform movement identified with the Puritans sought to 'purify' the Church of England from any sign of Roman Catholic observance. . . The seeds of Puritanism first flourished in a controversy over ritual, vestments and the use of a prescribed liturgy; later the movement became more radical, seeking to abolish the episcopacy" (9). Puritans under the Stuarts did not fare well. Moira Hook and Arthur MacGregor. *England Under the Stuarts*. Oxford: Ashmolean Museum Publications, 2003.

2   As a religion, Calvinism is based on the belief that the Bible (the Old Testament) is without interpretation, and is absolutely the word of God. Calvinism is a Protestant religion and one that stresses the absolute ruling of God over a person's life. Free will does not exist in Calvinism; one is predestined at birth to the path of Hell or to the path of Heaven.

lay possibly only on the exterior surface, and might be lost if she penetrated too far. Indeed, with what unlooked-for dangers might not further discovery be accompanied, and with what surprises! Something in the memory of that rude firm grasp of Macgillvray's arms upon her was fraught with terror; his simplicity and directness were in themselves an alarm, so brusque was he, yet so tender.

'I am very, very angry!' said Jessamine.

And even as she said it the moment came back in such strong appealing sweetness that it overwhelmed the wrath. Thus one thought, with harelike cunning, doubles on another that pursues it.

'My God!' murmured the girl, with her hand over her eyes, in an inexplicable medley of emotion and in very real fear.

Being Sunday, Jessamine was banished all day to the parlour. She wished the McKenzies were not such rigid Sabbath-keepers, and that she could have surrounded herself with the cheerful atmosphere of the kitchen, and broken the monotony by activity with pots and pans, for her restlessness increased. As it was, she had no resource save reading, so she took out a novel from the book-case. It was a book considered by the sick nurses of Propriety as eminently suitable to the virgin mind. The morning dragged away, the afternoon came, and Jessamine closed the book with a sense of nausea.

'Something has gone wrong with this author,' said she; 'I used to like her. All this talk of duty and good manners now seems to me sickly and rotten. I don't think Dr. Cornerstone would approve of it. I even believe he would call it "invalidish."'

She threw it aside and went out into the wholesome air and sunshine. As she put her hat on she told herself that Macgillvray was not in her mind. Yet she took the way to Dalfaber. Instead, however, of passing the cottage, she walked down to the loch, and sat upon the bank to watch the flow and sport of the ripples. About her spread the fields of barley and of oats; she looked on them as Colin had done the night before, yet with different eyes; already the barley ripened on the stalk, and she knew that the harvesting must begin. Then, again as Colin had done, she looked to the hills; the afternoon light pinked out every bush and rocky angle, and deepened the shade in the crevices, and burnt into the tints, so that the hues of the heather became more roseate and the grass and mosses greener, and flames of colour stole like still fire hither and thither; a delicious undertone of flapping water, scarcely heard and yet apparent, lulled her ear; the wind was in the trees, but not on her; the sun flung light and shade, as seed scattered from a sower's hand, upon the loch, and the clouds (beautiful players) moved, floated, changed, catching the light and hiding it, throwing it over the hills and withdrawing it, with the noiselessness of serene nature, the great sweet sport of universal beauty at one with itself, content.

Jessamine looked and listened. All day she had been trying to goad into activity the small fry of conventionality, but the effort died out; she fell instead under a grave and strange presentiment. For there crept upon her mind the dim consciousness of a difference in herself; it lay there like a weight, with the heaviness of an unborn child. But, also, it was accompanied with a sense of physical well-being, of oneness with the very heather on which she sat, so that she stretched her bare hands out and lifted her unveiled face to the sunshine and the sweet blowing of the wind. And that vague pleasurable emotion which had wakened with her in the unguarded morning hours returned thrivingly in the sunshine.

Suddenly from the west, like a trumpet-call, shot up a red flame, and lit a beacon upon the hills. Jessamine shook off her dream, rose to her feet, and took her way back to Macgillvray's land. With more active movement a buzzing of discomforting ideas returned. She pictured the peasant as coarsely and consciously reminiscent of yesterday's occurrence, and portrayed to the eye of her mind the offensive smile with which he might greet her. The blood flecked her cheek, and again a spark was in her eye; she made ready such weapons as she judged would tell. On gaining the top of the slope from which Macgillvray's cottage looked down, she beheld him approaching at a distance. He came through a narrow path in a field of oats; his collie ran to meet him; the shrubby birch-wood flanked the field in a half-circle; there was no other figure in sight.

Jessamine walked towards him firmly and deliberately; she meant to incline her head with the indifference which had been in the old life her daily practise, and which was of all things the most fitting in the manner of a highborn lady towards a rustic. Her lips touching each other without any grimace of firmness, yet held the onlooker distant, and when, as Colin came near, she raised her eyes, their shafts were icy.

Here, however, the Unexpected tripped her up.

The face her glance swept contained, as she saw at once, no hint of consciousness, nor of any recollection which was touched with levity. The man's eyes were raised and onlooking; a serious gentleness lay upon his lips; his brow had its old aloofness. The impressions of the Sabbath evening service had not passed from him; he had from that sparse sowing reaped richly of his own spirituality, and he carried still about him his own thoughts. So that Jessamine's prepared demeanour stumbled, as it were, against the massive unpreparedness of a preoccupied mind. She received—even before her own condescending little gesture was ready—the courteous dismissal of Macgillvray's hat-lift and the grave glance of his eyes in her direction. Then he relapsed into meditation and passed on.

CHAPTER X

THE small hours of Monday morning were washed with showers. When Colin opened his cottage door, the clouds had cleared and the sun shone; but a fragrant smell of rain lingered in the air, and a grateful moisture intensified the hues of the heather, the myriad tints and flash and flame of colour.

'It will rain again before noon,' said Colin, his eyes fixed on the clear hue of a distant hill, behind which a small but ominous tail of cloud streamed up into the ether.

'Ay!' said old Rorie, staring about with open mouth to supplement the dimness of his eyes.

'Lad, are ye remembering how ye promised John McKenzie to take the cart up to Drynock?' called Mrs. Macgillvray, a woman with a voice sharpened by retrospective grievances.

'I'm not forgetting,' returned Colin.

And he stepped out on the moor, and went towards the fields, his head up, his brow stern with some tenacious resolve. But his eyes were soft as they followed the long lines of the oat-fields, the green still faintly sprinkled amid the gold, and the blades bowed with the heaviness of ripening, tawny red.

When the dinner-hour came, Colin appeared again in the cottage. There was an unaccustomed weariness in his face, and he wiped the sweat from his brow, though he had not been putting any great force into his work, and though the morning was fresh. Indeed, new clouds hurried up in the sky, and a wind had arisen. Mrs. Macgillvray pushed a smoking plate of porridge towards him as he seated himself at the table. He took a spoonful, and dipped it in the milk, but he did not eat with appetite.

'Ye were taking the cart to Drynock for John?' asked his mother, her eye anxiously fixed on old Rorie's somewhat uncertain operations with the spoon.

'I was working in the barn,' returned Colin.

'Aweel, lad!' put in old Rorie. 'John will be ill-pleased with ye.'

'Maybe,' answered Colin.

He fed himself again with the porridge, but his hand was unsteady, and underneath the ruddy sunburn his cheek was pale. Presently he put his spoon down, and stared fixedly at the closed door; then he rose, opened it, and looked out. This happened twice.

'What will be ailing ye, laddie?' cried his mother.

'I was thinking somebody was knocking,' returned Colin confusedly. 'Mother, I've done, and I'll be going out to see after the horse.'

'But ye are not through with that porridge!'

'I have done, though. A body need not be eating more than he wants.'

'It will be a sinfu' waste.'

'It will be a worse if I was choking myself.'

'Gude save us! the laddie's ill! Staring at the door like a bogle, and leaving good porridge on the aschette!'[1]

'I'm all right, mother,' answered Colin, correcting some confusion of face by a smile.

Then he went to the outhouses, and fetched a halter, and walked down amongst the heathery hollows, where his horse stood thrusting his nose into the purple tufts and cropping them short. Colin brought him up to the cart, and harnessed him.

'It will be an easy thing,' said he with a grim look, 'to see the way clear when a body's in the kirk,[2] and when nothing comes betwixt the talking of the heart and the Lord. I was meaning John McKenzie to fetch the cart himself to Drynock, and to go for the coal his lane. When a body is clean daft, he must be his own keeper, let folks think what they will. But Gude save me if I can bear her knocking at my heart and at the door of my cot[3] any longer, and not make an answer!'

Then he took the way to Drynock.

'You are late, Colin,' said McKenzie, as his friend pulled up the cart in front of the creeper-covered porch.

'I am late,' he responded shortly.

'Aweel, there will be the whole afternoon before us, and time enough will be as good as any time, I'm thinking.'

'Oh yes!'

'You will be coming with me? We can load the cart quicker together.'

Colin leaned back against his horse, and did not immediately respond. His eyes sought through the open door of the kitchen for a glimpse of the bright presence of Jessamine. The kitchen was empty. Mrs. McKenzie's dolly-tub stood with some of the wet linen hanging on the side; a heap of unwashed things were tossed on the settle.[4] He glanced round the yard and the garden, and then he caught sight of Mrs. McKenzie standing near the road and look-

---

1   Bogle: "an ugly or terrifying ghost or phantom" and Aschette or ashet: "an oval serving plate" (*CSD* 52, 17*)*.

2   Kirk: church (*CSD* 342).

3   Cot: cottage (*CSD* 117).

4   Settle: a bench (*CSD* 581).

ing up it, her hand shading her eyes. Before he had responded to McKenzie's request, she turned round and walked towards them, some perturbation of mind disturbing the habitual serenity of her brow.

'Colin,' said she, 'you were not passing Miss Halliday along the road as you were coming?'

'I was passing no one,' returned Colin, his heart thumping.

'I'm fretting a bit over her. I'd very much rather she would just be taking her walks about the moor and the roads, but she was ever very wilful since she came. And this morning she would not hearken to counsel.'

Colin did not reply. He looked hard at Mrs. McKenzie, and it seemed to him that he was staring at a dark place whence words, which he knew beforehand, would issue ominously.

'And so, for all I was saying,' continued Mrs. McKenzie, 'she must take her way this morning towards the deer-forest and up beyond to Craggan More, carrying her bit lunch in her hand.'

Colin turned sharply to McKenzie, as though to respond to his request.

'I have work to do,' said he; 'I will not be coming with you.'

'Bide a wee, Colin!' cried Mrs. McKenzie, 'Will the deer be getting dangerous? The lassie has been gone a weary time and a storm is gathering.'

'Ay, they will be getting dangerous.'

And without another word he turned on his heel, leapt over the fence, and ran back towards Dalfaber and on to the deer-forest at the top of his speed.

*   *   *   *   *

That morning Jessamine had waked with a sore heart.

'I will not work,' said she; 'what does anything matter? I wish there were somewhere for me to hide myself and lose myself, that I might cry all the tears out of my heart and no one see. It is horrible to be despised.'

Mrs. McKenzie prepared for the weekly washing after breakfast, and put the cups and saucers aside for Jessamine's share of the work. Then she set the inner door open, and, presently looking up, saw the girl standing there, the dark, dusty little staircase down which she had just descended throwing off her profile, with its delicate pale despondency, the rays of spare light tenderly touching the curves of her cheek and the ruffled rings of her dark hair, and tracing the fair, slim lines of her figure.

Mrs. McKenzie, looking at her penetratingly in the brief moment when she dangled her hat in her hand before raising her eyes and speaking, read in her mien a total disruption of the morning's arrangements, and sighed. Then occurred that little passage between good counsel and wilfulness which she had described to Colin. When the girl had taken her basket and passed out, Mrs. McKenzie stepped to the door and looked after her with the steady benediction of her motherly eyes.

'The lassie's young,' said she, 'and it's an ill thing when one's young to get properly acquaint with one's own heart. Seems like as though we started life with a stranger in the bosom, who will be taking up a deal of our good time. When we're a bit settled down in life we get used to it, and leave taking so much note of what will be going on in our own insides, and we will just be remembering that others' insides will be in the same ill-chance as our own. Gude send she comes to no harm!'

Jessamine, whose small bark of experience was far from being anchored by this tranquil wisdom, was attracted by the width and silence and loneliness of the fir-woods, and fancied that she could sit all day amongst the trees and solve the problems of the heart by thinking of them.

The wood was fenced on one side; there was a road through it, but the gate was locked. Therefore an entrance into the place involved a climb of some kind. The locking of the gate—which was done to the high inconvenience of the people of the place—was the act of the proprietor, a man who lived in the country for one month in the year and shot over the land. But the road had been closed for many weeks beyond this one month, and when Jessamine had climbed the fence she found about her an untrodden wildness which delighted her. The road was heather-covered, the cart-ruts showing only as deep lines of shadow amongst the rank purple blooms; spiders' webs woven from tuft to tuft glittered with the rain-drops which the sun had not yet licked up; and the bluish translucent mist, which hovered beneath the thick growing branches of the young firs, was pierced with shafts of brilliant untouched colour—purple and crimson heaths, emerald ferns, carmine fungi, blood-red cranberry leaves, rich browns, and pale variegated lichens. Above, between the fine lace of the top-most branches, the blue of the sky was of unfathomed depth, and over it the hurry and disorder of wisp-like clouds kept passing at intervals like the ranks of a flying squadron. Amid this undisturbed loveliness the girl went slowly with her graceful, dainty tread, swinging her basket in her hand and lifting her fair face to receive the painting of the sun. It was lonely to eeriness; but her health was splendid, and in nerve and fibre she was strong. As to danger, inexperience forbade her to conceive it possible.

The road wound upwards almost to the top; here bare crags escaped from a dwindling edge of trees and lifted their scarred sides to the sky. The point of the hill was called Craggan More, and it was Jessamine's first design to reach the summit; but before she was half-way up she saw, between the branches, a place almost clear of the wood, and where the heather spread bare and purple. Then she left the road, and, pushing through the thicket, reached the heather, and flung herself down to rest.

From her position she commanded a good view of the country; amongst the more familiar landmarks, she saw the loch that lay below Dalfaber, and, on the moor above, the brown thatched cottage. Fixing her eyes upon it, she clasped her hands round her knees and began to think.

This was her first half-conscious recognition of the fact that she was nearing her own life-problem. She had been instructed by Aunt Arabella into the duty of a girl to repress feeling, to hold herself poised between relative advantages until the event culminated from the outside. As to her own nature, of that she had heard nothing; passion, she had been taught, was an offensive word and an unladylike allusion. But dicta of this kind have been proved before now ineffectual when genuine emotion is in question. What she was feeling might be right or wrong, decorous or indecorous; *that* was not the point. She partly realised that she did feel, that her heart, hitherto cold and virginal as snow, was melting and opening beneath an influence that was as new as it was strange. So self-conscious a creature as Jessamine could not wholly miss this change in herself, nor the subtle delight of the entrance of the fresh experience within. She was far more inclined to yield to and dally with her sensations, than to direct them. There were not in her whole repertory any reasons at all for conduct one way or another, except the reason that a course was *comme il faut* or not *comme il faut*,[5] as the case might be; and this was not likely to prove efficient before the strongest of the natural impulses. It was true she possessed a vein of hard appreciation of the advantageous as distinguished from the disadvantageous in a worldly point of view. That, however, if it ever came to a severe struggle between inclination and moral force, was only likely to weaken the decision by confusing the issue. Great decisions are won only upon clear, simple lines, and it is merely a sign of feeble character to take too many points into consideration when resolutions have to be made.

Jessamine had just reached the phase when the stirring of her nature—like the rising of sap in the spring—threw her upon an unusual activity of mind as well as body, her whole self putting out new buds and leaves, here and there and everywhere, of thought, and feeling, and beauty, and health. She was occupied at present with the unmixed delight which characterizes

---

5 *Comme il faut:* as it should be.

the opening of a passion before the more difficult stages are reached. But her acute little mind seized at once on that general opposition which is sure to meet an individual excursion from the realm of the accustomed, and she felt it already as an injustice, as a too great demand upon personal sacrifice, to be required to keep to a beaten path which she had had no responsibility in shaping, which she had been taught was advantageous, but had had no means of trying for herself, and which, indeed, in the initial stages she already cordially hated. Unawareness mingled with the perceptiveness of her thinking; it was pictorial rather than reasoned, yet the sense of contrast between this dawning spontaneity and the flat range of her former ideas of life was clear enough, and she discovered it to be alluring.

It was scarcely a deliberate meditation into which she fell; thoughts hitherto strangers passed into her mind without her knowing how or why; a sense of greatness overshadowed her, of isolation, a prevision freed from the tiresome details which she had been wont to call 'considerations.' For when Nature is very near, she has a hand with which to touch the remote springs, and to bring to the surface hidden and unspoken matters which lie slumbering within.

CHAPTER XI

A HIGHER wind came suddenly in the fir-trees, and a drop of rain fell upon Jessamine's hand. She looked up, and saw clouds hurrying from the east, and long trails of rack[1] stretching over the sky, and shadows rolling upon the hills. A shower descended visibly over the furthest range, and drew across it a glittering veil. The glow of colour was changing into silvery grays and duns, but the sun still rode high in the heavens, shooting shafts of light into the heart of the mists, and keeping the air around wonderfully clear, so that the nearer landscape gathered in distinctness, and Dalfaber, with its loch, its fields of corn, and its brown thatched cottage, stood out like an etching of Dürer's.[2]

Jessamine did not move. In spite of the threatening drop upon her hand, she sat still to watch the contention of light and shadow as the mists encroached upon the valley, and it pleased her fancy to see how Dalfaber shone like a jewel on a sombre nebulous garment, chancing, as it did, to concentrate the bright scarce rays upon itself. Her dreaming was over; the whole encampment of vivid images stole away from her heart, and left it sadder and more desolate than before.

Luminous thinking was rare with her. To see anything in its essential simplicity and incontrovertible verity was, with her, as a rift in a cloudy sky that closed again. Upon a mood of clear intellectual activity and of genuine discrimination followed the accustomed parodies of those powers. She had never learned to look anything in the face, or to concentrate herself upon it; the eyes of her mind glanced hither and thither. So that after any short spell of thinking, before she knew it, a host of distracting by-thoughts and fictions ran into her mind with hot pattering feet and perplexing rapidity, and all that she possessed of native genius remained but to assert itself in a sad foreboding of martyrdom, and a more mournful prevision of personal apostasy.

'I cannot think,' said Jessamine, whimsically pointing what is a common experience to her own case, 'but the Aunt Arabella in me gets into it and spoils it.'

---

1 Rack: "driving mist or fog" (*CSD* 537).
2 Albrecht Dürer (1471-1528) was a German painter and printmaker from Nuremberg. He was a very prolific artist; he was also a scholar of mathematics and human anatomy. Dürer's etchings were extraordinarily precise and detailed, so that what was in the forefront of the etching was just as distinct as what was in the background.

It must have been close on noon when her reverie permitted her for the first time to distinguish from the slow regular rustle of wind in the branches, and the occasional fall of a rain-drop, the sound of something stirring near at hand. She turned round with a start, to behold, amongst the trees behind, the red side and branching antlers of a stag. It was cropping heather, and was partly hidden by the interlaced foliage of the firs, so that it did not see her. But this sudden apprehension of alien life close beside her was infinitely uncanny, and a remembrance of Mrs. McKenzie's warning made her look upon the creature with alarm.

'If I keep very still,' thought she, 'it will go away without seeing me.'

The stag, however, showed no signs of retiring, but continued to crop the heather with short snatching noises. For full half an hour she sat in a silent tension watching, the situation pressing upon her with a more and more painful sense of loneliness; the hurrying of the clouds overhead seemed inconsequently to increase the feeling, while the sight of the unattainable refuge of Dalfaber, lying below in homely security, made her heart yearn hungrily. As the moments dragged on, it began to appear as though she and the stag were hung midway between earth and heaven in a world of their own, which to her was terrible.

Then the stag raised its head, and saw her. Her heart leapt when those strange wild eyeballs rolled upon her own. For full ten minutes the forest creature stood motionless, gazing at her with a pair of humid, startled eyes, its branching antlers proudly lifted; and Jessamine in mortal fear stared back.

And still she was acutely aware of Dalfaber lying below, with the smoke curling steadily out of the old chimney. It seemed to her that her spirit flew out of her body, and flung itself knocking and crying at the door.

The stag began slowly to move round and round in a circle. She followed it with her eyes. Sometimes it got behind the trees, and she lost command of it for the moment, and then her nerves shivered in an extremity of expectation. Presently it began to make its circle smaller and smaller, and to gradually disentangle itself from the trees. She dared not stir, but still trusted to quietude and the steadiness of her own glance; but at last the creature stopped, stretched out its throat, and gave an angry bellow. Jessamine, who was wholly unprepared for the sound, was startled out of her self-control, and she sprang to her feet with a cry. Then the creature levelled its horns, and trotted towards her. She flung her basket at it, and fled towards the shelter of the trees. For the moment the basket saved her. The stag stopped, and gave her time to reach the thicket; but Jessamine, as she pushed her way frantically through the close-growing branches, saw over her shoulder, with sickening horror, how the beast tore and trampled on the basket until it was in shreds. Desperate now, and completely unnerved, she rushed through the wood at exhausting speed, over the hidden boulders and treacherous clumps of heather and fern, breaking her way through the interlaced branches as best she could, her clothes torn, her hands bleeding, and her face smarting from the frequent striking of twigs against it. Her aim was to reach the old heather-covered road, for when in it she would know in what direction to run, and fancied that fleetness might carry her safely to the fence in time. By good luck she made her way through the thicket pretty straight to the desired point. The trees became larger and wider apart, and she saw the road through them; but as she neared it, the mad crashing sounds in her rear—which had been to her like the goading of a nightmare of terror—suddenly seemed in front. Halting for a second to listen, she heard the stag somewhere to the left, and before she had time to effectually conceal herself, it bounded out into the road, and stood still, turning its head about, and snuffing the air; then again it bellowed.

Jessamine's heart leapt in her body, and her throat was so dry that her breath hurt her; her limbs began to fail, and she clung to the shelter of a large tree, and gained a moment's respite. But the stag saw her immediately, and trotted in her direction. She darted from that tree, and reached another, glancing frantically round to see if there were time to scramble up and take refuge in the branches. But before her trembling hands had grasped the lowest twigs the stag was rushing forward again, and she was compelled to flee towards a new shelter.

'Oh, Colin, Colin!' cried the horror-stricken girl.

For an hour of time, with limbs that seemed each moment less capable of sustaining her, and with straining eyes that grew more and more blind, and ears that were deafened by the horrible singing in her head, Jessamine saved herself from the onslaught of the beast by the expedient of darting from tree to tree. She hoped by degrees to near the fence, but the creature still followed her, and she seemed no nearer the confines of the forest than when the desperate game began. Then the sense that a moment must come when her strength and her wits would inevitably fail began to sap the little remaining courage which she possessed; and finally the thing she dreaded most of all happened—she lost her footing, and fell headlong over a clump of heather, only saving herself from rolling helplessly over and over by snatching at the friendly trunk of a pine-tree near. Unable to regain her feet, the most complete despair settled upon her, and she uttered shriek upon shriek of anguish that tore her throat. Then the strength even to do that failed; she yielded herself to the bitterness of death, and lost every kind of sense and consciousness saving an extremity of horror and darkness, and a quivering of the flesh in terrific expectation.

But the fate she waited for delayed; it began slowly to dawn upon her benumbed senses that the crashing sounds of the stag's progress were arrested; then she heard it snorting angrily at some yards' distance. Opening her fainting eyes with half-terrified hope, she found that it had entangled its antlers in the crooked, close-growing branches of a tree, and was for the moment a prisoner. Relief brought back more of her sense and strength, and then she was enabled to distinguish the reiterated shout of a man's voice somewhere in the wood. No flute-like music could have sounded so sweet as that rough sound, and, gathering her forces together, she managed to give an answering cry. And then came the rending and tearing of the underwood again as someone frantically fought a way towards her, shouting as he came. The stag, frightened both at the sounds and its own imprisoned condition, made frantic efforts to free itself, and at last broke from the branches, and bounded away into the thicket at the very moment when Colin's form became visible amongst the heavily-massed foliage.

Jessamine was struggling to her feet as he came up, and he put his hands out to help her, bending speechlessly towards her with a white face. She burst out crying when she saw him, and caught at his coat, clinging to him and hiding her face until the horrible shuddering was over-past. And he held her silently, his mouth set and grim.

'Oh!' moaned she, lifting her head at last; 'to die like that—to die like that!'

'Ay,' he said; 'young and so bonnie!'

Then he threw one arm round her, and helped her along, while with the other he beat back the branches. When they came to the road, he lifted her like a child in his arms.

'Cannot I walk?' asked Jessamine.

'Not until we get to the highway,' he answered briefly. 'Put your arms about my neck; I will be carrying you easier that way.'

She laid her arms about his neck as he bade her, and closed her eyes. And then she heard him give a great sigh, and it seemed to her that for a moment he pressed her tight against his heart. When they reached the highroad, he set her again upon her feet. By this time the rain beat down in a wild shower. He stood so that he could shelter her a little with his body, his hands being thrust into the side-pockets of his coat.

'Bide a wee,' said he; 'a cart or something must be passing along in a moment. There are a good few every hour.'

'Oh!' cried Jessamine, her eyes still wide with terror, 'if you had not come the stag would have killed me. I could not have run another yard.'

'If it had got you,' said he shortly, 'there would not have been a bit of dry heather left unfired in the forest by morning.'

She looked up. His face was still white and grim, and in his eyes was a sombre desperation which could not be lightly banished, and which affected her with a sort of fear. She made no reply, but cowered by his side, while the rain poured down in sheets before them, washing out more and more of the landscape, and, by obliterating their surroundings, concentrating the consciousness of the two upon the small dripping spot of earth which they occupied together. Jessamine shivered, not only with retrospective terror, but with foreboding fear. Glancing up again to his strong figure, and taking an indelible impression from the quiet force of his face, her heart ran down to some remote place of weakness in her being, and it seemed to her that she had been snatched from death only to be set upon some dim-washed islet of earth, where a tremendous and inexplicable claim grasped and held her.

Both of them were relieved when a cart rumbled along, driven by a man with a mackintosh cap pulled over his nose and a mackintosh cloak pulled over his ears; the rain ran in rivers over him. Colin stopped the cart, and, briefly explaining what had happened, begged the driver to take the exhausted girl back to Drynock.

'Indeed and I will,' was the gentle Highland response.

And, while Colin helped her into the cart, the driver unbuttoned his mackintosh to spread over her. It seemed to Jessamine to make everything that had passed more dream-like and inexplicable, that Macgillvray had altered his manner to the old distant respectfulness.

'Stop!' she cried, as they were about to start. And, leaning over the side of the cart, she stretched her hand to Colin, who came up and took it reluctantly in his own. 'If you had not come,' she murmured, gazing at him with eyes that were still dazed, 'the stag would have killed me.'

She had intended to thank him, but nothing save this lame phrase would rise to her lips.

'I'm thinking,' returned Colin, 'that we will be quits now.'

A faint smile played for a moment over his white lips; but he withdrew his hand instantly and signed to the driver to proceed. The last Jessamine saw of him, he was walking along the road, his head turned aside, the inextinguishable grimness still in his face. Then the showers washed him out, and left nothing save a blurred shadow. And she crouched down in the cart under the mackintosh, with her hand pressed tight against her heart.

CHAPTER XII

MISS HALLIDAY liked her colours in half-light; the hues she preferred were pale primrose, cream, or wan yellows. Nevertheless, one morning, about a week after the stag incident, and when she had entirely recovered the event, she was to be seen ransacking her drawers for a knot of rose-coloured ribbon. But her drawer contained no such thing as a bit of bright ribbon; though she turned the contents over with eager hands, nothing of the sort was to be found.

After searching in vain, she stood still in the middle of the poor cottage chamber, the clumsy beams near her head, the little window letting a chill draught stir the skirt of her dress. It was the gray woollen dress with the straight unadorned folds. Her hands were loosely linked, and her body so poised upon thought and so still that it looked like a lovely statue, and the wonderful female face was lifted like a flower.

Suddenly, with a sobbing exclamation, she stretched out her hand and unhooked from the wall the small looking-glass which formed the sole substitute for the splendid mirrors of yore; it hung in a dark corner, but she carried it to the window and looked critically at the reflection of her own face. Macgillvray, who continually set her in a new light to herself, made even her beauty a matter of interrogation, so that her gaze into the glass was both penetrating and anxious. Out of it looked back to her a small oval face, with a dash of colour in the cheeks, exquisite lips, red like cherries, a short dimpled chin, and, underneath the wing-like eyebrows, a pair of large dark eyes with storm in them. The colour and the storm were new. She took a knot of pale primrose and then of cream ribbon and tried them against her cheek, but neither satisfied her. A bit of red sweet-william with other flowers stood in a vase on her mantelpiece; she tried that. The rich deep velvety hue suited, she saw in a moment, the flame-like signals in her cheeks, the new ripeness of her lips, the wild strange light in her eyes. There was an amazing magical something in her face which the colour intensified, and she threw the dejected aesthetic hues (which so ill-suited this leaping up of life within her) away, and, putting on her hat, slipped out without pausing to excuse herself to Mrs. McKenzie, and walked many miles to the nearest shop, and purchased two or three shades of bright-coloured ribbons.

On her return, she hurried up to her bedroom again, and tied her ruffled hair up in a little heap above her head, with a tiny knot of the ribbon showing like a spark in the midst, and she fastened a handkerchief of the same colour under her collar and long white throat. The walk had flushed and animated her, and when she looked again into the glass a laugh of triumph parted her lips, making her pearly teeth glitter, and dimpling with tender mischievous touches the pretty curves of her chin and cheeks. She threw down the glass and lifted her lovely arms, clasping her hands behind her head.

'I am beautiful! beautiful! beautiful! cried she in a strange fervour of conviction. 'Ye gods! why have I been made so beautiful?'

The moment after, her arms sank again to her sides, and her body fell into a posture of lassitude, while her brows slightly contracted over some brooding thought.

'So beautiful,' she murmured, 'that it frightens me!'

After which she shook off the impression and went out demurely, without any covering on her head (as she had seen Mrs. McKenzie do), to ask if she could not set her hand to some work.

In the field opposite the house McKenzie was occupied with his stack;[1] he was covering it with fresh green rushes as a defence against the rain. In the same field Mrs. McKenzie was spreading the morning's washing out to dry. Two cows and a horse pastured near them; the field had a little curving path through it, and a slope of rising ground; the fowls picked their way across the road towards the stack, with the air of trespassers who trust a preoccupied world may imagine that they come upon affairs of importance. Mrs. McKenzie, looking up, saw Jessamine, with her red ribbons and uncovered hair, unfastening the wicket gate and approaching; McKenzie, glancing down from his ladder, saw her also, and greeted her with the smile of indulgent amusement which was his invariable salutation. She lingered near the stack for a moment, her eyes entreating for a recognition of her beauty, and her lips asking all manner of questions about the rushes and his mode of fastening them on, and what was the most excellent way of preserving a stack from harm, and whether the hay would last all winter for the cows. A cow meanwhile, neglecting its pasture, stretched a moist muzzle over the fence towards the stack with vain and improvident appetite. McKenzie, looking down from his ladder to answer her inquiries, perceived that the play of sunshine on her bright ribbons and wavy hair was a beautiful thing to the eye, and smiled the more because of it. Jessamine turned away satisfied, and passed down the field towards Mrs. McKenzie.

---

1   This is a peat stack, which is "a large pile of dried peats erected out-of-doors as a fuel-store" (*CSD* 481).

In Mrs. McKenzie's roomy nature, the most astonishing event settled down after a time into composure. She had put forth a maternal tendril or so the more on Jessamine's account, and when she saw the girl approaching with the bright ribbons in her hair and a new and nameless grace upon her lips and brow, she raised herself slowly from her stooping posture and looked her over steadily. And she saw, as in a picture, a way opening before her—the most mysterious and dread of our existence, save death itself—and Jessamine passing down it alone and unaided. Men call it the way of Love. What erratic, fitful light gleaming out of the astonishing depths in Jessamine's eyes touched her Scotch nature with vague premonition, it would be hard to say; but the quietude and sobriety with which she received the girl intensified in her gaze, as though she would have thrown out some steady anchorage to her help.

'Lassie,' said she in a caressing, grave voice, 'are ye fey?'[2]

'Fey? Oh no! See! I will help you with the linen.'

And she dragged a sheet with effort out of the basket.

'I have been away all morning,' she added. 'Have you been busy?'

'Ay. In this hard country we must be doing all we can, and taking every chance that comes. There will not be any time too much.'

'Where I came from time dragged.'

'Ay. It is all one hour; but a body here will be saying "Bide a wee," and a body there will be saying "Go straight on like the lightening." He is aye ill-treatit is old Time; he pleases none.'

'And here it is never dreary,' murmured Jessamine, with a certain cadence in her voice like the colour in her cheeks.

'When the wunther comes it will be dreary—especially the wunther evenings.'

'And when time is dreary, what do you do?'

'Indeed, we just pass it away as well as we can.'

Jessamine looked round; the sweet country out-of-door life, the shafts of sunlight, the stir of work, the ripples of laughter from the children who played in the road, filled her heart with melody.

'In the winter it does not look like this?' she said.

'In the wunther it is ever bleak and cauld; there will be little work to do, and long dark evenings to be sitting still. And the wind drives cauld down the chimney.'

'Have you books to read? There must be something.'

'A few books; but John and me will not be great readers. We have the singing class, though, and that will be something.'

---

2   Fey: "portended by peculiar, *usu* elated behavior" (*CSD* 195).

'You sing? Ah, I remember! But how about this class?'

'The lads just meet at each other's houses, and then we sing in parts. It passes time away.'

'Does Mr. McKenzie sing?'

'John is not so much at it. He will not have a very good voice.'

'Do you sing in the class?'

'Oh yes! whiles.'

A pause, during which Jessamine's heart ran on and then tripped up.

'Does—Mr. Macgillvray sing?' asked she with a throb in her voice.

Mrs. McKenzie shook out a shirt and held it up in her brawny arms.

'Colin will not be knowing much about it. He does not know how.'

'Does he not like music?'

'Oh yes; he is very much taken up with it indeed.'

'Why, then? Hasn't he a good voice?'

'Oh yes; he will have a good voice. But he doesn't know anything.'

'Is he not a reader? I am sure he is fond of books.'

'Colin reads a little now and then; but he is not a scholar; he does not care. He just does his worruk.'

'He is a good farmer,' said Jessamine, a shadow on her face.

'He does not care to improve his farm; he has not any ideas. He just does his worruk.'

'He built those good barns,' said Jessamine, an inconsequent fury in her heart.

'The old ones fell down, and he had to have them built up again. The barns are better than the house,' insisted Mrs. McKenzie with her ordinary deliberate composure.

'The house with the thatch roof is very pretty, I think.'

'It is a poor place; he might improve it. The top story is just nothing. But Colin does not care. He just does his worruk. That's Colin.'

'He is good. He has a face full of kindness. I cannot think he would ever be unkind.'

'Colin is a kind man; he will be always kind. He keeps himself very respectable. He just does his worruk. That's Colin.'

And Mrs. McKenzie moved farther off, bending her matronly figure over the basket, and setting the large wise prose of her mind to make the more expedition in that she had wasted time in words.

Jessamine, on the other hand, stood idle and reflective, looking at the sheet she had spread upon the grass, with minute care as to the mathematical squareness of its shape.

Meanwhile, Maysie McKenzie and her small allies had tumbled over the fence into the field, and had begun to play near. At this point they made themselves conspicuous by silence; they stood in a row, hand-in-hand: Maysie with her yellow hair and velvet-brown eyes, her discreet manner and brain fertile in mischief; Mary Grant with still fairer hair and blue eyes—a tiny toddle, whose little cooing voice perpetually asked for consolation; Larry Grant, a pale-faced, large-eyed creature, with immense wisdom of demeanour and a facility in following evil counsels; Willie Macniel, the eldest, a red-haired, gray-eyed lad, whose sweet elastic little body was never still, but who ran and leapt and bounded with the grace of a young deer. They stood now, hand-in-hand, gazing with round grave eyes in one direction. Jessamine, wondering what attracted them, looked too.

Down the little curling path, which ran through the field, came slowly along the figure of an old, old man. He was dressed in corduroy, and his clothes, though good, were ancient and greasy; he wore no collar, and his woollen shirt was open at the throat; he had a crushed wide-awake upon his head,[3] and in his hand a staff. His hair was white and his beard was white; it was tossed and wild, and his ruddy face was stained with peat-smoke and ingrained with dirt. He had large hooked features, and a certain ancient and uncanny air, which made him an astonishing though not attractive picture. At him the children gazed, and Jessamine with them. The old man came on, setting his staff on the ground with a little blow as he went, and staring about him with open mouth and with the slow, dazed stare of the aged. As he neared the stack McKenzie came down the ladder and leaned over the fence to say a word or two to him.

'Who is it?' asked Jessamine of Mrs. McKenzie, looking at the old peasant with horrible misgiving.

'That will be old Mr. Rorie Macgillvray Dalfaber—Colin's father.'

'Mr. Macgillvray will be wanting you, Annie,' shouted McKenzie from the stack. 'He is going into the house.'

Mrs. McKenzie left the linen and hurried after old Rorie, who was walking on and smiting the earth with his staff as he went. The children, as though some joyous event had come and gone, began to play and scream with renewed zest. Jessamine for a few minutes went on unfolding the linen and spreading it upon the grass; and then a feeling of sudden illness overcame her. She dropped a sheet in a heap at her feet, and stood staring dazedly before her; and then she walked right away up the little path, down which old Rorie

---

3 A wide-awake is a man's hat, which is low-crowned and made of felt. It is also known as a Quaker hat.

had come, out of sight of McKenzie and the children, until she reached a knoll covered with birch-trees. Here she sat down in the shade, her body bent together, and her arms folded across it.

Beneath her the little path curled, and beyond spread the waving gold of an oat-field ready for the harvest, and beyond that was the tumultuous grandeur of the hills, over which the afternoon light scattered itself in a golden shower, and above which the clouds slumbered in a silver haze. But her eyes strained themselves along the path that, like a twisted thread, crept about the purple flank of moor, breaking off now and then in a shredded heap of gray stones, or sinking into a hollow of sparse grass, and finally vanishing round the corner of some farmer's cottage beyond.

We go on and on, knowing neither how nor where; and in youth this irresponsible wandering of untutored feet acquaints us again and again with the strangeness and suddenness of human experience. That road is undiscovered land to each young soul; a myriad feet may have paved the way beforehand, but to each human being it is as an unpenetrated desert, a venture into new worlds, a sailing on unnavigated seas. There was none to whom Jessamine could appeal and ask, 'Whither leads this road?' Her mind opened and shut, opened and shut, letting out formless flitting ideas of youth and passion, life and love; but side by side with every aerial-tinted image went the repulsive figure of old Rorie, staring with open mouth, and smiting on the earth with his staff.

The heavens, wide as hope and clear as the thoughts of a god, are above us, but our feet are entangled in narrow ways.

Down the curling path, afar off, scarcely distinguishable at first from the brown side of the cottage, appeared at length the figure of a man. Jessamine strained her eyes towards him; it was as though she had expected the form to shape itself upon the little curling path, and to come walking towards her. A feeling of blindness fell upon her as though the whole world were blanched out and the twisting path alone were left with the figure approaching. On he came with poised deliberate walk, his head up, his limbs moving from the hip, his great shoulders straight. Jessamine knew without seeing how clear and serious were his eyes, and how his lips were folded one upon another. And presently he was near. His face smote like a brown-red cameo against the translucent blue of the distance, and smote itself like a fiery seal on the heart of the watcher.

And just then he looked up.

A gray birch-tree with a pallid lichen-covered stem and the indiscriminate gray shadows of many other birch bushes crowded together, and drowning colour in a cool umbrage; a grassy knoll, close-cropped and juiceless, a gray heap of granite; and against the lichen-covered stem a soft gray dress; and above, a little face, with sparks of red under the chin and in the knot of hair, and a flame in either cheek, and in the eyes an unutterable something which made the world reel suddenly.

Colin's steps dragged; his hand automatically sought his cap; but he saw nothing, knew nothing, save the face which had opened like the heart of a flower out of the dim gray wood for him alone.

The great world gave a leap as the two pairs of eyes met each other.

And then a voice, quavering and impatient and coming from afar, broke the spell and veiled the moment. It was old Rorie shouting irritably for his son. Colin with an effort forced himself away, and passed on without speaking. Jessamine slid like a shadow into the wood.

END OF VOLUME I

CHAPTER XIII

JESSAMINE felt herself to be as one sitting on a bare jet of rock, round which the tide creeps closer. And yet she thought that she could still escape.

For two or three days she saw nothing of Macgillvray. In the mornings the first touch of the sun woke her to immediate gladness of existence, and she would spring from her bed, an ecstatic sense of youth and health coursing through her limbs, dyeing her cheeks and shining in her eyes. At such moments she was as an untired swimmer in a sunlit sea, ungirt by visible shores, but leaned upon by a limitless sky.

She worked so hard and with such a flush of exuberant energy, with eyes so hopefully expectant, that Mrs. McKenzie, watching her one morning at the ironing-table, felt prompted to speak. She was sitting behind, nipping and pressing the edge of a cap with her fingers, and as she looked at the creeper-covered window, with the back of the slim girlish figure—over which, she fancied, the sun seemed glad to play—silhouetted against it, a maternal solicitude began to trouble her mild eyes.

'*Two* will be in that task, I'm thinking, lassie,' said she.

Jessamine was pressing the iron upon a shirt of Mr. McKenzie's. Mrs. McKenzie, watching her steadily, saw the little ear and the curve of the cheek—just then daintily edged with light—flush; the gentle swaying movements of the ironing continued, but the figure seemed to quiver with consciousness.

'Will someone be gathering and giving you the bit of white heather?' continued Mrs. McKenzie in a low voice.[1]

There was no answer; the iron came down on the shirt-sleeve with the deft firmness which had been learnt from Mrs. McKenzie herself.

'They say,' remarked the latter as firmly, 'that luck's in marriage.'

These words hazarded, she looked for their effect. A second flush beat into the cheek and ear—one so deep that they must have smarted as from a blow; then it drew away, leaving pallor. Mrs. McKenzie's eyes filled with wistful alarm, but the patting of the ironing went on, and was continued until the shirt was folded. Then Jessamine turned round, and Mrs. McKenzie found herself confronted with a pair of sad, inscrutable eyes, and the manner of the Dominant class.

---

1 Heather is a prolific flower in Scotland, but white heather is still rare. White heather symbolizes good luck for all events in life, but especially for marriage.

'I have finished the shirts, Mrs. McKenzie, and will go upstairs for a little. No; no one has gathered and given me a bit of white heather.'

In Jessamine's appearance for the moment was a curious resemblance to her Aunt Arabella, and upon this metamorphosis Mrs. McKenzie gazed with eyes of penetrating mildness. Then Miss Halliday left the kitchen, the other remaining to her reflections.

These were almost immediately broken by the appearance of John at the outer door. He had a spruce and brushed-up look, his skin shining above his dark beard, and his eyes cheerful with the prospect of adventure.

'I must be going, Annie,' said he; 'but where will the bonnie wee lassie be?'

Mrs. McKenzie moved her head in the direction of the inner door and staircase without speaking.

'She might be wanting something from town. Could we be calling her?' asked John, with the hesitating awe of high quality which still perplexed the more familiar relations.

'John,' said Mrs. McKenzie, rising, 'it seems to me as though I was seeing trouble coming.'

'A-weel,' said John, his radiance unabated, 'if trouble's coming we will just be sitting still and biding for it; we will not be saddling a horse and going out to meet it.'

'But,' said Mrs. McKenzie, 'if we could be turning it into another road?'

'Depend upon it, Annie, if we try, it will be making us carry it here oursels. And what will be ailing you to talk of ill-luck?'

Miss Halliday's light step upon the stair dispersed Mrs. McKenzie's slowly gathering answer, and the moment afterwards the bright innocent face in the doorway shot a reproach right into her bosom. Jessamine walked up to John with a little bit of paper in her hand, and he greeted her with a smile of indulgent liking.

'You are going to town,' said she. 'Will you do me a small errand?'

'I will be most pleased.'

'It is only a little one. You see this name on the paper? It is the name of a journal which you can get from any of the large railway-stations, if you will be so kind as to call there for me. It costs one shilling.'

'Oh, certainly!' said John, taking the paper, and feeling in his pocket for his book; 'but I will be losing this scrap of writing, and, indeed, I had best be setting it just down in my book.'

He drew forth a pocket-book, and turned over the leaves.

'Let me see,' continued he; 'where will I be? Oh, here! "Sale of Corn at

Righchar. Longhorn Calf at Bulnabruick." That will be it. And now what will I put down?' He examined the scrap of paper. 'Oh yes! *Society's Whispers.'* He wrote the name down under the calf. 'Oh yes! Indeed, I will be most pleased to get it for you, Miss Halliday. And I will be bringing it back to you to-morrow, whatever!'

Then he went out into the yard, and Jessamine followed to pat the horse on the nose, and to watch Mr. McKenzie get into his trap and drive away. The red of her cheeks and the shining of her eyes caused him throughout the journey to smile again and again unwittingly.

When he had gone, Jessamine returned to the kitchen, where Mrs. McKenzie was bending over the fire to throw vegetables into the broth she was cooking; but when Mrs. McKenzie caught sight of her standing in the cross-light between the door and window, she looked her over steadily once more, while she continued stirring in the pot with a large wooden spoon. But she said nothing.

'Let me peel the potatoes for you,' said Jessamine caressingly.

CHAPTER XIV

'LUCK'S in marriage.' Those had been Mrs. McKenzie's words, and they echoed over and over again in the girl's mind during the rest of the day, filling her with indescribable alarm. Was the question really before her again? If so, this time it was indeed an unvarnished demand—one of simple and austere purport, having no part concealed by flattery and adroit artifice.

Jessamine recoiled with a feeling of offence.

When Mrs. McKenzie's back was turned she would glance at her with fitful gloom, and her lips were proud. But Mrs. McKenzie made no further reference to the subject.

'John came home last night, and was looking for you everywhere,' said she next morning.

'I am glad he is back. I missed him,' returned Jessamine.

'And he was not forgetting what you asked him to bring. Here is the paper.'

Mrs. McKenzie handed her a pink-covered journal. The very aspect brought back London and ennui. She seemed to see the corner-table in the drawing-room at home, on which the papers were wont to lie; she depicted Aunt Arabella coming into the room in an elegant tea-gown, and sitting down upon the arm-chair by the fire, and placing her gold-rimmed pince-nez upon her high-bred ridge, and retiring behind the pink sheets. These involuntary reminiscences caused her a shiver; she glanced at the journal with distaste, and went on with her dusting.

Mrs. McKenzie, who by this time was too much accustomed to the girl's moods to notice them, carried the pink paper reverentially out of the way of the dust, and, unremarked by her, placed it on a side-table in her own room.

Thus it happened that *Society's Whispers* lay for a day or two unopened in the little square chamber, its pink satiny covering looking very much out of place there.

During these two days the ways of Jessamine were beyond calculation, and there were moments when good Mrs. McKenzie gazed surreptitiously at the inscrutable lassie with awe in her eyes, so mysterious did the swiftness and variety of her changes appear to the even-natured Scotch woman. And during this time Jessamine kept herself very much to herself, going little abroad, and doing much hard work.

On the afternoon of the third day she came into the little square sitting-room, and caught sight of the pink paper. Whereupon she approached, and stood gazing down upon it gloomily. Her eyes had a hunted look, and at the moment a mask-like coldness lay like a blight over her lovely features.

'Come,' said she, 'let me peruse my Aunt Arabella's favourite pages.'

Erelong she was absorbed. The sheets really contained a good deal of piquant matter, skimming, as they did, cleverly along the edge of libel. It appeared that some scandal—the nature of which was insinuated rather than told—would shortly involve two exalted families in very unpleasant law proceedings, and the members had vied with each other in scattering well-seasoned particulars abroad. *Society's Whispers* had a few delectable passages of its own—dark hints, *on dits,*[1] and spicy innuendo; the jaded interest of society in the dull season being very well whipped up, and every means resorted to by which a return to town could be rendered enticing. The journal really had a peculiar interest. Jessamine, who had been shut out, so to speak, from 'life' all these months, was quite astonished to see how many names of men and women, whom, in the great world, she had pictured as mirrors of deportment, appeared to be trembling on the brink of some scandalous exposure. To a quite unsophisticated eye, to an untutored mind, it suggested that society might be troubled by some vicious cancerous growth, whose far-spreading roots could not by any possibility leave any member untouched.

'It really will not astonish me,' said she, 'if, when I turn the next page, I find that my Aunt Arabella has been discovered in a not very reputable locality with some antiquated person of the bluest blood.'[2]

The list of marriages was particularly interesting. It was headed by an account of a very grand ceremony and important alliance. This was between a middle-aged man of enormous wealth, who was familiarly recognised in private circles as—next to Lord Heriot—the biggest rake in Great Britain, and a beautiful girl in her teens, whose family were permeated with hereditary insanity, and who was herself said—in strict confidence—to have had her moments. The object of the alliance was to connect two splendid land properties, and to unite the blue blood, which it was said the bride brought, with the immense amassed capital of the bridegroom, with the further object of producing a single unit of the race to inherit in his own person all these pleasing consolidated privileges. The alliance had received the highest and most signal support; royalty had appeared at the ceremony, and all the best nobility had been present. As to the clergy, they had assembled in such august

---

1   *On dits:* gossip.
2   Bluest blood: "descent from nobility or royalty" (*Webster's* 154).

and overwhelming numbers that there had hardly been a sentence apiece for them to read over the happy pair. The law also had been assiduous in confirming the alliance, and in tying the two together in a complication of bonds and red tape.

Jessamine dropped the paper, and looked up and shuddered. It was like a breath of poisonous air. She caught sight of the sky, and the glint of occasional timid sunshine on the wet eaves of the barn, and the big tree near it. The fowl cackled below, and Maysie shouted in the garden.

She recalled the image of Lord Heriot, the greatest 'catch' in Europe, and the most debauched of men—of Lord Heriot, with his *'Hee-hee-hee!'* his moist palm, his vile eyes, and his heavily scented apparel. She thought of his drunken younger brother, of his sister, a microcephalous idiot,[3] of his father dying of paralysis and ungovernable temper.

And then she thought of Colin. Oh, Colin, 'my Jo,' with your sturdy planting and hoeing, and eyes that purely and tranquilly peruse the skies!

'The greatest catch in Europe!' The hateful face was driven out by that of her noble peasant. And then she stretched her young limbs in their light clothing, and threw back her head to laugh in pure joyousness. She would go out presently to Colin's farm, and, though she happened to know he was away, she would spend the remainder of the afternoon in treading where his steps were most frequent.

But there the fear of old Rorie stopped her. Her cheek blanched at the thought of him, and she stared aimlessly at the wall.

Presently she was back again upon the page, and that with great absorption, her work neglected, and the dishes lying unwashed in the kitchen; while Mrs. McKenzie in Scotch patience glanced at the doorway again and again, and sighed.

Alas, poor Jessamine! Society has a thousand scourges for those who disentangle their will and escape to live a human life humanly. And its corruption clings; it is a disease not to be vanquished by the sincerest willing; it eats into the nature, plays havoc with the constancy, and vitiates the best intention.

The next portion of *Society's Whispers* contained a summing-up of the work of the Parliamentary Session. Members had dispersed very late after their exhausting efforts. As far as one could judge from the report, these endeavours had been directed in a really hard tussle to prevent the rights of

---

3   Microcephalous idiot: a genetic "condition in which the head or cranial capacity is abnormally small" (*Webster's* 807). Retardation usually accompanies this genetic abnormality.

humanity encroaching upon the rights of society, and they had been successful. Besides which she learned that the political world had been thrown into
agitation, because one honourable gentleman had called another honourable
gentleman a liar, and that considerable time had been spent in arranging the
matter. There was not, it appeared, much question about the lie; but a nation
trembled to see Parliamentary etiquette endangered.

She turned from that impatiently to the 'Ladies' Column,' and learned
that the laws of fashionable beauty demanded a large excrescence to be carried
on the back, and waists to be three inches longer, and the heel more in the
middle of the foot.

After this came 'Gossip.' 'Gossip' occupied ten pages of the journal, and
it was these ten pages which really absorbed Jessamine; they ate into her mind,
they obliterated the present, they altered her sweet face into a semblance of
Aunt Arabella's, as she bent over the page. Scotland, the life of the last few
months, vanished, as she perused detail after detail of the familiar world from
which she had absented herself.

Habit and familiarity have a terrific power. The redeemed tramp, they
say, will leave his model lodging-house and return to his rookery, the re-
claimed drunkard to his cup, the assisted pauper to his wayside begging, the
reformed thief to his practises, the civilized savage to his nakedness and toma-
hawk, and, as St. James long ago remarked with vigorous perspicuity, 'the
sow to its wallowing in the mire.'[4] Habit makes slaves of us all. The least little
clean reach forwards or sideways or upwards out of the old rut, and after an
austere attempt to maintain the new adjustment, back we drop to the ancient ways with relief and even ecstasy. More mournfully tragical than these
mysterious personal chains are the inherited tendencies with which we are
born, the preformed habit which is in us at our birth. Who that has striven
against some evil inheritance, that has lifted himself out of it by main force
of will, does not know the rapture of a relapsed moment? Nature mocks us
with this trick of reversion. Behind the mounting steps of Evolution creeps
the stealthy shadow Atavism, like old guilt which can never be repudiated any
more.[5] Now and then our assured humanity is terrified by seeing an indubi-
table startling seal of ancestry set on the ill-starred frame of a fellow-man. We
behold ourselves in him drawn back as with irresistible force to our abhorred
beginning, a woeful reminder of lineage branded on the common frame. But

---

4 This is not from St. James, but from St. Peter in which he says, "But it is happened unto them according to the true proverb, The dog *is* turned to his own vomit
again; and the sow that was washed to her wallowing in the mire" (2:22).
5 Atavism: "appearance in an individual of some characteristic found in a remote
ancestor but not in nearer ancestors" (*Webster's* 87).

though atavism be rare in the body, no mind can call itself safe from the reversionary principle, nor dare to say it has fathomed the possibilities within itself, nor even affirm that it has never been startled and confused by some unpremeditated action of its own. One half of us seems running backward to embrace the unspeakable ancestor, while the rest reaches forward to the high level of posterity.

This is why arguments and preaching are secondary and comparatively useless matters. To make real way, the child, the plastic soul, must be taken and set from early years in the rut which on the whole will run to righteousness. No soul beating upwards from maimed early years, with the common hounds of ancestry pursuing him along the road, but cries out against the social scheme which lent him no fair start at the commencement. To see to it that every man and woman child shall receive a chance in the running, the little feet being directed straight from the starting-point, is work for the statesman and philosopher; and the man who is sturdily striving to raise the average of the common mass does more for his nation and his age than any other form of work can do. But while we are thus every one of us racing a mad race, with the whole wild jumble of our horrible predecessors in full cry behind, and while we know that our own heart is apt to play the traitor to us as we go, calling to us to turn back and join our 'own flesh and blood' in their lairs, we yet commonly permit the early training of a child of rank to be a simple pampering of the mouths that will devour him in the end, and, for the humbler little one, we make the starting-point a sheer throwing of the young soul to the kennels, so that he finds the whole ill brood abreast of him ere yet he has set out on the way.

Jessamine read and read with absorbed interest and burning cheeks. The life that had been leapt into prominence from the recesses into which it had been thrust: the luxury, the triumph, the round of varied excitement, the flattering crowd of acquaintances and lovers. The paper instructed her in the movements of a host of well-known figures. Society life, with its intellectual strain, its heart-burnings, its peacock pride, its corroding personal ambitions, its triviality, its splendid prizes and dominance, its lion-hunting and intoxicating incense, its grace and fastidious elegance and the sense of the upper circle, its sentimentality and perfumes, its clever talk and learning and piquant gossip and dangerous half-breed immoralities—all these things, the whole of this subtle, penetrating, highly-charged atmosphere, returned upon her from the skilful pages as heavy perfumes after purer airs.

She looked up presently, glancing out upon the gray landscape with eyes that discerned it not. The farm-yard, with the loose horse cropping such spare grass as he could find, the road, the stack in the field, and the winding path that crept away to the farm near the fir-wood, the hills behind, with wisps of pale chalk cloud lying along them and gray mists hiding their heads—of all this she saw nothing. Her mind had run through the printed page back to the noise of the West-End. One pink finger rested upon a single paragraph as she sat motionless, staring blindly from the poor little window.

She had set it there with an eager little start, with a shooting of surprise and burning anger into her cheek and eyes; and with the same emphatic feeling she held it there now.

'Out, damned spot!'[6]—not an act, but a tendency; not a deed of blood or shame, but the taint of the whole nature, the inherited and educational hue of the mind!

She sat there with a frown on her brow and a hard contempt upon her mouth, a sombre fury blazing in her eyes, and her figure strangely erect and unbending. Then she looked down again, and re-read slowly, and with narrow bitter attention, the paragraph which had lashed the tenderness out of her face. It ran as follows:

'Lord H . r . . t, we understand, has taken his yacht to Norway. It causes some surprise that his beautiful *fiancée*—with whose name, we presume, we must not make free to adorn our pages— does not accompany him with her mother. But they say the lovely *blonde* is not a good sailor, and the ladies have preferred a quiet trip to the German baths to reinvigorate themselves after the arduosities of the season. Some are ill-natured enough to remark that he secures his last few weeks of liberty before entering the bonds of Hymen;[7] but these are the misanthropes, the misogynists and envious. Certain it is that the distinguished nobleman has, during the last few weeks, consoled himself from the access of despair which he pre-eminently shared with society in the early spring, owing to the sudden and mysterious disappearance of the *then* queen of society, Miss J. H . ll . . . y. We regret to say that beyond hearing that she is well and happy society is permitted to know nothing of the whereabouts of that divine *brunette*. They say the house in —— Square, so well known for its elegant appointments and *recherché* gatherings, will be closed during the

---

6 This is from Shakespeare's *Macbeth* in which Lady Macbeth speaks and says, "Out, damn'd spot! Out, I say! One—two—why then 'tis time to do't. Hell is murky. Fie, my lord, fie, a soldier, and afeard? What need we fear who knows it, when none can call our pow'r to accompt? Yet who would have thought the old man to have had so much blood in him?" (Act V. Scene I.). Lady Macbeth is sleepwalking and struck by guilt because she and her husband have killed King Duncan of Scotland.
7   In Greek mythology Hymen is the god of marriage ceremonies.

next season. Whatever can be the motive of the truant fair, certain it is that her abdicated throne is admirably filled already by her majestic blonde rival.'

The thing, all claws and fangs and horror, leapt like a wolf on Jessamine's new-born passion.

CHAPTER XV

THE girl did not immediately make up her mind to return.

That glimpse into the old world did two pieces of mischief. In the first place, the slowly-growing purity in the springs of her motives was again sullied. In the society she had forsaken, multitudinous smallness served the purposes of serious concerns, and it was all recalled over-vividly to her mind. Again, the perusal of the pink sheets had given her fictitious strength by accentuating the sense of contrast. The atmosphere of the *grande dame* returned to her, and surrounded her by what she felt as an invincible and enchanted circle.

This inward assurance of being in possession of an infallible charm against danger resulted in nothing but an encouragement to play with temptation. That is the most subtle of delights—to toy with the alluring. From the moth to the man it is so. And we should all flutter round the seductive if we were absolutely certain of escaping without a burnt wing. Jessamine told herself that her pinions were free, and that at any moment she could beat them out upon the air untrapped.

It follows inevitably that the creature existing merely as a source of pleasing emotion in others, and educated to conceive of herself only in that aspect, shall find herself particularly susceptible to the thrills of sensation when, in her turn, she is the victim.

So that she did not fly. The present was delectable, and in actual ascendency. London was far, and by no means so attractive. Moreover, the season was long since at an end.

It was the middle of August now, and the days were shorter; about nine in the evening dusk gathered. But one evening, before the sun was low, Jessamine went out. She took her way across the moor; the purple undulations of colour spread on every side, mingled with patches of brown where the cattle had cropped a meal. The light throbbed on the red stems of the pines, and the sun's burning flame alternately lit up the dusky canopies, and let them sink again in shadow. A rosy glory like a fisher's net spread everywhere, and in the midst the girl walked with her face lifted, her inscrutable eyes large and quiet, and her elastic step treading the heather daintily.

And Colin, who had been watching and waiting day and night, slipped from the cover of the birch-trees, and followed her.

'For,' said he, 'if I may see her face once more, and hear her silver tongue, I will lay me down and die most thankfully.'

Thus it came about that a long shadow crept up from behind to the side of Jessamine, and Macgillvray, with his lifted cap, came by.

'Good-evening,' murmured Jessamine.

'It will be weary for you on the moor your lane.'[1]

'Yes.'

'And night comes quicker now.'

'Yes.'

And then silence—the silence which speaks so much faster and more swiftly than the tongue. And while there was silence, it seemed to Colin that his spirit went out from him and kissed her on the mouth, and to Jessamine that she clung about his neck.

They spoke again in fear.

'In June the evenings were long enough.'

'Oh yes! it was grand weather in June—grand!'

'Shall you begin the harvest soon?'

'Well, I think we might be cutting the barley in a day or two.'

'I should like to see it cut.'

'I—we—shall be most pleased, whatever.'

Then again Silence took them by the hand and walked between, and whispered the same thing to either heart, until the tongue leapt out to divide them.

'Will it be a good crop this year?' asked Jessamine.

'Oh, it will be a very light crop this year, indeed!'

'I am sorry for that. How is it?'

'The dry, hot season does not do for this sandy soil. It will be taking a deal of wet.'

'But we have had some rain.'

'Just a shower or two running about, but nothing to make any good.'

Meanwhile, they reached a gate leading to Dalfaber, and Colin paused and laid his hand upon it. He told himself with an ever fainter resolve that just such a manner of man he was, and no other; and that just such a manner of woman—made to shine in some world which he surmised but could not picture—she was, and no other.

But when he paused Jessamine paused also. He leaned against the gate, his hand at the latch; she stood before him mute, exquisite. She felt him there, his influence falling like rays upon her. Her eyes could not lift their lashes; she

---

1   Your lane: "on one's own, solitary" (*CSD* 356).

knew his sought her face. Then she felt him withdraw them, and, looking up, found that he had turned them upon the moor.

'Good-night,' murmured Jessamine.

'Bide a wee!' cried Colin suddenly.

And Jessamine, following his glance, saw in the midst of the brown and purple land a little tuft of white heather, growing snug and small, close to them. Colin vaulted over the gate, and stooped over it. He gathered it prodigally, leaving not a twig behind. Jessamine, with the words of Mrs. McKenzie going up and down her mind, waited. She saw the moor stretching from side to side, and in the midst the man stooping to gather the symbol of his love. He came back presently with the white sprigs in his hand and a great emotion in his eyes.

'Will you take it?'

She stretched her bare, soft fingers, and, white and warm, they rested for a lingering second upon the peasant's coarsened palm. Then, without a word, she took the sprigs, and turned away.

Colin stood by the gate watching her as she passed, in the straight gray dress, on and on along the bare moor road, until he lost her in the mazy confusion of the evening light.

'Oh, God, God, God!' murmured he, his passion struggling for utterance, and throwing itself out of his silent nature, in the word that for him comprehended the highest mystery.

CHAPTER XVI

IT was twilight in the little square sitting room; a peat-fire smouldered on the hearth, sending out a small red glow, for the evenings were apt to close in coldly after a hot noontide. The windows in the sitting-room were low and small, but through them one saw the moon sailing slowly towards the west, and drawing after it a procession of pale ghostly clouds; the road glittered, and the moonlight came into the room carrying a chequered shadow.

The shadow was of a tree, and it fell over the figure of Jessamine seated motionless by the window. She wore a loose white wrapper, and her head leaned against the pillows of the chair; she was as still as death; her loosened hair fell over her shoulders, and her hands, lying in her lap, covered something jealously under them. Sometimes the shadow of the tree moving in the wind climbed as high as her breast and fell down again.

There was no sound at all save the singing of a little wind in the eaves, and the figure in the chair against the window, with its flowing white robe and deathly stillness, looked ghostlike in the dusk light of the chamber.

Suddenly she moved and opened her fingers, and, bending over them, raised what was hidden there to her lips and kissed it reverentially.

It was the white heather which Colin had gathered.

Then she dropped the sprigs back upon her knee, covered her face with her hands, and, bending her body in a heap together, appeared to tremble convulsively. The chequered shadow of the tree covered her as with a net.

It is a pretty fiction, and one traceable to a simpler and more primeval era of emotion, which paints Human Passion with a child's body wearing coloured wings. That might have suited less introspective and less complicated times than our own. Ours it will not suit, not even cases less civilized and distorted than this of Jessamine Halliday. For us to-day the legend and the allegory are otherwise.

For us Human Passion resembles a sphinx-like woman, with a gray hood drawn over her eyes. She goes about the world groping inexorably for human heart after human heart. When she has found what she desires, she comes close with a riddle upon her lips and a long knife in her hand, and she propounds the riddle. While we are thinking of it we see and feel the long knife ready. If we guess it rightly, we are rewarded—that is, she hands us a dish of herbs of mingled sweet and bitter, and clothes us in the garb of a pilgrim, and sets our feet in a path which is sufficiently rough and cruel, and in which, at times, the stones tear the flesh as we tread; but down this path forthwith we have to march. If we fail to read the riddle right, she plunges the knife into the heart up to the hilt and leaves it there. Nor can we die immediately, but by slow degrees, expiring of pain by inches.

Nor is it possible to assure ourselves that we will avoid the torment of that discipline. One day we shall look up and see the figure of the Gray-hooded Woman going along the road in front. We see the long gray shadow there, and we try not to think of it; we turn straight out of the road to avoid it; but there it is in front of us again, the Gray Hood bent, the backward parts so mysterious and attractive that we draw nearer and nearer until we are close by. She does not turn her head. We go ourselves and peep under the Gray Hood—an irresistible something compels us—for a little, little moment to see what is there. And she looks at us with her eyes.

And then we move away no more. We stand gazing at her, and secrets pass out of those eyes and out of that austere brow and sink down into the heart. She looks at us; she takes hold of the conscience; she roots up the being; she rakes it from end to end; there is not the hundredth part of an inch, the remotest or most insignificant corner, that she does not haul over and sweep out. And then, when we are shaken to pieces and have not a solid foothold left, when every preconceived idea is smashed on the head and every ancient staff a broken reed, she propounds her riddle and presents her knife.

That is Human Passion to an introspective and developed race.

Jessamine raised herself again with an effort and left her chair, and began to move slowly up and down the room, pressing her handkerchief against her face and eyes, words every now and then escaping her lips unconsciously. The white gown swept the ground, her hair tumbled about her in a dusky curtain, and her face lying between like a small silvery disc, caught the moonlight. The red glow in the peat-fire shot a broad red ray up the folds of her dress as she passed.

Every now and then she stood still, and then the face, turning towards the window, appeared cold and frozen as in dismay, and the same dismay stared from her eyes.

'Jessamine, pink of perfection!' once she burst out; 'own niece to your Aunt Arabella! Is it true, or is it a dream? In love? In love?' She hesitated, and then twice repeated a magical name. 'Colin Macgillvray! Colin Macgillvray!' she said. 'A *peasant!*'

Tears rushed to her eyes; the large dark orbs swam and glittered in the moonlight, and two drops hung on her lashes; her lips quivered.

Penetrating further into the realm of Reality, she found herself face to face with the Unexpected. It became apparent to her that one is not always master of the event, nor in the position towards it of a graceful enchantress managing the sequences with dexterous wilful fingers. The event, she perceived, might trap her in turn. She had a frightful sense of bungling absurdly. With that, in a sudden change of mood, she raised one hand, and rushed forward a step or two angrily as though she would strike some foe in the face.

'No one warned me!' she cried. 'Oh, I am trapped!'

Again her anger melted. The rosy moment of love was still in her memory, and her dazed eyes softened again at the thought. She was in an enchanted place, a place where the wits are distraught by visions, but where Prudence kept plucking at her with a cold, cold finger. There were moments when Prudence prevailed, and held her agonized and chilled. And then she told herself that she must *think;* and with that she would shut the moonlight out with her hand before her eyes. But her brain was a blank place, and, while she sought eagerly for an idea, her fingers thrilled with a sudden tormenting memory of the palm of Colin, on which she had permitted them to nestle.

Shivering again convulsively, she moved towards the table, and, drawing a chair close, sat down beside it, leaning her arms and body upon it, so as to gain the perfect quiescence which was needed before she could cope with her thoughts and emotion. Her raised eyes were fixed on the slow depressing drift of thin clouds in the path of the moon.

'Of course I must go home at once,' said she; 'back to—*Aunt Arabella.'*

So spake the well-taught school-girl to the growing woman. But her whole nature cried out in rebellion against her tutored tongue. Her mind, suddenly active, inquired why such a return was obligatory. The mere statement of the commonplace inevitable remedy called into being a hundred reasons for not accepting it. Some ways which decorum presents to us as right ways, offend the nature by their miserable union of the obvious and the distasteful. We tell ourselves that flames and swords are better. Besides, Jessamine's revolt against Aunt Arabella had been a movement of the best part of her nature, and was she to stultify it now by a return? Circumstance suspends us by the hair over the lake of pitch from which she has drawn us, and puts her choice to us in the moment.

Jessamine had a love of adventure, and within this adventure were alluring possibilities which thrilled while they terrified. Every prudent dictate was rimmed and confused by a coloured halo of sweet reminiscence and still sweeter promise; in her heart were both delight and fear, longing and foreboding, at once. She tried to summon into clearer prominence the chiller self-repressing prose, but the thrill triumphed; she was young, and it was her first taste of a common human experience. While her lips shaped themselves to cool resolutions, feeling overflowed.

'Oh, oh, oh!' she cried in sudden mighty emotion, as primeval as that of Eve, 'let me give myself to him, or I die!'

The words out of her lips, she snatched herself together with a shrinking gesture, as though someone hailed blows about her ears. Impossible—impossible! Most miserable Jessamine! Hush!

Whereat her heart rushed welcoming towards that very word 'impossible!' and accepted it. For the one seductive and ever more seductive thing is the impossible thing. Once let the heart fix *there* its desire, and it may not relinquish it again. Jessamine opened the window of her mind, and drew the bird within, and held it in a full-grown grasp, recognising her treasure, even while she let fall the feeble tears of a girl.

For, indeed, bitter slow tears began one by one to drop over her cheeks.

'I *cannot* understand it,' murmured she; 'God is mocking me. Supposing *they* knew—my Aunt Arabella and all those!'

Even as she told herself she could not understand, her heart began swiftly to spell the heart's own lesson.

The impossible is the important thing in life—the thing that carries us furthest, that gives us power to achieve or power to resign, that shakes all our thoughts apart and discriminates.

But this emotional creature had no defences of the mind. She had been taught not to discriminate, but to ignore; neither had she been trained into any heroism of will.

The new phase of her love was introducing already strange companions within, conjuring them out of her maimed nature as by some cruel trick. All the soft luxury into which she had been trained revolted against the austerity amidst which the dazzling figure of Love had chosen to alight. She could not support the conditions which were offered, nor carry the burden imposed.

Neither could she endure, on the other hand, to set the knife at the root of her happiness. She was a divided thing, and each part cried against the other.

Moreover, what she had of clear and truthful in her undeveloped character asserted roundly that her duty to Colin forbade her to undertake a position for which she knew herself to be unfitted. There! Close on that, too small to be flung out, subtle, dark, came the suggestion of a sweet falseness to Colin, to decide nothing, to drift on and on—to what?

Jessamine laid her hand over her eyes, and moaned as she learned her lesson—the lesson of over-mastering feeling—reading the inconceivable thing within herself in lines too plain for her mistaking. The moonlight could not quench the crimsoning of her cheeks when she looked up again.

'There are two *Me's*,' said she in a frightened whisper. 'There is the Jessamine that was ready to sell herself to Lord Heriot for a title and the diamonds, and there is the Jessamine who is ready to throw herself at the feet of a peasant to-morrow.'

The words being spoken, her lips shrank to a narrow outlet, recoiling from the thing they had uttered; and she clapped her little sunburnt hand over them, as though to entrap and enforce what had escaped, while her wild eyes, conscious of the world, cast timid, fearful glances about the chamber.

In truth, she had fled from her London experiences only to fall into as indecorous a piece of human passion as ever startled the world. There was 'nothing in him than his worruk,' his genuineness, and massive simplicity; and she, with all her undisciplined impulses, fought frantically against but one part of her surrender—that is, the chain.

'I can't see anything,' she said; 'I can't tell one thing from another. Is this passion? Oh, my lover—my lover!'

The moon slowly edged out of the window opposite which Jessamine sat, and the shadow of the tree climbed in gigantic effigy up the wall.

The girl had withdrawn her hand from her mouth. What was the use of laying it there? The words she had uttered returned to her from the sides of the chamber, and they escaped out of the window and were anyone's possession. She leaned her chin upon her hands and stared into the darkness, and heedlessly muttered and murmured on. Before her on the table lay the white heather.

'I think,' she said, 'if I think of it at all, that God must be too great to mind—to be angry. Oh, my God! I feel that I could sell the world for him! And if I went to him because of the drawing of my heart, and clung to him, would it seem a wicked act for which I must be punished? Oh, my God! my God! you should have made me different, if so! For I feel him drawing me, and I long with every nerve to go. And if I did my duty and ran away from him, and to-morrow in a church married myself with the clergyman's blessing to Lord Heriot, would it seem a good act for which I shall be rewarded? Oh, my God! if that is so, you should have made me different!'

Her praying was revolt. And that was the first earnest petition to invisible powers which had ever left her heart. The conventional being broken through, she found sincerity within, and with it rebellion. Not the mere teasing wilfulness with which she had delighted to confuse society, but a heart-felt resistance to an order which she suddenly found was laying a cold prosaic claim upon her intimate devices for warm and natural joy.

And order to her was summed up in the figure of Aunt Arabella. God and the social laws *might* lie behind, but Aunt Arabella officiated in the foreground. The idea of this hated incarnation of religion and society, piercing, with her small metallic eye, to her own scene of disorderly tumult, thrust her upon a harsh mood. She struck her hands sharply upon the table, breaking the sob in her throat by a laugh.

For, indeed, a sense of the inadequacy of all she had been taught, as a guiding principle, suddenly affected her—the incommensurateness of any reason for goodness with which she was acquainted, with the difficulty of the effort. Goodness to her was synonymous with prim negations, and she glowed with life. It made her bitter to think with what a defenceless heart and ill-furnished mind she had set out on her quest for reality, and how amongst her range of acquaintances there was scarcely a friend whose wisdom she could trust with a priceless secret.

'I have never had anyone to tell things to save Aunt Arabella and'— she paused, struck dumb for the moment by an idea of import—'and—Dr. Cornerstone.'

With the thought of Dr. Cornerstone her emotion passed into a new phase; her heart leapt in her breast, and her face became transfigured. Whatever this phase of emotion was, it appeared to carry her from the realm of agitation and struggle. She remained perfectly still, intent upon something which erased the whole problem by diverting the attention to a plane of thought beyond it; but not for long. These abstract uplifted moments could never be sustained ones in her mind.

She caught her hands up with a frightened cry, and sank forwards, burying her face within them.

'I dare not!' she cried, 'I dare not! My whole nature chooses him before all the world for my lover. I prefer his strength and his simplicity and his wholesomeness to all the culture in London. I am sick of culture. But I *dare not!* DARE NOT! It isn't because I am good. I am not good any more.'

To be in revolt was the recognised form of evil, and Jessamine had nothing in herself to oppose to the idea. A code of rules is the least useful baggage with which the character can set out on its mysterious journey; it will probably find them to be pure impedimenta. What is wanted is a furnishing in qualities, and then the conscience may be trusted to solve its problems for itself. Disaster and error spring not so much from what is done, as from hesitation in the will and fevered incoherency in the choice.

Jessamine was conscious of temptation either way. It had been easy to escape from the Heriot entanglement in London; but in view of the temptation which met her here, and the fearsome attraction of it, the Heriot entanglement (with the Church and clergy behind, and the support of society) appeared almost as the path of virtue.

How was she to discriminate? Everything within herself appeared ready to play the traitor because she had no notion to what she should be true. Her mind, however, retained energy enough for that self-derision and sorrowful candour which dictates the terms of treacherous capitulation which the soul makes.

'At least, let me be true,' said she mournfully to herself; 'let me be true as death for once. It isn't goodness in myself that guides me. I haven't a guide. I haven't a reason. There is nothing that I know about by which I can direct myself and control myself, except just vanity, and custom, and fear of Aunt Arabella and her set. If I escape, it is not because I am good; it is because I am vain. Praying is no help. When I pray, I pray that God would help me to Colin. As to Dr. Cornerstone, I cannot confess to him. I am afraid—because—I am sure I don't know—but something tells me he might say something that would help me to be—set things in queer fresh lights that seem good lights—help me—help me——'

She snatched herself suddenly from her seat, horror—the horror of outraged vanity—in her face.

'*Like any housemaid,*' she whispered, with a thrill of fear and disgust.

From which terrible moment she gathered herself at last. To act in common with common natures was the one thing which the particulars of her education caused her clearly to repudiate. The word 'housemaid' conquered for the moment. She had been taught to credit common people with feelings unworthy of herself. That decided her—for the moment. And yet the less conscious self, which haunts with criticism the more conscious, deciding, acting self, did not acquit her now. She had no comfort nor release from self-disdain. Rising from her seat with a soft rustle of her garments, and with a composed, undulating movement of her figure, she approached a second and smaller window of the room, about which a little moonlight still played. Her face was tired and cold as snow that has lain three days, and her voice was bitter and thin.

'Of course I shall keep straight,' she said; 'of course I shall go on right enough. Not because I am good, however, but just for vanity's sake. I *must* have praise.'

Then she turned and walked to the door. Her hand was on the latch, when, with a new impulse, she looked back on the little room which was so dull, but which, nevertheless, glowed with so much thought and feeling, and her eyes swam again with tears. A presentiment lay heavy on her heart, a clear foreboding of the inevitable lying before her, of something towards which she was destined to advance, and which, beyond this present turmoil and colour, waited fatally and cold. Would she have the power to escape it? The question shot beyond consciousness, dimly hovered in her brain, disappeared, and left her heart and her eyes empty and distraught.

Then the door closed, and the small square chamber was left silent. The shadow of the tree had long been expunged, and the moonlight was drawing slowly away from the second window.

CHAPTER XVII

THE next morning Jessamine went about like one benumbed in feeling; exhaustion for the moment had emptied her of passion. Mrs. McKenzie watched the girl's face, sealed as it was by a new reticence, and shook her wise head.

When the mid-day meal was over, Jessamine went out. It was a real harvest day—a day of delicious heat and quiet airs; the farmers had been up from the earliest hours reaping, and the fallen corn lay about the fields in yellow bundles, while everywhere along the standing edges passed in persistent rhythmic movement the figures of mower and gatherer. Jessamine perceived that the harvest had really begun, and remembered that Colin would certainly be cutting his barley. Yet she turned up the road in the direction away from Dalfaber. Had it been possible to lie down under the trees in some sequestered spot, and softly to sleep herself out of existence, she would have been thankful.

The way she chose was one not much frequented; it led over the moor-covered side of one of the hills, and gradually dwindled to a mere straggling path which vanished amongst heather and boulders. At first her idea had been to reach some high crag, and at least to lift herself as far as possible beyond the region of her turmoil and passion, but her limbs refused the task; she was enfeebled by yesterday's emotion, and needed quiescence from effort. So that midway up the path she paused, and sat down upon a heather-covered rock. The place was not far from a small cottage—a tiny tumble-down house which had no pretension to be called a farm, but where, nevertheless, the morsel of surrounding land showed signs of cultivation. It was more like a picturesque hovel than anything else, and yet had an aspect of comfort. There was even a little outhouse, and one or two other accompaniments to the meagrest form of agriculture. A burn[1] tumbled down the hill by the side, and a water-butt placed across the channel served to arrest the stream, and to form a convenience for washing purposes; and then the water leapt out of the other side of the butt, and continued its flow with a cheerful murmur.

Jessamine liked the sound; of late the vast silence of the country had oppressed her, and now she sat down willingly within hearing of the brook's chatter because it broke up and dispersed the settling of thought upon speculative ideas and uprooting questions. After she had been seated there for some

---

1 Burn: "a brook, stream" (*CSD* 74).

time, the door of the cot opened, and a little child came out, and ran towards the burn. She had a tin pail in one hand, and in the other a rag and two or three common spoons. Upon her small face was a look in miniature of house-wifely bustle. Having reached the side of the butt, she dipped the pail in, deft-ly preventing herself from following it headlong, and pulled it out again full. Then she sat down, and drew it cautiously between her sturdy bare legs, and forthwith proceeded to dip the spoons in the water, and to rub them clean with the rag. All her actions were deft and careful—a delicious parody upon grown-up humanity—and Jessamine watched with increasing interest and admiration. Her beauty and vigour were great, and she appeared to be but five years old. She had firm limbs and a velvety golden-brown skin, through which showed the healthy red; her hair of dark brown curled about her head, and underneath the pretty tangle looked out an alert pair of brown eyes; but it was the content of the child, the happy activity and the unconscious joy in being and faculty, which best expressed the exuberant wholesomeness of her nature.

Jessamine watched the little creature with growing admiration, and then with yearning. An inexpressible look came into her eyes—one which may be seen often in the eyes of women, but which was new in Jessamine's; she con-tinued to watch until all the spoons were rubbed up to satisfaction, and with every movement the mingled delight and longing increased.

'Little one,' she said at last in a coaxing tone.

The child turned her brown curly head, and opened her eyes wide in the direction of the sound. Perceiving the beautiful smiling stranger, she stared unwinkingly for full twenty seconds.

'Come and speak to me,' called Jessamine from the other side of the burn.

Then the child very slowly and deliberately drew her sturdy legs up, rose from the ground with great care as to upsetting the pail, lifted it, and, carry-ing it to a safe distance, emptied away the dirty water. After which she picked up the wet rag, and put it in the pail; then she took the clean spoons in the other hand, and, having now finished her preparations, approached the burn and stood on the side opposite to Jessamine, with her bare legs and firm little feet well planted, staring reflectively. Jessamine smiled, and sought for a coax-ing phrase. But the child saved her the trouble. Without removing her eyes she uttered an ecstatic crow, and shouted:

'Granny, come and see the bonnie wifie!'

This summons was followed by the appearance of a woman at the cottage door. Seeing the beautiful stranger, she hurried forward with apology upon her lips.

'Oh, Bessie, that's a naughty bairnie![2] Staring and talking to the bonnie leddy!' said she.

'Don't take her away,' said Jessamine; 'I like to see and hear her. Come over the burn, little creature.'

But the child shrank behind her 'granny,' and peeped out roguishly from her skirt, shutting up her eyes and making a little mouth, and playing off her coquetries in the manner of babies.

Jessamine laughed, and turned to the woman.

'What a beautiful child she is!' said she. 'What glorious eyes—when she is kind enough to open them! What fine firm limbs! How old is she?'

'Three years, ma'am.'

'Three! I thought she might be six, and was certainly five.'

'Ay, she's a bonnie bairnie and a good one,' returned the woman with pride; 'and she can do for me already. Ay, she knows how to make herself useful!'

'Is it your grandchild?' asked Jessamine, looking at the splendid little creature with renewed admiration.

The woman did not immediately answer; she lifted her apron, and appeared to wipe off from her lips some shrinking apology, while her eyes deviated for a moment from Jessamine's inquiring face. Then they returned, with a glance which shyly appealed to a possible knowledge within the beautiful lady's breast of matters which are frankly human, but which do not come under the range of the respectable.

'Well, no, ma'am,' she said; 'I'm just caring for the bairnie. I'm no relation, but she calls me granny because I'm fond of her. She is not a legitimate child, ma'am.'

'She does you credit,' returned Jessamine with feeling.

And then she turned away with misty eyes that looked at some far-away thought.

'Have her parents forsaken her?' asked she presently.

'Oh no, ma'am!' returned the woman, scandalized; 'the father is very much taken up with her indeed. He comes every week and brings me the money. He is a carpenter in the near town, ma'am, and the mother is in service at Edinburgh. She sends me the money regularly, and she will just be coming to see the bairnie when she will have a chance.'

'Are they going to be married?' asked Jessamine, with the astonishment of one taking a peep through the open threshold of a new world.

'Oh no, ma'am. The mother is just in service, and the father is just a man

---

2   Bairnie or bairn: "someone's child; an offspring of any age" (*CSD* 27).

busy at the carpentering and keeping his old grandfather.'

'Is he a good man?'

'He will be very steady and hardworking, ma'am. And he will be very fond of the bairnie.'

Jessamine sat silent, her eyes full of thoughts. The woman, after looking at her hesitatingly, drew softly away to her work, and the child began to play. With the cheerful inconsequence of three years, she chose to dig up the ground with one of the three spoons she had just so deftly cleaned. But presently a wonderful thing happened. The beautiful mysterious stranger crossed the brook and came close to her, and dropped upon her knees, and encircled her with her arms. It seemed to the little child as the closing of soft scented wings and shadowy sweetness and delicious wonder about her.

'Will you kiss me, little one?' asked the tenderest voice she had ever heard.

And she put out her red lips, and nestled her red cheek against the marvellous face with the swimming eyes, and kissed it readily enough.

How Jessamine loved the beautiful little mortal who had been born into this world out of wedlock! The thought, like some waif and stray into an ancestral mansion, ran into her heart and hid there. She got up and went down the hill, and took the way towards Dalfaber.

It was getting towards evening, and the reaping day was almost over. She walked down to Macgillvray's land, as was her custom, and seated herself upon a bank near his barley-field, in order to look on. As she sat there watching from afar, she felt like one upon the edge of the river of death, who turns a last look at life. And the picture of life which she saw was calm and beautiful, and weaved from Nature's quiet moments.

She saw the yellow waving corn, into which the mower thrust his scythe, and at his feet were the fallen glittering heads; leaning across this more distant picture was a rowan-tree, with dark leaves and scarlet berries; on the right was a gloomy edge of forest-covered hills, and on the left a beautiful bright soft range meeting them and fading into an exquisite farness of blue and opal tints; above that were the piled-up clouds and brilliant ether. The figure of the mower passed along with a strong swaying grace of movement, and the sunburn showed on his cheek and neck; over him the sunshine rested like a homely benediction; it caught also the figure of the woman following after him in her dun-coloured dress. Macgillvray was a favourite with children, and, when he worked, a little cluster of bare-legged mites were apt to play about him; they pattered after him now, their fair hair and bare legs twinkling in the light. Two older boys stood motionless side by side, the sunshine on their heads and about their bare legs, absorbed in admiration of the mower.

Over all the net of light fell with its softening and uniting power, and through all ran the sense of people at wholesome work, joyful, kindly one to another. The brown thatched cottage also was near, and a white kitten came and played about the peat-stack; behind, two red horses, attracted by the fallen corn, came lumbering up to stare from a distance; and round every part was the softer background of blue hills, and pine-woods, and tinted moors.

Against this beautiful sober picture Jessamine rested her over-tired heart as one who earns a little respite, but who hears a sound like the running edge of the deathly river.

Presently the picture changed. The woman in the dun-coloured dress left off gathering, and rested her arms on her hips. Colin stopped also, and drew his scythe out from the corn and leaned upon it; Jessamine could hear his voice as he talked with the woman. Then the latter began to move away from the field, calling and beckoning the children as she walked, and these went running in a little fluttering cloud after her. Colin resumed his work alone. But it seemed to Jessamine that, as the woman moved away, he had turned and looked at her. And she got up from the bank and went slowly down the field towards him. She fancied as she came up that he welcomed her with the old air of courteous indifference, and at this, with the most inconsequent of chills, she felt that the agonies of the few past days had been gratuitous, yet longed to be assured that they were not.

For not one of the human kind, having tasted it, would barter love, with all its sharpness, for an empty peace.

'It is a grand harvest day,' said Macgillvray, desisting for a moment from his work, and lifting his cap.

'Yes. The woman has left you. Are you going on alone?'

'Well, yes. I am bound to finish before night; but the harvest day is really over, and the little ones went in for supper.'

'The sun shines still.'

'And while it shines I must be shearing.'

'You have no one to gather for you?'

'No one.' He smiled. 'I must gather for myself after the shearing is done.'

'I could gather for you.'

He raised himself from his leaning posture and stood erect, looking at her with a ray in his eye that reached her heart. 'It will be too tiring for you.'

'No,' said Jessamine with desperate joy; 'I am strong.'

'But you will not know how.'

'Yes; for I watched.'

'Indeed, you do not know how it will tire you.'

'Let me try. I cannot bind, but I can gather,' said Jessamine meekly.

'Thank you; you are most kind.'

He resumed his work without further argument, and she placed herself behind, as she had seen the woman do, and followed, picking up the corn as it fell from his scythe and laying it aside in a large bundle. It was very still, not a sound could be heard save the long swish of the scythe through the barley; he did not speak, and when they reached the end of the row he merely stopped and glanced over her work with a smile. Then he went back to the other side of the field and began again. Not much remained to be 'sheared.'

After an hour's steady, silent work the corn had all fallen, and mower and gatherer rested from their toil. For Jessamine the hour was one of benign calmness, a restoration to sanity, a beautiful tranquillized moment, within which she would willingly abide. The air of the fields, the peace of Colin's kindness and presence, the delight of necessary work shared and accomplished—these things sufficed, because the whole kingdoms of the world have nothing better to bestow.

'I cannot bind,' said Jessamine, standing still and pushing at the last fallen sheaf with her slender foot.

'No; I will just do that myself, and then I must stook them.'[3]

'Show me the way, and let me bind too.'

'Very well—if you are not tired.'

'I am not tired.'

'See, then. You will just take a little bit of the straw first.'

Jessamine knelt down and pulled a piece out as he directed. Macgillvray, stooping near her, did the same.

'Now watch,' said he.

And he put two ends together, and by a deft wrist movement twisted them into a secure straw-rope.

'I can do that. How easy it looks! Now see!'

She tried and failed, with a pleasant ripple of laughter. Macgillvray laughed too, and came nearer, his shadow falling over her and his bronzed hands out-stretched.

'You just did it wrong, indeed, for you turned your wrists the wrong way.'

The words were small, the voice rich and deep; it seemed close to her, as she looked down disconsolately on the unattached wisps of straw, he laid his hand upon them to take them from her. And at that moment she raised her head with a smile at her failure. Close to her was Macgillvray's strong bronzed face under his straw hat; close to him was the lovely face of Jessamine, pink,

---

3   Stook: "a shock of cut sheaves . . . set up to dry in a field" (*CSD* 673).

dimpled, the eyes swimming with pathos and wistfulness. He looked into them intently for three brief seconds, and then a kind of blindness smote into his own, and he stooped forward and kissed her on the mouth.

For Jessamine the earth seemed to leap as the fire of his kiss burnt to her heart; she knelt motionless, staring at the corn in her hands; and then a sudden inconsequent fury seemed to erase the whole problem of her passion, and to leave her free and untouched. She looked up, dropping the corn, and turning a face of anger upon him; had there been in his the least trace of swagger or triumph, the anger would have endured. But she found that he had withdrawn a step, and was standing a little apart, his arms hanging by his side, his face dark and soft with a fathomless remorse; and before it, the anger and remnant of her resistance vanished. She caught her hands to her burning face and covered it, and knelt trembling above the unfinished sheaf. Had anyone seen that kiss? The world was full of it.

'You will not be needing,' said Colin in a low, desperate tone, 'to be looking at me like that. You will not be needing to cover your bonnie, bonnie face. I know what I have done. I am one just not fit to live. And I will not be living any longer if it harms you. I cannot wipe my kiss off your lips. But I can go and drown myself, so that you need not be thinking at it again, or flushing red like a rose because of my being alive on the same earth. I can go now. I am not caring any more to be alive if I have hurt you.'

The words in their quiet desperation reached Jessamine's ear, and sank every one of them to her heart, and created there, every one of them, an added circle of joy. When he ceased to speak she made no answer, but still seemed listening; she felt like one lulled safely on a small islet about which tumbles an infinite ocean of disaster. Would he speak again? A woman fears to spoil the music of the first love words by any utterance of her own. But he said no more; she fancied she heard his feet move from her through the stubble. And then a misgiving, lest she should miss her moment—the golden moment of life—and drive him with that look upon his face to some despairing deed, sent thrills of terror through her. Keeping one hand over her eyes, she stretched the other out towards him with a passionate gesture, and cried:

'Oh, Colin, Colin! I am not angry.'

He caught her hand in his own as she rose and stood before him.

'Not angry?' He waited, looking anxiously at the lovely living cheek and quivering mouth. The hand still covered her eyes. 'Do you know what you will be saying? Jessie, bonnie bird! "Not angry" means you love me,' said he, trembling exceedingly, but pressing the question home with grave insistence.

'Let me go!' she answered, waking up to the thundering of those waves of disaster in her ear.

'No,' returned he firmly; 'since we are come so far we must go further. If you bid me I will drown myself for what I've done. I'd rather that than shame you, Jessie. But a man does not throw his life away for nothing. I will drown myself if I hurt you with my kiss. But if I did not hurt you, tell me, and I will live. I must know before I let you go.'

'No, no; you did not hurt me, Colin,' said Jessamine, shivering.

'Why, then, should you tremble? Ah, my wee bonnie do'e![4] why would you be looking at me as one not fit to live?'

His voice thrilled, and shook with hope; and in her heart was so strange a commingling of joy and complete despair, that it seemed to her beyond the slightness of her frame to bear it. She found no words.

'Let me see your bonnie eyes.'

He laid his fingers timidly upon the wrist of the hand with which she still veiled her emotion.

'Jessie, Jessie! when a man trembles on the edge of a great happiness and on the edge of a great trouble, much may be forgiven him.' He used his strength with reverential gentleness; her hand dropped into his, and her eyes opened upon him. 'My God!' said he, with a great tumult in his heart, as he read what was written there.

'Now let me go,' she murmured, drawing away from the passionate force of his embrace; 'be content, and let me go. Colin, Colin!'

And as his arms relinquished her, she fled like a frightened shadow through the gathering dusk of the field.

---

4   Colin calls Jessamine his "bonnie bird" and "bonnie do'e" or dove.

CHAPTER XVIII

IT is no delusion which makes true lovers feel that their own passion fills the world. For the world itself is interested.

As a rule, the affair of love, the grave meaning of human union, is lost sight of in the fuss and prettiness of an engagement; sentiment and elegance serve for passion, and morality is exchanged for conventionality. If there be a white dress, a wreath of orange-blossom, a train of bridesmaids, a church or conventicle,[1] and an officiating priest, the union is moral—that is to say, society leaves a card upon the couple. If these things are missing, the union is considered immoral; society does not visit.

An abnormal situation, however, throws us upon our own resources. We cease simply to breath in and out the exhausted atmosphere of society, and, retiring to some isolated peak of genuine thinking, brace ourselves up to a nobler tenour.

Once more the square little chamber was the scene.

Jessamine paced up and down like a caged creature animated by a hope of liberty. Sometimes she leaned against the wall, her hands behind her and her head thrown back. Colin's kiss still glowed on her lips, and the pressure of his arms about her body, while the certainty of his love snatched her, as in a chariot of fire, out of the ordinary world which she had trodden so long with disdain.

'I am happy,' said she; 'I am in heaven! I am alive for the first time.'

The little chamber could not hold her. She folded a woollen 'cloud' about her head and throat, and went out. At the back of the house a path led a short way up the hill; it was moonlit now, though the light was crossed by the frequent overshadowing of birch-trees. Up this path she walked, continuing the ascent until she saw a birch-tree growing higher up and apart from the rest, larger than them, and with a trunk so divided as to form a natural seat. Leaning against this, she looked across the dusky heads of companion trees— the foliage sown as by a silver coinage—to the land of shadows beyond. There was nothing to hear; the breeze of the day, so valuable to the reapers, had fallen, and the quietude was absolute.

'I am happy,' said she, 'because the thing has happened to me which

---

1   Conventicle: A small meeting house or chapel for religious worship.

happens to few women. I have found with my heart the very man my heart would choose out of all the world, and he loves me.'

She nestled down in the forked trunk of the tree, leaning her head with the knitted shawl about it against a branch. Twinkling leaves hung motionless about her, but her feet and gray skirt were scarcely to be discriminated from the ground on which they rested.

'It is because he is so real that I love him,' said she—'because it is all so removed from the lies I lived in down there in London.'

She crooked her arm around a branch of the tree, and settled herself more securely.

'Also,' she added with a gasp, 'because it is so shocking and ill-regulated—such a frightful smash up of everything I know about. Oh, oh, oh! how happy I am!'

She closed her eyes dreamily, the moonlight falling placidly upon her face.

'Colin the peasant kissed me,' she said.

Her heart beat and leapt with mingled fright and ecstasy. She was like an antique Sicilian girl, whose lover seeks her in the woods, and says nothing about ceremonies nor makes any bargain. Jessamine's idea of a bargain was for ever connected with her London experiences and the detested Heriot. Her revolt into sheer nature and primeval emotion, following upon that, was a wild and fearful joy. For the moment, at least, she had got hold of the undivided man, the simple beloved, unattached to a banking account, to an elegant position, and fine upholstery. She was nearer to nature than most women. And this, for the own niece of her Aunt Arabella, was a sufficiently wonderful matter.

'Supposing other girls—other professional beauties—were like me,' she said; 'I wonder what would happen?'

Her face, with the eyes now wide open, gleamed with a little terrified fun, across which mournful shadows kept flitting.

'I wish,' she said, 'that the thrusting out of my finger'—here a small finger like a little white line appeared from amongst the shadows—'could topple down the whole hateful fabric of London society. Yes; I do wish it. Suppose that, hidden away in this Scotch birch-tree, I had such a power with my enchanted finger. Would I not use it?'

To desire this social upheaval was equivalent, with Jessamine, to a wish for the destruction of every moral law for the furtherance of her own chance inclination. A want of discrimination gave her wild fancies the criminal touch, which properly was no part of them, her mood becoming that of reckless self-abandonment, without regard to the innocence of her projects, or even their beneficial tendency. It was the consequence of her want of brain that she fell into so immoral a spirit, and turned to evil a situation which by no means necessarily involved it, though it certainly demanded a powerful choice.

The thing which had happened to her argued, she thought, an impropriety within, and perceiving this, all the footsteps to joy appeared to her as a flight downwards. Whereupon her mirth faded to mournfulness, and she tenderly considered that to reach her Colin, who was so good, she, his 'bonnie do'e,' could only be bad—a frightful situation that turned her young heart cold. For the instincts of deep affection detected in this the irreparable spiritual separation from the thing beloved.

She drew her hand back within the shawl, the scornful daring finger seeming, in fancy, to turn against herself, and sat with her head downcast, musing.

To be sure, she was born under a curse, for wherever she turned she was beaten back. When it touched her marriage with Lord Heriot—the splendid wedding supported by every possible prestige—Dr. Cornerstone, who was in a sense her exterior conscience, had looked, she recalled, upon the proposal with a sort of Satanic wrath that became him and heartened her.

As to the next step—the kiss in the cornfield exchanged with the stalwart peasant—her ears tingled and her cheeks smarted already with the hootings of an indignant world's outraged propriety. How could she keep her head in face of an assurance of so multitudinous a condemnation? It is a hard thing to be a woman and heroic. Jessamine's resource was recklessness and a meteoric shooting forth of unguided will.

'Oh, mad, bad, miserably happy Jessamine!'

There was no smile on her face as she raised it and gazed up into the vastness of the sky, which night and the moon were filling with changing cloud-pictures. But night is night; and some of Nature's great influence dropped on the weak, forlorn heart beating beneath it. A thought came east and a thought came west, and softly fell upon the confusion of her mind, and for a moment it seemed as though that delicate, little-used thinking apparatus of hers would interpret it, and would move under the impulse of a genuine idea.

'Forsake the artificial and accept the true, the rose with the thorn.'

She put out, as it were, feelers, half blindly but wholly earnestly, towards a true solution. Her prerogative as a human being kept breaking upon her in momentary light, startling her mind with apprehensions too great for its grasping, too great for a definite response, but leaving her with an aching, beating, aspiring heart that stretched and yearned she knew not for what.

It is a terrific experience, and Jessamine at best was a slight creature.

Her position on the tree became presently too restrained for her emotion; sliding out of her seat, she stood erect, pressing the knitted shawl upon her breast with both hands.

The prevision upon her was of the universal which touches us in every personal experience, the call to be, through any single event, something which belongs to us alone, and which yet is for all. To miss the significance of the unique moment! That is desolation.

The girl's heart grew under her passion to a half sort of cosmic apprehension; the wide setting, which rims our remotest act, being suddenly surmised by her, but never for one moment so clearly comprehended as to leave her free to think. She drew the long quivering breath as of a vaguely rising resolve, and stretched her hands out searchingly towards the night, looking up as she did so with solemn asking eyes.

'What must I do?' she said. 'What must I do?'

Then she paced the small space of ground beneath the tree with agitation, forcing her thoughts to marshal themselves in regiments that ran with too restricted an aim. Better to have gone on lifting a passive heart to the skies.

'Colin knows nothing,' said she. 'Need he ever know? He knows I am beautiful, and he vaguely knows I am something beyond the McKenzies' farm-help that I choose to appear to be. He knows it just in the way the McKenzies know it. But he never dreams that I am rich, that I am socially altogether out of his ken.[2] He does not picture, has not the faintest flash of an idea of, my real position and surroundings. How should he have? He is just simply a man who sees in me a woman; he, and he alone, has found *me*—has found Jessamine; I am in a sort his creation. I am just what I should be if he were Adam and I Eve. All the rest seems to fall away when I am near him and see his clear-looking, truthful eyes, and feel him loving me.'

Why was he not Adam and she Eve? What shuts the gate of Paradise against them? She stood there knocking at the doors with a timid but ever more and more importunate hand, until the whole night filled with her appeal, and she sank upon the earth kneeling, with extended arms and uplifted face.

It was to all the old-world mythologies she cried this time, not to the rigid spectre whom Aunt Arabella had set up as god. She cried to everything primeval to which men from time immemorial have carried their wants, and, like any pagan girl, asked her impossible heart's desire from earth and skies.

'Oh, good God, forgive my thoughts,' she cried, 'and fulfil them!'

---

2 Ken: "ancestral stock, familial origin" (*CSD* 340).

She drew her hands back, pressing them against her breast and shivering, but still cried on to that whole mythology of Nature.

Then she rose, and restlessly paced in the shadow of the tree, staring round with a fearful face—a face ever too conscious of a prying and derisive world. The pictured mockery drove her to severe lengths of thinking, to a self-flagellating imagining. Mentally she leaped her abyss and landed on the other and grim side, and there summoned before her the shallow world of critics whom she knew. Her thought, shuddering beneath the weight of its own temerity, pictured the thing that might be. A return after an interval—that interval too dimly sketched to be anything but a blissful terror, in which heaven and hell were strangely commingled, and from which her thought shrank hurriedly away.

But afterwards the return! London and the old circle of flattering friends, with ominously silent faces and a pinlike curiosity in the eyes.

'To these,' said Jessamine, 'I speak frankly. I force myself to do it. I carry in my arms my little baby, and I say, "This is the child of the man I love, and for whom for ever, though I see him no more, I shall live as a true wife. He was the best and truest man I ever met, and the finest to look upon; and he took my heart by storm. He was a peasant, and lived in a sort of hovel, and worked in the fields with his own hands; he looked splendid when he was reaping the corn. He had been educated, but it was a small matter; he did not read much: he said quiet, wise things instead. I'm afraid he knew no poetry, but his eyes were poems in themselves. He had no adventures, neither had he any vices. He was wholesome, from his sunburnt skin to the inmost core of his heart. There was not a spot in his whole nature from which you had to turn away your eyes. Such a power of goodness went out from him that he had but to look at me and I grew better. I could not marry him, because I was not fit for the duties of his wife; but, yes, I loved him so that I united myself to him with trembling joy. And this is my baby." Supposing I said this.'

Pausing in her walk, she rested again against the birch-tree, while her eyes and features lent themselves to the expression of some deep natural yearning; it grew in her face as though she saw something far off, as a star is far away, with which she had some intimate connection. It seemed that she became enwrapt even to partial unconsciousness, for her arms involuntarily extended themselves as though to receive a gift.

The yearning in her eyes increased, and she drew her arms together—empty as they were—and curved them towards her breast. The fashioning of her face under the spell of the idea was wonderful. Presently, as she gazed down enwrapt upon her empty arms, a rain of tender tears fell from her eyes.

Then a little wind came in the tree, and the fluttering of the leaves waked her. She glanced up with a distraught look, upon which smote sudden anguish.

'I dare not! *I dare not!*'

And she fell to the ground shivering and sobbing, and drew the shawl over her head and smothered her face on her gathered-up knees. The moonlight drew away behind the hill and left the place in shadow.

CHAPTER XIX

THE morning brought apathy and a passive inclination to let things drift. The performance of household duties in itself helped to carry the moments on-wards, one by one, in soothing activity without too much leisure for thought.

'Where is Mr. McKenzie? I have not seen him to-day,' said Jessamine in the course of her labours, turning to Mrs. McKenzie.

During the morning her eyes had more than once wandered to the open door and the gate in the yard, in vague expectation.

'Oh, he is just away again. Colin Macgillvray was calling this morning, and John was to go with him to the sports of Righchar.'[1]

Jessamine's cheek burned as she sedulously rubbed up a chair.

'Mr. Macgillvray was here, then?'

'Oh yes; he would be here early, lingering about just like anyone daft indeed.'

Jessamine felt no offence; she smiled at the criticism.

'"Colin," I was saying,' continued Mrs. McKenzie, '"ye will be resting ye at the wrong end of the day whatever." And Colin he was just laughing.'

'What are the sports?' asked Jessamine, knuckling up her white hand and leaning her pink cheek upon it. 'Has Col—I mean Mr. McKenzie—gone away to them?'

'Oh yes! John was to go with Colin. It will be a change for them.'

'What will they do?'

'Oh, it will be a very grand affair indeed! They will play the pipes, and they will dance the Highland reel, and they will run and jump and throw the caber and the hammer.[2] Just all sorts.'

'Does—Mr. McKenzie join in them?'

'Oh no; he will not be joining.'

'What will he do, then?'

'Oh, he will just stand round and watch.'

'Does Colin Macgillvray just stand round and watch too?'

'Colin Macgillvray will be trying for a prize. He was ever the best at

---

1   Mrs. McKenzie is referring to the traditional Highland Games. This is a "meeting consisting of athletics, piping and dancing" (*CSD* 224).

2   Caber: "a heavy pole, a long slender tree-trunk." To "toss the [caber means to] throw the heavy pole as in *Highland Games*" (*CSD* 78).

throwing the hammer. Colin is a strong man whatever.'

Jessamine dropped the duster and came up to Mrs. McKenzie blushing like a rose and wearing a coaxing face.

'Mrs. McKenzie, I want to see the games. Am I too late? Can I get there? Will you let me go?'

'I should think I will let you go, indeed! No, you will not be too late. But it is not fit for a wee bonnie lassie to go her lane.'

'It will be fit for me, Mrs. McKenzie, because I am not a Highland lassie, and because I am very canny and know how to take care of myself.'

'A-weel, that will be as it may be,' said Mrs. McKenzie with a sigh. 'Ye can be seeking out John amongst the crowd, and ye can be standing near him, and he will just be looking after ye.'

'Can I go now?'

'Just as soon as ye like indeed.'

Righchar was a town fifteen miles distant; the station was five miles from Drynock; Jessamine would have to walk so far, and could then take the train for the rest of the journey.

Her dressing for the occasion was studiedly different from the costume of gray with which the villagers were already familiar. She hoped to escape detection in the crowd, and to watch Macgillvray in his action amongst his own people when he was unaware of her presence. The dress she chose was a simple one of black with a tight-fitting jacket; the costume had been made for an unfulfilled purpose of hospital visiting in the old days, and it was finished by a close little bonnet and a veil over the face.

She did not reach Righchar until the day was well advanced and the games—in spite of Highland ease and dilatoriness—more than half over. The scene was in a field, and the arena, which was extensive, was simply marked out by placing the spectators in a circle. In the centre of the space thus formed a number of handsome Highlanders—some in national costume and some not—were expected to display their prowess in feats of strength, or grace, or agility, or in musical skill. At the moment of her arrival a reel in costume was going on;[3] but a glance sufficed to assure her that Colin was not one of the performers; indeed, neither he nor John was to be seen. A few carriages drawn up on the edge of the ring had enabled her to approach unobserved; these were surrounded by groups of respectably-dressed people, and, placing herself near, she trusted to her proximity to them and to the newness of her dress to conceal her from notice. The spectators were, with the exception of the few gathered near the carriages, composed almost entirely of peasants,

---

3   Reel: "a lively Scottish dance" (*Webster's* 1192).

and she soon detected the feeling of association and familiarity which leads a community of equals to call the members by their Christian names, and to recognise each one in his individual character and capacity.

In due season the reel—the weird grace of which delighted her—came to an end. The bagpipes, however, by no means concluded their operations; they retired behind a wooden shanty, from which the prizes were to be handed, and then each piper, with a strange and quite magnanimous toleration of the rights of others in the matter of music, continued to play each one his own instrument in cheerful and uncomplaining independence, marching about the while in plaids and kilts and unabated dignity. But the dancers having made their bow and disappeared in a picturesque and medley group, a new group of men came now into the centre. These were hatless and coatless, and clad in jerseys and short cotton drawers. Amongst them Jessamine's heart leapt up to recognise Colin. The feat to be performed was tossing the caber; and two men appeared bearing what looked like a small tree, denuded of its branches, and about eight feet long. Two or three Highlanders each in turn raised it, only to let it fall again; whereupon a great laugh rippled round the circle of spectators, and a man carrying a saw and dressed in ordinary working clothes came forward. Amidst the holiday-makers he had a certain irrelevant and prosaic air, and he applied his tool stolidly to the caber, and made as though he would shorten it. The crowd tittered. But then Colin walked forward with his grave nonchalant bearing, and pushed the workman aside. The people clapped in anticipation; as for Jessamine, when she saw him stand there in the pride and ease of his strength, the heart within her stirred with a delicious surprise.

Macgillvray took the caber, planted his feet firmly, and poising it, small end downwards, on his right hand, stooped low, and then, with a mighty movement of his arms and body, projected it forwards in the air. The caber went up a great height and then turned and fell to the ground at a considerable distance onwards, big end foremost. The spectators clapped and shouted, and Jessamine drew her breath with a quiver. It was the sense of achievement this time that dazzled her.

'Yes! He did that!' said she. 'He sent that great thing, that I could not lift, high and far in the air. And he looked beautiful as he did it—as though it were a trifle. He can do things that I cannot imagine.'

The unconscious Colin retired modestly after his achievement amid the plaudits of the crowd, and the eyes of Jessamine followed every one of his movements.

The exploit next on the programme was leaping over the bar. It took the good Highlanders a considerable time to erect first the two poles and then to balance the bar across them. However, they were up at last—after falling down three separate times—and the game began.

Colin took no part in the leaping; but upon his return to the ground there was a marked difference in his demeanour. Instead of his former collected air, a certain restlessness was to be detected; he held his head high and walked about with his figure consciously drawn up to its full height. His eyes, too, shining lustrously, darted hither and thither over the crowd, and he laughed and talked more than his wont. After the leaping came 'putting the weight';[4] one or two men walked into the square, and acquitted themselves moderately well. And then it was Colin's turn once more.

'A Macgillvray against a' the Macphersons!' was the cry.

Macgillvray shook his hair back, and presented himself, his face smiling, and in his eye a curious excited light. He took the stone and placed himself in the square. The stone weighed about twenty-two pounds; having this in his hand, and standing on the back line of the square, he raised it to the level of his shoulder, keeping his elbow directly under it and close to his side. His body was balanced on the right leg; the right shoulder being drawn back, the left leg was raised from the ground and, with the left arm, thrown forward to help the poise. In this attitude he crouched somewhat, as though pressed down by the weight of the stone, and then raised it up slowly two or three times to the full stretch of his arm; then he took a quick movement forwards, and, both feet now on the ground, but the weight of the body still on the right leg, and the right shoulder still held back, with a sharp spring and rapid half-turn of the body—a movement of exceeding grace and strength—he propelled the stone, holding himself strongly back as his right shoulder swung forward, and as his right foot touched the 'scratch' line.

Jessamine saw him, after the fine and rapid changes of his attitude, with white, set face, and strongly-thrown-out arms, and well-controlled body held back from 'following' his shot. The stone, as though it had been veritably projected from some powerful spring, whizzed through the air and made its first pitch at a distance of about thirty-five feet.

Jessamine did not know that the 'put' was unusual, and would be announced in every sporting paper in England, nor was she aware how great a part the influence of her own personality had in it. But a roar of applause, accompanied by hand-clapping, burst from the crowd, and her heart beat high with pride and joy.

---

4   What Brooke describes Colin participating in is like our modern day shot put, with the exception that Colin is lifting an actual stone and not a metal weight.

'It's no canny!⁵ the lad's fey!'⁶ cried out an old fellow who knew Macgillvray, and was accustomed to his quiet and cautious ways.

And Colin, the excitement playing over his face, stepped back a pace or two, and stared round as though dazed by his own achievement. For, indeed, in that moment he touched, as it were, the high-water mark of his life, throwing out, in the way most possible to him, a sudden expression of that fuller personality which lies latent and hidden under the every-day character, to escape but in those rare hours when some deep stirring of the nature carries it forward for an instant to a higher plane of action.

Then he ran laughing from the field. A group of peasant girls near Jessamine were shouting with delight, clapping and cheering with might and main, and what they were saying sank suddenly upon her ear.

'Ay, Colin's fey!' they cried—'Colin's fey! See the big mon running through the field like a bit laddie! Ay, it will be no canny! Colin's fey!'

Jessamine felt the interest and exhilaration die suddenly out of her heart. She wanted to escape and to get home. Slinking out of the crowd, she hastened to the station, determining to take the next train back. But arrived there, she found there was an hour to wait, and time had to be passed in the waiting-room, which was as dreary as such places usually are. A time-table of the Highland railway hung on one wall; a bundle of texts in Gaelic upon the other. In her heart, instead of any pleasant thinking, went the peasant girls' cry of 'Colin's fey!' In and out of the room came an occasional passenger. Some Highlander in costume returning slightly intoxicated from the games; some dull respectable Scotchman of the Lowlands travelling on business; a family group dragging about with them a half-witted member; a laird and the laird's man. There was nothing in the surroundings to mitigate the sense of horrible dulness, or the prevision of evil, which had fallen upon her. 'Colin's fey!' still rang in her ears, and with it the inevitable sequence.

'People are "fey" in Scotland before a great calamity falls. What have I done to Colin?'

It was getting towards dusk when she arrived at the end of the short railway journey, and stepped from the train; and then a walk of five miles lay before her. The road was long and lonesome and silent. To begin with, the banks on either side were high, for the road ran through a cleft of the hills, and they leaned close upon it with an overshadowing of woods which made it gloomy. After a mile or so the small cleft widened to a broad valley, the hills

---

5 Canny: "favourable, lucky, of good omen" (*CSD* 83).

6 Fey: "other-worldly" (*CSD* 195). Colin is like one possessed and exhibits unusual strength and dexterity during the Highland games. The meaning of "fey" here is set in a positive light and not a negative one, as Jessamine assumes it to be.

retired on either side, and the road ran as an exposed white line over a moor-covered and partially cultivated country. Just now, when a break in the woods permitted her to see it, a beautiful light lay on the tops of the hills; but this was drawing away, and the sky above her gathered already in depth. She met few people; one or two traps overtook her, and once a group of gipsy tramps passed by, but the traffic was small. She had walked on for about a mile, and dusk was really closing, when a dogcart shot past her at a great rate; looking after it, she recognised the figures of John McKenzie and Colin Macgillvray.

'They did not notice me,' said she, 'and I am glad.'

Another quarter of a mile brought her to a fir-wood—it closed the road in upon either side—and leaning against the fence under the shadow she saw the figure of a man. She advanced with some feeling of trepidation, but as she approached the figure came out, and stood in the road confronting her.

'Ah, it is you!' said she with a quiver of mingled gladness and timidity.

'I'm thinking it will be me,' said the low, laughing voice of Colin.

He stood in front and stopped her. The heart in her breast was agitated, and yet felt heavy as lead. Looking up with an effort, she realised at once, from the expression of his face, the magnitude of the change which yesterday had made in their relations. A word, the touch of human lips on each other, and causes are started which go palpitating on, with the whole of life for their circuit—perhaps with the infinite space of ages.

'It's me,' repeated Colin, 'and I'm just hungering for you.'

'Shall I take your arm, and shall we walk down the road together?' asked she timidly, with the sense of warding off some greater proposition by a less.

'That will not be enough,' said he.

And before she had time to surmise his intention, he gathered her to his breast, lifting her in the fervour of his embrace almost off her feet. She gazed up at the strong, masterful, tender face with something like terror. It was all so different from her expectation.

'I am frightened. Set me down. Let us walk on,' she murmured involuntarily.

'Na; there will be no one coming. I could carry ye as I was doing before. My arms ache for ye.'

'Oh, no, no! I—it frightens me, Colin!'

'You have given me no kiss.'

Her heart beat terribly. Present to her thought was the strong direct strength he had both of mind and body—the fierce candour and simplicity before which she was helpless.

'Colin, I have something to say,' said she, grasping for safety at straws.

'A-weel, Jessie, my do'e.'

'I saw you at the sports.'

'I'm thinking you did. I saw you just as the leaping began, and it was like wine in my heart. Nothing would have been too high for me to-day.'

'Colin, no, no! Let me walk by your side.'

'Ay, a maid knows well how to plague a man.'

'You must not talk that way. They were saying to-day when you threw so well that you were fey.'

'Fey was I? I was to believe them, I'm thinking, if they were saying so a while ago. But not after yesterday, Jessie. Fey or no, I have all I am wanting now, and more than my best dreams.'

'Was yesterday so much?' asked she, at her wits' end.

'Oh yes—yes! Why, lassie, would it be small to ye?'

His voice held a disconcerted tone, and that was as intolerable to Jessamine as his unquestionable claim upon her.

'No, Colin, no! It was not small.'

'Look, my wee bonnie Jessie,' said he tenderly; 'I love you true. There will not be a corner of me that does not love you. You just will be my heart.'

'Yes, Colin; thank you. I like to be your heart. You passed in a dogcart with Mr. McKenzie just now. How was that? Did he see me too?'

'No; he was not seeing you. I saw you. I just thought that the machine would do verra weel without me, and I said to John I would just be walking the rest of the way.'

'It was quite dusk, and I was close to the hedge, yet you saw me!'

'I'm thinking I would be feeling you if you were near, whether I saw you or not. But I saw you, Jessie, my dearie. There are eyes in my heart.'

'Are there, Colin?'

'Yes. Now for my kiss.'

She raised a vainly protesting hand.

'Jessie,' said he solemnly, and he pushed the hair back from her brow with one hand while he held her with the other arm, 'you must love me true.'

'Oh, Colin, I do! I do!'

He gazed down upon her face with a long, grave, yearning look. The eyes that opened wide upon his after his kiss were dim with something like terror. He vaguely perceived it.

'Ye will be trembling, lassie,' said he tenderly.

She made no answer, but caught at the lapel of his coat.

'A-weel. Trembling will just be the way of a maid. Come closer, and ye winna tremble.'

'No,' said Jessamine, in a choking voice; 'let us go on.'

'And ye're greeting,[7] lassie! For why? What will ye be greeting for?'

'Oh, Colin! Perhaps that's just a maid's way too.'

'Perhaps. But I'm thinking we will just make the most of to-day, for to-morrow I shall be away.'

'Away! Where?'

'Oh, it will only be a sale of corn to which I'm bound to go with John.'

'When shall you be back?'

'Oh, by evening.'

She walked on a short distance in silence. They reached the open road, and then she pulled him by the sleeve.

'Wait a minute; there is something to say. Listen to it now.'

'Ay, Jessie! What will it be, my lo'e?'

She was so white that a vague apprehension dawned on his heart. 'Will you remember what I am going to say always?'

'I will remember it. What will it be, my do'e?'

She placed a hand on either shoulder and looked him full in the face.

'It is that I love you, Colin, and ever shall and ever must till death comes. Believe it always, remember it always—*whatever happens.*'

He took her hand down from his shoulder and held it in his own.

'It will be a great matter to say that, Jessie, my wee wife. But it will be true, for I feel it in my own heart.'

After that they walked on soberly together, speaking little. But her hand rested on his arm and his feet trod on air.

For herself, the unexpectedness and directness of his love-making were at once a terror and a charm. He appeared not to dream of circuitous preliminaries; gift-bestowing, court, fictitious distance, and compliment-paying seemed not to enter his head; the simplicity and ingenuousness of his passion, now his reserve was once broken down, had in it something inflexible and austere; his love-tokens were the pressure of his arms, the thrill of his voice, the look in his eyes; and these signs in himself he evidently considered sufficient, and that with them she should be well pleased, just as in her they were for him all-satisfying.

---

7   Greeting: "weeping, tears" (*CSD* 247).

CHAPTER XX

Old Rorie Macgillvray, sitting in the nook by the kitchen-hearth, fancied that his dim eyes caught sight of the fluttering of a woman's garment past the window. The rain beat slantwise across the smoke-stained pane, but he had an impression that, with the rain, the wind had puffed some loose gray streamer over the blurred outlines and mist-washed shapes of the mountains. It made him stare and open his mouth wider, and turn his head and his ear in an endeavour to supplement one failing sense by the failing power of another. Then the idea of the fluttering shawl touched some association, and he sat thinking of it, his mouth still open and his eyes perusing the smouldering peats on the hearth, upon which, in comfortless fashion through the open chimney, grimy raindrops fell in frequent spurts.

His 'auld wife,' a plaid[1] about her shoulders, and an umbrella—or, rather, a blue roof[2]—in her hand, had set out at an early hour on a five-mile walk to the 'merchant's'—that is, to the store of the universal provider of the place, an emporium warranted to supply all human wants, from curling-irons down to a ha'porth of treacle,[3] in addition to which large enterprise the 'merchant' had undertaken to manage the post-office necessities for ten miles round. Those who possessed their souls in patience were really likely to get their needs supplied at the shop, for it was well stocked. But the drawback of a monopoly is that it breeds an insolence of spirit which rebels against the routine involved in business habits. So that the customer arriving hot and breathless from a long and burdened peregrination over the hills was as likely as not to discover the postmaster and manager nodding in the back parlour in a hopelessly bewhiskied slumber, while a slow and confused boy pottered over the post-office business, from which no entreaty could seduce him; and the girl, engaged in farm-work at the back, would peep in to acquaint herself with the customer and, ten to one, would disappear again with a final air.

Old Rorie, therefore, from prolonged experience, did not expect the

---

1   Plaid: "a rectangular length of twilled woolen cloth . . . *formerly* worn as an outer garment *esp* in rural areas, *later* also as a shawl by women in towns, and *now* surviving as part of the ceremonial dress of members of the *pipe bands* . . . of Scottish regiments" (*CSD* 499).
2   Blue roof: "a canopy" (*CSD* 573).
3   A half penny's worth of treacle.

return of his wife for hours to come; as for Colin, he was attending the sale of corn with John McKenzie. So that the old man's mind, roused to momentary attention, trotted off again tranquilly to fifty years ago, when the things that happened had not so dim and vague an air, and when the fluttering of a shawl—by no means belonging to the present Mrs. Macgillvray—had been an incident of consequence. The world was not so good as it had been, old Rorie frequently remarked; events had little interest. Whisky, it is true, retained its fascination, and while his eyes twinkled at the peats in the delights of disreputable reminiscence, his old hand sought at the shelf by his side. There is reason to believe that the old fellow had been left at home alone on parôle, for Mrs. Macgillvray held it a disgrace to be drunken at the third hour of the day; nevertheless, his fingers were just nearing the recess where the whisky-bottle stood, when a knock came at the door. Old Rorie's hand was jerked down by frightened conscience, much as the hand of a child is snatched back from forbidden sweet-meats, and he stared hard at the direction of the sound. It came back again. Then he felt for his staff, and slowly raised himself, showing as he stood up on the kitchen floor a not inconsiderable height, and went to the outside door and opened it.

A little figure in gray stood there, at the sight of which he jerked his head forward in an attempt to surprise his senses into grasping its full meaning, and then, lifting himself to as erect a posture as possible, made the salute of the peasant. He did not in the least recognise in Jessamine the McKenzies' farm-help, of whom he had heard much, but he did recognize the air of a great lady.

'Is Mr. Colin Macgillvray at home?' asked Jessamine, who knew very well that he was not.

'No, mem;[4] Colin is away. He went west this morning, and he was taking the horse and cart.'

'Will he return soon?'

'I'm thinking, mem, that he will be back this evening. He was going to a sale of corn with John McKenzie. Him and John will be great friends, ye see.'

'I am sorry not to find him in. It rains fast.'

'It's a very bad morning whatever. Will ye come in, mem, and rest ye a whilie?

'Thank you.'

Jessamine stepped forward without alacrity. She had been gazing at old Rorie's face with fascinated interest, and yet with horror. It was so fine and yet so grotesque, the civilization faintly veneered over the obvious barbarism.

---

4   Mem: "madame" (*CSD* 409).

His features were of the Scandinavian type, the racial markings still as pro-nounced as in the age when the Viking harried the coasts.[5] The upper classes pare away the traces of their ancestry; the rustic peasant startles the fastidi-ous by retaining them unmodified. Moreover, these wild though grand tribal features of old Rorie's were not clean, nor were his manners pleasant; his corduroy clothes were greasy, and his woollen shirt was open, revealing a shaggy breast. The course of ages and the surrounding of a gentle-mannered people had, as it were, trimmed the claws of the ogre; old Rorie was incapable of cruelty, he was hospitable, and had a strong sense of personal dignity; he possessed with this a conservative though independent respect for the Laird and the great world of which he knew nothing; he believed in the election of the saints, and had no doubt of his own salvation; and, though his youth had been somewhat tinctured with the disreputable element, and in the matter of 'whusky' he was still an impenitent, on the whole he was reckoned amongst the highly-respectable members of society. But, then, Culture had given but the hastiest daub to his once splendid animal physique; of all that manifold limitation in air, speech, gesture, which we call 'good manners,' and which is woven out of an inherited and acquired knowledge of that which is pleas-ant or unpleasant to our fellows, he knew nothing. The Unlimited and the Dubious render intercourse impossible; disparity of manner is as disparity of race—an incalculable thing. Jessamine therefore followed old Rorie with trembling; she would have shivered to have followed a Red Indian into his wigwam, or a Zulu into his kraal,[6] or an amiable gorilla up his tree, and her sensations were not materially different now.

Still, she was resolved. He was Colin's father.

'May I see your kitchen?' asked she, as old Rorie turned to the room on the left, to which Colin had ushered her on her first visit to Dalfaber.

'Oh yes, mem!' answered Rorie; 'it will just not be cleaned up the morn, ye see. But ye can come in and welcome.'

He opened the door into the kitchen, where he had just been sitting. It was a square room, with low wooden rafters, and the rafters and ceiling were black with smoke. The floor was of stone, and so was the hearth. This last was simply a flat surface raised two or three inches, and extending across the room; the arch of the chimney hung above it, and was merely an immense

---

5   Old Rorie's lineage draws from people who attacked the coast of Scotland; though this is his ancestry, he has learned to rise above the extreme savagery of his forefathers. *Webster's New World Dictionary* provides a concrete definition of the Viking: "any of the Scandinavian sea rovers and pirates who ravaged the coasts of Europe from the 8th to the 10th centuries" (1584).

6   This is an enclosure for livestock, usually cattle.

cavernous aperture—the size of a small room—which, without diminution in its proportions, opened to the sky. The shelterless nature of such a contrivance was exemplified now by the dribbles of wet which came down the soot-covered wall and fell about the hearth. Old Macgillvray, however, evidently regarded his chimney as a show; he beckoned Jessamine to approach the hearth and to look up. She did so, and saw four stone walls festooned with soot; above them, a gray sky, across which trails of rain-cloud swept; a thin spiral of smoke was whirling about towards the top in momentary indecision whether to rise or descend.

'Surely,' said Jessamine, 'you are smothered with smoke on windy days?'

'Oh ay!' answered old Rorie; 'we will just be smothered. Ye see, the vent's too large. Ye see, the smoke blaws down back into the room, and that makes the rafters black. And, ye see, it will be verra cauld in the wunther time. But,' added he, 'we're used to it.'

His smoke-ingrained skin well testified that Time had lent the clemency of habit.

As for the rest of the room, there were good presses against the wall; there was a table, a wooden bench, and a chair or two, shelves with pots and pans, and an indescribable piece of furniture, which Jessamine suspected to be a bed.

'Will your Highness like to see the other room?' asked old Rorie, throwing in a title which he judged commensurate with his guest's distinguished air.

'Thank you,' said Jessamine, unwilling to confess to a former visit.

'We live mostly in the kitchen, ye see, for comfort,' explained old Rorie; 'but we have the parlour.'

And he led the way to the other well-remembered room. There was the bed in the alcove, the clothes tossed aside as Colin had left them that morning; a couple of tables, a few chairs, a rifle leaning against the wall, a small looking-glass (for Colin was something of a dandy),[7] one or two books, a vase or two upon the mantelpiece, a small ordinary grate. The floor was without drugget,[8] but everything was neat and orderly.

'This will be the parlour, mem, and that will be Colin's bed. Colin sleeps here, mem. This will be his rifle, for Colin was joining the volunteers, ye see.'[9]

---

7   As a dandy Colin, perhaps, pays a little too much attention to his clothes and his appearance.

8   Drugget: "a course woollen cloth" (*CSD* 162). It would seem that they do not have rugs on their floors.

9   The Volunteers (this was a named group, and therefore should be capitalized) were men who joined "uniformed rifle clubs . . . that flourished throughout Scotland"

'Colin is your only son?'

'Colin will be our only son, mem. He will be having the farm after me.'

Here old Rorie assumed a confidential air, and approached close to Jessamine, who felt exceedingly alarmed; nor was she at all encouraged by the laying of his hand upon her shoulder.

'He will be a solid man, ye see, mem, with money at the bank. I'm telling ye this, mem, not to boast, but that ye may just know that Colin will be something. He was ever a very quiet lad with his words.'

'You live very simply,' said Jessamine, edging back nervously from the old peasant's confidences.

'Oh ay! verra simple. Just porridge and potaties, with a kipper now and then, and milk. That will be it—a verra good diet, ye see. Folks will be overheating themselves with meat.[10] Oh ay! I'm often saying that porridge is the finest diet in the world.'

Jessamine smiled. Not even the terrible presence of old Rorie could quite overshadow the wistful strangeness in her heart at standing in the room of the man she loved. She leaned against the window-frame, looking out upon his beloved landscape, and ineffectually envying his austerity and simplicity.

'Ye must excuse me, mem,' said old Rorie, seeing that she made no answer, 'if I am not speaking the English right. Ye see, I'm not verra good at the English.'

'Oh!' said Jessamine, 'do you speak Gaelic?'

'Oh ay! We will just be talking the Gaelic at home. I can go into more things in the Gaelic. I must ever be looking for my words in the English, your Highness will understand.'

Jessamine looked up quickly, a pink spot in either cheek.

'Do not call me "your Highness." I am—the McKenzies' farm-help at Drynock.'

Old Rorie's jaw dropped at this information. His mind had a long way to travel from the title of his invention to the simplicity of Jessamine's claim, and her aspect belied her words. At last, while she rather tremulously watched him, the bewilderment passed from his face. He made an emphatic gesture

---

and would be ready to fight alongside trained soldiers if there was an invasion (12). Scottish soldiers were particularly supportive of Queen Victoria and participated in building, through active battle in various wars, the British Empire throughout the nineteenth century (1-12). Edward M Spiers. *The Scottish Soldier and Empire, 1854-1902*. Edinburgh: Edinburgh University Press, 2006.

10 Old Rorie's comment on what he and his family eat reflects their level of poverty. Even on a farm, it would be hard to keep too much meat. If he did have meat, it would most likely be dried or salt cured.

with his hand, bringing it down to his side with a slap.

'A-weel,' said he—'a-weel, the farm-help at McKenzies'. It's come on me of a suddenty. Dear, dear, dear! I'm no verra good with my eyes, and I was taking ye for a grand leddy. Ay, but ye are bonnie; I'm no so blind but I can see that. Ye are bonnie. Lads will let ye know it, I'm thinking. Ay, ye'll be trailing a good few at your heels! Ay, I was hearing of ye—a bonnie wee lassie at McKenzies'! But ye'll no be much hand at the working?'

'I am strong. I can do as much as most. Mrs. McKenzie thinks I have learnt a good deal,' said Jessamine, feeling rather as one who has swept down all defences with her own hand.

'Ay? Ye will just be learning, so as ye can manage your own farm, I'm thinking.'

He turned rather a cunning eye upon her.

'Perhaps,' said Jessamine; then she added hastily: 'And are you able to work upon the land yourself still, Mr. Macgillvray?'

'Oh ay! I can plant and hoe and lift potaties myself verra weel. But Colin, he will be rare at the working, mem.'

He looked sideways at Jessamine, a cunning thought visibly changing his features, and he nodded his head more than once.

'Indeed,' said Jessamine.

The old man approached again with his terrifying air of confidence. Jessamine's little start backwards did not discourage him. He came and laid a patronizing hand upon her shoulder.

'Ay, Colin will be an awful clever lad! When he was a bit bairn, and a charge was laid upon him, he was aye on the alert. Oh yes! he will just go straight on, and ye won't be stopping him. He will have the farm when I'm gone, mem. And Colin will be a great match, mem—a solid man with money in the bank. Ay, ay, I was a saving mon[11] in my day! And Colin's bonnie, mem—bonnie!'

Still with his hand on her shoulder, he looked into her face, grinning confidentially.

'Yes,' murmured Jessamine faintly.

'The lassies was ever running after Colin!'

He gave her shoulder a pat as he spoke, and then drew back, and expanded himself into the joviality of reminiscence.

'I was a great mon for lassies when I was young. But that will be a great while ago, mem.'

'Yes.'

---

11 Mon: "man" (*CSD*, 421).

'Eighty years, I'm thinking, or more. But I was ever for lassies. And Colin will be his father's own son—favours me, mem, in his features. But he will be quieter.'

'Yes.'

'Lassies will be ever running after him, though. They will know a bonnie lad when they will see one. I was saying to Colin: "Colin," I was saying, "ye'll be choosing a lass one o' these days."'

Old Rorie chuckled.

'Yes.'

'And Colin was just laughing.'

Old Rorie bent himself together in a quite inexplicable ecstasy.

'Yes,' said Jessamine.

'I'm saying to him sometimes: "Colin," I am saying, "ye will be choosing a lassie and bringing her home."'

Again he approached Jessamine, and, laying the tips of his fingers upon her shoulder, stood leaning back and chuckling with a lively mirth. She gazed at him with fascinated intensity, tracing, through his dirt and grotesque manners, the curious faint remains of Colin's 'bonniness' and grandeur in type of which he had claimed the parentage. Suddenly he withdrew his hand, and crumpled up his smiling features into a shrewder look.

'Ye see,' said he, 'we will be wanting a lassie about the bit hoosie now. The auld wife she's ageing fast, and we would be glad—verra glad—of a thumping lassie to scrub round and gather and hoe a bit. But my Colin, he's slaw, I tell ye; slaw and canny[12] my Colin will be.'

He shook his head with affected gravity and great concern.

'Ay, my Colin's slaw. But I'll just be telling ye ae thing. And I'd no be telling it to every lassie. My Colin will stick. A lassie will just be dealing skeelfu' with my Colin, and he'll stick. Slaw he may be; but he ever was for sticking since he was young.'

He surveyed her to see the effect of his words.

'Yes,' said Jessamine.

'And I'll tell ye ae ither thing. My Colin's ay very tender in his feelings. Gude bless ye! I was myself when I was young. But a mon wears a bit better when he will be eighty year. My Colin he will be tender. And a lassie will just be saying "snap" to his "snip." A lassie will if she was skeelfu'. And my Colin he will stick.'

Having delivered himself of these predicates, old Rorie drew a deep

---

12 Slaw: "in a leisurely way" and Canny: "cautious, careful, prudent" (*CSD* 628, 83).

breath and gazed down at the 'lassie' before him.

'I am rested now,' said Jessamine, whose eyes perused the ground, 'and I think the rain has stopped. I will go now, and I thank you very much.'

Rorie disentangled his mind with difficulty from its preoccupation, and with a very dignified air opened the door to let Jessamine pass. As she did so she glanced up the staircase, which disappeared into some nondescript region above.

'That is your bedroom up there, I suppose?' said she.

'Oh na! That will just be a make o' loft. Me and my auld wife we sleep in the kitchen—just for comfort, ye see. But,' he added cunningly, 'I'm not for saying that Colin wouldn't knock up a bit room upstairs for the lass and the bairnies when they come.'

'When Colin is married, you and Mrs. Macgillvray will remain here, then?'

'Oh ay!' returned old Rorie with the tranquility of full assurance; 'he wouldn't be turning on his old father and mother whatever.'

'No. I will go now, Mr. Macgillvray. Thank you, and good-bye.'

'Good-morning to ye, mem,' said the old peasant, standing on the threshold, and involuntarily saluting the high breeding in Jessamine. 'I am most pleased to be seeing ye, and we will be verra pleased if we was seeing ye again.'

CHAPTER XXI

THAT evening Jessamine stood in the small enclosure which contained McKenzie's barns and outbuildings, her hand resting upon the railings.

It was the place in which she had first become aware of Colin's existence. Her face looked worn and pale, and she grasped the rail firmly, so that the knuckles of her hand looked white under the skin; this was the sole sign of the tension of her mind. All day she had done no work. The storm of the morning had ended in a steady drizzle of rain, and it was chilly enough; the landscape was gloomy, the nearer details sordid under the dripping wet, the hills covered with shreds and trails of chalky mist, and over-weighted with the heavy roll of black clouds of moisture upon them. Jessamine's eyes looked steadily southwards. The stern and unillumined front of a hill, down which the storm-rack crept with chilly clinging hands, intercepted her gaze; but there was an expression in her eyes as though this natural barrier had melted before their penetrating rays, and they saw something beyond and far off.

She wore a gray Glengarry bonnet[1] and a gray plaid about her shoulders; her position was uncomfortable, but she had chosen it rather than endure the closeness and dulness of the little square chamber; the air, at least, was fresh and sweet. But it was silent; everything that runs or flies, chirrups or sings, and lends its little being to help make up the cheerful intermingling of sound and movement, seemed to have sought its lair or to have hurried beneath the ground; the very rain fell without its usual jovial tinkle; it was but the noise-less emptying of one of those cold and chalky clouds, and its drip washed out rather than intensified the colours of the grass and heather and foliage.

Suddenly Jessamine gave a violent start. Her eyes flashed and dilated, and a glow as from some reflected sunlight burned in her face. She withdrew a step from the railing and looked to the right. A cautious step amongst the bushes had been to her heart an unmistakable signal; and now, from the mist and grayness of the birch-wood, Colin's form appeared and stood out on the green knoll near. He looked at the house for a moment and then discovered her. She was gazing at him with a curious panting fear in her eyes.

'Jessie, my do'e! Ye're waiting!'

---

1   Glengarry bonnet: "a kind of flat-sided cap or bonnet (shaped rather like a modern forage cap) pointed at the front and back and *freq* with two ribbons hanging behind" (*CSD* 236).

And he ran down to her. The fence was between.

'No!' said she, drawing still further back and speaking almost sharply; 'I thought you were away.'

'A-weel? But ye're here, and it makes no difference.'

'Have you bought your corn? And has Mr. McKenzie returned?'

'Oh yes. We bought a stock for seed. John will not be back yet. He was staying at McKenzie Craigowrie's—his cousin, ye'll understand.'

'He will be returning, Colin, and, if so, he will see me. I should not like that.'

She made as though she would withdraw, and a blank look drove the radiance out of Colin's face.

'Oh, Jessie! Ye maunna be going![2] Why, lassie, I was not seeing ye all day!'

'Is that so very necessary?' asked Jessamine, mournfulness chasing the sweetness of her smile.

'I'm thinking it's likely ye need be asking that! Jessie, I'm coming over the fence!'

'No, Colin, no!'

'Ay, Jessie, ay! I'm no for bearing these bits of iron between. I've had no kiss.'

'Colin, stoop your head. I will give you one.'

'Your own self, lassie?'

'Yes.'

He stooped his head over the fence, and Jessamine, pulling at the lapels of his coat, stretched herself up and touched his mouth with her lips. It went to his heart like a sting. In another moment he was over the fence and had her in his arms.

'Colin,' said Jessamine, 'let me go! You are crushing me to pieces! I thought I forbade you to come over the fence!'

'Ye'll be forbidding the sun to shine, and the wind to blaw, and the burn to run down the hill, winna ye, lassie?'

'Perhaps Mrs. McKenzie has seen you from the windows.'

'Then, lassie, I must be making my bit explanation. I have got, ye'll understand,' he added gravely, 'to be telling McKenzie soon.'

Jessamine, who, after an anxious scrutiny of the road, had retired to the protecting angle of a barn, stood with her back against the wall. Her face was red enough now, and her breast rose and fell; Colin, the very picture of a handsome and triumphant lover, stood looking down upon her, his eyes wandering over the flower-like face, and his heart a mere suffusion of mingled

---

2   Maunna be: "must" and "an unavoidable necessity" (*CSD* 404).

tenderness and worship.

'Colin,' said Jessamine, in a rapid entreating tone, 'promise me something.'

'If it's no against nature, lassie, I'll promise ye anything. I'll no promise not to kiss ye again in a minute.'

'I want you to listen in real earnest,' said she anxiously. 'You said you would promise?'

'Ay, lassie.'

'Promise me not to tell Mr. and Mrs. McKenzie anything at present.'

There was a moment of silence. If Jessamine had looked up, which she did not do, she would have seen in Colin's eyes a little flash of pained astonishment.

'*Not* tell? A-weel, Jessie, that will be as ye like, my lo'e. Come,' he added tenderly, 'a little nearer. I cannot see your eyes.'

As he spoke he put his arm out and drew her close to his side. The pressure was more like that of a protecting husband than of a passionate lover. And Jessamine yielded to it tranquilly, laying her hand in his, and looking up to his face with eyes swimming in tenderness.

'*Not* tell, my lassie?' he repeated as he bent down to look closer into them.

'You do not understand,' said she, her lids drooping for the moment.

'That may be. But it will be my part, I'm thinking, just to—to—be seeing that folks about gets no wrong notions into their heads.'

He loosed his hand from her small clinging fingers, and, folding both arms about her, pressed her jealously to his breast. She lay there with her cheek pressed against his coat, and her eyes looking up at him with a sad inscrutable gaze.

'We see things differently, Colin,' murmured she.

'Oh ay! Ye will be versed in many things that I was hearing nothing of. But if ye love me it will be all one.'

'I do love you, Colin,' said Jessamine with sudden emotion.

And she lifted her arms and tightened their grasp about his neck, and once more startled his lips with the soft fire of her own.

'That's well, lassie,' said he, the grave depth of his voice intensified by tenderness; 'it is like the opening of heaven's gate to hear it. Many and many's the time I was thinking of love; but I was never seeing the lassie that could just make me in love with love.'

'But when you saw me, Colin?'

'I was just set of a sudden out of earth into heaven.'

'Yet you thought ill of me at first—the day you came into the yard and stood staring at me, Colin, so as quite to frighten me.'

'Ill of you? Na! na! I was thinking that you were a make of lassie I was just not seeing before, and that a man had need to be cautious—'

'Cautious?'

'Ay! Cautious when wraiths and witches were about.'

'You were right!' said Jessamine with bitter energy.

'Right was I? Well, I'm no saying but there's witchery in your kiss, lassie—my ain, ain lassie! But wrong, because you love me.'

'Do you trust me so much, Colin?'

'Oh ay! What else would I just be doing?'

'Yet you know little of me. Perhaps—it is just possible—I am different from your ideas.'

'Oh, may be. It will just be a verra pleasant page to learn, I'm thinking.'

'Colin, you always seemed canny—cautious. Yet you're taking up a new book, and thinking, like a child, that it will be all straight reading and pleasant.'

He laughed. Then he laid his hand against the curve of her cheek and chin, and lifted her face a little, and kissed her mouth and eyelids. It was so small and flower-like a face, the figure in his arms was so slight, the locks of hair ruffled against his breast were so fresh and curly and child-like!

'I'm thinking I'll just risk all that's written there. Once I've folded ye to my heart, Jessie, I'm not the man to go back on a tough bit or two. I'm thinking that I'd rather like a wrestle with ye.'

'Colin, Colin, be warned!'

It was almost as though a bird should chirp out a caution, or a child exhort its elder. What in her was there which he could not master?

'Warned?' said he, with a low murmuring laugh; 'I'll show ye how!'

'Colin, Colin, you frighten me! I cannot breathe. You must not kiss me again to-night.'

And she struggled in his arms until he loosened them and let her slip from him.

'I saw your father to-day,' said she, rearranging her plaid, and beating the wet out of the Glengarry bonnet, which had long since tumbled on the ground.

'Did you?' said Colin, his face lighting up with mingled surprise and anxiety.

'Yes.'

'You called there?' asked he, with a dubious air.

'Yes.'

'Well?'

'Your father is a splendid old man.'

'Oh ay! You saw my mither?'

'No.'

He waited for more, a vague unrest troubling his heart. He scarcely liked this independent call at Dalfaber when he had not been there to soften its asperities. His eyes were downcast. Jessamine watched his face with remorseful sympathy.

'Jessie,' said he, looking up at last, 'ye're but a bit lassie. Ye shall have a servant when ye're my wife.'

Jessamine looked away with a curious creeping of blankness over the love-light and colour in her face.

'Thank you, Colin,' said she softly.

'I'll be telling my father and mither to-night,' said he.

She glanced at him quickly, alarm shooting into her eyes.

'No, Colin. Promise me you will do no such thing.'

He came nearer, and looked longingly at the little bit of warm white throat he could see between the folds of her plaid; but he made no effort to kiss her.

'Have you ever a mither, Jessie?' asked he, with grave tenderness.

'No; I have no mother. I never knew what it is to have a mother, Colin.'

A vision of Aunt Arabella, of her high-ridged nose, the elegant insipidity of her visage, rose to Jessamine's mind, and sharpened her tone as she spoke.

'That will be a verra great loss, my do'e—a verra great loss. I'm thinking I will have to be mother and man to ye both.'

He looked at her leniently, as one looks at a child who needs directing. She looked at him with the sad, unfathomable eyes of those who are learned in life and the world. He took her hand in his own. She turned her head away.

'Jessie, lass, it will be sweet to me to carry a secret i' my breast, and share it just with ye alone.'

She made no reply, but the leaping of colour to her cheek showed that she listened.

'But I'm like a partly drunken man with wine still before him when I see ye, Jessie.'

A smile like a meteor lit up her eyes.

'And I'm kind of jealous of myself. I'd like to build a church about ye.'

Jessamine shuddered.

'Oh no, no! I should not like it.'

And, turning her face, she suddenly lifted her eyes to his with a soft, mysterious, tempting light in them.

'Bonnie, bonnie bird!' he murmured.

He stretched his hand towards her, but she drew a little further off, and stood gazing into the murky, misty gray where the South was. She was so still that Colin did not venture to interrupt her thoughts; she stood lifting the drenched plaid to her chin, and slightly shivering now and then. With her great beauty still before him, he had not room in his mind to discover how inscrutable she was. At last she spoke. Her eyes lifted themselves no higher than the top button of his coat, and her voice, in its low, firm tone, seemed driven out of her by a studied effort of will.

'Colin,' said she, 'I will give you leave to tell John and Annie McKenzie and your father and mother, in three days' time from this—if *you still wish it then.*'

'I see no harm in that delay whatever. And I'd willingly lengthen out my joy, for it will be a joy to steal round and see ye, Jessie—to know ye're all mine, and no one else to guess it.'

'You feel it so?' she asked, with a low wild little laugh and a darting look.

And then she shivered again.

'Good-night, Colin; I am going.'

'Bide a wee. I'm no saying that I can wait these three days and not see ye! I must see ye, Jessie.'

'Well, where?' said she, with a sudden fierceness of intonation.

'Could ye trust me, lassie?' asked he hesitatingly.

She looked in his eyes with a wild challenging smile—triumph and dread in one.

'Ay, how ye look! Lassie, every glance ye give me goes straight to my heart. I feel partly mad. But if ye can trust me, come to-morrow night to the new barn by the stack. Come, and ye'll find me waiting.'

'I'll come—I'll come!'

Her eyes were meteors.

'Gude bless ye, my lassie! But—but——'

'What, Colin?'

He raised his hand, and laid it confusedly upon his brow. Jessamine crept near again, and leaned against him, watching him. Her looks were wild, her lips were parted by quick breaths, and her bosom panted.

The man gave a great sigh, and dropped his hand.

'Oh, naething! Ye'll just come,' he said, in a faltering whisper.

CHAPTER XXII

WOMEN, when they are frail, are so in great measure because they have not been instructed in the nature of choice, nor taught the art of selection, nor the meaning of responsibility. Wilfulness they may know, but not too many are acquainted with will.

Jessamine's mental debate was in an ever-increasing darkness—if, indeed, it could be dignified with the name of debate. She was merely a prey to varying strong impulses, a thing passively delivered over to a struggle between opposing inducements. Shaken with longings and terrors either way, she stood wondering whither her fate would lead her at the last. There was an element in her passion perhaps unusually strong. She longed definitely and deeply after motherhood. Her thinking upon this point was no more the precise reasoned thinking of a man than on others; it was a brooding pictorial feeling on the part of a very feminine type of brain. But it coloured all her love for Colin, and was not distinct from it.

In Jessamine it was not so much that natural feeling lay as a rich residuum beneath a cultured mind, as that she was a pagan creature covered up in artificiality. In character development, with all her pretty cleverness, she was far behind the level of her age. She and other women like her move in a world for them 'not realised,' and beyond their understanding in its serious claims. But this fact does not exempt them; the serious claims are made upon them, nevertheless—fair neglected children as they are of the centuries of moral training which have never taken them in hand.

None of the girl's overpowering emotions were relieved by the consolations of intellectuality, or the dignified sense of a possibility of firm choice. Had the life she had condescended to in a freak proved too lofty for her? Or was she infected by the element into which she had come, to something lower than herself?

Neither question was she able to decide.

'Give yourself to Colin!' cried the strong voice of Nature.

Jessamine did not discern whether this voice came from an angel or the devil. All her thoughts were contradictory. At moments she found herself girding about her the armour of Aunt Arabella's instructions; at others, whipping herself up to the catastrophe almost as the virtuous whip themselves up to virtue. Beaten thus between two hesitations, either way the result would be simple frailty, and not decision.

And, out of frailty, nothing of good in this life was ever won.

All the next morning she moved about silent and distrait. Mrs. McKenzie watched her, and read her with her quiet motherly eyes. Trouble had come to the wee bonnie lassie, but its nature she could only faintly guess. Yet, since matrimony is the way of bonnie lassies, she ventured upon that subject at last, her soft voice throwing around her a region of temperance, safety, and peace.

'Jeanie Macbain will be making up her mind at last,' she ventured with cautious irrelevancy.

Jessamine started at the quiet voice, and blushed at it because of its mild contrast with her own tumult. The cup she was washing slipped from her hand into the wooden bowl with a clatter.

'It isn't broken, Mrs. McKenzie!' said she penitently.

'I won't be saying that I thought so,' persisted the good woman. 'Jeanie Macbain will be making up her mind, whatever.'

'What to do?' asked Jessamine timidly.

'She and Willie Dallas will be married soon.'

'Willie Dallas, of Sluggan Granish?'

'That will be he.'

'A very well-to-do man, I suppose? I am glad if Jeanie is happy.'

'A-weel, I'll not be saying so much about that. She will be ever very moderate. But it will be a right thing for her, whatever. Willie he was ever very backward and melancholious, and Jeanie she was laithfu'.[1] But they are making it up at last, whatever.'

'I am glad. Jeanie is not very young.'

'She will be getting on in years indeed. Many a weary body would ha' had her, but Jeanie she was ever very back-with-drawing. And I said to her one day, "What will you be thinking of Willie Dallas now?" And she said, "I'm thinking he's getting gray." And I said, "Grayer than yourself?"'

Jessamine reached down a tea-cloth and began to wipe the cups and saucers. The slop-stone stood under the window; she had been stooping over it with her back towards Mrs. McKenzie; but she turned from it now and leaned against it, her slim figure in the short blue linsey gown defined against the light, and her face downcast and rosy. Every ripple of the matron's tones, as she sat opposite knitting by the hearth, contained a gentle admonition and personal application.

'Yes, Mrs. McKenzie?' said the girl softly, seeing that she paused.

'It'll be best for a wee bonnie lassie to be wed. Lassies weary in time of

---

1   Laithfu': "reluctant" (*CSD* 354).

jinketing[2] round. Best get a gude mon while they may.'

The tone was firmer and more direct. Jessamine said nothing, and rubbed carefully round the plate.

'It will ever be a comfort,' continued Mrs. McKenzie, 'to find a straight road. It will be a comfort just to run right on without a sight of wonder and uncertainty. Whiles there will be turmoil in a lassie's mind. And I've noticed it gets settled down when a lassie buckles to with a douce quiet mon to do for, and bairnies aboot. That will be just a woman's way. There won't be so many roads for a woman as for a man. It's aye a wise dispensation, for they're but ill-shaped for roving. Seems like, the hearts in our breastsies need harbouring and resting. Oh, indeed! It was ever better with me since I took John. It stilled a sight o' thinking. A douce quiet mon and bairnies aboot will be the best thing for a woman, whatever.'

Mrs. McKenzie ended her speech with some sense of surprise at the un-wonted length of it.

'It is the best thing for a woman?' repeated Jessamine gently and slowly.

Mrs. McKenzie, raising her mild glance for a moment, was startled to find the girl's eyes dark as with a veil of trouble thrown over them, and with a face now as wan as it had been rosy. So unspeakable and deep an air of misery had rarely met her eyes before. She dropped her knitting and planted her hands upon her knees and leaned forward, not in excitement, but with a large comfortable inquiring air of sympathy.

'What will be ailing the lassie? She will be greeting the nicht through.'[3]

'Nothing ails the lassie,' repeated Jessamine gently, a twisted smile tremulously altering the lovely mouth, 'nothing—nothing at all. I am, I think, almost terribly well, Mrs. McKenzie.'

The wild wan eyes rested hungrily upon the good woman's face.

'A-weel!' said the latter, 'I'd not be one to be finding fault with the good health, whatever! It's a gift of the Lord to be thankful over. Lassie!'

'Yes, Mrs. McKenzie.'

'You'll not be saying a worrud over the sports. Did you like them?'

'Oh yes, very much. Oh, I liked them!'

The thought of Colin ran with a thrill through her voice.

'Colin Macgillvray he went west to the sports too,' said Mrs. McKenzie deliberately and with a quite infecting calm.

All Jessamine's glowing thoughts scampered as startled wild things to their lair when they saw the trap thrown out for them. The rustle of them

---

2   Jinketing: to "flirt" (*CSD* 327).

3   Greeting the nicht through: weeping all night (*CSD* 247).

seemed to her scared senses audible.

'Oh, he was there, of course,' she responded hurriedly, 'and Mr. McKenzie too. And—and—there was a very good piper there, a short man who played better than anyone.'

'Oh, indeed! You'll not be so very much taken up with the wee bit chappie with the pipes, I'm thinking.'

Jessamine, trembling and frightened, laid aside her tea-cloth, and turned away to place the cups and saucers on the shelf. It was notable that all the skilled society fencing, to which she was accustomed, failed her in the wise controlling eye of this wholesome peasant woman. Mrs. McKenzie's atmosphere threw everyone around her back on simple virtues.

'Mrs. McKenzie,' faltered the girl presently, when the last saucer had been put by, 'shall I not sprinkle a little salt in the porridge?'

'Just a thought, lassie,' responded Mrs. McKenzie, 'and you might be getting the platters down.'

Jessamine reached up for the wooden salt-box. But her fingers were trembling and awkward, and her eyes were blind. She pulled the thing forward on the shelf and let it fall, scattering the white contents over the floor.

'Oh, that will be wanchancy,[4] lassie!' cooed Mrs. McKenzie in scarcely a raised voice, and more sympathetic with Jessamine's ill-luck than sorry over her own loss—'very wanchancy, whatever.'

'Wanchancy?' reapeated Jessamine, staring at the white heaps on the ground.

'Oh, indeed yes, lassie! Very wanchancy, whatever.'

After the mid-day dinner, the rain, which had fallen heavily all morning, cleared off a little, leaving the atmosphere warm and damp; and Jessamine restlessly wandered out to the yard at the back of the house, near which she thought she heard John McKenzie at work. She found him building up a peat-stack[5] near the shed under the shelter of the projecting roof.

All the summer at odd times he had been sawing and preparing wood to build the shed, and, with the aid of Colin and other friendly neighbours, it had gradually risen from the ground, and now presented the appearance of a tolerable building. To-day he worked alone at the peat-stack, piecing the black blocks of fuel securely together so as to form a convenient heap, and this in the leisurely enjoying manner of one not concerned to take Time by the forelock, nor to perform any astonishing feat of empty celerity. The acrid

---

4   Wanchancy: unlucky.

5   Peat-stack: "A piece of the semi-carbonized decayed vegetable matter found under the surface of boggy moorland, *usu* cut into brick-shaped pieces, dried and burned as fuel" (*CSD* 480).

pleasant smell of the peats filled the air; and Jessamine, strangely soothed and secure as she always felt in either of the McKenzies' presence, drew nearer and nearer, until the man's busy glance took her into it. Whereupon he welcomed, with his usual pleasant glance, the lovely presence which he was now so accustomed to see lurking furtively about the edges of his daily labour.

'Won't you sit down and rest you a whilie?' said he gently.

Jessamine climbed on to a heap of fallen wood, and perched herself on the top. For a moment the turmoil that filled her life was stilled. She breathed in good odours, she watched healthy labour, she was conscious of kindly companionship, and, somewhere deep down in her nature, of the love that gives richness and glow to all life.

'We've had bad weather lately for the harvest, haven't we, Mr. McKenzie?' she began, identifying herself as usual with the interests of the place.

'Oh, indeed, and it's very bad weather,' returned McKenzie, with the patient glance at the sky characteristic of the Highland farmer.

'Will the corn be spoiled?'

Jessamine was anxious, and opened very grave eyes on McKenzie's face.

'We'll be waiting to see that, whatever. We've got it in the stooks, and we shall carry a bit soon.'

'I'm glad if it is not spoiled. That peat is the winter fuel, I suppose?'

'Oh yes! In the summer we will be building the stacks, and in the wunther we will just be burning them.'

John threw a pleasant glance up as he spoke. The peace, the monotony, the day-by-day living and labour, soothed her sense more and more.

'Where does the peat come from?' said she.

'Side of Craig Ellachie,' said John.

'Above the fir-woods? That's a long way to go. How do you bring them down?'

'Just with the cart and the horse.'

'But the road through the deer-forest is closed.'

'Whiles they close it, whiles they open it. It will be open when we will be casting the peats.'

'But it is so rough—scarcely a road at all.'

'Oh, it's a very bad road, whatever. It's awful hashing for the horses and the harness.'

'And you have to go so often to get enough.'

'A-weel,' said John, 'a good few times.'

'How tired you must get with the long journey up and down!'

'Oh yes! A body gets very tired and hot.'

'I think the laird should mend the road. It knocks the horses to pieces.'

'It will be very hashing to them. But whiles I'm not so sorry to take the roan. He was ever a very wicked horse; he will be for rushing even in the plough. And it will quiet him a bit.'

'But the roan is a good horse. You made some new turnip drills in the old hayfield. "Hadoof," you said, "hi, whisht!" and the roan turned, or stepped to one side, or stopped, and was, I thought, very clever and obedient. I wonder how you can make the horses understand.'

'Oh, we just teach them. They just learn by degrees like the scholars in the schools. Whiles the roan will be good enough. But he was ever very nervous; since he was young he was a nervous beastie.'

'What a long time it takes to build a peat-stack!'

'Oh, I'll soon be through.'

Jessamine leaned her pretty head against the side of the shed. It was a moment of ease and forgetfulness, of genuine peace, and of that unmarked happiness of which we make too little, because it is only a level of quiet thoughts and gentle composed sensations. For the time she forgot even Colin and her passion; the thought of them may have sung a little gently at the bottom of her heart, but they were merely an intermingling of colour with that hueless woof of pleasant thinking and sensation. John's very unconsciousness of, and his aloofness from, her personal turmoil helped her to forget it; it passed for the moment into the comforting obscurity of things unconsidered, the outdoor life, with its health and large calm, soothing that too intense feeling of the personal, and setting it in truer relation to the rest of nature—a relation which few attain to even in moments, and none securely hold throughout a lifetime.

Out of such moments, if any activity arises, it will be sweet and generous. Jessamine felt a desire to be genuinely useful to the good and kindly folk among whom so long she had resided; the sense that she had power, *might* have power to help, was strong within her, and she found no reason why she should not use it. She forgot on what the power was founded and its accompanying humiliation—if, indeed, she were capable of feeling this last—and she forgot, too, her carefully preserved disguise. It was with a little grave considering air that she spoke next.

'The land is poor,' said she, 'and it would be better if you had the hill with the fir-wood on for pasture.'

'Oh yes! it is a poor bit of land,' said John tranquilly, 'and if we got the fir-wood from the laird for sheep pasture, it would be a very good thing for us, whatever. We could be keeping more sheep, and helping ourselves that way. Oh, it would be a very good thing if we had the deer-forest again. Whiles there was no deer-forest.'

John, without pausing in his work, glanced up at the long wide range of the hillsides, where the land, which might have sustained a village, was covered up from use by the mantle of fir-trees that formed part of the deer preserves for the amusement of one person. Then his glance fell again, and he fitted the peats together sturdily.

'When I go back,' said Jessamine composedly, 'I shall speak to the laird. I shall ask him to cut down the fir-woods and to give the deer-forest to the people for the sheep. And I shall ask him to open the old road and to mend it.'

When John heard her speak thus, he left off his work and stood still, leaning his arm over the peat-stack, and looking at the morsel of humanity before him. She proposed, it appeared, in her own small person, to bring about what was to him and his interests a sort of millennium; she proposed to do it by the simple process of asking the laird.

He had not the faintest idea of the commercial value of that bit of exquisiteness perched on the heap of his cut wood, her head against his newly-built shed. He was unaware that lovely women were bought and sold in the London marriage market very much as Circassian slaves are sold to a Turkish harem,[6] nor could he form any notion of the prices lairds and others might be willing to give for their possession—even for their momentary favour. The genial twinkle of his face—and it was always there when this pretty whiff hovered about him—broadened to a forbearing smile.

'That'll be a rare bit of work for a wee bonnie lassie to undertake,' said he. 'But you'll not be talking of going back yet a whilie, lassie? We'd be after missing you if you did.'

Jessamine started. What had she said? *Go back! Stay!* What terrible meaning was locked in either simple phrase to her! For her what alternative was there which was not hemmed in by terror?

She darted a wan, frightened look at the good quiet face before her, and slipped down softly from her seat.

---

6   "The Circassians were a tribally organized people of the Caucasus who lived under the Ottoman rule" (48). Toledano, Ehud R. "Shemsigul: A Circassian Slave." *Struggle and Survival in the Modern Middle East.* 2nd ed. Ed. Edmund Birke and David N. Yaghoubian. Berkeley: University of California Press, 2006. The Circassian woman slaves, in particular, "occupied a special position in domestic slavery, being legendary for their pale beauty and much sought after for the elite harems and the palace" (132). Reina Lewis. *Women, Travel and the Ottoman Harem: Rethinking Orientalism.* London: Tauris & Co. Ltd., 2004.

CHAPTER XXIII

THE evening cleared up more determinedly, though not with any settled tendency towards finer weather. The moon sailing high in the heavens wore a beautiful watery halo, and was followed and crossed and surrounded by a court of ever-changing, chalky, wraith-like clouds, the whole appearance of the sky being of hurry and preparation for a coming downfall. Every now and then they dispersed and drew back, leaving the tranquil disc, with its coloured ring, peaceful and lonely in a deeply-coloured, cold, clear night, over which again presently that noiseless tumult swept and hurried. In the upturned leaves of the birch-trees went the sound of a little showery breeze, and the winding paths showed in the silvery light as cold and slimy tracks through the fields or heather, while the sides of the barns and sheds exhibited also the same silvery shining wetness.

It must have been towards nine o'clock that the door at the back of the McKenzies' cottage softly opened, and Jessamine slid cautiously out into the night.

She had her rough gray skirt drawn high above her slender ankles, and her gray plaid twisted about her head and shoulders; save for the exquisite face lying like a carved bit of ivory between the folds, she might have been taken for any village lassie creeping out for a tryst with her lover.

Slipping cautiously round the corner of the house, Jessamine peered towards the kitchen window, and saw that a faint ray of light came from under the door and from the chink in the shutter, and lay upon the wet pools in the yard. The McKenzies, then, had not yet retired; but the house was closed up for the night, and there was no chance of disturbance. The gurgling sound of water in the gutters, the dropping from the eaves, and the cold swish of the trees, threw an indescribable feeling of discomfort around. Jessamine shivered; she half drew back, went forward a hesitating pace or two and paused, and then ran desperately on.

Her light step was indistinguishable amidst the various noises of the night.

There was some distance for her to traverse, and once across the road in the safe loneliness of the fields and open space, the girl sped recklessly onwards, uttering every now and then a sobbing incoherent word or sentence that seemed to throw itself out of her agitation without her will and purpose. For whither were her hurrying steps bent? They carried her not over the heather merely. Her spirit, as a skiff broken from the anchor, leapt and bounded forwards on uncharted seas, scudding before the winds and at their mercy. Each beat of her foot upon the ground thrust the familiar world behind her; the new, the irrevocable, the wild adventure lay before! An intoxicated sense of loose moorings, an exaltation of the mind at her own daring, the thousand vivid allurements of the moment, sped whirling through her brain. In one spot a complacent whisper hummed, an assurance that the future still lay in the future and that the possibility of safety was not yet snatched from her; the seductive could be dallied with, yet find her adamant in the last resort. Another corner concealed a reckless thing, which told itself that the cup was there, and that the lips should drink it every drop, nor pause till it was drained; and just there it was that the wild fiery throb kept burning, and stabbing, and thrilling her through and through.

Somewhere on the edges of all was a whisper, cold and gray as the dim shade that uttered it; this murmured of the consequence, and muttered warning. But who listens to a thing dreary and chill? That was the place of the anchor and the mooring from which she bounded away, and behind it was an old world in collapse, with faint thunders of falling cities growing less and less in her ears.

'I care for nothing! I care for nothing!' Some strange voice floated that out on the air, and suddenly she stood still. She looked up; the greatness of the night and the streaming rack with the moonlight leaping upon it, arrested her. With it some answering greatness, some womanly foreboding, rose within. She stared up to the sky, clenching her hands. But her eyes and cheeks were wet as the night itself. Again she sought wildly over the heavens, and again nothing like prayer would come—nothing save that sick revolt against the purposeless convention, which was all the goodness she had ever learned. She raised the clenched hands upwards and cried out again:

'I care for nothing! I care for nothing! There is no meaning anywhere—save *this*. What was I born for if this is wrong?'

Out of the air rose her cry, and, shrinking from the silence that followed, she darted on with renewed recklessness.

Macgillvray's land being reached, she walked more composedly, casting as she went searching, fearful glances about the bushes, and this because she became suddenly seized by an unreasoning fear that old Rorie would start out from them and claim her with his terrible courteous welcome. The barns—the new substantial buildings, so much handsomer than the cottage of their owner—were presently to be discerned, their slated roofs shining in the mingled wet and moonlight. By night they seemed larger than in the daytime, and the little path was swallowed up in their shadow. She paused confusedly, wondering which way to turn in order to reach the door in the front, and as she paused, she inconsequently blamed Colin that she was thus left to hesitation and permitted to wait alone.

The next moment, just as inconsequently, she shrank at his presumption, because she found herself encircled by his arms.

'I was waiting for you, lassie mine, for a whole long hour,' came the warm rich voice through the chill night-air. 'Many a weary time have I stepped over the bit field to the road, and looked and waited. There will be a hunger in my heart indeed, for it will be a night and a day since I was seeing you. And your promise made the time seem longer.'

Jessamine sank against his breast suddenly still; she heard over and over again the echoes of his voice. Everything was done, then? There was no more any struggle left, neither decision nor hesitation, but mere drifting and helplessness. The thunders, and voices, and hurry in her mind were at an end. Silence came with his touch. She slightly shivered.

'Take me to the barn,' she murmured.

In a moment he had lifted her in his arms like a child.

'It'll be wet for your wee bit feet, lassie. And oh, my lo'e, I canna draw thee close enough.'

She clung about his neck stiller than ever. Thought, anxiety, terror, were annihilated. There was nothing left in all the world but *this*. The moment! the moment!—that was all. No peace was ever more complete.

'A nicht and a day,' he murmured, with his lips against her cheek as he walked.

'Only so long?' the sweet mouth breathed back in the lowest whisper—so low a whisper that the words seemed to slide from her tongue to his ear without the medium of sound, and with no more will than is thrown into a sigh.

'And long enough, my do'e, my wife!'

'Only so long,' stole the tiny musical murmur again. 'I thought it was a week—a month.'

The phrase uttered, her eyes closed softly. Was ever love-making sweet as this? He strained her to his heart with such an upleap of wonder and of thankfulness that utterance overflowed into silence and was lost.

Treading gently, strongly, and slowly, so that the tender moment might not be overpast too soon, he brought her silently at last within the shelter of the barn.

'Set me down,' she whispered when she felt the dry rafters over her and the warm air about her.

In her heart was no other feeling than that of a helpless sliding, strange, delicious, fatal—and full, full of that peace.

There was a homely smell of hay and seed—a mild agricultural odour—and from somewhere beyond a partition came the soft, wholesome breathing of cows.

Instead of obeying her, Colin seated himself upon an upturned wooden box which he had prepared for the purpose, and drew her to his knee. A single lantern swung from the roof, sending a meagre though steady light, which disclosed the middle part of the barn-floor carefully cleared and brushed by Colin; in the centre was the improvised seat, with a rug thrown upon it; some gleamings from polished metal showed the harness hanging in the dark corners, into which also various simple agricultural implements were pushed; and the sides of the barn were decorated with scythes, hay-forks, bunches of herbs, and repositories for seed-stock, save one side, which was a bare partition with apertures, whence came the quiet rustle and the warm breaths of cattle. Above all, the lantern's steady ray illumined the group in the centre—the woman lying still as death in the arms of the man, her face with closed eyes against his breast, while his head leaned down to touch hers.

For full a quarter of an hour, speechless and motionless, the two remained locked in an emotion apparently as simple, primitive, and undivided, as though Time had run back for them and borne them to the age of Paradise.

In truth, Jessamine was in a half-fainting condition, will and thought obliterated in the strong reaction after struggle, of which, indeed, the sole survival was a faint surmise—a surmise indefinitely circled by that peace of acquiescence. She lay with her face, like a bit of exquisite carved ivory, against his rough coat, her long black lashes resting on her cheeks.

Colin's face, with its deep conscious life, presented to hers as strong a contrast as it is possible to conceive. He had spent the interval between the last meeting and this in a way of his own, and the mark of it remained with him. He leaned above that half-fainting, acquiescent feminine frailty upon his breast with a look of reverence, the impassioned tenderness of his eyes undivorced from the strong quiet curve of the restrained lips and delicately harmonizing with that, and the thrill of his arms over their burden subordinated to the slow, massive and accumulated power of his will and conscience. Thus, within this seemingly mutual trance of emotion, difference was already at its work, the woman slipping darkly and helplessly towards some moral abyss, and he with his will anchored, as it were, to the stars.

The stirring of a heifer beyond the wooden wall, and a sudden prolonged and plaintive low, aroused the pair from their impassioned stillness, and set the tongue to its restless work of speech.

Colin had his thoughts to impart, and these had been lashed to unwonted speed by the sweet confession which had fallen from Jessamine in the moment that he raised her in his arms.

'Lassie mine!' he murmured at last.

The lids at which he looked longingly and reverently, raised themselves suddenly to a wide-open gaze of suspense that startled him. He looked into them until his heart almost swooned with bliss and pain.

'We need not be waiting long, my do'e,' he whispered—'not long.'

His utterance was slow, unwilling, and bare, because of the mighty restrained emotion behind.

The dark unfathomable eyes stared at him, the very breath suspended, and the heart almost ceasing to beat.

What could he say more? Where seek for and hit upon true expression amongst so much? He failed to discover fitting words at all.

'I'll be after knocking up the wee bit chamber for you,' he murmured; 'there's nothing money will buy but I'll get it for you, lassie!' he continued, impulses of extravagance shooting across his canny Scotch thriftfulness.

At this she made a movement. She laid her hand on his coat, and pulled herself to a more upright position—still with that wild suspended gaze. It shook more words from him.

'You'll be telling John McKenzie, my own sweet lo'e?' he said. 'And we'll be looking for the wedding bells before the month is out. Thank God,' he added in an eager whisper, 'I'm a solid man, and there's naething need keep us twain waiting and apart. I'll fix it up, Jessie, this month. We'll go straight on, my lassie, like the lightning. Love,' said he, 'canna be waiting too long—too long.'

But to this he earned no response. Had all the love been breathed out in that one sweet whisper, whose echoes still stirred live and warm in his heart?

She sat straight up now, looking into his face—his face all tremulous with tenderness and reverent devotion—and she placed one hand on his shoulder, while the other lay limp in her lap.

'You'll not be saying me nay,' he pleaded. 'Lassie, I canna wait. My heart's pulled in two with loving when I'm my lane. I cannot be my lane, sweet Jessie, any more. I'm needing you snug in my life, and no more good-byes nor good-morrows. I will never be knowing what love was before. It is,' said he, trembling a little, and looking away from her and up to the rafters where a dove or two sat, 'a great—great matter.'

Whereupon, at that, suddenly she slid from his knee, and stood upright on the floor beside him. He rose too, and came close to her, and, impatient of distance, drew her again unresistingly within his arms. She leaned against him, but still she did not speak.

'I cannot fetch it into my mind,' he continued, 'that I'm deserving of this great gift, whatever. But I'm thanking the Lord indeed. Seems like the fiery chariot of Elijah that went by.'[1]

He looked away from her again, and raised his hand, moving it gently in the air, and seemed bereft of further speech in wonder.

'Colin!'

The tone was scarcely natural. It was thin as well as low.

'Oh, my wee do'e! What your voice is to me,' he murmured, overjoyed at hearing it; 'tell me you'll be saying "Yes" to your own man. Tell me you'll be coming to me—drawing into my wee bit housie like the sunshine that you are; that you'll be resting there, and making it summer, wunther and all.'

'Colin!'

'My lassie?'

'Don't—don't say that! Not about the chariot of fire.'

'Why not, lassie mine? I'm fair whirled away into a heaven of my own—caught up and carried. I'm lifted up from earth.'

'Oh no, Colin—oh no! Not that—*not* that.'

The voice wailed, with helpless tears in it. The engrossed tenderness of Colin's face changed a little to surprise.

'I'll not be saying ae thing that my lassie will not be liking,' said he briefly.

'I don't like it!' gasped Jessamine, with her hand against her throat; 'it—it—*frightens* me.'

'It will just be what I was feeling. But I'll be saying it no more.'

The girl stood clutching the lapel of his coat, and staring at him speechlessly. The echoes of his silver tongue pierced her ear and touched her heart; his face and his eyes overcame her. But all around and about this fair image of manly love beat chaotic miseries, and the religious fervour of his wooing and his simple conscientious aims drove her cruelly back upon them, and divided him and her, and froze up that acquiescent glow within her heart of hearts into a nipping grief. What was the simple natural issue to him was just the clear impossible to her.

---

1 The story of Elijah and the chariot in the New Testament is as follows: "And it came to pass, as they [Elisha and Elijah] still went on, and talked, that, behold, *there appeared* a chariot of fire, and horses of fire, and parted them both asunder; and Elijah went up by a whirlwind into heaven" (2 Kings: 11).

Not yet could she fathom or dare to realise the abyss between them. But the feeling of it crept near already, cold and cruel as death.

'Colin,' she began again, her voice hoarse with a fear beyond words.

'Jessie?' he responded.

And then he looked at her gravely, with more attentive interest and scrutiny—a scrutiny which was not so much blinded by his own emotion as before.

The terror and entreaty in her eyes began forthwith to become apparent to him. His head leaned forward a little, and with a puzzled look he gazed into them.

As for those eyes of hers, they searched everywhere over his face and over his whole nature, in a wild and desperate appeal. Just such an appeal had she made to the dumb mythologies of all times—just such an entreaty against the laws of life and fate, that crushed and threatened her.

Her own feeling became darker to herself and more overwhelming; the intoxication was past; each thought was an abyss, each breath a slip downwards. She shrank in ignorant terror from herself and in shocked amazement from her remembered thoughts; but more than all she shrank from the religious fervour of his wooing, from the austere tenderness which made so terrible a claim upon her, and up to the level of which she knew it was impossible for her to rise. How should he see that every word conjured up images of distaste and unbearable hardness—that behind the face and eyes, to which her gaze might have clung with supreme and satisfied love, hovered, to her mind, an austerity that terrified? All the best gifts he had to offer seemed to her as fetters and a dungeon. Her love had the quality of self-abandonment, but higher than that it could not rise. Shame she would have accepted, but noble endurance was, as yet, beyond her.

So the pair of human souls, chained together solely by passion, divided by everything that remained, gazed into each other's eyes, silent because the darkness and the separation were invincible. Yet some reflection from the terrified phantoms that stole up and down the edges of Jessamine's mind, and did duty for thinking, crept into the mirror of her eyes, and suddenly into the midst of them Colin's quick words were interpolated.

'I mean fair by you, lassie!' he cried.

The tone was anxious, hurried—even *business-like*. Before it, the sick heart of the girl swooned afresh with a wound.

The contract—the contract! How should the honest, fair-dealing man dream that the terms of the bargain are not for ever the main thing in the heart of the impassioned woman?

To his quick, short sentence she offered no reply save a gasp. She continued to stare up in his face as a dumb child might to a mistaken parent, as a lamb to the slaughterer, as human nature to an irresponsive God. The silent searching fear of her face, the desperation of her mute appeal, moved the man beyond expression. It drove him from love-making to asseveration. A spirit as of the ancient Covenanters[2] wakened in him—a remorseless, puritantic, self-sacrificing austerity.

'Woman!' cried he sternly, 'as I live I'm meaning fair by you.'

Whereat, hearing the sternness of his voice, her own wild daring tender love fled, and sank away somewhere out of sight abashed and horrified. The rose in her heart froze in a moment. The man—her own lover—had detected it, perhaps, seen it—*and reproached her!* She was wrong then—bad in *his* eyes?

Ah, *there* was something more awful than Society's tongue-wagging!

For Love's sake, leaping in her own experience over some abyss—the nature of which she but faintly comprehended—she had alighted at the bottom, only to meet with the furies of disdain!

Chaotic sounds rang in her head and ears. She uttered a broken cry, and threw herself upon his breast, grasping his coat with her hands, and sobbing in an emotion as incomprehensible to him as it appeared to be inconsolable. No penitent but disgraced wife could have felt an anguish more acute than did Jessamine as she lay there. Colin held her firmly, quietly, concerned now chiefly, in the beneficent habit which he extended to every living thing, to still and soothe this emotion away. When he believed it to be subsiding, his own tenderness broke out again in the only speech that he knew of which might be likely to touch and heal this fear, and draw her again within a circle of reassurance.

'Why do you greet, lass?' he murmured with unutterable gentleness; 'why will you not be speaking? You understand me, Jessie, bonnie bird? You will be trusting me, your Colin? I mean fair by you—honest as a man can mean. What do you fear, my lo'e—my do'e? Wee, wee wife of mine!'

He spoke with difficulty, his bronzed strong throat quivering with tenderness and sympathy, and his heart heaving with the great faithful tumult of his passion. He passed his hand over and over her dark hair in curious

---

2   Covenanters were Scottish Presbyterians who first rebelled against the Roman Catholic Church in the 16th century and then the monarchy in the 17th century in order to keep their religion as the sole religion of Scotland. The Covenanters were relentless in their insistence that Presbyterianism be the only Scottish religion; wars were fought and bloody battles waged in order for their beliefs to be won. In 1790 the Presbyterian religion was declared to be the official Church of Scotland; it remains so today.

worshipful delight, and his thinking was a single unmingled vow of devotion, protection, and plighted troth. It was the highest he could conceive of love's surrender—for Colin, too, had prized his freedom—and he held it a cheap price indeed.

She kissed his muscular sunburnt hand every time it neared her lips, and—shuddered at his words.

That shudder he felt, and he marvelled the more. His slow mind, quickened by love, moved from all its well-anchored points, and sought far and wide over all his knowledge and experience for some solution to the trouble that shook her, and his tongue gathered up into unwonted words the tender distresses of his heart.

'Jessie, my lass,' said he in a firmer, graver tone, through which ran a hint of reproach, 'you must be leaning on me, trusting me. Colin,' he added, 'would never shame you.'

Whereat the slight figure trembled like a leaf, and the head drooped like a withered flower. She had abandoned herself and all her preconceived ideas to meet with blank rejection, and cold reproof.

'Gude save us!' cried the man in intense agitation; 'I will be always holding you high. You will never need be fearing, nor flying off, nor trembling like a shy, frightened bird. The angels above——' His voice choked and broke. 'It will be like that I am thinking of you, Jessie. My wife—*my wife!*'

Words could not express his uttermost devotion and reverence; speech altogether failed him. He lifted his hand and his eyes helplessly to the rafters, where the white gleam of the sleeping doves arrested him with a sense of harmony that answered for him.

But then the half-swooning girl, lashed by his words as by scorpions, terrified, ignorant, withered by shame, her very passion flying from her like a wild strayed thing from some immeasurable prairie-land of freedom, back whence it came, slipped from his arms, and tumbled suddenly to the ground at his feet, and lay before him in an abashed heap of tingling dismay.

Colin, startled beyond expression, his Scotch slowness and undemonstrativeness hampering him in the one brief second that was left, drew back a step before he stooped to raise his fallen burden. Did he for the first time apprehend something foreign, incompatible, strange?

Into that second of time rushed all the dividing legions that come between human souls.

When he stooped towards it, the form which had lain like a dead thing leapt to its feet ere he had touched it, and darted from him to the half-open door, and thence out into the night.

Colin, like a man amazed, hesitated for another brief second, and then rushed to the entrance, sending his voice after her in a mighty cry of tender entreaty.

But the night itself was cruel. Strangling clouds hung over the moon, and in the north the hurrying rack had sullenly coalesced, and from thence, blown by the risen wind, a blinding furious shower came and beat across his eyes.

He stood peering and calling, and waving his arms like one distraught. Then he plunged over the heather in a direction different from the one her winged feet had taken. And at length, struck by a sudden faintness of despair, he fell face downwards on the soaking ground of his own field.

Like a wraith she had vanished from his life.

END OF VOLUME II

PART II

CHAPTER I[1]

TEN years had passed away.

The beautiful month of May was in its zenith, and the parks of London were gay with flowers; jonquils and tulips were being sold in the streets, and the shop-windows of the great thoroughfares vied with each other in the display of feminine fashions for spring attire, and the other knick-knacks of tortured ingenuity which the hand of competition throws out to catch the eye of extravagance.

The main business of the hour was so to organize the interplay between permanent greed or neediness, and chance spendthrift desires, that the fickle stream of the latter might be caught and utilized, as by a mill-wheel, before it dashed onwards on its aimless play.

It was May, and it was night. 'Everybody' was in town; not to be in town argued one, in fashionable circles, as a country-cousin and an ineffectual non-entity. In the West-End, the atmosphere was charged with social and political intrigue, with intellectual strain, with all the pressure and confusion of a great world bent on struggling onwards, in pursuit of its own glittering, noisy aims.

The streets and squares were beautiful with their regular setting of the topaz-like gas-lamps or the imprisoned moons of electric light; with the moving stabs of colour in passing trams and other vehicles; with the suspended glows at tavern or theatre doors, in chemists' shops, night-abandoned road-mending, or other opportunities and tricks of illumination.

Fashion was, for the most part, in the theatres or concert-halls, or in the great drawing-rooms of favoured houses, or at least on its way to them within the safe protection of closed carriages, glimpses of the brilliantly-dressed, glittering, presumably happy persons flashing out through the windows as they

---

1   In the three volume edition of this novel, the third volume begins with "CHAPTER I" and not "CHAPTER XXIV" as one might expect. The final volume of the three-decker edition of the novel runs from "CHAPTER I" to "CHAPTER VIII." This is true also for the 5th one-volume edition of the novel. This is not true, however, of the American edition, which continues the chapter numbers with "CHAPTER XXIV." To be true to the reprint of this edition, I have chosen to follow the chapter numbers of the first through fifth editions, all published in 1894.

rolled by. The footpaths of the street were left, for the most part, to passengers of another kind. And in the labyrinth-like quarters that lie huddled and clustering behind and near the great thoroughfares, out streamed permanent London to its street-chaffering,[2] its leisured hour, its genial gossip, its despair, conspiracy, or crime.

It was an hour when the great city in all its parts is more restlessly awake, and in some more evilly active, than at any other time—an hour for the lover of the sensation of things to be out and moving, feeling beneath his feet the 'pavement of a great city,' or realising from the top of a tram-car the stir and pulsation, and the intoxicating sense of a tumultuous life and fateful destiny.

Being night, it was also the time when those whose hearts and brains are impressed by the deep and tragical reality of suffering existence which underlies the noisy and ambitious struggle above, become in their consciousness clearer as to the causes of things; more convinced as to the distinction between shadow and substance; more acutely discriminative between the barrenness of party aims and the import of those anxious demands which knock periodically and constantly at the doors of the nation, the hunger of starved souls and bodies in their ominous reiteration.

Invincible faith, rather than despair, is the characteristic of onlookers and thinkers such as these, the heart of patience and hope being retained amidst the central glow of pity and indignation which keeps their energy in the cause of the people at a white heat. To them the suffering outcry, and the more piteous dumb appeal of the oppressed, contain within themselves their own irrefutable reply. The unanswerable demonstration of any evil, endured by the inmate of a civilized state, is a matter which may wait long, but which draws its conclusion inevitably after it. Not the brilliant talent or the particular gift, but the ascertained need of the weakest and most broken of the children of Fate, is the fulcrum which determines how and in what direction the national will shall move; and the leaving behind, or the dropping out from social advantages and modern ease, of many—of some, of even a few—is the signal for the readjustment of national contrivances until these laggards in the race be drawn up abreast with average progress, and be reinstated in that place in the world to which chronologically they are born. For within the average mass lies the strength and fate of the nation, and the exceptional success of advanced skirmishers towards progress is immaterial, unless it be utilized in bearing forward that desolated and mournful fringe which drags down the average, by existing beneath it in the evil social conditions of fifty or a hundred years ago.

---

2   Street-chaffering: Literally "to chat idly" on the street (*Webster's* 234).

On such a May night a great Minister gave a great entertainment, and everybody who was anybody was there. It was a pure and beautiful evening, starlight and mild, and the coachmen, driving up their precious freight to the handsome house in the handsome square, blessed themselves in that they had not to sit there under a blinding rain or soaking fog. The stream of carriages was long and imposing; it obstructed the road for some distance beyond the square, but the cause was respectable and out of the arm of the law. So one by one, and inch by inch, they crept along until, after patience and manœuvring, aided by the dexterity of the police, each one deposited its burden beneath an awning amidst the breathless and solemn silence of an awe-struck crowd, who watched the guests advance up the crimson-laid steps and vanish into the brilliant hall above.

This silence and awe produced an effect as of a religious ceremony, which touched the imagination of a sharp-faced street-child of some education.

'Oh my!' came the shrill little voice through the sweet night-air; 'it's just like the C'lestial City, and the pilgrums, and the haingels wot took them in at the gaites—wot teacher told me on!'[3]

A burly policeman, with some sense of incongruity in the allusion, and feeling that it might be distasteful to parties concerned, here took the prattling little one by the ear and led it gesticulating away.

At that moment a hansom crept up—a common, vulgar hansom in the middle of the coroneted carriages!—and out of it popped a small shriveled, deformed gentleman, with an ugly wedge-like face and great burning eyes. He ran up the steps, looking as he did so like a curious beetle, and the crowd burst out into a hearty, irrepressible laugh.

An agreeable sense of pleasure suffused itself over the heart of the little gentleman at finding himself the innocent occasion of momentary mirth amongst the poverty-stricken gathering outside.

Mr. Carteret, when he found himself well within his sumptuous surroundings, committed at least three solecisms in tranquil unconsciousness before he reached the opening chamber of a splendid suite of reception-rooms. Near the entrance to this first apartment stood the host and hostess, receiving, with mechanical cordiality, the constant stream of arrivals who advanced, exchanged a few words of greeting, and were then carried onwards by the press into the apartments beyond.

Carteret, as surprised to find himself present as others were to see him, as whimsically conscious of incongruity in his person as any observer could

---

3   This is a reference to John Bunyan's 1678 Christian allegory, *The Pilgrim's Progress from this World to That Which is to Come.*

be, followed the loud herald of his own name into the dazzling scene, and
confronted his hostess with a short bow and swift, sarcastic, silent smile. The
high-born lady extended the momentary patronage of her graceful recognition to the man of genius; his host said a few apt and cordial words; and
Carteret— singular little blot upon a scene so gay—passed onwards with the
rest.

There were four reception-rooms opening one out of the other. The first
was upholstered in a faint yellow hue, which admirably suited the pale, dark
colouring of the Minister's wife. And this room was lavishly decked with the
most *recherché* and expensive kind of cream narcissus having the long golden
centre bell. The fireplace, the mantelpiece, the lamp-brackets (the myriad
lights being also shaded in faint yellow), and every available receptacle, were
heaped and covered with these delicate, highly-cultivated blossoms, each one
a miracle of perfection and beauty.

From this fairy-like scene the guest passed on to an apartment upholstered in æsthetic green and white, and decked with maiden-hair and Gloire
de Dijon roses in beautiful, lavish masses.[4]

The next reception-room was of well-toned tints, both enriched and softened by a show of delicate fantastic orchids, each one a wonder in itself, and
so disposed that the long, trailing blooms seemed fancifully etched upon the
bronze-coloured wall beyond.

And last, there was a large brilliant apartment in pink, or in some faint,
indescribable shade of that colour, the vulgar milkmaid hue being toned
down to something exquisite which could hardly tolerate its low-born name.
And this room was decked with gently-perfumed and marvellously-tinted
azalea blooms.

It was a scene of such enchanting beauty and taste that only the extremely
well-bred and *blasé* managed to pass through it without exclamation or remark, and with a mere determination to outdo the effect when their turn for
an entertainment came about.

Carteret, poor little blot, wandered—or, rather, was brushed on—
through the exquisite scene, his head thrust forward, his brows puckered, his
restless eyes searching and noting, his under lip pushed out, grimacing from
habit, and (again from lonely habit) unconscious and lost from himself, but
gathering up all that he saw and heard with his swift observant faculty.

People saw and noticed him, of course. Beautiful creatures—and under

---

4 Maiden-hair are delicate ferns. The Glorie de Dijon rose was introduced to England
in 1851 by Henri Jacatot (1799–1883), a florist who lived in Dijon, France. The colors of the rose are apricot, pink and cream.

the influence of the lights and the colour plain women appeared good-look-ing, and good-looking women beautiful, and beautiful women exquisite, ethereal angels, while everybody lost a decade from their age—beautiful crea-tures remarked Carteret as they passed; the silken and lace billows of their trains swept over his legs and knees as the wearers undulated onwards, and some of them glanced down on him with a faint amazement, and back again, as from something unpleasant and startling.

Men went past him whose shoulders obscured him; he noted broad backs and thick necks, with tight-cropped polls; gentlemanly, cultivated backs; weak, slanting backs, with irritable shoulders, and long-stretched necks, and unmanageable hair carefully distributed over bald heads; scholarly, university-men backs, slightly bent—every kind of back, and neck, and headpiece.

'Know lots of these faces,' muttered Carteret to himself. 'Punch—"Essence of Parliament."'[5]

In process of time—it took quite an hour—Carteret, with his observant eyes, had arrived at the last apartment—at the room, that is, decked with azaleas. From this there was a wide egress into an open space above the main staircase. The azalea-room appeared to be the favourite, partly because people were arrested in it by the fact that the egress, though wide, necessarily nar-rowed the stream, and partly because it really was the most beautiful portion of the scene. Carteret, who was already getting bored and depressed, had contemplated passing out through this egress, which he had detected from a distance, and afterwards slipping away home.

He paused at last near a lounge, constructed to hold two persons in a pleasant tête-à-tête.[6] Looking towards the outlet, he found that it was blocked by silks and satins, dress-coats, and their wearers. His frail body was too much fatigued for him to attempt the standing, waiting, and dexterous pushing necessary before he could get out; so he sank down on the lounge, took out his handkerchief to mop his face, and resigned himself. Two young married ladies came presently and stood in front of him, talking together in calm oblivion of, or indifference to, the fact that so insignificant a person as this small, beetle-like man could overhear every word they uttered.

'There she is!' exclaimed one lady to the other.

---

5   Punch, or The London Charivari was a famous British weekly journal that began in 1841 and ended its run in 1992. Punch was notorious for its biting humor; nothing was sacred to Punch writers, including many parodies written about the New Woman during the 1880s and 1890s. "Essence of Parliament" was a weekly editorial (humor-ous, of course), and/or cartoon that made observational and detailed descriptions about parliamentary actions, decisions and behavior.

6   Tête-à-tête: Close "conversation" (Larousse 521).

They turned their heads, and stretched their necks, and looked keenly in a particular direction. The tone in which the three words were uttered was noticeable; evidently a show person of some kind was approaching. Carteret got up, stood upon a footstool, and looked too.

He caught a glimpse of a tall and slender figure, of a magnificent dress, a perfect coiffure, glittering jewels, and an oval cheek.

Then the crowd closed over the form; Carteret got off his footstool and sat down again.

'It is quite too sad how she goes off!' said the first lady, in that make-believe sympathetic tone which barely smothers self-congratulations.

'She manages to be very, very beautiful still,' returned the second in rather a longing voice.

'Thirty, if she's a day, I suppose!' said Mrs. Four-and-twenty disdainfully.

'Well, yes! But at thirty a handsome woman is handsomer still,' returned No. 2 a little anxiously. 'There is *esprit,* experience, a *je ne sais quoi* that younger women miss. It isn't her age.'[7]

'Oh, I am aware she poses for originality as well! One has to do so much nowadays to be anything.' The speaker sighed. 'It is all wear and tear. The demands on one's resources are continual.'

'All the pewter gilded and rubbed up to look like gold, and everything set out upon the counter as in any trumpery shop!' said No. 2 with unexpected asperity.

'Well, I don't know that I should care to be as severe upon her as that!' returned the first dexterously, taking refuge from the hit in a fold of the garment of Charity.

No. 2 coloured slightly and was silent.

'What, now, is the special peculiarity you referred to?' asked the first lady, in a voice warmer for the sense of momentary victory.

'I think I was alluding to the oddness of her charities. You are aware, I suppose, that she takes a particular interest in women who—*are no better than they should be,*'[8] replied the second in a lowered voice.

'Dear me!' Is *that* all?' returned the first in an indifferent tone. 'But it is the fashion to take up that sort of person now. It makes such splendid platform material.'

'Oh yes! But it is not in the way. She does not exactly *take them up.* She

---

7   *Esprit:* This is literally "mind" in French (*Larousse* 203). The observation here suggests that Jessamine possesses her own mind and thoughts. *Je ne sais quoi* means that Jessamine has a certain something that other women do not.

8   The reference here is to prostitutes.

sympathizes with them.'

'Openly?'

'Well, of course!'

'You call that *charity?*'

'I did.'

The back of the first lady expressed, from Carteret's point of view, a rigid sense of her own virtue; the ear and cheek and neck of the second, a sense of confusion. No. 2 was no match for No. 1; she had a habit of blushing. Women over fifty have been known to retain the trick, but they are not usually social successes. It was No. 1 who hardily returned to the topic.

'How does she exhibit this—*sympathy?*'

'By never assuming any superiority, and by holding out a friendly, helping hand where she can. I like her face. I rather like her odd ways. She is so inoffensive and gentle—*and strange.*'

'H'm! Look at all the men trooping after her!'

'Oh, well, of course! She is a great society belle—almost historic.'

'Nothing, I suppose, of a scandal in her own life?'

'I assure you—*no.* There have been odd freaks, but no scandal whatever. She is considered exemplary—a perfect model as——'

At that moment the on-coming stream moved up so determinedly that the speakers were gently brushed aside, and Carteret lost the end of the sentence. He remained seated as before, and was presently glad to observe that the lady who had formed the subject of so engrossing a conversation neared the spot, and stood for a moment in front of him, exactly as the late speakers had done.

Carteret looked at her attentively—at so much of her, that is, as he could see. To him she presented an appearance made up of soft colour, lace, mystery, sweet odour, flowers, and jewels. There would have been nothing more than that for him, had it not been for the words which he had overheard; she would have been a shining something outside his ken and his world—something with which he had better not trouble himself, had it not been for these. As it was, he surmised the human being beneath the ethereal wrappings, and peered somewhat curiously at the slender, graceful neck, with its splendid diamond necklet, and the irrepressible small rings of dark hair which would escape from the jeweled pins to prettily intrude themselves upon it.

Presently she moved a little.

'Let me sit down,' said she, in the softest and most weary voice which Carteret had ever heard.

She addressed herself to the man by whose side she had advanced into the azalea chamber. Carteret sprang up and moved aside, and the dark lady seated herself, submitting as she did so patiently to a certain fussy assiduity from her companion, who, however, immediately left her—almost, Carteret thought, with an air of relief.

It was then that the strange thing happened to Carteret. He had relinquished the idea of escaping, and stood by the lounge looking down on her. He was vaguely conscious of a buzzing pressure of men around and near him—as bees press round a honey-laden flower—and he himself was lost in the quiet, almost religious, contemplation of the beautiful face near him. It was over-wearied and too languid, but beautiful—how beautiful! Suddenly—he could scarcely say how it happened—he felt that she looked at him and had noted his appearance. That was followed by a faint though unmistakable sign—he hardly knew how to characterize it—that she wished him to take the seat by her side.

Carteret placed himself on the lounge.

He had no scruple in watching her. Was not she there to be watched? Indeed, her attraction was so great that he was not able to prevent himself from doing it. She leaned back in an attitude of indifference, her long lashes on her cheek, and her hands idly holding her fan. It was doubtful whether she saw the azaleas, whether she saw anything of her surroundings. Her beauty attracted more and more of the passing people; they made excuses to pause and look at her. Carteret became convinced that everyone knew her or recognised her; her name, he perceived, was whispered from tongue to tongue, though he did not catch it. To all this, to all the stir which her appearance and presence excited, she seemed, however, blind or indifferent. The deepest respect was in everyone's bearing, but some there were who envied Carteret his seat.

Carteret remarked this; but he refused to budge. Inconceivable, incomprehensible though it was, he was convinced that he had received an invitation to seat himself by her side. While others buzzed and paused impatiently around, held off by the invisible barriers a woman knows how to raise, he was permitted to remain snugly beside her, a delicate fold of her drapery intruding over his knee—he, the odd little blot on the brilliant scene.

Men began to cast angry glances at him; but Carteret sat on. He sat there speechless, his arms folded together over his bent figure, his eyes fixed on a definite spot in the leg of the trouser of the man in front of him, and his under lip shot out. The sarcasm of his face, the crumpled figure with its stubborn pose, held them all at arm's length as effectually as did the cold graces of the lady.

'Beauty and the Beast,'[9] murmured over his head a faultlessly attired wag, with more shirt-front than brains.

At that moment a hand was laid on his shoulder, and he raised his head to find leaning over him the genial face of the first friend he had met that evening—the friend to whose good offices he owed his introduction to the scene. Carteret's mouth puckered good-naturedly.

'Lucky dog!' whispered the friend.

His eyes glanced across to the beautiful woman and laughed back at the little man.

'Just so,' said Carteret.

'Won't you come out of this and have a chat?'

'No.'

'Well, I can't say I wonder. By the way, old man, have you seen Cornerstone lately?'

'Cornerstone!' repeated Carteret. 'Have I seen Cornerstone? Why don't you ask me if I've eaten and drunk and slept and clothed myself lately?'

'I see. All right, old fellow! Don't go up in a balloon! We're all mortal! But just tell him I've got the new microscope I spoke of, and ask him to drop in and look at it. And, Carteret——'

'Well?'

'Just come out of this and have a chat. There is something particular I wish to speak of.'

'I don't budge.'

The friend laughed, and passed on.

Then Carteret started again. A hand was laid on his arm from the other side.

'Sir, I beg your pardon!'

Turning quickly, he found the most perfectly beautiful face he had ever seen anxiously bending towards him. The eyes were remarkable—even star-tling. Wide open as they were now, and dark as night, they appeared to him to be dashed by an incomprehensible and haunting look of horror. So deep were the pupils, so marvellously transfixing in their look of human entreaty and fear, that Carteret gazed back at them for several perceptible seconds silently.

'You mentioned—I thought—you mentioned a name?'

'Yes; I mentioned the name Cornerstone. I spoke of my friend Dr.

---

9 *Beauty and the Beast* is a fairy tale originally written in French by Madame Le Prince de Beaumont in 1756. The English translation was published in 1761. Jack Zipes. *Fairy Tale as Myth*. Lexington: The University Press of Kentucky, 1994.

Cornerstone,' replied Carteret, attuning his voice to unaccustomed softness.

'Is he living? Is he well? Do you see him?'

'He is living and well, and I see him every day of my life.'

'Then you will give him a message?'

'Willingly.'

'Sir, I *trust* you. I do not know who you are, but I trust you—*not to forget.*'

'I will not forget.'

At that moment a shadow fell upon them. The beautiful woman felt it, and shivered before she looked up. Carteret, shrinking instinctively, also raised his head. He had heard the speech before he saw the man.

'I'm going directly, don't you know,' said a voice whose minutest tone was saturated with mental disease and feebleness. 'Take my wife home, don't you know.'

The speaker bent over the sofa, disclosing to Carteret a tall head with retreating forehead, bald at the temples, the hair limp, fair, and thin, the nose small, narrow, and mean, the eyes old, and the lips wandering and feeble. He put out his hand, and took hold of that of the beautiful woman. Carteret expected her to wince.

Instead of that her hand rested quietly in his, and her face was attentive and no more.

'Don't you think you've had enough of it? Shan't you be tired? I'm deuced sick of the thing myself. Do you want to stop, or will you come?'

There was a note of anxiety in his appeal.

'I will come.'

Her voice was a little dazed, and her eyes, still with the strange look in them, wandered back to Carteret.

'Well, then, come now,' returned the husband querulously.

She rose, dropped her handkerchief, and, as Carteret stooped to pick it up, stooped also, and contrived to whisper in a wild, hurried voice these words:

'Tell him—I entreat you not to forget—tell him to come—beseech him—pray him to come!'

Then she took the arm of her husband ungrudgingly, and they turned away together quietly, amicably, as any other united pair might do.

Carteret rose and followed them. She had neglected to give him her name, and it was necessary that he should know it. He watched narrowly to see if she would shrink, would snatch her hand away, or whether either of the pair would exhibit signs of that connubial impatience which is, of all earthly experiences, the bitterest and most hateful. Nothing of the kind. The ill-assorted couple kept as close together when no one was watching as when they were being observed, and it was to her husband she turned, when the costly wrap was to be hung about her shoulders.

Whatever this hidden tragedy might be, it had elements in it not of the common sordid kind.

As the pair stood waiting in the hall, surrounded by footmen and the bustle of departing guests, Carteret fancied that a certain mysterious isolation marked them out, discriminated, and united them—as some pairs have been united in the imagination of all time—within the circle of the peculiarly damned.

Presently a splendid menial came forward and announced: 'Lady Heriot's carriage stops the way!'

And then the pair moved forward together, and together vanished.

CHAPTER II

DR. CORNERSTONE had moved his place of residence. He had left Bloomsbury, and taken a house in the district of West St. Pancras, not far from Regent's Park. Here he could give his wife and children the advantage of a beautiful open space, green trees, and some picturesqueness, and yet not be too far from the centre of things, that being, in his eyes, the East-End.[1]

In West St. Pancras, close to, and yet isolated from, the main thoroughfares, with their noise and traffic, one comes on the unexpected oasis of a quiet street, of a little nest of pleasant detached houses, each with its own bright garden.

In this street, Dr. Cornerstone had settled himself with his wife and children. He had selected it because the atmosphere was bright and healthy, and this he knew to be essential to proper development and happy existence.

Dr. Cornerstone had no mind to embrace in his own person, and in those nearest to him, the misery from which he daily saw others suffering. He preferred to maintain a high though simple standard of comfort, and he would no more have attempted to improve and assist a suffering world by adopting in his own person any portion of the scandalous poverty and degradation inflicted upon the struggling hordes of the workers, than he would have tried to save it by assuming the wicked luxury and degradation of the superfluous rich. He regarded it as his first duty—as it is, indeed, that of every responsible citizen—to keep himself, and those whose well-being depended upon him, sane in body and mind; the pursuit of wholeness was the aim by which he determined his daily personal conduct. His second duty was the work which he had cut out for himself in life, and that was—the rescue of others from the high misdemeanours consequent upon either poverty or wealth. That work occupied all his time and energies.

Dr. Cornerstone's practice had increased, and as it included the rich as well as the poor, he found himself in a position to give more and more of his

---

1   The East-End is where Dr. Cornerstone ministers to most of his patients and in the nineteenth-century it was a place of poverty and slums; moreover, at the time that Dr. Cornerstone is healing these patients, "there were far more cases of fever and consumption mortally affecting the older part of the population than in any other region of the capital" (vii). Peter Ackroyd. Introduction. *The East End: Four Centuries of London Life* by Alan Palmer. New Brunswick: Rutgers University Press, 2000.

advice gratis where it was most needed.

His name had become a well-known one, so that the idle rich would appeal to him when, beaten by the diseases that follow in the train of ennui, excess, and self-indulgence, the human nature within them revolted against its own sickliness and yearned for a tonic. This the caustic tone of the uncompromising Doctor was sure to present, for it was his habit to commingle heart-searching advice with medicinal prescription.

To sick women amongst the rich, Dr. Cornerstone habitually mingled mercy and tenderness with his firm truth-speaking, save in a few instances. There had been cases when the dealings of the Doctor with his feminine patients had been, indeed, awe-inspiring.

There was no doubt that he regarded all disease as being somewhat of the nature of moral delinquency, or, at least, as being closely connected with it. This somewhat severe idea was really the occasion of the optimism which was unexpectedly found to colour his otherwise grim appreciation of the misery amidst which he found himself. Possibly he needed a strong imagination to support him under the burden of human woe. And his imagination was of the kind which extracts from desolating facts a reason and a cause, and which possesses an invincible faith in remedial application. Dr. Cornerstone could never persuade himself to accept evil when he saw it, or to pause on the indulgence of mere emotion; the sight of evil invigorated his will, stirred up his brain, and drove him on to that kind of beneficent action which is named hard-thinking.

After some particularly heart-rending experience amongst the wretched and forsaken of mankind, he would come home and sit with knit reflective brows, dreaming dreams, and seeing prophetic visions, until at last he would shake off his depression in the startling declaration that old age and death themselves—those two unconquerable items of our fate—might, for all he knew, lie finally in the hands of the Race, so magnificent a latent power to work out his own salvation did he discover enclosed within the brain and heart and will of man.

On a soft, warm evening, a day or two after the Minister's great entertainment, Dr. Cornerstone sat on the veranda of his house with his friend Carteret.

The windows of the sitting-room were thrown open behind him, and every now and then a child or two stepped out, ran to play in the garden, and ran in again. There was an attraction in the sitting-room that called the little ones constantly back to itself. The mother sat there with her work; her soft movements, the snip of the scissors, the laying down of the reel,[2] the rustle of the material, the gentle voice speaking to the children, came through the open window to her husband's ear, and accompanied his thoughts and conversation.

The ten years which had passed over Dr. Cornerstone's head had changed his brown hair to silver; his eyes were tenderer and more attentive than they had been, and his mouth a trifle firmer, otherwise he was unaltered.

Near the pair a laburnum hung its delicate, beautiful flowers; the trees were covered with fresh and beautiful green, and the sun turned the well-cut lawn into a carpet of gold. Around in the air the roar and jar of traffic was all too close, yet not so near but that the softest tone might be heard, and the pants of the children's breath from their little red mouths as they ran, and their light foot-fall in the race.

'The age,' Dr. Cornerstone was saying, 'belongs to the common life that flows through our streets, and not to rank, riches, nor genius.'

'I am aware that we are destined to sit under the footstool of the mob, and hob-a-nob with the tramp,' responded Carteret meekly.

'When I see anyone adorning and yet more adorning his own life, and refining and yet more refining his own spirit, and comforting his spiritual imagination for this world and the next——'

'You yearn to bundle him and his fads off this serious earth,' interrupted Carteret with his usual dry air. 'But when the virtuous recognises his kin in the commonplace sinner, and the man of genius does not exalt himself against the fool—what then?'

'There you are at your ineradicable individualism again!' said Cornerstone testily.

'Oh, take all the feathers out of all my caps!'

'A good brain is, in justice and right, a communal belonging. It owes rent to the community, just as the possessor of a good field, or a mine, or any other special advantage, owes rent to the rest to make the balance even.'

'This intrusive age!' sighed Carteret; 'it leaves us no privacy, nor any private property—not even our own heads!'

'Those least of all. The better furnished one head is, the less is there left for the rest.'

'I decline that!' said Carteret.

'I insist!' returned Cornerstone; 'there are limitations everywhere. If we use up the national capacity as a forcing-bed for the few, we draw off mental power from the rest. The best individual brain falls off somewhere; so of the

---

2 Reel: "A frame or spool on which thread . . . is wound" (*Webster's* 1192).

national brain. I seem to see——'

'What?'

'I seem to see each man of genius and capacity amongst us dogged in his steps by the pauper, the imbecile, and the rogue. Assuredly, the crime, imbecility, and degradation we find beneath, stultify the refined product above. What national pride can we have, so long as one degraded specimen is left to run like a rat to a hole at the tread of a policeman? Our symposium at Westminster is cancelled by our thieves' quarter, just as a City feast in November is cancelled by the hunger of the unemployed. In these things we are debtors.'

'But how to get at the complaisant consciences of the mentally endowed?' asked Carteret.

'Would that I could do it!' returned the Doctor. 'Would that I could bring your man of abnormal brain power into contact—genuine spiritual contact—with some of the broken and degraded, and say to him, "*There* lies the blot to your personal civilization, this savagery shames your development, this noisome shadow dogs your advance and belongs to it. Wipe out that blot, change these shadows, cancel this shame, or *your* presence in our midst, and not *theirs,* is the worst of our national disgraces."'

The Doctor stretched his arms out and got rid of the irritation of shirt-cuffs, while he gazed at the setting sun. It burnt slowly down through the trees opposite, and sent flames of colour up into the London sky. A child ran suddenly forward and leaned a round pair of arms upon its father's knees, looking up into his face silently and happily. Then it darted away to its play.

'Cornerstone!'

Carteret's voice was sad and musing. An unwonted depression had characterized him during this interview. The Doctor turned and looked at his friend.

'When we have harried all the rogues off the face of the earth, and solved all our problems—the *women* we have always with us.'

'Ah, I for one decline to speak of that difficult problem as an insoluble one. I will never allow that natural law is so stubbornly adjusted, as to leave one half the race under a real, permanent disadvantage.'

'Of late an odd thing happened to me.'

'Out with it.'

'I went the other day to a great entertainment. I was present at Lady Shunland's the other evening.'

'Poor strayed sheep! Poor fish out of water!'

'It was there the odd thing befell me. I saw there the most beautiful woman in England—or in Europe, for the matter of that.'

'H'm!' said the Doctor, with an uneasy frown. 'In my opinion there's no beauty left since——' He broke off suddenly, and that with a regretful eye. 'Well, proceed.'

'I saw her, and she exhibited towards me a certain favour.'

'The deuce she did! The jade! *That* was your odd experience, eh?'

'She held all the men at a distance. None might come near her, saving myself; I was the favoured one. I might sit by her side with a fold of her dress over my knee.'

'The Jezebel had heard of your book, Carteret. They'll take up with *any-body* when they fancy it increases their power.'

'I found myself touched, Cornerstone.'

'Devil take her! Pooh! Did I swear? Don't let my wife hear!'

The Doctor here cast a rather fearful glance towards the sitting-room, whence now came the gentle click of knitting-needles.

'I was moved by her, Cornerstone—moved as I rarely am by a woman. I suspect them all—range myself against them all by instinct. With this one, on the contrary, I took sides against the world.'

The Doctor shook his head.

'This is bad, Carteret, bad! You are advanced in life, but that makes the case worse. Change of scene might, however, be effectual.'

'Every since I saw those eyes of hers I have been dreaming.'

'Heavens and earth! What of!'

'Of mortal ruin and despair.'

'Ah—h! I see, I see. This is not a common case—no mere outbreak on the part of an elderly fellow who ought to know better! Proceed.'

'There was something in the eyes that went straight to my heart. I could believe that I had heard the cry of a lost soul. My bodily ear did not receive the words, yet they haunt my mind as though they had been spoken: "I am lost beyond hope! But soothe my soul with one drop of human comfort before hell swallows me up for ever!"'

'Indeed! indeed!'

'I am tough enough, yet I cannot endure the memory of that woman's eyes.'

'Poor soul! she was in the usual feminine predicament? Sucked in by love and passion into some moral morass?'

'I hardly think it.'

'What, then?'

'There were certain indications that the case was peculiar.'

'Well, her name?'

'Her name! *That* is a thing of disgrace—a name to scald the tongue!'

'Pretty company for you to be in! What name was it?'

'A great name as the world goes. She answered to "Lady Heriot."'

'Ah, my prophetic soul!'[3]

The Doctor set both hands on the arms of his chair, leaned forward, and stared silently in Carteret's face.

'Did you know of this thing, Cornerstone?'

'It is far off now—the marriage, I mean. I have put it out of my head as much as possible, seeing that it was unalterable. I heard nothing from her since I received the long letter I told you of, prior to her disappearance. A little more than a year afterwards, I read in the paper that she had married that revolting brute.'

'He was there with her.'

'Well? And she has made her discoveries?'

The Doctor was a little pale about the cheeks, and his jaw looked square and black and ugly.

'She has found out *something*,' returned Carteret; 'some more than ordinary experience has produced in her eyes a certain look of unfathomable sadness. I should call it more than sadness. Some sight she has seen, some shock she has received, has impressed itself permanently on her mind. Of this I feel sure.'

'Did you speak to her? Were you introduced?'

'I was not introduced. Yet we spoke together.'

'Anything of note?'

'It was confidential. For once my withered hideousness was of service with a woman. She wanted *me* to sit by her and protect her from the nauseous assiduities of sexual admiration. Poor wretch! poor wretch! They educated her into sexuality, until it is impossible for her to avoid exciting the corresponding sensual in our coarser natures. With me, however, she was safe. She detected it by instinct. And how unerring have her instincts become on matters such as these! By me she sat contentedly, at rest.'

'How did you know it?'

Something burnt for a moment in the eyes and withered face of Carteret, something that was like a flame from a long-repressed smoulder of pain at the

---

3   This quote is from Shakespeare's *Hamlet*. Hamlet has just learned from the Ghost of his dead father that he was poisoned by his father's brother. Hamlet proclaims, "O my prophetic soul!" (Act 1, Scene V). Brooke has made one change, the "O" to an "Ah".

centre of his being. But his voice in replying was commonplace and quiet.

'Because,' he said, 'usually women cast a hasty glance at me and—scuttle away. I am so accustomed to it, so prepared for the inevitable moment of repulsion, that the slightest variation appeals to me as a plain word. Lady Heriot's lovely eyes noted me and my deformity as I made room for her to reach a lounge, and as she seated herself, she indicated by a look, by a movement of the hand, that the place beside her was vacant. That in itself was an event to a man such as I am. It was a greater, when she did not withdraw the trespassing fold of her gown, nor shrink from me into the remotest corner.'

Dr. Cornerstone drew his handkerchief out and dried a drop or two that stood on his forehead.

'You comprehend,' he said, 'that the inimitable Jessamine was the most precious of my patients?'

'Well, as I said, she spoke to me.'

'Yes?'

'A friend of mine mentioned the name of someone with whom she was once acquainted.'

'That would be me.'

'Just so. There is some tragedy behind—some weight on her mind. She found the occasion to send you a message. She whispered in my ear: "Tell him to call. Tell him to come. Beseech him! pray him!"'

The sun was edging slowly out of the sky; nothing but a red half-disc remained. Dr. Cornerstone leaned back in his chair and stared at it.

CHAPTER III

THE sexes suspect each other. Even the heartiest sympathy falls short of sympathy in proportion as there is therein an admixture of good-natured tolerance. And much of the sympathy between sex and sex is no more than a purposed toleration of probable weakness little understood.

There was a note in Jessamine's message pitched too high for Dr. Cornerstone's comprehension. Even his insight into her probable misery could not account for it, and it irritated him.

'She can go away. She can break the tie. Let her free herself,' said he.

To those not within the delicate meshes of some difficulty, action seems always possible.

'It seems easy, doesn't it? The odd thing is that everybody's individual mess is a sort of charmed circle, out of which he does not find it so simple to step,' returned Carteret. 'Shall you go?'

'Yes. Hysteria and wretchedness are my business.'

It was getting dusk next day when Dr. Cornerstone found himself alone in the private sitting-room of Lady Heriot. A single lamp covered with a shade served rather to add to the obscurity than to illumine it, but he saw that the room was furnished with every possible luxury. It gave him a sense of oppression to be there; the wretched hours spent therein by an unhappy soul burdened the atmosphere. There seemed no escaping the infection; the breath sucked it in, and it lay heavy on the heart. He sat down to await her coming; he thought of her as of one who had left his guidance to learn life's merciless lesson by herself. Some deep experience she had conned alone. But *that,* he said, *is* life. And here, after ten years, he sat on her hearth watching the light stealing from the window and giving place to shadows, and the lamp glowing more and more to a ruby redness. Loneliness, he said, and isolated experience are the great facts; many are conscious of the rod above—the rod that falls when errors are made—but each spells the lesson alone. The rest—sweet mates and the play-hour—is palliation and exception. It is a dream, haunting the heart against all knowledge to the contrary, when we say to ourselves that, one day, we shall sit hand-in-hand with some lost beloved creature, the barriers broken between, hearing without reserve at last—at last—the untold history.

O groundless hope! he said. Time shakes the sands down in the glass, the thief Age strips us of our opportunity, and Death steals on and hems the way at last; and still the heart, befooled with visions, holds to its goal and runs. One day—so we picture it, he said—we shall overtake the vanishing moment, catch up the long-sought friend, and, as self to self, bend and listen to the story, feeling no need to pardon, or forbear, or excuse.

To visions impossible as these, was there a substance and a counterpart? He thought, perchance, it might be so. He thought that he who silently loves his friend, without one breath of the word 'forgiveness' in between, who wholly loves, accepting utterly, comes nearest—for all dividing space and years and facts—to that most unattainable and sweetest of dreams.

A curtain, Dr. Cornerstone observed, hung over one corner of the room. To that his eyes wandered from time to time uneasily. Would it be from such a pall-like symbol of mysterious years that Jessamine would step? He thought of her past as lying huddled behind it, and of her face straining towards him in speechless consciousness of what was hidden there, the eyes full of the eternal, voiceless cry of the human creature: 'Oh, fellow-soul! There lies the irrevocable thing behind me! Is there hope? Has life taught you that there is consolation anywhere?'

He fancied he caught the faint rustle of a garment—a step. No; there was nothing. The air was full of steps; they walked and pattered through his heart, departing—departing. As hopes unrealised, that come and pass beside the waiting heart and go, as steps of those that move away, they beat despairing rhythms in his ear. Oh for the steps that pause and enter!

He imagined that he heard a sigh. That went, he thought, through a frozen world, wherein the voices of all nature were stilled. Of all earth's once myriad cries, there remained only this thin and broken sigh, the lasting thing being grief—unresting grief. When Earth is dead, and the sun has perished, some poor belated and lost soul, heaven-banished, hell-rejected, will wander hitherwards, and come back, and sigh like that, he said.

Looking again towards the curtain, he saw now a white hand thrust between—a hesitating, timid hand—which slid away again.

His head drooped. So had he seen a tiny promise creep towards a life palled with sorrow, the dull monotony of grief fluttered by a beckoning finger, which vanished when the frozen heart began to beat. Strange torturing trick of fate!

When he raised his eyes again, he became aware of Jessamine's presence. A woman clothed in a long white gown held the folds of the curtain apart, and stood between, darkness behind her. When their eyes met, she dropped her hands, and came a step forward, and paused and looked at him again.

The weight of years was in her face, and in her eyes questions deep as death.

He rose from his seat. More startled than he could have conceived possible, he barely managed to murmur her name.

She advanced, and placed her hand in his.

'It is you—at last,' she said, in a small, low voice, about which, as on a weak string, hung heavy beads of most impressive tears.

'Jessamine!' he repeated, drawing through the name the lingering memory of what had once been bright and fair.

She turned aside as though her little strength gave way, and, sinking down, laid her face against the cushions of a chair, like one for whom the storm has been too cruel.

Life had its ghosts, it appeared; the woman before him was but the ghost of Jessamine. He bent above her, searching in her face, and fighting all the time against the mournful influences which seemed nipping the heart out of his courage, and his impulses of healing and of help. She turned suddenly, and gazed at him with her dark eyes.

'Doctor, Doctor, Doctor!' was all she said.

At which, he found himself forced to walk some paces through the room, oppressed by the distracting, desolating hopelessness which infected him from her eyes and paralyzed his resources. He did not remark that, when he turned, she rose and followed him, casting as she did so many an anxious, flitting look upon him. When he paused she paused too. They stood together, the slender woman's form against the sturdier male shape—the ever symbolical pair, whether united by love, friendship, or mere chance position, the world's cruellest enigma, the two who hide between them secrets which forever they strive to impart the one to the other, and have not the power to disclose.

He was startled when she touched his arm, and he heard her voice close beside him.

'I am not mad, Doctor,' said she; 'my mind is clear. I am not mad.'

'No, no,' said he.

'You will help me?'

'If a man can. If there be a way.'

'There is a way.'

He placed his arm about her, and led her back to the chair.

'I try to get this look out of my eyes,' she said anxiously, 'but I am not able. Once I tried to smile.'

She laid her hand on the lace and cashmere about her throat and bosom, and looked at him.

'I understand,' said the Doctor soothingly; 'I know.'

She shrank back against the cushions and moaned. It was like the moan of some trapped animal, and beyond what is human in its despair.

'Come, come now,' said Dr. Cornerstone; 'tell me the whole history. I am here to help you. Do not hide anything. Tell me the whole from the beginning.'

'I shall hide nothing from you.'

'That is well. I was a little overcome at meeting you again—at finding you in distress. But there's a way out of the heaviest trouble, you know.'

He drew upon his resources of wholesome cheeriness. Yet it seemed to him that the hopes he threw out fell with a hollow sound. In the atmosphere of that room, the little lamps which experience, will, and philosophy light for the human soul burnt low indeed.

'I have lately seen that there is a way—just one,' said she. 'So far, for many years, I thought that there was none.'

'Tell me,' said he, 'how did you come to make this marriage?'

'Ah, why?' said she. 'It is too late now.'

'Too late?' he repeated. 'It is never too late to pluck up will. We may shake ourselves free from our worst error. I do not say without loss or suffering.'

'Is it so?' said she. 'No; there are errors which are as living nerves, into which we dare not cut.'

'Jessamine, my child, you over-estimate your sorrow. Your will and strength are broken for a time. Take courage. Tell me all.'

She looked at him with meek eyes of unfathomable moveless grief.

'Listen,' said the Doctor, apprehension hurrying his speech: 'you think—many women do—that a marriage is an eternal thing which cannot be broken; but that is a mistake. We live in the nineteenth century, and not in the Middle Ages. You can go away to-morrow if you wish. Pluck up a will and escape.'

His own words chilled him with an incomprehensible sense of missing the mark.

'Is that your way—your help?' she asked.

'Jessamine, it is. I do not hesitate to advise you to act as I have said. This bond is breaking you. I find you crushed. Moreover, it is a degradation. Escape from it. I say that it is the only right step left for you. You had better be a crossing-sweeper or a scullery-maid than remain in this splendour—set to *this* work. Gather together your resources of courage and will.'

'Escape?' she repeated blankly. 'How is that possible? Escape—from what?'

'You fear the scandal?'

She looked at him in doubt, as one looks at a person who introduces an irrelevancy.

'Other women have done it,' he said.

'Yes. I have wondered,' was her simple reply.

The Doctor's lips parted for speech and closed again. An incredible idea stole into his mind.

'You do not love this man?' he asked after a little hesitation.

Something faintly rippled the settled mournfulness of her face; but there was no answer. The Doctor, from experience, knew that a woman's heart has strange, deep phases; he knew, too—had not Carteret reminded him?—that the individual experience is a charmed circle for the individual sufferer, and that no human help can avail, until the enchanter who lurks within gives the signal of release.

'I think I understand, Jessamine,' said he tenderly; 'the thought of your child keeps you—*now*.'

She cast a shrinking, suspicious glance at him.

'If that be the case,' said he, yet by no means certain that he had touched the right chord, 'I think you ought to face the suffering. As the law stands, it is true that the child is the father's, and not yours.[1] But I do not hesitate still to say that it is your plain duty to separate from Lord Heriot—to resign a life which is for you a degradation.'

He had been noticing the slim white hands, laden with rings, which lay in her lap. Faint suggestions came to him from the sight of them and touched his heart. He now remarked that the fingers twitched nervously.

---

1   Under the law, at this point in the nineteenth century, Jessamine does have some rights to her children, though they are fairly restrictive. The Infant Custody Act of 1839 "gave women custody of their children under the age of seven in cases of divorce or separation. Thereafter, the husband resumed control, though visitation rights were secured for the wife" until the child was sixteen years of age. However, "[t]he act modified but did not overturn paternal control, for any father had complete authority over his children, determining their domicile, the extent and location of their schooling, their religion, and their guardianship" (27-28). The Infant Custody Act of 1873 allowed judges to award children up to the age of sixteen to the mother in cases of separation and divorce only. If, up to this point in the century, the mother was found to be adulterous, the children would automatically be placed with the father. It did not matter whether the father was adulterous or not. In 1886 the Guardianship of Infants Act was passed; this gave "mothers the guardianship of their children upon the death of the father" (28). This Act also gave mothers the right to make decisions about who should take care of their children, if the mother should die. Susan Kingsley Kent. *Sex and Suffrage in Britain, 1860-1914*. Princeton: Princeton UP, 1987.

'The child!' she said, in a low, quick voice. 'No, no; it is mine too! The responsibility is mine as well.'

By this time dusk had gathered in the room. The glow of the lamp beneath its red shade was scarcely an illumination. He saw Jessamine as a willowy figure in white leaning back in her chair, the dark hair against the cushion, the pale, sweet face beneath with closed eyelids, and the slim hands moving nervously upon her knee. So far he had reached no further than surmise; he must break that mournful reticence if he could. He had no assurance that at present he had found the source of her trouble.

'Tell me about it from the beginning,' he said firmly; 'give me an account of how you were induced to enter into this alliance.'

She roused herself a little, and opened her eyes. He thought that they were always pondering some fixed intense idea.

'You wish me to tell you about it,' she said.

'It will be well that you should do so. Was it of your own will?'

Jessamine leaned her cheek on her hand, and seemed to be thoughtfully considering.

'It is a long time since then,' she said slowly; 'still, I remember. There were things in myself that terrified me—even then.'

'Yes?' said the Doctor.

'I recall a stupefied feeling—a numbness. I recall feeling as though everything were dead—as though I were one of those fallen autumn leaves which the wind blows where it will. The wind that blew me on, that kept me moving, was just restlessness—no more. I had something unsatisfied, hungry, in myself—something that kept driving me into action, display. I wanted to fill—to fill—what? There was a hollow place where my heart ought to be, a burning confusion where my thoughts should have been. There was nothing to which I cared to put my life. I think if I had fallen into good hands it would have been better with me. But I came back to my Aunt Arabella.'

'Ah!'

The Doctor's tone was significant.

'Do not blame Aunt Arabella,' said Jessamine gently. 'She and I are kin. There lies the root of the evil. What is in her is in me also. If it had not been just so, she would have had no power to influence me.'

'Ah!'

'She only interpreted my own self to me. It was that which made the dreadful thing happen.'

'Your marriage?'

'No. Must I tell you this also?'

'I think it best that you should tell me all.'

'It frightens me a little to recall it, yet I will tell you. Why should you not know me through and through?'

'It is well that you should tell me.'

'She worked on me when I came back.'

'Came back from where?'

A crimson wave rushed to Jessamine's pallid cheek, and her eyes became suddenly suffused with tears. She threw her hands before her face with a single helpless sob. Her grief was intense, and yet the sight of it relieved the Doctor, because it was the sharp natural grief of a woman, and not that strange, incomprehensible despair.

'Came back from the thing that killed me,' said she in a loud, hoarse whisper.

'Well, well!' said Dr. Cornerstone soothingly.

'It does not matter where I came back from,' said she when she had recovered her more composed bearing. 'When I returned I had nothing but this feeling of stupefaction, and—as though I had been braced up to something too high for me—a sense of relief in sinking back to vain, luxurious ways. Aunt Arabella worked on this last.'

'I can imagine it.'

'I was conscious of degradation, yet had not the force to resist. I am not sure that I wished. I saw, without putting an end to them, all her devices about Lord Heriot—my husband. The spring of my desire for goodness had dried up; I had lost my self-respect. Nothing seemed to matter. Such a vain pursuit of such a miserable social triumph as she placed before me seemed all I was fit for. But there came a day towards the end when my apathy was suddenly fired, when something—I know not what—rushed over me. She was talking to me. I was listening or not listening, as the case may be. Then she began to go on and on about my beauty. And all along vanity in me—*vanity*—ached like a diseased nerve. She spoke of Lord Heriot being in doubt between me and the blonde woman, of what people would say—were perhaps saying—as to my disappointment. And suddenly I seemed to feel my brain like a spot of fire. Wild anger and hate were in my heart. Hate against her and against myself for being like her, and against society for turning out such creatures as we were. And I wanted to end it in a moment. I had not any clear thought. I felt as though all the great cruel wrong, whether in me or outside me, was impersonated, and stood before me in the figure of my aunt. And a swift impulse of energy against it seized me, as though it were possible to destroy by one blow the devil in myself that was tempting and dragging my life down. At that time I was physically strong and vigorous. Have you ever felt the vanity of words and the necessity of flinging out acts instead? Men do, I think; but they disallow it to women. Well, I—*I*—flung out at the traitor within, who spoke to me by the mouth of the traitor outside. I felt a blaze in my brain and a blaze in the room. I don't know what I did, but it was over in a moment, and I sank back in my chair with every spark of self-respect dead within me. I did not know whether I had hurt, or perhaps even killed, her. And I did not care if I were hanged. I sat there looking away from her as she lay on the floor, and trying to get my own breath back. I think I hoped she was dead, because then the end would come; for I felt that now I had done *this,* there was no more anything to cling to or to live for. I wished to be put out of misery. So I sat looking away from the heap on the floor. But just then we heard James coming, and suddenly Aunt Arabella sprang up. She looked dreadful, and the first thing she did was to rush to a mirror. The one thing she thought of was that, if James saw her with all her toilette spoiled, he would tell. And then I perceived how complete was our degradation. We were too trivial and con-temptible, too shriveled and dead in our souls, even for hanging. And when she had got her hair right and her collar arranged, and was crouching in her chair, and James had come in to put on the coals and had gone out again, I turned to her and said just this: "Aunt Arabella, I will marry Lord Heriot as soon as you like." And at that she began to shiver and whimper, and thanked me, and praised her God.'

'So,' said the Doctor, 'you knocked Aunt Arabella down. And afterwards?'

'Nothing that I recall until one day I woke up from my stupor.'

'That was after your marriage?'

'Yes; months after. A tiny ray of hope—it was scarcely hope—came to me one day. It was a little thought—no more than that.'

'Yes?'

'I caught at it. You do not know the darkness that went before. Sometimes I think men do not guess what settles—settles down on a woman's heart when she is hurt—*that way.* But suddenly I saw that it was possible to live—a dif-ficult life, but still a life. Something—so small, so tiny a link it was, but still a link—came to me out of what I had lost.'

'What had you lost?'

'Hush! Do not ask. Let me tell you my own way. It was for the sake of *that* I strove to be good again. I realised that I had married Lord Heriot; I thought—"*That way* my duty lies." It was all the goodness I had ever learnt about. I thought it linked me on to what I had lost. And in that idea I lived. I woke up day by day and clung to it."

'You do not wish to leave Lord Heriot?' said the Doctor perplexedly.

She put out a trembling hand, and laid it on his arm.

'Wishes with me are dead,' said she; 'I find no way save through devotion to my duty. Once I learnt something better. I cling to the memory. But I see no chance of faithfulness to *that,* save faithfulness to *this.'*

He gazed at her with a frown of perplexity and doubt. Her eyes were anxious; she feared his words; her looks were weighted with deep questions which she shrank from putting.

'I married him of my own free will. My eyes were wide open—wider than you think—than you dream. I would not quarrel with him, would not go back on my steps—had self-respect enough to keep, not break, this tie—*even when I comprehended what it meant.'*

Her grasp tightened on his arm. She feared—he was certain that she feared—his words; yet the sources of her dread were dark to him.

'One day,' said she, 'the little cord of hope to which I desperately clung found a fellow. I began to dream of motherhood.'

'Yes,' he said—'yes.'

'Doctor, did you know, did you guess, that I had that feeling—that yearning?'

'No,' he said.

'It was my strongest passion,' she said; 'even my vanity was second to that. I *know* that it is so.'

'It will redeem you, Jessamine, my child,' he said.

She looked at him with an awful reproach.

'Ah!' he hastened to add. 'For years you have been disappointed.'

'*Disappointed?*' She leaned forward and stared at him. '*Disappointed?* Is that the word? From dreaming over it as a half-hope, I have come to think of it with concentrated horror. But I am chained—I am chained!'

'Jessamine,' he said, 'I have told you that to efforts of the will there are no chains that cannot be cast aside.'

'Death,' she said, 'will release me—death alone. Death is the solver of *my* problem, Doctor.'

'It lies with God,' said he, a sudden apprehension in his tone.

'The only way,' she said, 'is *death.* I have considered and found it so at last. What holds me back is cowardice and—something further. Oh, Doctor, Doctor! *Is* it so easy, then? Death even hides his face at times from me. Responsibility holds me like a vice, and breathes an icy breath upon my heart, and kills even *that* hope. I cannot yet resolve to leave my post—and die.'

She rose, and, advancing to the curtain, stood holding the folds back with both hands, and looking at him over her shoulder.

'*Is* it so easy, Doctor?' she repeated. 'Can we by one firm act undo our errors? They gather—gather. They strike root within. They live without. Come, come! You shall see the chains that bind me.'

*   *   *   *   *

He stood with her on the threshold of a wide and cheerful room, towards which she had led him. A woman dressed as a nurse had frowningly objected to his presence. She spoke of his lordship's strict command, of the secrecy of years. Jessamine, with gentle firmness and entreaty, broke through her objections. And then he stepped forward, and the secrets of the House of Heriot lay before him. The room he stood in was a nursery; there were one or two attendants—more than would be naturally required— and there were two children, aged respectively, he surmised, eight and six years.

He passed with rapid scrutiny and a horror-stricken heart from one to the other. On those frail, tiny forms lay heavily the heritage of the fathers. The beaten brows, the suffering eyes, expatiated in themselves the crimes and debauchery of generations.

'My children,' said Jessamine, with a look into his eyes.

Once, in a confusion of horror and shock, he put his hand out to touch the drooping head of the elder. And then the mother caught his fingers, and snatched them back.

'Take care,' said she in a dull and gentle voice; 'at times she is malicious. That is my boy,' she said, pointing to the other.

And he saw a poor malformed thing—a child who lived in pain, and whose eyes alone answered for him; and these, the Doctor thought, followed his mother up and down the room with an awful look of reproach.

Subdued and gentle, Jessamine walked amongst them.

No one spoke. The attendants, with their quiet, secret faces, hung back like gaolers.

The silence in the nursery was scarcely broken, save for Jessamine's few words, and the aimless scratching of the idiot girl's hand upon a little table by which she sat. Of all the scenes of anguish upon which his eyes had rested, this, in its repressed and concentrated horror, was the most appalling.

*   *   *   *   *

They stood again in the sitting-room. Dr. Cornerstone's face was white as a sheet, and he was speechless. Jessamine closed the door behind the curtain, and locked it. Then she went swiftly to the second door, and locked that also. After that she returned to the hearth, where the Doctor stood silent and smitten. He could not look her in the face.

'You understand me *now*—a little,' she began, in the same low, gentle voice—the voice whose grief was too deep for outcry. 'I told you that, when I waked to understand my own deed, I accepted it. I took up duty—clung to all I knew of that. For the sake of something in the past—out of fear of something in the past—I made it my aim to be simply a true wife to the man I had married. God knows that I meant rightly. It was what I had learned of right. Do efforts of right-doing turn to fruits like *those?* When I saw and understood the face of my first baby—when the little hope born of dreary patient effort turned to *that*—do you think I did not have my desperate moment? But there upon my breast lay the child itself, breathing perpetual warning. I dared not stir; terror and horror held me fast. I strove—good God, how piteously!— to do moment by moment all the duty and the right I knew of. I came to think—and there were reasons more than you know—that our first child was *my* crime, not *his,* my husband's. And a little hope and comfort lived on. You see the dreary years—the working on in darkness and suspense? The clinging to the only light I knew—oh, with such desperate fear! And then the answer. Dropped so slowly, Doctor. The awful sameness of reply! My God!'

She sank to the floor at his feet in a kneeling posture, bending her head, and crushing her hands against her breast.

'Jessamine,' said the Doctor, finding words for the first time, 'was it no crime to become a mother by that effete and dissipated race?'

Whereat she straightened herself a little, kneeling more upright, and seizing his hand and arm, to which she clung convulsively. She had the look of one on whom a dreaded blow has fallen.

'You say that, Doctor?'

'Alas! what else should I say?'

'Kill me, then,' said she sharply; 'don't let me live to commit it any more. Give me the means of dying, so that my baby does not see the light of day. I have seen—at last—that *this* was the only way. Of my own will I can do nothing. I am bound with chains. Give me the death which is my only release.'

'Will *that* undo the error?' cried the Doctor sternly—'*that* more than desertion?'

She caught her hands together, and laid them across her eyes and brows, and held them there while she considered. Then she rose softly to her feet.

'You are right,' said she. 'It would be useless. I was a coward to think of it.'

He saw her standing for a moment poised in thought, her finger on her lips, her mind concentrated upon the hideous problem of her own creation.

'The children,' she said. 'They live on and on—when I am gone.'

He stood silent; words would be fatuous; his uttered phrases struck him now as cruel; he was without resources.

She, with her facile, undisciplined brain—untaught, unguided—set to this torturing riddle, face to face with a situation so awful and supreme! He was silent indeed.

She looked up presently with dark, interrogating eyes, and pointed a question swiftly.

'You believe in will, Doctor?'

'In will? Assuredly.'

'Ah, then—ah, then! You are right. In *will*. The only safe way is from within, outwards. From *within*.'

She repeated it slowly and emphatically, bowing her head as she did so.

She approached, and laid her hand gently on his arm. 'Do you know, Doctor——'

'Yes? What?'

'The *crime*—I think you called it so—came from within.'

'Alas! poor woman!'

'You said it was a crime? You are right. I see it. A *crime!*'

Her eyes darkened, concentrated, and the brows contracted as in strong mental effort.

'Crimes come from *within*,' she repeated.

'All is not lost,' murmured the Doctor.

'Because,' said she with sudden energy, speaking in a loud whisper, and tightening her grasp upon his arm, 'I will cancel it—from *within*. I will repudiate it—reject it—from *within*. If there is a crime, I will not connive at it. I will throw myself on the side against it. I myself will annul it. I shall *will*—and *will*—and *will*. God Himself shall side with me, and Fate be forced to have mercy!'

She paused, sighed, raised her arms high above her head, and looked up.

'I beat with my willing against the very door of heaven. I will tear my wish out of the centre of things,' she cried. 'Who has a right to his will, if not I? And I shall win it! There is nothing,' she said, 'stronger than a mother.'

CHAPTER IV

DR. CORNERSTONE sat in Lord Heriot's dining-room; his wine remained untasted beside him; he leaned his elbow on the table and his head on his hand, and fixed his eyes thoughtfully on the figure of his host.

There was ample opportunity for observation. Lord Heriot was asleep. He had fallen asleep upon his chair, the table-napkin spreading over one knee, his hands dangling, and his legs crossed, the dainty shoe being pointed stiffly and with singular aimlessness upwards. His immaculate shirt-front, with the diamond sparkles at regular intervals, hooped outwards, and his head—the hair most carefully tended—nodded sideways.

'The best valeted man I ever beheld!' said the Doctor.

All that the tailor and a priceless personal attendant could do had been done to turn Lord Heriot into a reputable figure of a man. If starch, fine cloth, and shaving, could have erased the traces of a past, that past would have vanished under the applications as completely as breath on a well-scrubbed mirror. But Lord Heriot's past was a long one; it did not begin with himself. There had been a sameness in the history of the Heriots for generations; it was varied only by the differences in manifestation, caused by the different tastes and fashions of the time. The lines of the resulting contour cut deep. Violence and excessive animalism in the first instance—the unabashed and muscular tiger who founded the family—had, in the inevitable processes of time, degenerated into meanness, irritation, and vice, in such members as did not reap their heritage in insanity, disease, and shocking malformation.

That the Heriots had survived at all, was the result of the extraordinary advantages in sick-nursing which wealth had permitted them to enjoy—that is, the hot-bed fostering and care which go to cherish an enfeebled stock. That cause, and one other, had prevented their natural extinction, the other cause being the alliances into which their wealth and titles had tempted England's fair daughters from time to time. For generations the Heriots had purchased handsome women as wives, in much the same way as an Eastern despot buys the inmates of his harem. Had it not been for these two measures, the family would have died out as quickly as the generations of the vicious are said to perish in the slums of London. And, in effect, the force of the original cause had, by this time, over-mastered the antidotes, and the natural doom had reached them, settling upon the present representative in a horror which appeared to him inexplicable.

While he slept Dr. Cornerstone watched him. In imagination, he took this instance of the unfortunate semi-criminal loafer, and placed him in the position that suited his capacity—subtracting him, that is, from the House of Lords and setting him down in the Casual Ward.[1] Thus clothed upon by circumstance and rags, he presented, to the eye of the mind, a consistent image.

Suddenly the sleeping nobleman awakened; his eyes opened in an empty stare upon a world of which the uppermost reminiscence was of jaded appetite and ennui. Catching sight of the Doctor, troubled recollection passed into his face, while his hand betrayed him by seeking the decanter; but he recalled the action, snatching back his fingers, and turning his head nervously aside, the consciousness of temptation being writ in his eye and profile, as in a dog's face one may see the consciousness of a forbidden bone.

The Doctor still perplexed him by his watchful glance, and at last uneasiness waked him up completely, so that he sat upright on his chair.

'Beg pardon, Doctor,' said he confusedly. 'Been having forty winks, I'm afraid. Trouble. Sleepless nights.'

He opened his red, pale-lashed lids, and stared before him at misery. In truth, there were causes and to spare for desolating reflection. A sort of whirlwind had passed over the House of Heriot during late past months, and if the confused mind of the master was still capable of entertaining a ray of hope, it was apt to be obscured or hunted down by images of terror. The truth was, that the secret chambers of the mansion were empty and open now. In one moment of fierce horror, the brood concealed therein had destroyed itself, the hand of the idiot girl having been lifted suddenly and dexterously against her helpless brother. After the event, the fair mother had sunk into a condition of mental and physical collapse, from which she had not yet revived. As to the noble lord himself, only one form of collapse was possible, to which he immediately betook himself; the restraining, guiding hand of his wife being

---

1   Sally Mitchell, in her excellent and fascinating work, *Daily Life in Victorian England,* gives a wonderful explanation of the casual ward which I cite in full here: "The workhouse also had (often in a separate building) a 'casual ward,' which gave food and lodging for one night (or, in some cases, three nights) to people with no money and no fixed place of residence: tramps, poor people walking to another part of the country to seek work, seasonal labor, seamen who had spent their pay and were heading back to port for another ship, navvies moving from gang to gang. The casual ward also served as an occasional shelter for the urban homeless who did not want to claim relief because they preferred to live on the streets. They would take a night's lodging once in a while when they wanted to escape bad weather and get a morning meal" (95). Sally Mitchell. *Daily Life in Victorian England.* Westport: Greenwood Press, 1996.

withdrawn, the careful artifice of his reformation tumbled to pieces, and in her enforced absence he plunged into every downward-tending consolation which his diseased taste could devise. Just at this moment, when he sat under the Doctor's eyes staring at misery, his conscience crept with memories and superstitious foreboding.

'Not been called yet, Doctor, then?' said he presently, rousing himself and recollecting that he was a Heriot and noble.

'Not yet,' was the obvious reply.

The Doctor's tone was gentle; this was not a case for abuse: his sympathetic finger was, as it were, on the pulse of that dim bit of humanity before him.

'Is there any chance?' asked Heriot, setting forth his importunate hope in a nervous question.

'What of, my lord?' returned the Doctor.

'You know,' replied the other after a sulky pause—'you know what I want.'

The Doctor made no answer. The man's willing and desiring was too lamentable a spectacle in the face of the universe.

'It's deuced hard on a man to be thwarted in his ambition and wishes,' went on Heriot, the flood of complaining being loosed. 'I seem singled out for misfortune. And yet all I ask to make things complete is an heir to my name.'

'Yes,' said the Doctor; 'you seem singled out for a particular misfortune.'

Lord Heriot took the reply for encouragement. He had ideas to lay before the Doctor; they seemed to him an imposing logical array, if only he could get the right one uppermost. He took a silver fruit-knife and beat with it upon the table to aid his speech.

'I want,' said he—'I want her ladyship to pluck up heart and courage. I tell her it rests with her.'

He glanced up cunningly to see if he had said something impressive. The Doctor, gazing at him with quiet, speculative eyes, was striving to draw from his appearance a further clue to Jessamine's mysterious faithfulness.

What hidden argument sufficed to hold the wife to her unloved bond, to make her, to this diseased and ineffective creature, a miracle of self-sacrificing patience?

Receiving no answer from his silent guest, Lord Heriot drew out his handkerchief and mopped the moisture from his brow.

'Lady Heriot has been a good wife, Doctor,' said he querulously; 'I've nothing to say against her. I wouldn't have anything happen to her for half my fortune. When I married her she was a pack of whims; but I liked that. It's wonderful how she changed after. Steadied, you know. Well, I don't mind telling you she set herself to reform me. Hee! hee!'

He rose a little in his chair, tilted the knife up, and lifted his other hand with the weakly spreading fingers, and showed his teeth in a mirthless laugh at the Doctor. The latter pursued his silent observation.

'I'm not given to sermons myself,' continued the noble lord, dropping back to an unbraced attitude; 'don't like them. But when it's a pretty woman preaches! Eh? Don't you know?'

His watery eye, seeking sideways for sympathy in the looser suggestions of his mind, came in contact with the Doctor's collected mien.

'I give you my word, I haven't tired of her yet. Come! Nine years!' he jerked out in a burst of confidence, the man within him appealing to what he conjectured of the man over there.

'N—no?' said the Doctor with uncommitting caution.

'Fact!' returned the other.

He drew together the sides of his dress-coat and absently fastened the bottom button; while he contemplated this unusual instance, a faint surprise at its existence in himself rose to a noticeable sensation. It gave weight to his following disclosures.

'Look here,' said he mysteriously, 'I knew *you knew!* She told me. Well, I didn't want a scandal. See? Kept it all deuced dark. That is why I sent straight for you, when the crash came. Now, look here,' he repeated, opening one hand, the fingers widespread, and laying the tips of the others upon it to indicate the logical force of his conclusions, 'I don't pretend to be a religious man; but I believe in a thing or two. I believe in *Providence.* And when I see how, at one stroke, Providence cleared away the whole difficulty, swept the place clean of trouble, I feel myself to be specially marked out for—something or another. Do you see? I believe in Providence. It would be ungrateful not to trust for the best. What did He make a clean sweep of things for? Why, that we might begin afresh, of course. I don't pretend to be a religious man, or claim more than I should. But that's how I look at things.'

He pulled his waistcoat down, and tried to fix his dim eyes on his guest, making them seem as points of watery light. God! how the face was marred! What frightful excess was written all over it, what bestial memories! Where had he been during the months that his wife lay ill upstairs? Again, the Doctor saw by inference the martyred patience of the woman who had borne the chains of the marriage she had made, during the nine years of which *he* boasted.

The powerful concentrated gaze, which Heriot's attempt at a steady look encountered, seemed to swallow it up. He did not know whether his disordered soul had touched on comfort or not. His eyes wandered off shiftily and nervously, the feeble lids fluttering with weak apprehension. He started off on a new topic.

'Yes; she took me in hand,' he began. 'A powerful mind, Doctor—a powerful mind.' He shook his head sagely. 'I assure you'—here he stretched his spreading fingers over the table confidentially—'since our eldest was born, I've been a reformed man—that is, to be accurate, until lately. She regularly talked me over—frightened me a bit, I don't mind saying. I was deuced cut up when they told me the girl wasn't right. But she bore it like an angel; got me to promise all sorts of things—regularly took me in hand. You'd not think a man like I am—experienced, you know, Doctor—could be talked over by a woman? Well, I was. Don't mind owning up, either.'

He rubbed his mouth with the table-napkin, and flicked an imaginary crumb off his knee. Though silent for the moment, his lips were parted as though the babbling of his fragmentary thought could scarcely be retained. The massive silence of the Doctor shook speech out of him as no questioning could have done.

'If the brain of the woman had but matched this extraordinary power of endurance, the magnitude of this conception of duty!' thought the Doctor.

'Well, I don't mind saying it over again,' babbled Heriot; 'she fairly frightened me. She's not the bullying kind, you know, Doctor, or, by Jove! I'd have made her feel it'—a curious impress of his tigerish ancestor crept out on to his mean face. 'No; Lady Heriot is the right sort—gets hold of a man the right way. Pretty woman, too—though I say it that shouldn't. And I promised her there and then. I promised her, if she'd help me to keep to it, and—and—be good to a fellow.'

Here he wept into his handkerchief, falling suddenly into an access of grief. A slight frown wrinkled the Doctor's forehead. He had a shrewd idea that this trickling of tears was as much induced by feeble remorse as anything else, and Heriot presently confirmed the impression. He stammered out his wretched confessions; they comprised a long history of resolutions, which in themselves it was a shame to have made, but some of which, under the assiduous care of Jessamine, it appeared he had kept until the illness induced by shock removed her from his side. Oh, then, indeed, he had gayly plunged!

Every confession of the wretched man was accompanied by praise of the woman, whose commiserating care had availed to drag him out of his more conspicuous wallowings, and to place him even so far on clean, firm ground as he had reached—before, that is, her withdrawal lent him the opportunity to relapse.

'I'm not fit for her, you know, Doctor—by Gad I'm not! But I mustn't lose her. You must see to that, you know. Only set her on her legs again, and give me my heir—an heir to the name of Heriot, you know, Doctor,' he continued, with fatuous and grotesque pride—'and I'll show what I can do in the way of reforming.'

The Doctor's frowning silence continued. The important thing was not that Heriot should reform, but that he and his race should pass into annihilation. Virtue itself meets some too late, and the best to be hoped for is painless extinction. But that the pale, exhausted woman upstairs should have pursued, through such dark and fetid ways, for years, a quest so useless, wrung the Doctor's heart and amazed his intelligence. What force had not been expended in kindling the tiny rushlight spark, to which the titled loafer confessed?[2] What paths of horror had she not traversed in hunting after his worthless soul? What motive lent the impulse to a spiritual expenditure so enormous?

'Brain,' said the Doctor to himself—'brain is wanting. This meaningless strength and sweetness excruciate the heart that contemplates them.'

As to the wretched creature before him, hardness and contempt were scarcely possible. In the awful degeneration of the race of Heriot, a depth too low had been reached for even the tonic kick of mankind. Besides, mingled though it was with grotesque vanity and selfishness, the sincerity of the broken creature's attachment to his wife was evident, and turned aside severity.

His lordship, copiously weeping into the fine cambric handkerchief, scarcely seemed to expect a reply to his asseverations. He possibly did not remark the Doctor's silence. Regaining his composure, he sat quiet, turning his weakened face sideways, and contemplating presumedly bleared images of his own creation.

When at last the Doctor rose to go, he also sprang from his seat, and, nervously seizing his guest's hand, broke into an explosion of incoherent murmurs.

'Do your best for me, Doctor,' said he in a helpless appeal, feeling that his moment had surely arrived, but that Providence was, after all, capable of scuttling off in a base desertion, and that in the strong hand of a friendly man was his final trust. 'Any pay, Doctor!' continued he, appealing now to mammon.[3]

---

2   Rushlight: This is also known as a "rush candle [which is] made with the pitch of a rush as the wick" (*Webster's* 1248).

3   Mammon: "[R]iches regarded as an object of worship and greedy pursuit; wealth as an evil more or less deified" (*Webster's* 859).

'I'm inclined to think the other fellows bungled. Do your best.'

The Doctor pressed the wretched man's hand quietly, pity and loathing meting out his heart about equally between them. Then he turned towards the door.

Heriot sank down on his knees by the table in a whimpering access of uncontrollable grief and fear.

'Don't be long, Doctor!' he cried; 'help me—I mean her. It's—it's—an important moment. By Gad! if we fail this time! Heir. Delicate female.'

His words scattered themselves off into sobs. The Doctor looked back for a moment at the spectacle. Even Jessamine's singular faithfulness could not endow this titled loafer with any halo.

'He has been drinking badly—badly,' said the Doctor to himself as he closed the door behind him. 'He'll rot down to the grave in six months.'

CHAPTER V

A SMALL rim of safety and an abyss below. The terror of that abyss was still in her heart; but a hand, rough and sudden, had plucked her thence and thrown her to this edge.

So it seemed to Jessamine.

She still feared what lay below. Down there they had pinned her to a place of torture in the centre of a whirl of fire and noise. There were shapes and cries, regiments of creatures, waves of fire, and wide shouting mouths with fangs that darted out and fastened on her heart. But the great dread was that which lay behind.

Somewhere beyond that wheel of discord and suffering lurked a shadow—small, still, insignificant, but containing within itself monstrous possibilities. The consciousness of this was worse than the sharpness of the severest pain; it lay like a stone, black and heavy, dropped through space from a distant star—something that was meant for her, which lay still enough now, but which the pressure of a myriad miles was not sufficient to hold down.

That was the horrible, uneasy dread. Suppose the thing moved, or grew, or uttered sounds? Her heart, bare to those other fangs, trembled at this surmise with unutterable fear. The dread was secret too; she stifled it, kept it down, looked away from it, dared not protect herself or confess her horror, lest she should arouse the treacherous shade. And yet, while holding her fear at bay, she knew it was in vain.

Little by little the tiny murmur began—a low, fatal whisper, full of foreboding. Through all the nearer clamour it reached her ear.

And, then, did not the thing grow? So small, so shapeless, and so dim, it waxed and increased! With averted eyes and an agony of will, she denied that it was so; said it lay still and tiny and harmless; was but a stone and nothing more.

Little by little the murmur increased, and the shape became greater. Her heart was cold with apprehension; her blood ran ice; her nerves crept and quivered. While the whirl of fire went round and the fangs fastened on her, that murmur gathered volume, that shape heaped on vastness, until the heaven itself grew black.

Then it moved! Now her secret dread was held at bay no longer. It turned to frantic panic. Better surrender to the fire and the whirl and the fangs, than await that treacherous horror beyond. For she knew, she knew! All that mountain of dismay had been gathering through ages for her and her alone. She was the object, the victim. It came to claim her—on and on—slowly; then more swiftly; and at last with bounds.

With it, drew onwards the murmur, and this altered as it neared, and formed a word—a single word, that would break over her in a clash like thunder, and let some dreaded secret into her ears.

Defend her against that word!

The Thing overshadowed her! It had wings and eyes and claws that fastened on her heart. And then she understood. It was the outward embodiment of what she hid within. The Thing knew about the nerve of nerves, the hidden, sensitive fibre, the secret place. It was part of that, the inevitable, necessary consequence. As she had nursed the one into being, the other—black and horrible treachery—had been coming too; it intimately belonged to her, it had an irresistible, irrevocable claim. The citadel of citadels was open to that ill-omened Thing; that was its place; no remotest corner was safe or could be safe from its rifling beak; bars and defences, will itself, were vain.

It was close upon her. She felt it swooping down with wings and claws. Horror and black darkness overwhelmed her. Yet she turned to defy it. She fought the demon with puny hands of unimaginable despair, clutching the red throat open at her. She would stifle the spoken word, choke it in the utterance, break it off, though the talons slew her. Heavens! how she dreaded that word, how the idea of the unknown Thing appalled her! There! A wrench! A crash like thunder in her ears! A shriek that tore the sky! A horrible moment! And then, when all was lost, the mighty hand—rough but merciful—snatching her away to toss her here apart on the narrow rim of safety.

Hell was over.

She lay still. A sound like the tramping of departing armies, the rustle and beating of hundreds of wings, was all she heard. The orderly, regular tread, the shiver in the air above. But the sound lessened and sank to a quiet, distant hum. After the terror there was peace.

'Jessamine!'

Whose was the voice? It came from an unimaginable distance. Must she, indeed, arise already? Ah, yes! She was too near the abyss. The Thing might overtake her yet. That rim of safety was a small shelf, from which she might fall back. Besides, did she not know that a journey lay before her, and that the way was long and the time too short? Moreover, what was the Secret? The Word that crashed in her ears was overpowered by sound, the meaning lost in thunder. She must seek it yet, seek and find it for herself. She no longer dreaded it; it was the way she dreaded, the going thither where the Secret lay hid. Her feet were lead, her limbs like those of a corpse, her hands feeble. Yet she must go; the Way lay before her. How terrible! how weary! An upright series of enormous steps, cloud-like, rough-hewn, with no apparent ending. That was the Way. Weak and beaten, up those she must climb and cling, until she reached the summit.

Her feeble limbs essayed the fearsome progress. With leaden, aching efforts, with nerveless hands, stumbles, and hair-breadth escapes, on and on she pressed, clinging, climbing, dragging herself on hands and knees, and this for ages. On and on till Time was gray. Then invisible hands raised her, and the effort was over.

There was a Plain, wide and desolate, and full of twilight. Afar off lay a range of mountains. It was there that the Secret would be found; and miles and days of weary journeying lay between. She sat alone and mourned, her head in her breast; she drew the veil closer about her face and sorrowed. It was because of those who she knew would pass by; because of the steps that were coming and the eyes that pressed towards her. Fain would she hide from those eyes.

Behind lay a Vista of the Ages—the Ages of the future and the unborn. Faces, little faces, came up from them; her ears were full of the tread of little feet; little hands clutched at the veil and dragged it from her; eyes, the eyes of unborn children, looked at her with an awful reproach. They came and touched her with cold hands, and looked, and passed. Little feet and little hands and eyes that were dreadful. Each had the eyes of her suffering boy; each had the impress of her husband.

She rose and tottered on. Tears rained down her cheeks. By her side walked another Shape—something unknown, yet intimate. She had no fear, but knew not who it was. Her hand locked in that other's. And she heard the tread of little feet before her, yet saw nothing.

'The children!' she said, 'the children! I am smitten by the eyes of the children!'

They toiled on towards the mountains.

And suddenly there fronted her the walls, as it were, of a City with Gates in the midst. And this she neared; but always before her ran the sound of little feet hurrying.

'The children have gone first,' she said, 'bearing their accusation. They carry,' she said, 'my sins—my crime!'

She would have fled and turned back. Fear of the children overpowered her. Fear of the little cold hands, of the feet that made such haste before, of the eyes that told so much! But her palm was pressed by iron fingers.

'That is fate!' said she.

The Gates swung back before them, and she saw a light beyond.

'Is it over?' she said. 'Am I dead?'

'*Dead*,' said a voice close to her ear.

* * * * *

Dr. Cornerstone stood by the bedside of the exhausted woman, watching her face anxiously.

What he saw was a marble-white countenance, with pinched, worn features, lying like a carved ivory wedge between two heavy curtains of flowing, dishevelled hair. The white lids and long dark lashes hid the eyes, and only by the tiny, laboured, whistling breath did he know she lived. The hand, slim, feeble, in a strangely-tired attitude, lay outside the coverlet. Every now and then he took the unresisting wrist in his and laid his finger on the pulse.

So still she lay, so nerveless and beaten, with so much the look of a creature that has abdicated from her place and resigned all effort—the hand itself abandoning its toil—that, from hour to hour, he could hardly have said whether she lived or not. How should he know the agony of effort through which the poor soul passed, the torment, and the weary expiation? Not all his insight and his sympathy could teach him. He saw only the small, worn face lying between the masses of the hair that tumbled over the pillow.

From watching her he directed his attention elsewhere. His patient lay in a spacious room which opened to an antechamber. It was night, and the curtains were drawn. The fire and the lamps brought everything to a beautiful subdued glow, and the quiet of a perfectly appointed sick-room was only broken by the sound of the fire and the hum of a kettle. On the hearth sat a young woman in the dress of a nurse, her quiet face turned to the glow. She sat—significant fact—with idle hands.

A young but experienced nurse she was, with an aptitude for difficult cases, who attended Jessamine for the first time.

The Doctor walked towards her. She rose respectfully, yet, as it were, tempering her subordination with a sense of merit.

'She will do for the moment,' he said; 'but I shall remain until I see clearer signs of consciousness.'

A little hurt dignity flecked her cheek. She knew so well her own capacity, was so ready for emergencies! Indeed, in sudden difficult moments she was sure that she excelled. A hundred instances rose to her mind.

'Certainly, Dr. Cornerstone,' she replied with studious gentleness; 'but in any case I should know how to evade her questions. I have had cases before where tact was called for.'

'Just so,' said the Doctor absently, and passed on.

The nurse rose and hovered near the bed, deftly keeping an eye on the patient without troubling her. Her step could not be heard; her movements were soothing and wholesome. But her feeling was sore towards Dr. Cornerstone.

The same room saw the tragedy of Jessamine's soul, and the small upset dignity of the nurse who was assured of her qualification to treat it.

About the catastrophes of life play all sorts of tiny shafts of the smaller kind—the little affairs of irrelevant minds all unconscious of the depths they shoot across.

That is the little worldliness, intermingling itself, as ever, with the mystery and reality of life.

Meanwhile Dr. Cornerstone, unwitting of the flutter left behind him, raised a curtain and passed into the antechamber.

This, too, was warmed and lighted. And here, too, a second nurse sat idle and silent on the hearth. Not all the warmth nor all the light could warm that which lay within the handsome cradle, coldly pushed to a far corner. The chill of it was in the air.

He stood contemplating the hundred nursery appliances which had been prepared for the last hope of the House of Heriot; the luxuries and comforts which should have coaxed and cosseted the small life onwards to its splendid destiny; the material angels which should have carried the heir in their hands over perilous years, and landed him securely at last in the heritage of his fathers.

The heritage of his fathers! He had gathered that already. Dr. Cornerstone walked up to the cradle, which in its baby magnificence was shaped for a lord, and drew the silken curtain aside. The heir and the heritage of the House of Heriot both lay there together.

Thus had fallen the answer to the will and the designing of man.

The Doctor returned, and took his place by Jessamine's bedside. No patient in all London needed his care, his consolation, so much.

The nurse sat by the fire thinking of her merit, and telling herself anecdotes of her past achievements. And so the hours of the night went on.

After a time, when the silence was heaviest, when it lay like a weight in the midst of the warmth and light, and when, like an unwelcome ghost, a chill ray of early dawn crept through the closed shutters, she saw the Doctor bend close to the face of his patient.

'Jessamine!'

The eyes, locked so long beneath the half-moons of their lids, opened and gazed at him in an astonishment that slowly altered to suspense.

*　*　*　*　*

The Plain and her companion had vanished. Jessamine's consciousness of earth and of herself had returned. She lay still in her own chamber as she surmised, but her senses were numb, so that she could neither see nor hear, neither could she move or speak. Her mental power was, however, the clearer for that darkening of the rest, and her brain conjured up thoughts with a force and directness hitherto unknown to her. Memory especially was active; pictures of her past life rose before her, clear, defined, yet passionless. The emotion which had accompanied each scene had faded; they lay before her in the calm light of the judgment and reflection. 'Here and here,' said she, placing the finger of her mind upon this and that, 'I stumbled—I missed the way; deliriously I chose wrong.'

She went backwards from the last scene of all, which, blurred and terrible, struggled into her unwilling remembrance—the scene which had blotted out her mind for a time, and from which, onwards, she recalled nothing. Slowly, with effort, with shrinking reluctance, she reproduced it—the wide, bright nursery, the sudden unlooked-for fury of the idiot girl, the fear of the helpless cripple, her own falling form, with the flash of tables and chairs and common objects in the last glance of her eyes, and the shrieks that were suddenly silent to her ears.

Yes; she remembered. From that time onwards she must have been ill.

And now her mind dropped the memory wearily.

From it, she wandered far away to the days when hopes of many kinds, varied, bright-coloured and glittering, danced through her heart like merry children through a playground. In those days all her thoughts were little shouts of laughter and victory. Out of the mirrors of her mind looked the young, fresh, fatal beauty.

'My bitter fate! The way I missed! Where was the way?' she asked.

Surely it was where duty lay. With clear, unfailing memory she recalled the nine years of her steady adherence to that path.

Those who weaved beheld in the woven tissue some reward to their labour; those who ploughed and sowed reaped a harvest; those who persevered reached a goal. But for her nothing; the narrowest, most carefully followed path led to disaster.

'What is duty?' asked the sick woman. 'Who taught me how to find it?'

Her lids were heavy and hurt her eyes; her lashes hurt as they lay on her cheeks.

'I see nothing; I am too weary,' she said.

One spot of earth, and one alone, was dear to her in memory—the very pain of it was sweet. Time discriminates for us the reality of our treasures from the show. We may come to take pain as our dearest possession, not distinguishing it from happiness, because it is the one thing which, if we lose, we lose, as it were, the Self—the Soul.

That memory lay at the bottom of her heart; it was a hidden consciousness which, for ten years, had neither sunk beneath the horizon of vivid recollection, nor passed the bars of her lips. For her, the pastures of a distant land were ever moist with morning dew, and the harvest was still growing towards completion, while the everlasting hills lay silent above a human drama.

She retraced that past. One by one the kindly, gentle faces rose before her—all, that is, save the one face. His face—from the day she had fled to this—neither in dreams nor in memory had she ever been able to summon before her again. It had been blotted out. He walked through her mind always with head averted.

She sank for a time into something that seemed like slumber—or, rather, it was the unforced wandering of the thoughts. She was back in the heaths and fields of Dalfaber. She felt the sun smite hot between the rows of stooks in the barley-field. She heard the wind ringing the music from the nodding heads; she felt the breeze blowing over the heather; the melody of the quivering birch-trees was in her ear, the scent of fir-trees filled a sunny air. And suddenly out of the midst of it all—clear, vivid, and real as reality—the long-lost and unseen face, which her treacherous memory could never conjure, bent over her, looking in her eyes with the smile of his old love.

'Colin!'

'Jessamine!'

That was not his voice. Slowly the vision faded; but she had time to learn his features afresh.

CHAPTER VI

IT was cold, early dawn—the gloomy presage of a gloomy day.

In the antechamber the attendant drew back the window-curtain and looked out. A drizzling rain fell, and she saw the leaves of the trees in the square beaten by it and dropping from the twigs in silent, helpless surrender. 'Earth to earth' was their birthright;[1] but they fell on the stony pavement, where no soft mould sucked them in, but where the remorseless gray light found them out with its cold glitter, and warned the unburied things that, for them, there is no resurrection.

In the inner chamber, the nurse stirred up the blaze and drew the curtains close over the door of the anteroom, and made a cheerful stir of life and movement. The sick woman lay with her great eyes wide open, and fixed on the warm light nestling here and there on the canopy of the bed. The eyes were too conscious and far too full of thought for the satisfaction of the little nurse, who had made up her mind that the beautiful Lady Heriot should be restored, through her good offices, to her enviable position in society. And Jessamine obediently turned her head when required, and opened her lips to the food offered her.

But it seemed to her that the needs of the body were over, that she had dropped Life—dropped it like a heavy stone down some fathomless well of the past, on the edge of which she herself sat waiting. There was no reason why she should go on living. Life was a memory, a book she had read; she could turn the leaves and look at it now, as though it were the tale of another.

Every now and then she dozed. Waking, she found Peace, too long a stranger, hovering near her pillow. Peace whispered that it was over.

The Doctor, who had been absent some hours, returned at noon. Jessamine welcomed him with a smile.

'It feels,' said she, 'like a fresh spring day to me. The flowers are growing.'

'It is late autumn,' said he.

'No—spring,' said she; 'the year is beginning.'

---

1   Part of the Christian burial rites is the phrase, earth to earth, ashes to ashes, dust to dust; however, the King James version of the Bible does not cite this text, but another: "In the sweat of thy face shalt thou eat bread, till thou return unto the ground; for out of it was thou taken: for dust thou *art*, and unto dust shalt thou return" (Genesis 3:19).

He touched her wrist and looked at her features. They were altered and pinched; an invisible hand moulded and prepared them afresh. The eyes grew larger and softer every moment, and there was no longer either horror or terror in them.

'My life lies back from me as a dream,' she said; 'it is something I have passed through. It is all shadows, and they roll away like a curtain.'

'Yes,' said he.

'I am so free,' she whispered.

Later in the day, Dr. Cornerstone saw fit to summon into the chamber the incongruous figure of Lord Heriot. Like a beaten hound, conscious of delinquencies and of the direst failure, he crept up the magnificent staircase of his mansion, and in at the door of her room. He came like a shameful shadow of the past, bringing with him his tainted memories. But she looked at him steadily, nor shrank as he approached the bed, nor resisted when he took her hand in his. Nothing in this present belonged to her any more. He evaded her eyes; over the hazy something which he called his mind, his conscience scribbled scores against him. His shifty glance fell on those mental records with dismay, and he hurried into such refuge as could be found in words.

'It's an awful business, Jessamine!' he said.

And the ready tear, the symbol of unbraced will, stood in his eyes.

She answered nothing. Their two wills were two whole worlds apart, and hers had triumphed. In that moment, she realised what a frenzy of willing she had thrown into her desire that the baby should not live; fixing her thought on it, clamouring hour by hour against Nature and God, casting the wild gauntlet of her single rebellion against Fate, and filling day and night and space and time with the relentless demand for the extinction of that life and the effacement of her crime. And the baby had not lived; it had fallen out as she had resolved. Her husband came with eyes red with tears and wine, and face flecked with the pale lines of failure and shame, to meet her looks fixed on him with the first quiet sense of achievement she had ever experienced.

That frightened him. It set him in so isolated a region. With trembling lips, and shaking hands, and eyes that searched an empty heaven, he essayed once more the refuge of speech.

''Pon my word, it's a bad business!' he stammered. 'There isn't a Heriot left to take up the title! 'Tain't your fault, Jessamine,' he stuttered; 'I married for an heir. And, Lord knows, I thought I chose well! It's our infernal ill-luck!'

She lay in unassailable silence. Death, the Angel of Mercy, had passed his hand here and there, and cancelled her sins. There were no terrible vistas of the future. The horror was washed out of her eyes. That frightened him more.

The one point of union had been their mutual responsibility in parentage. But now her eyes set him apart. His conscience winced at the thought of what a headlong plunge into the mire he had taken, once the prop of her presence had been withdrawn.

'I feel it badly, Jessamine—'pon my word I do,' said he, shivering.

He was astounded to see the look of peace deepening in her eyes, and to feel her hand unresponsive within his.

It lay there quietly, it is true, for her mind retained its proud habitual attitude of gentle acquiescence in the deed of her own doing. But as she looked at him, she knew that that too was over; his very appearance dwindled and dwindled to an immense distance, for all their touching fingers. The feet of her soul travelled fast and sure. She was terribly silent. At last she withdrew her hand.

That frightened him more and more. The perspiration stood on his brow, and his heart went cold with dismay. Her solemn fixed eyes were awful, and he looked away from them. A horrible sense of inability possessed him; the world was in flux.

'You aint going to leave me,' he stammered anxiously; ''pon my word I can't do without you.'

'We have to stand each one alone,' said she.

Stand! Why, every footstep was a slough! There was only bottomless morass everywhere.

But she looked calm and strong. Her eye, in its secret peace, forsook him.

And then confession tumbled out of his soul headlong; there were neither locks nor bars left in his character, and the mere suggestion of a closed door in another mind set the deficient portals of his own flapping. He confessed out of mere ineffectiveness and inability to retain. He tried to catch her hand, but missed the pure, slim fingers, and, burying his head in the pillow, whispered, between choking sobs, his catalogue of offences, and the ready promises which were but an added sign of looseness in the soul. She listened tranquilly, her mind withdrawn. That also was part of the dream and the past. It was as though she heard the history of the dead and pitied it.

Afterwards he slipped from confession into murmuring complaint. He uttered laments against destiny, and denounced the fate that singled him out for disappointment.

'What is the use of being good when you can't get what you want out of it?' he asked.

'There is no use,' said Jessamine.

The Doctor stood behind the curtain and watched.

'Go now,' he ordered.

Heriot rose to his feet. He mopped the moisture from his brow, and looked at the still face on the bed.

'Get well,' he said, 'and come down. It's damned lonely without you.'

Vaguely in his mind lingered the ineradicable impressions of his superiority as a man, of his prerogative as a husband, of the magnificence of an alliance with the Heriots; it hovered on the surface of his thoughts that he would encourage her with assurances that he still hoped, that he would let her know that she need not be down-hearted, because he intended to be as kind to her as ever, and they would jog on together as before, and so forth.

Something—perhaps the mesmeric eyes of the Doctor—prevented this speech. He began to want to get out of the room. He was quite ill and weak with the outburst of weeping and confession, and the unusual moral exercise; his mind was already on the bottle as a restorative, his thought stealing to the indulgence and laying hold on it, while the more surface and open portion of his mind lingered on the luxury of good resolution.

'Ta-ta!' he said; 'see you again to-morrow.'

And he shuffled to the door, opened it, and closed it again behind him.

A thin wooden partition it seemed. It was the door of eternal separation. The material click of the latch might have startled him like some magical trick, such untraversable space did it set between him and her.

When he turned away, she had followed him with her eyes, and in them was a faint astonishment. The husband of nine years was so complete a stranger! More shadow-like than all the shadows, she felt him pass away into annihilation.

She lay and looked quietly at one place in the canopy of the bed. The whole of life—save one spot of it—became more and more to the eye of her mind a colourless region.

'What do you see, Jessamine?' asked the Doctor.

'Oh, my good friend! come here, and I will tell you. Hold my hand.'

Then it was that, for the first time, Jessamine opened her lips upon the story of the Highlands. She told the tale by degrees—sometimes with broken utterance—but she hid nothing from the Doctor.

'You understand it?' she said anxiously. 'I wish you to know that I am not better than some others. All that was wanting was the skill to win.'

She trembled a little, still shivering under the cold, mailed purity of the man, who could not guess the nature of her surrender.

'I do not know,' she said, 'what I was born for. On looking back, I cannot see what path was meant for me. Everything coerced, but nothing taught me.

I have been perishing ever since I began to exist. There has never been a way for me at all. I have rushed from extreme to extreme, and found—*nothing.*'

She drew a long, deep breath.

'Ah, dear Colin! He hurt me,' she murmured.

The Doctor sat staring before him silently.

'Poor women!' she said. 'That is what came into my mind when I heard of a fall. And—*I envied them.*'

The Doctor stared hard at the curtain and said nothing.

'It took the bitterness out of my heart when I went down to them, and sat with them hand-in-hand, and counted myself one with them. It soothed the pain in time—*a little.*'

The mouth of the Doctor was grimly closed.

'I strove to be better from henceforth, but God knows I meant no harm even then. I have been a dutiful wife to Lord Heriot,' she murmured. 'It was for Colin's sake. *I feared to lose Colin out of my soul.* God! the way was long.'

Her voice was weak now. Presently it ceased, and she seemed to slumber. The Doctor sat by her holding her hand. His mind was heavy with thought— thoughts of life and death, of choice and conduct, and the ways of men.

Later he noticed a restlessness and fever about her. He saw a flush in her cheeks, and that her eyes shone. She appeared more beautiful than before, but the white lids had opened with a strange look of expectation. He bent over her, watching her carefully; and when she saw it, something, between assurance and perplexity, passed into her face.

'Lift me, Doctor,' said she.

He obeyed, and Jessamine, clinging to his arm and shoulder, made shift to peer anxiously over the side of the bed. In her eyes was the piteous hungry look, and upon that followed a wan look of disappointment, and then she sank back upon her pillow as though convinced. What had she sought? What had she imagined? A lump rose in the Doctor's throat, for she turned her face to the pillow, and he knew that she was sobbing. He took her hand again in his own, and stroked it gently. The new phase of grief and excitement perplexed him. Presently the tears ceased, but then he was assured that she looked and listened again, and that for something hidden from himself.

'Tell me what you seek?' he asked.

'Doctor,' cried the weak voice of the dying woman, 'is there nothing by the bedside?'

'No, Jessamine—no, my dear.'

'Oh yes!' said she; 'surely there is.'

He replied more warily.

'And what is it?'

'Is there no little child there?'

He mistook her idea altogether, and answered quickly:

'No, no, my dear.'

'Yes,' she cried anxiously; 'a little boy, Doctor, with steady eyes of a yellowish brown, and sturdy red limbs, and crisp hair that curls over his brow.'

'There is none,' faltered the Doctor; 'rest, my dear.'

She struggled up again, and clung to him, looking imploringly in his face.

'Yes, yes,' she said; 'it is there. It must be there. It runs by the bedside smiling. Oh, sweet little face! I carried it as a baby ten years ago. It lay in my breast. I saw it. It gurgled and smiled. Eyes of a yellowish brown. And all through the years I watched it growing. When I walked alone through the passages, it ran after and tugged at my skirt. Crisp curls over the brows, Doctor, sturdy limbs, and a red, red mouth. It grew older. Sometimes its little arms were tight about my neck. At evening, when I was alone and all was still, it sat on a little stool, with its head on its hand, reading a picture book. And now it runs round the bed smiling and beckoning. Surely you see it too!'

'In—in—the next world,' he faltered; 'yes. I see it too, Jessamine.'

And he turned his head away, stifling a groan. But the half-delirious woman was satisfied. Hearing the last words, she rested in them. She lay with closed lids, a smile parting her lips. Presently the Doctor saw her feebly—very feebly—moving her left hand slowly and with effort towards the edge of the bed. She lifted her fingers and dropped them softly, tenderly, upon the little head she pictured there. And as she raised and let them fall, from the thin finger slipped the wedding-ring, and rolled away unnoticed.

The Doctor sat by her side holding the other hand in his. He would not leave her now until the end; in all London, no one needed him so much. No creature was so lonely as this admired queen of beauty. In all London, he was the one friend she possessed.

The nurse sat by the fire and nursed her grudge. She was unjustly robbed of the prestige she had hoped to earn by close attention on the brilliant and envied Lady Heriot. The Doctor plainly distrusted her.

Death, the Great Messenger, was the other inmate of the chamber. He stood there waiting, felt, yet invisible, with mercy in his eyes.

CHAPTER VII

IT was summer again; and it was summer in that most beautiful of all places, a fir-wood. It had been hot for a week, so that the air was full of a most sweet, aromatic odour, and the fallen needles of the pines made a sun-warm bed, and glowing light hovered over every leaf, and blade, and petal, and the flash of it was carried on the furry backs of squirrels and the wings of birds. In the air was a murmur of insects. Bees droned their music close to the flowers, and the flies made theirs higher in the shadow of the trees, and the wind in the topmost branches was continuous and very soft, with a roll in it like the tumble of far-off seas. And yet the volume of sound thrown out was low to human ears, so that the patter of a dry leaf on the ground could be distinctly heard, and the noise of the squirrel's clinging feet on the bark of the trees. Every now and then came the cooing of a dove, or the cry of a woodpecker, or the scream of a jay. The rooks flew silently, save for the rustle of their passing wings, and now and then for a soft complaint which did not rise to a caw.

It was the place for a summer holiday, and Dr. Cornerstone, his wife, and friend Carteret had found it out. The Doctor leaned back against the trunk of a fir, Carteret was silently measuring the spaces between the branches of a tree with absent eyes, and Mrs. Cornerstone, more thoroughly awake than either of the others, was bending her quiet, meditative face—full of home memories and peaceful joys—over some hand-sewing: and this, upon examination, proved to be a muslin pinafore, to which she was adding the motherly tribute of embroidery.

She it was who broke the silence.

'When you were telling us the story,' said she, 'you always spoke of her as "the superfluous woman."'

The Doctor opened his eyes and glanced at her.

'And you never told me her name,' continued she, still stitching.

'She was called by the beautiful name of a flower.'

'Then I, if I had known her, would have told her she was no more superfluous than the beautiful flower she was called by. I would have shown her how to believe it.'

'But I am not quite sure that it would have been true,' said Dr. Cornerstone.

Mrs. Cornerstone looked at her husband reproachfully from beneath soft brown eye-brows.

'We must be careful,' said Carteret; 'it seems we might easily slip into treason.'

'I am just a little fearful that my wife will touch this matter too romantically,' said the Doctor.

'Oh no, indeed!' returned Mrs. Cornerstone in surprise, and with a hint of indignation in her tone.

'I am rash enough to think so,' replied her husband.

'I did not think you would ever call me romantic,' said Mrs. Cornerstone.

'Prose is so cold and unattractive,' said Carteret. 'I am afraid when women discover how prosaic equality is, we shall not get them to accept it.'

He glanced at Mrs. Cornerstone with a twinkle in his eyes; but she, a model of composure, sat on her seat of fallen fir-spines without turning her head.

'I dislike chaff,' said she with gentle dignity; 'but you are—both of you—better than your own talk, and neither of you mean what you are saying.'

'I think I do,' said Cornerstone. 'But, come! let us, then, talk now as on an equality.'

She flushed a sudden warm colour and paused for her reply, tilting her head a little backwards, and contemplating the light that made the oak underwood blaze.

'As though we were three men?' said she, 'or as though we were three women? Go on. I will consent to listen. And in the end I shall perhaps decide whether to keep my own standpoint, or to condescend to yours.'

'Might we not begin by inquiring what inequality is?' said Carteret. 'Define it, Cornerstone.'

'Between men and men the only definition is, artificial inequality of conditions. Between men and women, it is enforced inequality of development.'

'Stop a bit!' said Carteret. 'That wants re-defining.'

'I mean that women, as a rule, are socially condemned to a too exclusive development of one side of the nature. Whereas the object in man is to bring out an all-round creature.'

'Yes,' said Carteret in a judicial tone; 'I think you are right. I believe I agree.'

'Wait a moment!' cried Mrs. Cornerstone in her turn. 'Is this natural or artificial?'

'This one-sided development? Oh, almost entirely artificial—hot-bed culture—*I* think! Others might not agree with me.'

Mrs. Cornerstone nodded her head once or twice emphatically.

'Cornerstone,' put in Carteret irrelevantly, 'did you ever search the dictionary for the meaning of the word "honour"?'

'I don't know that I have.'

'In Webster[1] you will find it defined under two heads. Honour for a man signifies integrity—*i.e.*, wholeness.'

'Certainly.'

'For a woman, however, it means chastity.'

'Is that so? A man is a man, and a woman merely a function.'

'That is a cruel thing!' cried Mrs. Cornerstone. 'Does anyone consider that such a definition is false? And a false definition may be accepted as though it were something final.'

'It is a cruel thing!' said the Doctor gravely; 'and the meaning of the inequality of the sexes was never better defined.'

'Is anyone to wonder, if a woman should adapt her moral conceptions to the idea expressed?' said Mrs. Cornerstone, with unusual heat in her tone.

'I fancy it accounts for some dry-rot in the ship's timbers all round,' said Carteret.

'Then,' cried Mrs. Cornerstone, opening her hands and lifting her face, 'I think I want a tempest to come!'

Neither of the men replied. Her work dropped on her knee, and lay there in a white heap; her thimble, a little bright spot, escaped, and rolled over the fir-needles until her husband caught it with his foot. The peace of the summer's day was apt to steal long pauses in between the conversation. A squirrel, holding a cone in its hand, ran along a bough near, peeped at them from its safe position, dropped the cone, and with a simulation of terror scampered away.

'The Lord will not be in the tempest,' said the Doctor, when the shadows were longer by a quarter of an hour.

'I suppose it is this stillness in the woods, for I protest I am glad to hear you say it. The dastard within me cowers at the thought of turmoil,' said Carteret.

'Why not a tempest?' asked Mrs. Cornerstone.

'Because,' replied her husband, 'I do not think that wholeness was ever won by clamour. A woman will conquer just as soon as she is in herself all she would desire to seem to be, and not one hour earlier. Equality is not a thing that can be given; it has to be won. Once won, I do not think men will

---

1   This is a reference to Noah Webster's *An American Dictionary of the English Language* (1828) in which "honour" is defined as: "any particular virtue much valued; as bravery in men and chastity in females". Also, Webster states that honour is a "distinguishing trait in the character of good men".

resist. For all its fortresses, the heart desires conquest, and loves no one like the conqueror.'

'That is a very pretty remark!' said his wife. 'But there are too many ugly things said on the other side for me to be able to believe it.'

'You are right, Mrs. Cornerstone,' said Carteret. 'Our manly egoism will defend itself against its death-wound.'

'Besides, I do not like fighting,' said Mrs. Cornerstone firmly; 'I do not believe good comes of it. What is the use, if we women add to the noise and turmoil in the world? We had better be quiet and suffer.'

'Oh no!' said her husband. 'You must not relapse into that.'

'It plays,' said Carteret rather dryly, 'too much into the hands of man.'

'Besides,' added the Doctor, 'I am not sure that the choice is left to you.'

'He means,' said Carteret, 'that the tendency of the age is towards equality, and its main business the break-up of monopoly. And no one can escape the influence.'

'I am sure,' said Mrs. Cornerstone, 'the spirit of the age cannot tell me to fight.'

'Possibly not in the way you mean. For the same impulse which urges women to take equality, urges men to yield it.'

Mrs. Cornerstone took up her work again, and her husband got the little bright thimble back and handed it to her.

'The aim is not, you know,' said he, as she pushed her finger into it, 'to take things and places the one from the other, but to have in the character the sort of qualities upon which the possession of them depends.'

'Ah!' said Mrs. Cornerstone, 'the struggle is not, then, between women and men, but between women and life.'

'Now, that fires me!' cried Carteret excitedly. 'There was a dream once that God became man.[2] The dream of the future is that all humanity becomes many-sided man.'

'Precisely!' said the Doctor. 'Give them but a headpiece!'[3]

'*Wait!*' said Mrs. Cornerstone. 'All this is still too masculine. You have not consulted me, and I am by no means certain that I am pleased with it. I

---

2   "God became man" is an interpretation of the following passage: "and the Word was made flesh, and dwelt among us, (and we beheld his glory, the glory as of the only begotten of the Father,) full of grace and truth" (John 1:14).

3   Headpiece here refers not to a hat or headgear, but to a "mind, [and] intellect" (*Webster's* 644). Through Dr. Cornerstone, Brooke is arguing that women must think for themselves. Yet, it is Mrs. Cornerstone who clarifies the matter right after this by explaining that women will choose their own ideas and paths to follow in life without the help of men.

will have a new headpiece if you like, but I will choose it for myself. And all women shall not have the same.'

Her husband laughed delightedly.

'That is, of course, what is wanted! Resist! resist! and choose your own.'

Mrs. Cornerstone, who had a many-changing face, softly responsive to clear thoughts within, bent over her work and gathered it suddenly to her breast.

'I have not yet said that I wish I had known the woman of your story. If I had known her, I would not have let her be beaten. I would have taught her that no man had a right to call her "superfluous." And tell me, in your heart, do you think that she was beaten?'

'I have asked myself the question,' said her husband.

'There was more in the end of the tale than in the beginning,' said his wife, 'and that is the most the best of us can attain.'

'Return to the general,' said Carteret. 'Need it be an execrable thing to be a woman?'

Mrs. Cornerstone smiled sweetly and leniently upon him.

'We must really beware of touching the problem too emotionally,' said Cornerstone; 'it is favour and flattery that blow women up into air-bubbles. Give them a fair field and no favour.'

'Hound!'

Mrs. Cornerstone turned her face—soft danger in her eyes and on all the points and tips of her features—to her husband.

'I accept the bargain for the whole sex,' said she gravely.

'I wish the rest of the world were of your mind!' said he. 'It is pressure that brings the good wine out, and we should avoid putting too much sympathy into the problem. The mischief with women is that they are too sympathetic. I am convinced it is an indication of contempt. I have remarked that every woman thinks all men beneath her, save the one she is in love with.'

'I am very much shocked at what you are saying, indeed!' put in Mrs. Cornerstone, blushing, however, in a way that looked as though she recognised some truth in the remark. 'Do not mind him, Mr. Carteret. He does not talk like this when we are alone.'

'But what is the average woman's conception of understanding men?' continued Cornerstone. 'Merely a facile adaptation of herself to his weakness, or possibly to his virtue.'

'The woman gives us just what our egoism demands,' said Carteret; 'we reward her by treating her as an angel, and alternating that by snubbing her as a growing boy.'

'Both are exceedingly disagreeable,' said Mrs. Cornerstone, 'and affect me as bad manners simply. I feel it difficult to excuse a treatment of myself as something that I am not.'

Her husband laughed.

'You must be more lenient,' said he, 'and pardon it. The rougher conduct is merely the sign of the advance of thought, man being more awkward than woman in accommodating himself to a change.

'I *think*,' said Mrs. Cornerstone playfully, 'that we shall be able to teach him we are reasonable and adults.'

'That is precisely what he longs—the best part of him—to be convinced about. Once make him sure of it!'

'I have always held,' said Carteret, 'that intellectuality is a necessary ingredient to fine emotion.'

'Yes; human nature is of a piece. What is our best is their best. The joy of earth is in *mind*. And we have not been choice enough in our pleasures.'

Mrs. Cornerstone listened with parted lips and a half-smile.

'Adam, you see, was the first coward, and was frightened of the apple that Eve dared to gather. He promptly invented the voice in the garden and set her under,' said Carteret.[4]

'Admirable Eve! Let her steal the apple once more.'

'And it is to be hoped she will give Adam the drubbing[5] he deserves.'

'I fancy not. Here and there, maybe, of course. But on the whole the creature is of a fine generosity. She has a noble honour. One day she will teach the meaning of integrity to man.'

'Oh yes, indeed,' said Mrs. Cornerstone softly to herself; 'so she will. Is he as perfect as he assumes?'

'We need a lesson!' exclaimed Carteret, who had not caught Mrs. Cornerstone's murmur. 'Do we not judge her life as of less consequence than our own, and her suffering of less account?'

'I am afraid that is true. I am afraid we must confess that we shuffle as much of our share of the burden of suffering as we can upon shoulders which it is convenient to us to name the weaker and to treat as the stronger. True— true. I have before now remarked that, so long as we keep in our eye Webster's definition of a woman's honour, and have not trespassed in that particular, we adapt the rest of *our* honour to the insignificance of the subject as we conceive

---

4   Genesis: "And when the woman saw that the tree was good for food, and that it was pleasant to the eyes, and a tree to be desired to make one wise, she took of the fruit thereof, and did eat, and gave also unto her husband with her; and he did eat" (Genesis 3:6).

5   Drubbing: "scold, abuse" (*CSD* 163).

it. What is a lie in a man's mouth to a man, is not a lie to a woman, and the whole masculine conception of integrity takes a lower tone when the question stands between him and one of the other sex. So that a man have not seduced the purity of a woman (*of his own class*), but have left her intact to some other man's thirst, he may cheat her commercially, break his word to her, insult her by a depreciating manner, under-pay her work, add to his own plenty from her penury, accept any sacrifice from her without repayal, cozen her with any sort of false promises, and ease himself cheaply at her expence on any opportune occasion. All this deleterious consequence to our manhood is the result of that Websterian definition of a woman's honour which man's fastidiousness has conceived. The distinction lurks at the back of every man's mind. Why, argues he, should I be whole in my conduct to a creature that has not wholeness in herself, who is there, not for herself or the world, but for me—for *me?*'

Mrs. Cornerstone rose to her feet, looking somewhat severe.

'Your tongue,' said she to her husband, 'is running away with you. This is really very extravagant language. Is this the place to debate matters with such extraordinary warmth? Listen! I protest I hear the woodpecker tapping. Oh, really, we have lost a great deal through not having sat silent. Do not, Mr. Carteret, allow him to work himself up to a white heat any more. For myself, I am going where I can be still. Is this a London drawing-room that we should talk so much? There have been moments when the sight of the winged creatures, over there in the tops of the trees, affected me as a kind of warning. "Only be still," they seemed to be saying. And, besides'—here she glanced upon her husband with a dewy eye—'I am convinced that only I really understand the story of that beautiful woman with the lovely name of the flower. I am going where I can think about her and not theorize. Perhaps—who knows?—I may discover that she is not so very distant from me, after all. If so, I shall have the opportunity I wish for of telling her that she is not superfluous.'

She glanced down again at the two men with a mysterious, reproachful look. When with a soft, undulating movement she passed down the wood away from them, her skirt turning the leaves and flowers as she went, they followed her with their eyes.

Upon her departing steps came silence. It was broken by the far-off cooing of a dove—a sound which stole the thought away to regions of leafy peace. Evening began to bring her deepening hues within the wood; every leaf burned with an indescribable ethereal glow; the atmosphere was golden and amethyst-tinted, and the light on the branches of the firs was red as flame. An unspeakable pomp and glory reigned, and neither had an inclination to break the embargo of silence which Dr. Cornerstone's wife had laid upon them.

Thus passed away an hour of silent enjoyment, the faces of the men changing and softening under the natural impressions.

At last with a mutual impulse they rose to go.

'She was right,' said the Doctor softly; 'I have the sort of perturbation which too much talking leaves behind. Have you any assurance that we spoke sense?'

'No,' said Carteret. 'But in the after-silence, I felt dreams, like startled birds, flying from my heart.'

CHAPTER VIII

IT was early autumn before Dr. Cornerstone began to make an end of holiday time. And he finished off his unwonted pleasure-taking by a lonely journey to the Highlands, where he penetrated to the remote corner of earth which Jessamine had described to him.

It seemed to him, when he discovered it, to be the one hidden nook in a world which is too public. But even here privacy was fast being driven from her last retreat; the place had been discovered by the tourist, and the story of the McKenzies' mysterious farm-help could not have been repeated a decade later than it occurred. The peasant of the district was himself becoming sophisticated; his canniness[1] began a little to overlap his primitive hospitality, and to threaten to submerge it. Were not the roving folks with long purses in their pockets created to supplement an ungracious climate with cash payments? And thus the hunger for relief from town civilization became here, as elsewhere, its own defeat.

The hand robs the nest of simplicity, and yet supposes that the brood will be reared; and restlessness chases repose from the land when undertaking to purchase it, by overbidding in a rising market.

Moreover, the spiritual outstretch of London, with its mingled good and evil, overflows by degrees to remotest corners. To be unsophisticated is a characteristic of ever-increasing rareness. It falls insensibly from the catalogue of modern qualities, and its possession, though refreshing, begins to argue an intellectual want. In truth, native unsophisticatedness of soul is being exchanged for that less fleeting possession, the simplicity which is the result of choice and of deep thinking. As old good things go, new good things come, and loss is mingled with gain.

The Highland village was changed. For one thing, the laird, not at all from a convinced or instructed mind, but out of deference to a force which he began to recognise as compelling, had reluctantly ceased to put up gates and fences, where the enterprising *Society for the Preservation of Public Rights of Way* as persistently pulled them down again.[2] The war, begun in bluster, was

---

1   Canniness: "shrewd; worldly-wise" (*CSD* 110).
2   I can find no record of this exact title for the society; the original title for the society was the Association for the Protection of Public Rights of Way, which is close enough to Brooke's modified title. The name has since changed, however, and the

dwindling to a tacit acknowledgement of defeat; and the secular 'machine' of the peasant farmer rattled over moor roads which formerly were proclaimed, by a sort of religious desolation and silence, to be consecrated to wild and, therefore, shootable nature.

Moreover, the common London Socialist left his literature behind him, and the peasant farmer picked it up and read. The modern spirit, the conception of thorough emancipation, struck a fruitful root downwards, and a man's vision became acute enough to detect shoddy in the pretenses of another, and to disperse the illusory halo surrounding purchased or inherited rights, the communal idea intruding upon and effacing the individualistic notion of 'his or mine own.'

That stretched the heart and strengthened the nerve fibres.

The canny peasant perceived that, in a world suspended upon Fortune's fickle wheel, his own depressed spoke might come up top at last. He cast firmer glances on the expanses of deer-forest which would be so convenient for pasture, and his eye was speculative of coming increase. When the glance of a peasant is so, the era of the deer-forest is over, even though the fir-trees still stand. Not to be so nipped, not to be so harassed, to have a little margin here and there, a little more life, and less expenditure of unrepaid effort— that, to the long-enduring worker, is heaven.

When Dr. Cornerstone dropped his knapsack at the little inn at Righchar, and prepared to walk over to Jessamine's village, Scotland entertained in him as revolutionary a guest as had ever visited her. He had a superfluity of disdain for shams; he knew of no worth save the worth of man. Where the laird and his 'rights' were concerned, instead of a conscience was a cheery jest; his sentences dispersed time-honoured claims; and he scattered his intensely modern spirit in words that dissolved the pious pretenses of property.

As to the genuine grievance and human need, he sought it out by tavern-tables and at the wayside, and the sympathy he gave was here, as elsewhere, tonic. He did not soothe with words of resignation and a reference to compensations hereafter, but used the laird's word 'rights' in strange contexts, and summoned up revolt in the heart by the suggestion of a remedy, leaving in the breasts of Scotch peasants, as elsewhere that he touched, the first dawning conception of free man and womanhood—the dawning of it in minds astonished at themselves, for what they began to harbour, but proud and secretly joyful.

Jessamine had been at rest for nine months before the Doctor found his

---

group is now officially called the Scottish Rights of Way and Access Society. The Society was founded in 1845 and still exists today.

opportunity of fulfilling his wish to visit Colin Macgillvray. The continued existence of the man was a matter of speculation; but knowing the persistent habit of the Highland peasant, he had little doubt on that score. He plodded over the long white road, where Colin and Jessamine had driven together on the occasion of the encounter with the sheep, and where they had sauntered the evening after the sports, without being certain that he followed in her steps.

And yet he found the road full of her.

The moors, the hills, the forests, the beautiful and desolate parts, were things on which her eyes had rested, and he saw them in the light of that thought. When the houses and the hovels became a little less scattered— and even to-day that was all which could be said—he knew that he neared 'Jessamine's village,' and her hiding-place.

Pausing by a large field that edged the road with a wire-fence enclosure, he scanned the near country. The fence was spiked to prevent the trespassing legs of truant children or of tramps, and a man drove a mowing-machine round the field, and the barley fell with a musical sigh.

'Mechanism even here,' said the Doctor. 'One would welcome the iron man, did the fruits but fall into the right lap.'

And then he hailed his agricultural fellow-mortal.

A shouted conversation ensued, in the course of which the Doctor seemed to encounter many shades of many McKenzies, the description of none of whom wholly satisfied him.

'There will be Peter McKenzie living west'—here his informant pointed vaguely with his whip in the direction from which the Doctor had laboriously trudged—'McKenzie Craigowrie they call him; and there will be Alexander McKenzie south.' Here he pointed over the valley and the river to a distance, beautiful indeed, but desolating when contemplated from the point of view of a journey of research. 'I don't know of any John McKenzie nearer than Muirton.'

That was thirty miles off if an inch.

'John McKenzie Drynock,' said the Doctor, falling into the country manner—which had been easy to Jessamine's tongue—of naming the peasant after his bit of hired land.

'Drynock? Drynock?' repeated the man. 'Drynock will be yon.'

Here he pointed his whip to the slight appearance of chimney-pots and the side of a barn, amid a cluster of birch-trees.

'Willie Macbain owns Drynock. And I'm not knowing any John McKenzie nearer than Muirton.'

Here he lifted his hat, shouted 'Hadoof!' to his horses, and the fall of the barley continued.

The Doctor walked on in the direction of Drynock.

He found a handsome modern farm-building erected on the ground where the McKenzies' curious dwelling-house, with its superfluity of doors and paucity of windows, had once stood.

He walked up to the entrance, knocked, and inquired for John McKenzie.

'There will be no John McKenzie here. This will be Willie Macbain's.'

The Doctor sat down in the porch and wiped his brow, though in truth the day was gray and cold, not raining, but reminiscent of rain, and ready to rain again.

To all inquiries after John McKenzie, all tentatives towards winning some lingering legend of his farm-help, the woman who had opened the door at Willie Macbain's was blank. Then slowly, almost fearfully, he inquired after the man whose name was the last spoken murmur on the dead Jessamine's tongue. The woman's face brightened a little.

'There will be changes,' said she, 'and Willie built the farmhouse and the barns himself. He will not be here long, you see, sir. But I'm minding it all suddenly. It was John McKenzie he took the land off, sir.'

'And John McKenzie?'

'Well, sir, I'm thinking he just went off to Muirton. He has a brother there in the timber trade, sir. And land will be ever very changeable. So he went—him and his wife, sir. John will be seeing a bit into the world, whatever.'

'And Colin Macgillvray, what of him?' pursued the Doctor.

'Oh, Colin, sir?' The woman smiled a little. 'There will be changes, but Colin will ever be for sticking. He's slaw, sir.'

The Doctor perceived from this that, whatever else he might discover in Colin, he was certainly not a prophet within his own country. No startling achievement had marked him out for the wondering admiration of his fellows, it was plain. And the quality of 'sticking' tells chiefly when it is withdrawn.

Dalfaber, it appeared, was in very measurable distance, and the Doctor, turning away, took the same road—the little path through the heather—which still to his fancy palpitated with the fall of Jessamine's flying feet. It might be that, to another heart than his, it ever beat to the same measure.

The aspect of Dalfaber struck him as dreary. Where all else went on, and gathered some of the fruits of modern progress, displaying a new idea in the shape of a good barn, or improved implement, or better house-building, Dalfaber stood arrested. There was precisely the same measure of application as before, without the faintest sign of an advancing notion. The barns, which had been built before Jessamine's day, because the still older ones fell down, were there, of course, but the worse for the beating on them of the winds and showers of ten years. And the patch of land—the six poor fields and the stretch of moor—had the pathetic look which land wears when the tilling is done by steady industry, without the aid of inventiveness. Plod and magnificent patience—that was the sum put into the land; mind was absent.

As to the small stone house with the great chimney, that was as before. Its capacity for improvement had not been taken advantage of; no additional building had been added, nor had one square inch of the moorland been redeemed for a garden. In the same primitive way as ten years ago, the fields were unfenced and unwired, and the straying cattle and hens were shouted off by a hired lad, though the acquisition of such a help must have been a difficult matter.

Over the clumps of heather, blossoming now into a rich purple, Dr. Cornerstone saw the shaggy, broad heads of the longhorns snatching bits of sweet grass here and there, and looking up now and then with wild, startled, threatening eyes; and the limping shapes of the farm-horses, painfully wandering in search of pasture with their fore and hind legs tied together.

Picking his way towards the door of the small stone house, pitched in such astonishing, ungarnished desolateness on the brink of the moor, the Doctor mightily wondered within himself what manner of man this winner, and rejecter, of the heart of Jessamine Halliday would appear.

As he approached, the smoke swept down the side of the house from the great gaping chimney in a malicious gust. He passed the dim stained window, where old Rorie used to descry the merest glimpses of a world other than his own peat-fire, and stood before the ill-hung door, and knocked.

It seemed a great while before his knock awakened any movement from within. Presently he heard a chair thrust back; the sound gave him the impression of an empty house, or, rather, of its being the lonely habitation of one. Slow, firm steps were followed by the opening of the door, and a man stood before him, lifting his hand and touching his brow in the distant salute of the peasant. The action waved him off rather than deferred to him, and the Doctor recognised at once a proud and solitary nature.

He was a majestic-looking man of about forty years, with a brown weather-beaten skin, and a broad pair of shoulders having a slight stoop, which appeared rather as a patient inclination towards the ground that nurtured him, than a defect in the figure. The face touched the imagination of his visitor at once. Slowness and firm patience were written on every feature—a temperate nature, with untold powers of endurance. The brow was proud and the lips kindly. As to the eyes—the yellow-brown orbs—when he opened the door to the Doctor, they looked at him full of a long-waiting expectation; they were the eyes of a person to whom something of import, long delaying, will occur at last. Such, indeed, was the impress of the whole face.

Save for this, it was clear from the signs of mental conflict; but hours and hours of waiting had writ themselves upon it; it was a face full of hope deferred and yet courageously cherished.

These eyes of his changed suddenly when they met the Doctor's. They widened, flashed, and settled into certainty. With that, holding them quietly upon his visitor, he awaited from him the first word.

'I come from London,' began the Doctor gently.

'Walk in, sir,' said Colin; 'I am most glad to see you.'

His tone was subdued, as is the tone of one to whom the feast of life is solemn. Nevertheless, as he spoke, the Doctor knew by the clearer brownness of his skin that the blood had forsaken his cheek, and that his heart was throbbing.

He followed him into the room, into which Jessamine had so timidly stepped on the occasion of her first visit, and sat down, as she had done, on one of the carved straight-backed chairs.

Colin stood before his visitor. He clasped the wrist of one hand with the fingers of the other, and looked out of the window, his eyes still finding, as it were, their home and inspiration amongst the hills. A man of massive strength and staying power both physically and mentally, and slow as he had been described. He did not hurry now, though every pulse beat thunders. He waited, with the same large patience as through ten years he had waited, reluctant to snatch hastily what he knew had come to him at last, reserving and ever reserving himself.

'You live alone in this wide and airy place?' said the Doctor, who was, indeed, impressed by the sense of boundlessness which Colin's unfenced fields suggested, flowing as they did over into the moorland tract, and on from that to the mountains.

'My father and my mother will be dead,' answered Colin.

'And you are not married?'

The yellow-brown eyes slid from the hills, and rested on his visitor a trifle startled. They were, the Doctor remarked, too full of light. The Scotch believe in second sight, and these eyes, the Doctor thought, possessed the faculty. Macgillvray did not answer the question put to him, but his lips were wistful. Vague poetry, wordless, yet done into ten years of patience, struggled in his heart. It was still torn by the moment of loss ten years ago. But, above the unseen wound, Colin kept his fancies. When all else fails, the lover finds the unseen bread on which to feed, loaves unmanufactured and unknown, a delicate and growing store that increases with the use—the guiltless faithfulness that never swerves, and which becomes in the end its own sustenance.

Colin without reply eyed the Doctor, with his face slowly changing under the stirring of deeply repressed sensitiveness.

'I bring you—a kind of message,' said the latter huskily.

'From Jessie?'

The long-unuttered name—the word too ever-present to be spoken—loosed itself from his tongue with trembling reluctance.

The Doctor inclined his head.

'She is dead,' said Colin with conviction.

'You had heard it, then?' asked the Doctor, both surprised and relieved.

'I will just be knowing it,' he returned.

And then he seated himself, as though he needed support under the strain of this conversation, but motioned with his hand that the Doctor should continue his story. And that was a difficult thing with a man who knew one burning chapter off by heart, who was in himself the essence of that chapter, but who possessed no clue to the beginning, or the end, of the volume.

Dr. Cornerstone endeavoured to hint, as clearly as he could, what position in the great world had been held by the McKenzies' farm-help. The man listened attentively, without exhibiting surprise.

'Oh yes, indeed!' said he; 'she will not be common.'

The Doctor came to her marriage. The patient brows of the peasant changed very slightly.

'I am just naething but a farmer,' said he; 'and he would be a great laird. And will she be loving him best? She was bonnie enough to be queen.'

His worship disallowed of jealousy. But the crux of the story lay here. With intense painstaking care, cutting the lines at each sentence a little deeper to make the impressions clearer, the Doctor strove to render truly the history of Jessamine. He was deeply conscious, as he spoke, of the incongruity between this troubled complex tale, and the massive simplicity of the nature that had the right to hear it. A silent mountainous greatness it seemed to him, akin to the scene in which the man had passed his days. But a nerve of Colin's nature burnt responsive to all that concerned Jessamine, and it is probable the Highlander understood more than the Londoner guessed.

'It will just open locked doors to me,' said he presently, when the Doctor had ceased speaking. 'Whiles,' he added, the sensitive reluctance creeping again into his face when he spoke—'whiles, I have felt as though it had all been a dreaming and a sleep, and as though I was just on the edge of waking. You'll not be knowing the feel of that, maybe, sir? I must just be getting up to open the door and look; I must just be turning my head over my shoulder, to catch sight of her slipping away like the wraith that she was.

'Whiles, it has seemed like a great lonely darkness, and me walking in it forever straight on, and nothing at the end. And then when I was fit to lie down with a sore great cry, sir—if you will excuse the liberty—I would just be feeling a wee bit hand in mine, and a tug against my shoulder. And—you'll not know the feel of it, sir—the loneliness filled up, and there was ever a flutter of a woman's garment after me, in the fields and on the moor.

'You see, sir, I changed nothing. I was ever fearing, indeed, to turn a clod that her wee bit foot had pressed. I was fearing to mend up and alter, lest I should take something that her hand had touched. And I was ever fearing in myself, sir, to lose her from my heart. It will be just there that I was building the new house for her, whatever.

'The neighbours laugh and call me slaw. It will seem no great matter to me. I'm thinking, whiles, that the roof that had her under it will be good enough for me indeed. I'm busy at another kind of worruk. My house and my land will just rot down with myself, sir, and my Jessie will be in them to the end.'

His hands moved with the first nervous feeling he had exhibited, and the Doctor surmised the stirring of mighty repressed emotions.

'You'll notice what I said of building her a house here, sir?'

And he laid both hands together with a gentle primitive movement against his heart.

'Yes,' said the Doctor.

'Aweel. It would be one evening last autumn that I was just dozing a bit by my fire, after the day's worruk was done. And I will hardly know if I was dreaming or not. But, indeed, and I was thinking that I saw her clear—face to face again—a wee bit white face it was, and it lay before me like a picture. I am not knowing if I was dreaming it or not, but, indeed, I sat looking, and fearing to move lest it should go. But it stayed with me, sir. And it was an uplift to a sair, sair heart. And an evening or two after I was sitting here again, and, indeed, I was thinking and waiting.

'And there came a little whisper. It will perhaps just be an echo. She would be saying my name whiles long ago with a bit of a laugh at the end of it—to get it right she would be saying. And I just heard her voice again in a little whisper:

'"*Colin Macgillvray Dalfaber.*"

'It went like the cut of a sword to my heart, and set me listening and shaking. I sat still as a mousie listening and looking—*looking*. God! how a body can look whiles! I was feeling her just behind me. I was seeing her in the ingle[3] or near the door. I was hearing the rustle of her dress past the window. And then I *knew* she was running over the moor to my house. So then I sprang up and opened the doors, and set them wide, and stood looking into the night, and stretching my arms for her. God! how a body can look whiles! I thought my eyes would cut the darkness open. God! how the soul can call when the tongue is still!

'I kept the door ever on the latch all these years, so that she could never be saying that Colin's door was barred against her. So that she could *feel,* wherever in the world she hid, that my door was open. But that night I threw it wide, and sat and bided. And presently it seemed to me that the house I had been building was full.'

The man's head dropped suddenly, and he covered his face with a great sigh.

'You will understand, sir,' said he in a low, quiet voice when he had regained his self-mastery, 'that I just knew she was dead, and had come to me that way.'

The Doctor said nothing; he stared at the hills. A great silence fell between the two. When Colin spoke again it was with his ordinary composure.

'And so my Jessie was a great leddie?' said he.

The Doctor marked the quietly appropriating pronoun.

'In the world's eye she was so. But not in her own.'

'She was just a wee bit thing, and it would be a sight of turmoil for her.'

'It was a great turmoil.'

'She loved me best?'

'She loved you only.'

'I'm just a common farming body. But she was true.'

'As steel.'

Explanations, definitions, excuses, and all the glosses necessary for a less balanced and less deep nature, were, the Doctor perceived, superfluous here. Colin had the sort of greatness which can see the thing in its essence, without the small despairing restlessness of those who curiously inquire into the imperfection of detail. The lasting and the eternal were enough for him; the passing flaws went unconsidered.

'It will be a sight of comfort,' he said—'a sight of comfort. But I was ever knowing it in my heart, though sore perplexed to understand. There will be

---

3   Ingle: "a fire on a hearth" (*CSD* 315).

things,' he added, 'a body does not go into easily.' He made one of his long, slow pauses. 'And now,' he said as though to himself, 'she has come home.'

The Doctor rose. Macgillvray rose also, wearing that hospitable manner which sat well on his proud and lonely nature. His visitor murmured something of finding his way there another year.

'I shall be most glad, whatever,' said he, with his gentle aloof air.

As he stood at the door, Dr. Cornerstone turned to get another glimpse into the yellow-brown eyes, and he saw that they glanced past his shoulder, and rested upon the mountains.

'The hills look butifully,' said Colin.

And then he raised his hand quietly in the peasant's salute.

THE END

APPENDIX A

Preface to the fifth, one-volume edition of *A Superfluous Woman*[1]

In sending out a new edition of my story, I cannot but take the opportunity of thanking my readers for their interest, and for the kind way in which they welcomed its first appearance. Its great success was unlooked for by me, and has been a deep pleasure.

While also thanking my many careful critics, I should like to disclaim having written with any special theory. I am no convinced theorist; and if the story has opened out problems and suggested a special moral, that is only what the recital of any human experience would do. A complaint has been lodged against my title. I may, perhaps, be permitted to explain that the designation 'superfluous' appears to me to belong to persons who fail, from whatever cause, to find and fulfil the function nature has intended them to perform in life.

I must add that my momentary popularity has disclosed to me that, however smiling a face Success may wear, the hair-shirt is concealed beneath. For in the moment of encouragement the strong light thrown upon my work by so much publicity shows me, in a way that nothing else could do, its amazing faults. I have, in the consciousness of them, a certain timidity in sending out my book again, and I can but commend it to the leniency of that kind public who, for the sake of what there is of merit in it, have already shown so much goodwill towards

THE AUTHOR.

June, 1894

---

1   Emma Brooke. Preface. *A Superfluous Woman*. 5th ed. London: Heinemann, 1894.

APPENDIX B - CONTEMPORARY REVIEWS

The Review of Reviews (January – June 1894), pp. 191-192

The passion of love in its most elemental form has been almost too much in evidence in very recent fiction; in this novel it is the one dominating influence, the motive that gives strength and influence to the whole. Yet it is so treated that the book is hardly likely to give offence to any but the foolish; while its tragic end, pitilessly pointing the result of libertinage and of marriages in which all wisdom, physical and moral, is forgotten in worldly advantage, is such a lesson as cannot be too often or too well learned. Artistically, there are points in which the story is unsatisfactory: that Jessamine Halliday should have wearied of a society in which hers always was the conquest, is credible, but that she should have adopted the advice of her mentor, Dr. Cornerstone, by hiding herself in a remote Scottish village and helping in the housework of a cottage, in order to show that she could do some good, some work, in the world, has many of the elements of farce. She meets in Scotland the young farmer whose magnificent, splendid manhood, making him so great a contrast to the men of her past, overcomes her, overbears all the dictates of prudence and convention, and, but for his honesty, might have brought about a catastrophe wrecking her future. It is in these chapters that the anonymous author presents primal passion, uncumbered [sic] of the trappings of shame and habit, with a simplicity and a directness unequalled in recent English fiction. Saved almost by accident from the consequences of her own folly, and terrified at the narrowness of her escape, Jessamine returns to London, resumes her place in society as its acknowledged beauty, and marries the peer, old and diseased, who anxious to provide himself with a legal heir, had for months persecuted her with his attentions. The tragedy of the marriage recalls the "speckled toad" episode in the "Heavenly Twins," and the obvious difficulties of presentment are here treated with a straightforwardness unexcelled even by Mrs. Grand. In short, "A Superfluous Woman" is a clever book, and a useful [one]. Whether it will attain the success of "The Heavenly Twins" is yet to be seen, but the good that it will do will be much on the same lines. The questions of morality and of women's position that it raises are ripe for solution, and their treatment in a manner so courageous cannot but be productive of good. Its most serious fault is its title, and that is grotesquely inaccurate.

The Literary World (February 24, 1894), p. 58

This novel, which is published anonymously, is written with earnestness, and is interesting both as a story and for its theories of life. The heroine, beautiful, young, and rich, was made for better things than the life of society dissipation to which she had been brought up. Afraid of being drawn into a loveless, mercenary marriage, she gives it up and takes refuge with a Scotch family in the Highlands, where she throws herself into all kinds of household and farm duties, seeking to find simplicity of life and to do serviceable work. Thus far there is nothing noteworthy in the book. The author has not yet gained the power to hold our attention from the outset, and the opening chapters have an incoherent, tentative quality; but here begins the love between the society woman and a simple Scotch farmer, and the chapters become strong, natural, and original in many respects. The character of Colin is effectively depicted, and his retrained devotion, to which he brings almost a religious fervor, is well contrasted with the passion of the young girl, who longs to give herself to the man she loves, but who cannot bring herself to accept his daily life. She leaves him to go back to London, and her later life is told in a few scenes, which one reads with interest, but which are not the strongest in the book.

The Athenæum (February 3, 1894), p. 144

A novelist whose most obvious purpose in writing a story is to proclaim to a corrupt generation his (or her) convictions about things in general is probably very young, and certainly very inexperienced, both with regard to society as it is and to novel-writing as it ought to be. Most people have at one time or other been possessed with a desire to preach a sermon. Many have found reason on reaching mature years to be grateful that no opportunity was afforded them of giving public utterance to a series of platitudes, or of generalizations which experience often proves to have been founded on rare instances. The author of 'A Superfluous Woman' has preached her sermon—it is too feminine a discourse to suggest the male pronoun. Her text is the law of heredity, which is in itself not a new one. Her theme is the wickedness of a girl selling herself in marriage to a vicious and effete aristocrat, the product of a race "outworn" physically and morally. The subject also is familiar; so is the conventional hero, who is, fortunately for our generation, more often met with in fiction or in melodrama than in real life. So depraved a creature as Lord Heriot is at any rate hardly to be taken as the type of an English aristocrat of to-day, and all the expressions used about him have a fine, old-world flavour.

Jessamine Halliday's restlessness and vague enthusiasm are far more usual in modern life than the exceptionally undesirable marriage which she finally elected to make. A turbulent and hysterical young woman who runs away from the hollowness of her surroundings to lead a higher life in a station to which neither God nor man called her, is not likely to profit very much by the experiment. Jessamine in fact did not, but had the sufficient saving grace to stop short of tying an honest yeoman farmer to herself and her whimsies for life. The last volume is full of lurid lights and coal-black shadows in which realities have little to do. Jessamine faintly recalls Miss Schreiner's immortal Lyndall at times, but she has neither the strength nor the poetry of that extravagant little spirit. The author shows some aptitude for writing, and would probably do much better with less indulgence in theory and more observation of life. A word of hearty praise must be bestowed on the charming binding with which the publisher has clothed the book. Its exterior is, at any rate, thoroughly artistic if the contents are not.

Lancaster Examiner (July 4, 1894), p. 7

Is it owing to the spread of democratic principles, or to a more truthful observation and delineation of real life, that writers of fiction have recently pulled aside more ruthlessly than they were wont the screens that too often conceal the leprous spots of "the upper ten?" Vice is not, of course, confined to the high in station, but it exists there as black as in the foulest slums, and it is more odious because mankind was trying to believe that wealth was the alchemist whose magic wand could transmute vice into virtue, or present it as an amiable weakness or an innocent pleasantry. Society wears a smiling exterior, but it has cupboards, and each contains a skeleton. Many of its customs are cruel as ogres, and hundreds of young lives fall yearly as sacrifices to the relentless monster. The anonymous author of this book has very touchingly illustrated this aspect of our much vaunted civilization: one charming girl offered on the altar of the insatiate Moloch,[1] whilst all the light and spring were for ever taken from the life of her disconsolate lover. The writer displays a wonderful power of emotional analysis, and is deservedly severe on those customs of society which outrage the natural outflow of pure affection, and wreck future happiness to gain coveted wealth or distinction that may be possessed by some vile, selfish, sensualist, of whom Dr. Cornerstone thought that the most important thing was not that Lord Heriot should reform, but that he and his race should pass into annihilation. It is an admirable tale.

---

1   Moloch: a god associated with child sacrifice.

The West Australian (July 17, 1894), p. 5

The authoress of "A Superfluous Woman" has chosen to hide beneath the mask of anonymity, but her book will not need the weight of a name to make it a success, or to smooth out the flaws, which in places disfigure a work otherwise beautiful. The first part is a love idyll, delightfully told, full of passion and power. The lady of high degree, rich, beautiful and accomplished, falls a victim to the innocent strength of character and unaffected tenderness of the peasant. Satiated with society, loved of her noble admirer, she seeks the Real, eagerly turning away from the world of shams and make-believe, to the Natural and the Actual. In the Highlands she suddenly meets with a stalwart peasant, stout in limb, sound in body, pure in mind. Before she is aware of it she has lost her heart to him. The moment she appeared he set her upon the altar of his affections and worshipped her from afar off. There are delightful incidents in the tale of their ripening love. It forms a pastoral in prose. The second part takes us away from the country, from the poetry and the beauty of the world. It confronts us with the rotten side of society, revolting and cruel, with the punishment of the children for the sins of the fathers. The first part of "A Superfluous Woman" will be read with pleasure almost enthralling, then the page turns to the distasteful subjects of hereditary disease and loveless marriage, and the reader regrets that the delightful introduction should have led to the perusal of a chapter of sin and its consequences. Yet it is not intended to condemn the whole of the latter portion of the work, the concluding pages—picturing connubial love and confidence—in a measure restore the mind to a happier frame, even though the worthy couple and their friends can find nothing better to discuss than the problem of sex. Still the discussion is pitched in a hopeful mood, and the book closes with a scene of real pathos, the portrayal of the bereaved peasant, in the calm dignity of a great grief, standing beside the cottage door, looking out on the blue mountains beyond, full of fidelity and constancy to the woman who has brought into his life his greatest joy and his deepest sorrow.

APPENDIX C

'Women and their Sphere' by E. Fairfax Byrrne

Our Corner. January Vol. IX (1888): 5–13 and February Vol. IX (1888): 64–73

WHEN the question of women's wages is under discussion, a variety of reasons for their unsatisfactory state are suggested. But as, when studying the question of all wage-receivers (male or female), one feels that the causes popularly alleged for their depressed condition are inadequate and secondary, and that they do not touch the root of the matter, so, in this particular department, one is conscious of superficiality in even the best reasoned popular writing on the subject.

Things that are continuously wrong need revolutionising and not patching up. And the preliminary to salutary reform is a searching question. Some such searching question as to the primary cause of the lowness of women's wages when compared with men's, we propose to ourselves in this paper.

What, then, is the primary cause of the lowness of women's wages when compared with men's?

To answer this question, we must ask a second which will carry us at once into the region of our simple and primitive emotions and feelings. The State is divided into two sexual halves: How does either of these two great armies of men and women regard the other in the light of use and value to itself? To which question, one must reply that, *primarily*, the value of women to men is their sexual value, their value as workers being a very secondary matter; whereas, *primarily*, the value of men to women is their capacity and power for work and defence, their sexuality being but secondary. It is not affirmed that the working power of women has no value in the eyes of men, nor that the sexuality of men has no value in the eyes of women for that would be an absurdity. The point is, that the *primary* value is reversed in the eyes of either sex when considering the other.

The effect of this disparity in the way in which one sex holds the other to be of value, is, in the first place, to retain the man's feeling of dominance over the woman at a time when prejudices of society, prerogatives of sex, monopolies of all kinds, are breaking down under the slow recognition of the true equality of the sexes, and of the right of the individual (whether male or female) to use his or her powers as he or she thinks best, for the service of the community. That which brought the woman into subjection to the man is not this matter of predominant sexual feeling; it was something different, namely, the exigencies of motherhood. But it is the former which, in spite of the light of modern ideas, retains her in subjection. It does so, through two effects: the first being direct, the second indirect.

The direct effect is that a marketable value attaches to her personality, and causes her to be brought into dependence upon an individual man or men—practically to be purchased and held as a slave or chattel.

The indirect effect is, that the commercial value attached to her personality lowers the wages which she receives for the performance of industrial labor, by opening to her a resource other than that of labor. For, economically, it is an accepted fact that when an expedient, other than immediate wages given for immediate work done, exists for any wage-receiving class, the effect is to lower wages. The effect of the old poor-law was to lower wages by opening to laborers another resource than that of remuneration for honest work done. It did not make a difference to individual laborers whether they availed themselves of this assistance or not; there was the fund, and it was so much deducted from their wages. So of women. Not all women are wives or prostitutes, nevertheless, the wages of all women are conditioned by their sexual resources; their sexuality is a saleable thing; marriage or prostitution is open to all, and a reserve fund being thus established in fact, their honest wages suffer.

Let us now pass on to ask, what posture does the State take towards the predominant sexuality of women?

The reply to this question is, that the English law does not concern itself with the value attached to women's sexuality, any more than the American slave law concerned itself with the value attached to the muscular force of a negro. The law, that is, does not recognise *the use to the State* of the negro's force, or of the woman's sexuality. On the contrary, the essence of a woman's sexual value and of a negro's muscular value is, in the eyes of the law, not their respective *uses to the State*, but their relations to individual men or masters; it therefore contents itself with merely regulating the conditions of the two forms of slavery. This being the case, it is merely logical and natural that the responsibility for a woman's maintenance and welfare, as of a negro's, should be made to rest upon the goodwill of the individual man or men, into whose power she passes. To sum up shortly: the law, not recognising the value of the sexuality of women in its use to the State, makes no national provision for the maintenance of wives and prostitutes; but recognising the value of this sexuality to individual men, regulates the conditions under which they shall have and hold it. Thus we get in some countries, State regulation of prostitution: laws which seem, to competent judges, inhuman and foolish and useless. Then we get laws regulating marriage: a code described by a French writer as, in England, so arbitrary that "the marital authority is made to press with an absolutely crushing weight upon" the wife.

In the early stages of human society, the exigencies of motherhood having brought the female gradually into subjection to the male, it is easy to conceive how it was that, starting from this natural function, a preponderance of the sexual idea gathered around the persons of women, to the detriment of that which is broadly human—the specifically feminine being developed to the loss of the common humanity in them. We are all, men and women, the products of that which has gone before, and we can on neither side bring railing accusation against the other; because the laws of a necessary past have shaped us, and have carried us through that unconscious foregoing darkness, to cast us, ready made and conscious, upon this shore of the present. Therefore it cannot be in the spirit of accusation that, looking into facts as we find them, we state, *First*, that the SEXUAL SPHERE—which has been gradually shaped about women through the preponderance of the sexual idea in their connexion, and back into which men continually and peremptorily press them—proves, when examined by the light of acquired reason, to be non-natural and arbitrary. And, *secondly*, that though the erection of this impalpable prison around them may very well have been the result of various necessities in the phases of development through which the race has passed, to wish to keep them locked therein in the present is the result of prejudice: that is, of the fact that all the individuals of the world, running the race of human development, do not touch the goal of the new thought abreast, but in lagging and disordered ranks, many being but halt and blind.

Women, however, have been found throughout historic time making continual efforts to shake off the preponderance of the sexual idea, and to stand in an economic world as free of it as man can be. But the cry of men to women has always been and still, for the most part, is: "Your value in our eyes is your sexuality, of your work we will have none."

The language used is not always so plain. We meet the idea sugared over with conciliatory sweetness or polished innuendo, until the meaning is well-nigh lost. A single and somewhat ludicrous instance will suffice. In a *Times* leader dated 1834, the following passage may be found; Harriet Martineau[1]

---

1 Harriet Martineau (1802–1876) was an English journalist, social theorist and political economist. She is considered to be the first female sociologist.

had, it appears, written an economic pamphlet on strikes—"We certainly," says the *Times*, "do not rank ourselves amongst this lady's general admirers; her subjects seem to us, for the most part, unsuitable to a female pen".

The opinion which divides activities, either mental or physical, into two sexual lines, is receding; in quality, that is to say, it is the same now as when the *Times* spoke, but in quantity, in mass, it is smaller. The fact that industries are less and less sharply divided into male and female, is a sign that the charmed circle of the sexual sphere is already giving way to the pressure of new ideas. Nevertheless, instances of complete and successful escape from it are at present few and rare. Many women, for example—a very great and increasing number—throw off the preponderance of the sexual idea sufficiently to justify by their works a right to stand independently of it, and of the assistance of male relations, in an economic world. They have, by so doing, prepared the way for great and beneficial changes; and the importance of their work cannot be exaggerated, every woman who frees herself from dependence upon others, being a pioneer towards the emancipation of her sex; for only be this economic independence can real freedom be won. In spite of these economically successful instances the sexual sphere, *in its purely sexual side*, remains almost intact. And it is the purely sexual side which forms the object of consideration in this paper.

Women are divided by the sexual sphere into three classes:

I Legal wives.
II Paid prostitutes.
III Celibates.

[We include under the head "Paid Prostitutes" those mistresses who are secretly kept by a large number of men.]

By the opinion of society a woman must stand in one of these three divisions. Irregularities, however, occur.

We can think, for the moment, of just two examples (though there must be more) where the complete escape from the sexual sphere has been successfully effected:—has been effected, that is, without loss of personal dignity, or injury to moral character. The allusion is to Mary Wollstonecraft and to George Eliot.[2] These women were capable of standing in an economic world

2   Mary Wollstonecraft (1759–1797) was an English author and supporter of women's rights, most famous for *A Vindication of the Rights of Woman* (1792). George Eliot (1819–1880) is considered to be one of the greatest women novelists of the Victorian era. Her most famous novels are *The Mill on the Floss* (1860) and *Middlemarch* (1871-72). Brooke's admiration for these two writers probably derives from the fact that both women supported themselves with their writing and at the same time chose to live with men outside of marriage.

on their own basis, and, in addition, openly broke through the sexual sphere and lived in their sexual life, in the eye of the world, outside of and apart from it. Whether they were "right" or "wrong", is a matter which individual minds will argue over. But few, if any, will venture to assert that the step they took was a retrogression in morals, or was undignified, profligate, or unnatural, or was even a step which could earn for them social contempt. The truth is that to very many minds, these two women stand out somewhat in the light of fore-runners.

Stress, however, must be laid upon the *openness* of their conduct. There are other irregularities, which cannot claim for themselves this singular success—this moral integrity kept intact while trespassing upon the conventional moral code. For these other digressions from the sexual sphere are secret ones, and are accompanied by the payment to conventionality of an ignoble tax in fear and subterfuge. Such irregularities point surely rather to an error in the moral judgment of the individual, than to wholesome and renovating force of character. Moreover, they cannot be of any use to society, but are, on the contrary, harmful as opening a door to the spirit of profligacy; and assuredly, we may take it to be the aim of all sexual reform to extinguish profligacy, and to establish noble manners; such manners as may render it every day easier for men and women to approach each other in the frank spirit of useful friendliness, without, on the one hand, the embarrassment of the predominant idea of sexuality, and, on the other, of that anxious, commercial, stock-jobbing spirit, which lies behind much of the social intercourse of to-day.

At present, however, many men and women oppose the breakdown of the sexual sphere for reasons which are perfectly comprehensible. On the side of men, is, *first*, an alarm that their resource, or wages, will be encroached upon—an alarm which is, economically, fallacious. And *second*, mere prejudice, a fear that the world will not be so pleasant, possibly not so moral, a place, when the economic independence of women has resulted in her personal and sexual freedom. On the side of women is, *first*, a shrinking from the effort and responsibility of continuous labor—a reason unmitigatedly bad. And *second*, another and much more serious reason, which is cogent enough to demand prolonged consideration.

Before touching upon this serious obstacle in the way of women's emancipation, it may be useful to give an analysis of the three divisions of the sexual sphere. The following is from an American paper:[3]—

"Class I. The man offers the woman love and maintenance. He asks from the

---

3   This analysis was found by the writer in Irma von Troll-Barostzani's book "Im freien Reich" [original footnote].

woman: the sacrifice of her own birth-name and of her independence, life-long service, the subjection of her own personality to him as a right of property, even to the
destruction of her health if he wishes it. Condition, marriage.

"Class II. He offers to the woman momentary maintenance. He asks from her:
the sacrifice of her good fame: a life of vice: finally abandonment, want and misery.
Condition, prostitution.

"Class III. He offers the woman sufferance and charity. She realises social insignificance. Condition, celibacy."

One is conscious of exaggeration in this analysis. It is exaggerated because it takes no account of exceptions—of the many who are happy and will
continue to be happy in spite of the sexual law they are under—and seems
to depict the whole female sex as plunged in misery. Which is an error. Take
Class III for instance. In this class, the risks of misery are less than in any
other. Under even a reformed system of sexual relationship many women
(as doubtless some men) will continue to prefer celibacy. Under the present
system, a large number have preferred as well as have been compelled into it.
And, under the present system, a great many gifted, celibate women, as well
as very many industrious, celibate, working-women, have won a high measure of freedom and consideration in the industrial world and are able to hold
their own and to raise themselves high above insignificance. In short, one may
be inclined to say that in this imperfect world, celibate working-women of
whatever kind have very little to complain of; they live, that is to say, full and
useful lives. But in thinking of the fortunate celibate women, we must not
forget her less fortunate sister who has lately been breathing her woes through
the pages of the daily papers, under the title of "Lady-companion". Such a
woman appears to taste the ashy fruit of insignificance as the daily food of
life, with deforming results upon her character and intellect. The analysis
is no exaggeration in its description when applied to her. But, whether the
celibacy is the cause of the disheartening result, or whether this cause should
be sought for in some other direction, it is not within the scope of this paper definitely to decide; distinctly, however, the opinion may be expressed
that celibacy has very little to do with the matter. No further, perhaps, than
this:—that the expectation of marriage in which girls are brought up, has
a bad effect upon their energies in other departments, and the anxiety and
disappointment consequent upon this monotonous restriction in the element
of hope, have a warping and stunting effect upon the temper and character.

Of Class II, prostitutes, little can here be said. The accounts of the sufferings of these women belong in the eyes of a Socialist to the catalogue of crimes.

De Toqueville,[4] in his "Democracy in America" makes a remark which calls, however, for comment. It is worth while to repeat and to reply to it, because it embodies an opinion which obtained a little time back, and which lingers still amongst the ranks of those who lag in the race of development. He says of these women that they should "be treated as foul sewers are treated, as physical facts and not moral agents". Few "all-round" modern thinkers will be inclined to endorse that cynical saying; the spread of Socialism is beginning to purge from the conscience the inclination to accept tranquilly the sacrifice of any class of human beings for another; and the spread of scientific culture has broken the force in such dicta as the following: "Prostitution has always existed and *therefore* must always exist". On the contrary, it is a growing opinion that prostitution is not a necessity, but merely a product of imperfect institutions, and that under an improved state of society, it will, whether as regulated by the State or merely as condoned by society, of itself dwindle rapidly away. At any rate, one may say with confidence that it is impossible to take a moral agent and treat him or her as an unconscious fact—be that fact foul or fair; and further, that if indeed prostitution be a necessary fact, then, in the light of the modern conscience, the words of De Toqueville require a strange expansion. For the new awakening conscience of the race cannot permit any human necessity to be laid as a burden on any particular class of men and women, so that from this or that class *alone* shall be levied the recruits to bear that burden—it cannot permit it whether the burden be that of labor or of prostitution.

The first class remains to be mentioned, that of wives. Here, more than elsewhere, the American paper will be charged with exaggeration in its analysis. And yet, it is just here than some such unmitigated statement is of special use. To say that a very large number of married persons are living together in happy equality, and that the woman is unconscious of the harsh conditions of the class she has entered, is an irrelevancy; it is simply to say that men are, for the most part, a great deal better than the laws they have made. The fact remains that, as John Stuart Mill says,[5] the law of this land does give into the hand of every male ruffian, a female slave to treat as he will short of murder. And though many happy women remain untouched by the legal conditions they have placed themselves under, there these conditions still are, ready to rise into painful prominence at any unexpected turn of events. Surely it is an

---

4   Alexis de Tocqueville (1805–1859) was an aristocratic French writer who is most famous for his work, *Democracy in America* (Vol. 1 1835 and Vol. 11 1840) in which he explores all aspects of political culture in America in the early nineteenth century, including: racism, class structures, the press, money, and the judicial system.
5   "Subjection of Women" [original footnote].

error—a sign of a most imperfect state of society—to bind legally the fate of any human being into absolute dependence upon that changeful, incalculable thing, the character of another.

When the best is said that can be said, it would be highly optimistic and certainly untrue to affirm that the majority of marriages are happy. Even if we allowed this optimistic view for purposes of argument, we must still grant that the provisos which some married couples find not incompatible with happiness, are retained at the expense of the torment and misery of others. And it cannot be denied that the concomitants of marriage, as for many centuries we have had it, are the subsidiary states of celibacy and prostitution.

Whether, however, the legal bond of marriage could be got rid of in the present state of society is a question demanding very serious consideration.

But we may venture to remark with confidence that in a better state of society the interference of law will be used in a precisely opposite direction from the present—not, that is, to keep people together whether they love each other or do not (for here interference is either superfluous or evil), but to provide escapes in case the ties of nature and affection prove weak, or become a torment and oppression.

BUT is it possible, looking on to a better state of society, to foresee a remedy—to cut the intricate knot wherein the sexual and economic positions of women are intimately blended together? Can a woman possess herself, and stand in an economic world and work therein as free from considerations of her sexuality, as a man can?

A physician has given the following as his opinion:—

"With all her bodily weakness when compared with man, the woman can accomplish more for herself and for her sex in this world of competition without his sympathy and with her freedom, than she can without her freedom and with his support and sympathy."

These are words of wide issues. It would be a hard thing for women to do without the support and sympathy of men, whether given in friendship or in love. *Yet it is impossible to find an equivalent for liberty.* And therefore one may take these words to be a moderate statement of a great truth. Indeed, it is more than probable, it is certain, that the difference in physical strength between the two sexes is greatly exaggerated by the unnatural conditions of civilisation. Having regard to what is already accomplished by working women, one may affirm that this physical debility, as compared with man, is not sufficient to found any argument upon, while the fact that women of all classes are ready to accept cheerfully, gladly, free competition in the work of the world on an equality with men, in spite of their physical inferiority, is a final reply to any objection that may be raised. They will accept their liberty with the risks.

Irma *v.* Troll-Barostzani,[6] in the book already quoted, gives five conditions which are necessary to the emancipation of women. They are as follows:—

"I. The complete social and political equality of the two sexes.

"II. Perfectly unconditioned freedom in the dissolution of marriage.

"III. The abolition of prostitution as a legalised or tolerated institution.

"IV. A fundamental reform in the education of the youth of both sexes.

"V. The education of children in the State institutions at the cost and under the guidance of the State."

Taken singly, some of these conditions have been tried here and there before. The important thing is that they should be tried simultaneously.

To try, for example, number two alone ("unconditioned freedom in the dissolution of marriage") would add to the miseries of women by throwing them into more anxious dependence upon their husbands. Many men, and still more women, strenuously oppose freedom in the dissolution of marriage, because they both see very plainly that, under the present conditions of society, this might merely issue in practically freeing the man from his share in the duties and responsibilities of the contract, while leaving upon the woman the penalty of her's.

Taking those five conditions together, however, we find the woman standing independently in an economic world just as the man does, and no more compelled to use her sexuality as a commercial resource than he is. But it is surely necessary to add to these conditions yet another in order that the emancipation may not only be won but be retained. And upon this last and sixth condition we may dwell at some length, the more so that it forms the woman's peculiar objection to sexual reform, referred to above.[7]

It has before been remarked, that the difference in the physical strength of the sexes is exaggerated. Yet in all discussions about the sexes, when advocating the absolute equality of men and women, one is haunted by the thought that, after all, there is an eternal difference which cannot be got over. This difference is the function of motherhood. The condition, therefore,

6   Irma v. Troll-Barostyáni (1847–1912) was an Austrian writer and feminist who was an advocate for women's rights. She was particularly interested in the education of women, marriage and family, and the public life of women. *Im Freien Reich* (1884) is an examination of social problems concerning women in various cultures and countries and how those problems can be solved.

7   It should be stated, that the objections come from the higher and middle-classes. Women of the working and lower classes would probably offer none [original footnote].

which it is necessary to add to the five set down above, is the following: That motherhood, the function of reproducing and nourishing the new life of the State, be recognised as a State function, and be supported and maintained by the State; and that the fruit of the union of two of the opposite sex be not regarded as primarily belonging to the parents, but as primarily belonging to the State. In other words, the sexual value of the woman (in so far as it differs from the sexuality of men) must be recognised by the State in its use to the State, and be therefore supported by the State. Obviously, however, the State must have the concomitant right of regulating the amount of motherhood— *i.e.,* of population—with which it will burden itself.

Looking back on the early natural life of man, we find that, broadly speaking, the work of the world was divided into two great parts. The man had the share of killing the life, whether of man or animal, inimical to the tribe or needed by the tribe; the woman the share of continuing and nourishing the life of the tribe itself. There was nothing arbitrary in this division, it was in itself a natural outcome of natural causes. What was arbitrary about it was that the man's work, being performed under more striking circumstances, and with more apparent effort and danger, drew to itself a certain prestige, which the woman's did not receive. Her work, on the contrary, was held in contempt. This arbitrary distinction as to the worth of different kinds of work, and the disparity of rewards, runs through all history and is linked, not only to the respective works of men and women, but also to the works of freemen and slaves. The same broad division follows us still in all our complicated civilisation; the man's distinctive share, very broadly speaking, is still to destroy life (it certainly is the part of men of the dominant classes); the woman's distinctive share, again broadly speaking, is to continue and nourish life. But these two broad divisions have now many accessories, and these last have become, as it were, overlapped; that is, in the accessory works of both kinds, both sexes now participate. The broad division, still, however, remains, and with it the other arbitrary condition; the distinctive work of man (whether now performed by male or female hands) gets pay and prestige, while the distinctive work of woman (whether in its accessories now performed by male or female hands) gets no prestige and little pay. For, whereas that work which is closely allied to the distinctively male part—the part of soldierdom, of destroying life—is State-recognised and very highly paid work, the nearer any other labor gets to the original distinctively feminine part, that of motherhood, of nourishing life, the less is it recognised as of State use, and the less is it paid.

This thought is not an adequate or proven one, or anything but merely tentative; and we can but dwell on it for a moment. Imagine a graduated column, representing the high wages of soldierdom; at the base is soldierdom, pure and simple, the merely dominant and fighting man, the chief, and the most highly paid. The nearer any industry is to the point at the base the higher are the wages; as industries remove from this base and reach the top of the column, the less do they partake of mere fight and dominance, the lower is the pay.

On the other hand is a column—graduated in a precisely opposite way—representing the low wages of motherhood; at the base is motherhood pure and simple, unrecognised and unpaid. The nearer any industry is to the point at the base—the more purely feminine it is, and the more it partakes of the life-nourishing quality—the less it is paid; whereas, industries that retire from the base, and reach the top of the column, are, in proportion as they lose the element of motherhood, better paid industries. In the industries removed from either base, both sexes participate. It might be an interesting matter to go into the question of these accessory industries; there is not, however, space in this paper. But one may observe, at least, that as civilisation advances, those works (or no-works) standing closest to the point Soldierdom, and representative of what is *now* pure dominance and destructiveness, will probably be shortly recognised by society as excrescences and superfluities, and will fall away. Thrones, dominions, powers, standing armies, landlords, capitalists and so on, seem already to have been marked "condemned" by the forerunning thought of the age. The industries closely accessory will probably be recognised as useful and necessary for a long time to come.

The mother, however, *as the type of that which nourishes life*, always remains and gathers under her direction more and more of the accessory industries of the time. Agriculture, commerce, the useful handicrafts, take in turn a new place and receive a new prestige. This calm and silent reversal of opinion as to the worth of the work, is one of the great lessons of history. Over and over again we find that the thing contemporaneously despised is the thing which receives abiding recognition. "The last", indeed, becomes "the first".

Motherhood itself, however, remains still unrecognised and still unpaid. More than this, it is actually looked upon as the symbol of the servitude of the sex, nature having, as it were, set this seal to the deeds of bondage. For it is this very function of motherhood, which constitutes the difference between the sexes which cannot be got over in the race of competition. A woman who is performing the function of motherhood is hopelessly handicapped; her force, whether she will or not, is going forth in an object apart from her own personal ends. This expense of strength is not over when the child is born, nor even after the first few months of its life have passed by. The child demands the care and close attention of the mother throughout the early years of its life, and to separate these two is cruel to both and a serious injury to the child. With the relations of the sexes one to another the State, in that future society to which we are all on-looking, will have nothing, or ought to have nothing, to do. But when a woman is a mother that is a different matter. One recognises that a woman who is a mother is something different from the individuals who form the rest of the industrial world. Besides her self-responsibility, she has become responsible for a life not her own. The question of bringing a new life into the world, and nourishing it when here, is of all questions *not* a personal one; it is a question of interest to the whole community—one which bears on future generations, on time to come, and on the welfare of the world at large. And therefore, it is one which the whole community is bound to look upon as a national charge, and a national responsibility.

It might be well to look at this question of the State support of motherhood, from two points of view: from that of the mother, and from that of the child. But in the short space of the present paper we must restrict ourselves to the point of view of the mother.

Let us suppose that the five conditions of the emancipation of women given above are established: that men and women equally educated, in possession of equal political and social rights, stand independently of one another in an economic world, and work therein. In this new society a woman unites herself to one of the opposite sex by the free choice of free affection: the man has no power to bind the woman to himself save the power of love, and the woman has no power to bind the man to herself save the power of love. Each continues his or her separate work, independently of their union with each other. A child, however, is to be born. The economic condition of the woman is instantly altered. The woman thus situated can no longer compete in the economic world *because she is already performing a necessary social function.*

Hitherto—it cannot be too often repeated—this natural function has been for women the badge and basis of servitude. Even in the present day, though sentimentally motherhood is endowed with dignity, it has certainly not been recognised in its important bearing as a responsible piece of social work; and even in liberal and sympathetic minds it is still looked upon, not as that which marks the woman as a social worker and sufferer of the most exalted kind, but as mournfully the indomitable mark of her everlasting pupilage and inferiority. This is said advisedly, and will bear examination. For what but this fact of motherhood, *in posse* or *in esse*[8] forms the distinction

---

8   Latin: *in posse* means having the potential to exist; *in esse* means to be, to exist.

upon which the inequality of the sexes is founded?

But in the future—in that juster social future for which we hope—is it likely that this necessary human work, this charge of nourishing and bringing forth the new life of the State, shall be the occasion of forcing the woman into renewed dependence upon individual men?

A statement of the case as it exists in the present, may possibly make the matter clearer. As things are, heroic lives of heroic women are consumed in the unremitting efforts required to raise up, under the best conditions possible, the future citizens of the future State. The husbands of such women may be either bad, incapable, extravagant, or simply unfortunate; their work does not suffice to support their families, and the burden lies heavily indeed upon the mothers who labor from morning till night, and often through the night, starving themselves, pinching themselves in body and soul, in order to keep the little household together, and to send forth the children so equipped into life, that they may prove good citizens of the State. If ever work was State work, national work, abidingly useful work, it is that of the good, wise mother of a household. Yet this is the work which remains absolutely unrecognised and unrewarded.[9] Lying at the root of all national life, the base of all those industries which go to the building up and nourishing of the life of the State, it remains unpaid work; and the performers thereof are often—one may say generally—the martyrs of duty. A celibate woman with far less labor, with labor pleasant to herself, with no pinching and starving of body and intellect, but yet with labor far less necessary and beneficial to the State, can earn a competency. The mother of a poor household, with all her heroic and unselfish efforts in labor upon whose results the future State is founded, cannot, *by doing it*, earn one sou to buy her sick child a little extra luxury.

It must be remembered that, as a matter of fact, *the majority of men do not support their wives and their families.* The wife, already exhausted with her special duties, has, in addition, to labor to bring a contribution to the household purse, and the children also contribute. These facts, however, do not take away the right which the law, and the opinion of society, give the husband of heaping constantly accumulating tasks and burdens upon the shoulders of his female companion, and upon the State the ill consequences of his own unreflecting sexual licence. It is a tremendous error on the part of some of the Socialist leaders, to preach in the wild and foolish manner they

---

9   One may say the same of the works closely accessory to motherhood and lying nearest to it—as nursing, household economy, early education, work amongst the poor, and other so-called womanly (but almost unpaid) professions [original footnote].

do against Malthusianism.[10] On their consciences must lie the lastingly evil results of such rashness, should their words prevail for a moment—as they will prevail with the Criminal, the Untaught, and the Pauper.

It is not within the scope of this paper to go into the remedies and methods to be applied against over-population and bad population. But one may point out one telling fact: which is that, whereas, under the present system, the responsibility for the birth of children lies in the hands of the stronger sex only, under an improved system—under a system where the wife stands side by side with her husband independent of him and in absolute equality with him—the responsibility for the birth of children will lie in the hands of both the sexes. And this cannot but in itself become a very adequate check. For it is in the last degree unlikely that a freed and intelligent woman would voluntarily incapacitate herself for the performance of the duties of life, by becoming a mere machine for the production of superfluous children. Yet should this natural check prove inadequate, it is certain that there will arise in the social world a very distinct and deterring opinion as to the extreme immorality of such a line of conduct, and should the State support of motherhood ever obtain—and under a Socialistic *régime* some modification of it cannot but obtain—the concomitant right of regulating the amount of population must become a leading duty of the State; the reformed penal code (in place of the decayed and useless laws protecting the rights and wrongs of property) inevitably containing some clause which will defend the industrial and self-controlled portion of the community, against the unrestrained licence of the producers of superfluous or diseased children.

For it is not lawlessness at which reformers in sexual matters aim, but an increase of the inducements to a moral response to scientifically binding law.

Yet in touching upon these subjects one is liable to misconception from the last two extremes of either party—from the party in favor of reform and the party against it. To the first one may say that it is surely a chief and foremost duty to guard strenuously against the appearance of conniving at the practices of vice and profligacy. The aim and object of the future is not to throw away law, but to find it—not to relax, but to brace up morality. Those who would attack the sexual institutions of to-day under the conviction that

---

10 Malthusianism is a political school of ideas derived from the writer, Reverend Thomas Robert Malthus (1766–1834) and his work, *An Essay on the Principle of Population* (1798). The essay explores the relationship between the growth in population and the inability to feed and provide subsistence as the population grows. Malthus argued that unless the population was checked by catastrophes, such as disease, famine or war, or moral restraints, such as abstinence or delayed marriage, the results would be widespread poverty and starvation.

they are bad and decaying institutions would do well to find some clear principle within their minds which can divide with accuracy the pure from the impure, the retrograde in morals from the progressive. It adds nothing to the advance of the question to be told in light and noxious flippancy that adultery is not adultery, that impurity is indistinguishable from purity, that a community of wives is a possible advantage, or that polygamy and polyandry are not retrogressions in morals. All this adds nothing but noise and ill-savor. Straining out of the decaying civilisation of the past faintly one discerns the fair face of a new time, and it is an offence to utter in that austere presence vaporing opinions gathered from a hasty survey of the manners of a long dead age, or of the possibilities within a coming one. Not an increase, but a decrease of sexuality is the aim and object of the reforming party—how best we may free men and women from the bondage of predominant sexuality, and set the sexual instinct in its right place.

That such an aim might be fulfilled successfully by the breaking of the sexual sphere seems probable. For when women stand independently of and on an equality with men in the industrial world—when their sexuality is no more a thing to be bought and sold—then, for the first time, sexual unions will depend upon no other consideration than that of mutual choice, a regulating element of feminine refinement and moderation will be brought into play, and a vast system of temptation will be removed from the lives of both men and women.

To the more conservative party there is little to say save to conjure them not to meet arguments with the mere charge of wantonness, nor to attack them in the spirit of those who have kept, with the faith, predominately "the passions of the faith". Words will establish nothing. It is time with its slow judgment that decides. On such judgment we are content to wait, reposing upon the tranquil and certain faith, that the good thing holds and the bad thing breaks, and that, inevitably, it is the more excellent matter which is established in the end.

Victorian Secrets

The Beth Book by Sarah Grand
edited with an introduction & notes by Jenny Bourne Taylor

First published in 1897, *The Beth Book – Being a Study from the Life of Elizabeth Caldwell Maclure, a Woman of Genius*, is a semi-autobiographical novel offering a portrait of the artist as a young woman. Grand's compelling story recounts in vivid detail the childhood of her young heroine, Beth, a spirited and intelligent girl who challenges the limitations of provincial life in Ireland and Yorkshire. Without the benefit of formal education, Beth must make her own way through adolescence, contending with a violent mother and an alcoholic father.

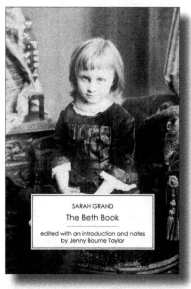

SARAH GRAND
The Beth Book

edited with an introduction and notes
by Jenny Bourne Taylor

Like Grand herself, Beth makes an early marriage to escape her unhappy childhood, becoming the wife of philandering doctor, Daniel Maclure. Disillusion soon turns to defiance, as Beth recreates herself as a woman of genius, with her rousing refrain of "I shall succeed!" After escaping to a room of her own, Beth becomes a New Woman, setting a high standard both for herself and for other women. The coming of age and sexual awakening of Beth broadens into a consideration of wider social issues, such as marital violence, vivisection, and the sexual double standard.

Includes critical introduction, explanatory footnotes, contemporary reviews, and extracts from relevant texts.

ISBN: 978-1-906469-31-3

Available in paperback and Kindle editions. For more information, please visit:

www.victoriansecrets.co.uk

Victorian Secrets

Victorian Secrets is an independent publisher dedicated to producing high-quality books from and about the nineteenth century, including critical editions of neglected novels.

All Sorts and Conditions of Men by Walter Besant

The Angel of the Revolution by George Chetwynd Griffith

The Autobiography of Christopher Kirkland by Eliza Lynn Linton

The Beth Book by Sarah Grand

The Blood of the Vampire by Florence Marryat

The Dead Man's Message by Florence Marryat

Demos by George Gissing

East of Suez by Alice Perrin

Henry Dunbar by Mary Elizabeth Braddon

Her Father's Name by Florence Marryat

The Light that Failed by Rudyard Kipling

A Mummer's Wife by George Moore

Not Wisely, but Too Well by Rhoda Broughton

Robert Elsmere by Mrs Humphry Ward

Selected Stories of Morley Roberts

Sowing the Wind by Eliza Lynn Linton

Thyrza by George Gissing

Twilight Stories by Rhoda Broughton

Vice Versâ by F. Anstey

Weeds by Jerome K. Jerome

Weird Stories by Charlotte Riddell

Workers in the Dawn by George Gissing

For more information on any of our titles, please visit:

www.victoriansecrets.co.uk

CPSIA information can be obtained
at www.ICGtesting.com
Printed in the USA
LVHW010633180620
658366LV00011B/915

9 781906 469566